MILK MONEY

JUDE E. MCNAMARA

Author Contact
Website: http://www.judeemcnamara.com
Email: jude@judeemcnamara.com
Facebook: Jude E. McNamara
Twitter: @judeemcnamara
Instagram: iamtwojudes

Two Judes Publishing
668 Stony Hill Road Suite 339
Yardley, Pennsylvania, 19067

CONTENTS

ACKNOWLEDGEMENTS

I am beyond grateful to everyone who was part of the process of creating *Milk Money.* Thank you to:

My loyal and diligent beta readers: Nicole Arnold, Jeanine Hillesland, Alexis Giostra, Donna Harden Nelson, Erica McCarty; all of who read multiple versions of the story, and provided me helpful feedback until I felt it was right.

A.D. Cooper at ADCooperBooks for designing the beautiful cover capturing the essence of my vision for *Milk Money.*

My editor: Michelle Phinney-Smith for all her work, without which there would be rambling and other grammatical offenses.

Donna Sebastian: the inspiration for the name Two Judes Publishing.

Britter, whose "bright green smiley-faced" note has been on my door for four years now and reads "Keep Writing"; it reminds me not to quit and to keep doing what I'm doing.

Candy Cane for helping me sort through tons of imagery for all things graphic. Your talents are never lost on me. I see you.

Tymoney, Diva, and Tootsie Pop: You're the best fan club ever.

A special thanks to Lani Diane Rich and Alastair Stephens at StoryWonk.com You guys are my first and my last word on all things story.

To my readers: To all those who purchased my novel and those who have shared my stories on your book blogs and with your book clubs, thank you for your unfailing love and support. You rock, and I am eternally grateful.

And last, but not least: To my mother for your undying love, motivation, and support throughout my entire writing life. To my father who is with me always in spirit.

DEDICATION

To JimmyMac, and the people I belong to . . .

Nicholas Becker, New York's Angel Investor extraordinaire, has the perfect life of wealth, power, and prestige. Almost. Gone is the missing long-time love of his life, Harper Carmichael Montgomery. She's the one woman immune to his charming ways, since their summer love went awry a decade ago. All grown up, Harper has become Nicholas's most ardent business nemesis.

Harper Carmichael Montgomery, daughter to a U.S. senator and heiress to the Carmichael Empire, is at the top of her game. CEO of her own company, Harper is now one of *Forbes*' top Thirty Over Thirty businesswoman. She's the poster gal for a successful single businesswoman's life. Life is good, except for the one thing she lost a decade ago, Nicholas Becker—the only man who ever held her heart captive.

While years have passed, Nicholas and Harper's animosity toward each other has yet to fade. The wedding of mutual friends draws Nicholas and Harper together long enough to discover they must compete yet again in a race to take over the Japanese conglomerate both prestigious family empires desire to possess.

Will obligation to family come first? Or will Nicholas and Harper heal old wounds and build a bridge to fulfill the desires of what they can only achieve together.

CHAPTER ONE

Nicholas

"The second best thing about this New Year's Eve night, next to my getting married, is the fact that you're my best man, Nicky. Thank you for standing up for me," Mico said, giving me a bear hug.

I tapped the rooftop of the limousine, waving my hand to let my driver Silas and my security chief Stephen Parks know that we were ready to head to Saint Patrick's Cathedral. Stephen was following behind us in the black armored Chevy Suburban. His security team was positioned ahead of us in another Suburban. Tonight's wedding celebration was a huge affair. My good friend Noah "Mico" Dunham was marrying Riley Nelson Cook. This time last year, my friend and his new bride's son had almost lost their lives in a serious motorcycle accident.

"Silas, get us to the church on time!" I yelled. "If we're late, Mico will put me in one of those famous headlocks he was known for at the Naval Academy."

"Yeah man, how's our time? Riley will have my ass if I'm late." Mico said.

"It's ten fifteen. Don't worry. Silas will have us there on time. Your bride is scheduled to arrive at eleven thirty."

"I take my vows at midnight, Nicky."

"Don't worry about it Mico. I've got the ring. We're on schedule."

Tonight was a big deal for my good friend. It was a bigger deal for me because I was standing up for him. Best Man. I wanted this night to go without a hitch.

"Here, take a shot to calm your nerves," I said, grabbing the crystal decanter off the limousine bar, pouring Mico and myself a shot of vodka.

"Thanks for the wedding present, Nicky. Loaning us the Milk Money jet so we can spend our honeymoon in the South of France is beyond wonderful," Mico said.

I could tell by his huge grin my gift had made him happy.

"Not a problem Mico. Riley's company was a great investment decision. I'll get it back from you one way or the other," I laughed heartily.

"Thanks Nicky. I earned major cool points with her when Milk Money took her company on as a client. That was a really good decision."

"Nah man. I should be thanking you for bringing Riley's business to my attention. Of the ten companies Milk Money has provided angel investment funds to this past year, hers has been one of the more profitable businesses on my leader board."

"Riley's worked really hard to make her business a success."

"Well it shows. That investment is showing lots of promise right off the bat. Even Lucia is happy," I said proudly.

"Well if Lucia is happy, then life is pretty good. Lucia is one badass woman. She is not to be messed with, Nicky."

"You're telling me? Dude, you're preaching to the choir."

"Does she ever chill, or does she always work herself into oblivion?"

"Rarely chills," I said, shaking my head back and forth.

What Mico didn't realize, was that "badass" didn't even begin to appropriately describe my business partner Lucia Falco's talents.

Lucia had been with me from the early days eight years ago, when I formed Milk Money. Together, she and I nurtured the firm, having started it on a shoestring budget. Today Milk Money was one of *the* most premiere angel investment firms on Wall Street. And Lucia Falco was central to the company's success. She was a beautiful, smart, no nonsense workaholic. When it came to business, we were a lot alike.

"Mico, I have nothing but good things to say about Lucia. She's a wonderful business partner. She keeps me on the straight and narrow. Lucia is the Yin to my Yang. I could not survive without her."

"Yeah, Beauty and the Beast," Mico grunted.

"Just like the POTUS needs a body man, Lucia is my body woman."

"Well somebody needs to keep you in line, Nicky. I suppose it might as well be Lucia," he said casually. "Everywhere I turn, you're in the gossip columns with this heiress or that model."

"Oh, don't believe everything you hear Mico."

"I don't. But I know you. No doubt, most of the gossip is true. You even give the foreign press a workout. Nicky, don't you think it's time to slow your roll?"

"Why should I?" I glanced at Mico quizzically.

"Look, I know you've got this whole 'I'm not going to commit to any woman' thing going on, but dude, you're forty-one."

"Give it a break, Mico."

"No Nicky, I think it's time you retire that 'playa' card of yours. Get on with it. Settle down. Tie the knot. Make some babies."

"Babies?" I said, choking on my drink. "Good Lord."

"You're Big Willie now. You are on *Forbes'* list of the top one hundred richest men. You are the most eligible bachelor in Manhattan. Quit the shenanigans, man, and settle down," Mico pleaded.

"Jesus man, you're starting to sound like Big Daddy." The mere thought of my kingpin father brought memories of his recent communication today.

"How so?" Mico said, glancing at his own watch, clearly getting more nervous the closer we got to the cathedral.

"I received a very lengthy voicemail earlier today from Big Daddy. He was dribbling on and on about why I needed a wife and kids. He claimed I need to focus on the family legacy."

"See Nicky, even Big Daddy and I are on the same page."

"Mico, please. You know there has only been one woman that has ever meant anything to me. And, she has managed to walk away with my heart. Matter of fact, she stomped on it, crushed it into a thousand pieces, and ground the heel of her pricey stiletto into it." I sighed and took a big swig of my drink, wondering how the hell things got so messed up between me and her. "And as far as Big Daddy is concerned, he wants me to do what he wants me to do, when he wants it," I babbled. "You know how he is."

"So?" Mico said sharply, shifting nervously in his seat.

"Sooooo, some people respect him, some people fear him. Big Daddy doesn't care which you choose, as long as you stay out of his way and give him what he wants. He forgets that *I'm* not other people. *I* don't have to give into his demands."

"Not the wisest move for you to be getting on the bad side of Big Daddy Blake Ross Becker II," Mico chuckled, putting full emphasis on my father's full name.

"Yeah, yeah, yeah," I said, waving my hand wildly in the air. I was ready for this conversation to end. I could hardly deny that my father was starting to put his foot on my neck over my state of singleness.

"Man, you best get with the program with Big Daddy. I'm not really sure you should be poking that bear, if you know what I mean. How hard can it be Nicky, for you to find a woman and settle down?"

"After Harper, I don't give my heart away anymore. She feels like unfinished business," I said solemnly.

"You've got to start somewhere Nicky."

"These other women don't really do it for me. They are just playmates on my playground, baby."

Mico shook his head. I knew that look. I'd seen it on his face too many times before throughout our friendship. It was the look of frustration when he felt he wasn't getting through to me. And there was a lot of truth to that.

"Harper doesn't get to rip my heart out and shred it in a thousand pieces a second time," I ranted. "Once in life is enough. I don't want to have to pull out the Uzis, throw handcuffs on her, and keep her on lockdown for a lifetime," I laughed.

"This is nothing to joke about Nicky. You and Harper ought to knock it off and call a truce. Why don't you cut out this sparring shit? It's obvious you two haven't gotten to a place of being done with each other."

Even I had to admit on some level that my friend was right. I never did feel like the relationship with Harper was over. I didn't have what last month's playmate said she needed from me . . . what was it? Closure? Yes. I didn't have closure. And, I didn't want anything close to closure either.

"You know you both have gotten down right lethal in your interactions. It's like a watching a bloody boxing match, except even the folks outside of the ring aren't safe. An onlooker to the two of you could easily end up being collateral damage. God forbid if one should ever get on either of your bad side," Mico sighed.

"It is what it is, man."

"Nicky man, what happened that summer at Martha's Vineyard was ten years ago. You both were young. But now you both are older, wiser, and a hell of a lot richer. You still can fix this, Nicky."

"I don't know Mico. Harper cuts my balls off at every turn. Have you forgotten how that woman operates?" I gave Mico my best "Are you crazy?" look.

"Look Nicky. Be reasonable. Your net worth is over half a billion dollars. She's pulling her own weight, pushing up strong on your heels three hundred million dollars later. Milk Money has been like a cash cow making money hand over foot in the angel investment market. You are heir to Becker Foods, *the* world renowned chicken processing dynasty second to none."

"And your point is . . . ?"

"My point is . . . financially, you've achieved almost everything you could ever hope for, frankly."

Hmphf. Not everything. What Mico didn't understand was that Harper was not in my life the way I needed her to be. *Everything* meant I would have *her.* And I didn't. I had everything, but nothing. My life was empty now without her.

"And Harper? Let's not forget her," Mico rambled further. "She's heir apparent to *the* Queen of Ketchup, Elizabeth Carmichael Montgomery of the Carmichael Ketchup conglomerate." Mico continued on with his lecture. "And her Daddy Warbucks father is the politically popular U.S. senator from New York. What more could you ask for with parentage like that? Harper would be the icing on your cake."

Well at least Mico had that part right. If I was the cake then she definitely was the icing. Chocolate icing on top of that. My favorite.

"Both you and Harper obviously have more money than brains because neither of you can admit that you still love each other. The two of you could put all those assets to good use. Roll with it Nicky."

Assets. Yeah, my Harper had a ton of assets—and I don't mean financial ones. Those big brown eyes, those sexy legs, those pouty lips. What I wouldn't give to have those assets under me right about now.

"There's a lot of dirty water under that bridge Mico. Not to mention Harper hates my guts. *And* she makes my blood boil half the time," I said, pouring myself another vodka shot before checking my watch.

I literally had to put myself on a back burner with a low flame whenever I was near Harper. Whenever I was close to her I wanted to fucking combust. "I wish I could turn her over my knee sometimes and spank that pretty little ass until it blushes," I growled. "That woman fights me at every turn. Hell, last year I couldn't even buy the little kids at the new community center in Harlem some decent artwork, without her stealing it out from under me."

"She didn't steal it Nicky. She outbid you," Mico said calmly.

"Yeah and then a few months ago, she did an end run on me with that little restaurant chain in New Orleans that I wanted Milk Money to take on as an investment."

"You beat her to the punch on those shares of Gilliam Global," Mico added. "She was paying you back. You pissed her off," he said, his voice raising a couple of octaves.

"And Lord, don't forget the time she fucking doused me in a vat of *Carmichael Ketchup* at that damn carnival my Mother's foundation gives in Martha's Vineyard every year."

"You fucking threw her in the water ball tank minutes before she was to show her horse."

"Man, I damn near drowned in ketchup."

"You ever seen a wet equestrian?" Mico asked. "What the hell Nicky?"

I shrugged my shoulders knowing that Mico was right. Harper and I had taken the passion we had in our love for each other and turned it inside out, directing venom at each other as if we were the couple in the *War of the Roses*. We both played our parts well too. She was a formidable opponent, I must say that.

"What was up with you two that day?" Mico asked.

"We were fighting over a very valuable piece of property on Star Island in Miami. Harper wanted to give it to her parents for their anniversary. I stole the deal right out from under her pretty little nose. Then I re-sold the property for a profit. She was beyond pissed. So I threw her in the water ball tank to cool her off."

"And you looked like a bleeding heart in your white linen suit doused in ketchup," Mico said, laughing out loud and shaking his head. "You two looked like a couple of spoiled overgrown rich kids acting out at the family picnic. The only thing missing was the crazy aunt."

"I swear to god that woman has made it her life's mission to fuck with me every chance she gets," I said. "And that mouth of hers. That cute little sensual mouth of her that oozes sex appeal, but never shuts the fuck up."

"Well it's not like your hands are clean in this either Nicky," Mico said shaking his head and laughing. "You broke her heart too. I repeat myself, Nicky. You *really* broke her heart," he said.

"She's making me pay in other ways," I scoffed.

"You know the deal. Hell hath no fury like a woman scorned, motherfucker," Mico laughed. "A rich one, I might add."

"No, that woman wants my head on a platter I tell you," I could feel myself getting rather animated. "She's got plans to stick a knife in me, throw an apple in my mouth, and serve my ass up on a platter for all the world to see."

Mico laughed even more heartily.

"Shit is not funny, Mico."

"Yes it is. And yes it's pretty much true she's making you pay," he said. "And, just so you know Nicky, *that woman* has been invited to the wedding tonight, so be on your best behavior man. Please. Do not start dueling at the wedding, because I can tell you right now Nicky, you would lose."

"I'll be on my best behavior tonight because it's your night. But losing against her is not an option," I kidded with Mico, but I was serious as a heart attack. Losing against Harper was not an option. I had a reputation to protect.

"Furthermore Nicky, I don't want to have to come save your ass because Riley would make me pay on my own fucking honeymoon, so try to put your weapons down for the night, my brother."

Ahhh man. I am really going to need another drink if Harper and I are going to be in the same space together tonight. This was going to test my constitution knowing I'd have to try to keep my hands off that beautiful woman. Hands that she would probably cut off with an ax blade if she had half the chance. I so missed what she and I use to have . . . who we use to be. I missed the days when we made love, not war. It was a lie that time healed old wounds. My wounds had never healed. My heart had a goddamn sinkhole in it.

"Man, I don't mind standing up for you and all. I'm honored to do so, but goddamn, I've got to deal with Harper tonight on top of everything else? Why man? Haven't I done enough penance?"

I could feel my old emotions starting to bubble up like a witches brew in a black caldron.

"Yes. You do have to deal with her tonight *and* her sidekick Mackenzie Rhodes. Mackenzie is doing the wedding photography."

"Shit man, that cock-blocker bitch Mackenzie is going to be there, too?" I grunted miserably.

"She's the devil incarnate herself. Whenever she's around, anytime I get near Harper, Mackenzie turns up like a bad penny. It's likes she's running interference for her or something. Do you think there is something going on between those two?"

"Are you asking me if Harper Montgomery is gay? Hell no man, put the vodka down. You know damn well Harper isn't gay," Mico insisted.

"Well how the hell would I know? Harper is never with the same man twice. She's gotten downright skittish about relationships, if she has them at all."

Oops, I shouldn't have let Mico in on the fact that I was keeping tabs on Harper. That might come back to haunt me. Loose lips sink ships.

"Rumor is she loves them and leaves them," I continued. "She's a no-strings-attached kind of woman now. It's like she's got a bunch of fuck buddies or something."

"How would you know? Are you keeping tabs on her or something? You haven't resulted to stalking her now have you, man?"

I walked right into that one. I could have predicted that was coming next. The truth was I pretty much knew her every move. Yeah, I kept a string on her business dealings. It was an added benefit to me that sometimes that meant I had access to her personal life as well.

"She has a whole slew of men after her. She leaves all of them on the side of the road for dead," I said calmly.

"Listen to yourself man. Do you hear yourself talking?" Mico laughed. "You're the biggest playboy in all of Manhattan. You're a regular Don Fucking Juan. And you've got the nerve to be judging her? You're the one plastered all over Page Six's gossip headlines several times a year with different women," Mico said.

"Are you calling me a manwhore?"

"Yes. Last I checked, you were in the arms of those supermodel glamazons and *Playboy*'s new playmate of the month. Are you really going to try to be judge and jury over Harper Montgomery?"

"Yes I am. Because she's a woman. It's different when you are a woman," I said. "And don't believe everything you read Mico."

"You should check yourself sometime Nicky," Mico said. "You're starting to sound like some of those old school chauvinistic commanders at the Naval Academy."

"So is she coming alone?" I asked. I was secretly curious. It was going to be hard looking at her in the arms of another man.

"I doubt it," Mico said. "All those invitations go out with a plus one. It's not my job to keep up with the women and their guests. Riley has already ripped my playa card up and set it aflame." Mico chuckled.

"Man, you haven't even walked down the aisle yet and you're whupped already," I laughed.

"The only thing I know about women these days is Riley," Mico said with a strong emphasis.

"Shit Mico, you have eyes and ears don't you? Don't you know how to keep them to the ground—at least when you're around your own woman?" I was starting to bitch at him.

"Or, you could have just asked my bride-to-be yourself," Mico responded. "After all, you are her angel investor. It's not like you don't have access to Riley."

"You know I try not to mix business with pleasure."

"Since the fuck when?" Mico laughed again. This is me you're talking to, Nicky."

Mico wasn't taking me seriously nor was he buying anything I was saying.

"Well one thing for sure, I did overhear Riley talking with my new brother in-law the other day. I heard Brooks's name mentioned. Harper might be bringing him," Mico said hesitantly.

"Brooks? Brooks Fitzgerald McKenna? Why in the hell would she be tooling around with that back-stabbing, steal-your-woman, arrogant, self-serving douche bag social climber?" I complained.

"Well, tell me how you really feel?"

"Seriously Mico. Why him?

"Uh, maybe because he's successful? Maybe because she likes him? Maybe because he treats her kindly?"

"Oh God no," I said, in total disbelief.

"Maybe because he's not always fighting with her all the time like some people we know who shall remain nameless right now."

"But Brooks Fitzgerald McKenna?"

"I don't know. Fuck it man. How the hell would I know why Harper would date Brooks?"

"I bet you my Ferrari he's only interested in her for her political connections and what he thinks she can do for him. He's spent all his life social climbing trying to keep up with the Joneses."

"Well, obviously he's done a good job of keeping up and climbing up," Mico said. "Brooks is pretty well off himself."

"That's only because he's a ruthless, deceitful, not-to-be-trusted-used-car-salesman, shithead for a businessman. I've heard the stories about him at the country club. I've crossed paths with him personally in my business circles."

"What formed your opinion of him?" Mico asked, genuinely interested.

"He tried to sucker me once a few years back on a deal. He insisted that I needed to be a part of the funding for some textile group. He positioned a very bright drop-dead gorgeous redhead at the center of this deal to try to help influence me. In the end, what he really tried to do was set me up for a fall and fuck me. So, I fucked him and I fucked her, but not in the same way or same order if you know what I mean." I laughed between vodka sips, glad I was feeling a much-needed buzz.

"Umm, a Nicholas Becker-style financial fuckfest," Mico laughed.

We gave each other a high five.

"Brooks was flirting very close to the edge of what could legally have been considered an insider trading scheme. He was coming in my back door with this woman threatening to involve my company. I wouldn't trust him as far as I could throw him. Well, at little less than that," I said, thinking I could throw that motherfucker pretty far given half the chance. Hell I'd throw him right out of Harper's life. The idea of her tooling around with him did not sit well with me.

"Word is he's looking to settle down and make a move,"

Mico said. "I think he's got her in his sights, Nicky. If you and Harper are truly done, you need to adjust to the idea, get over it and move on," Mico said with a raised eyebrow.

"No fucking way," I fumed, shaking my head and throwing back my vodka shot. "Not if I can help it. Not in this lifetime."

"I'm only telling you what I heard Nicky."

"I will bury the hatchet with her myself before I see her end up with that dirtball Brooks Fitzgerald Fuckhead McKenna. He doesn't have anyone's best interests at heart but his own. She's far too good for him and deserves better. I will personally see to it that she never ends up with that loser user," I grumbled.

"Listen to you Mr. Put Your Boxing Gloves On every time you see her," Mico howled. "I swear you two have a love/hate relationship."

"Hell we don't have a relationship at all."

"Yeah you do. You just haven't admitted it yet."

"No we don't," I said, checking my watch for the tenth time.

I could feel my blood boiling now. All I could think about was the fact that I needed to gird my loins if I was going to be dealing with Harper Carmichael Montgomery at this wedding tonight. Since that bittersweet summer ten years ago, our interactions have never been the same. Things were going to get doubly worse if she was going to be on the arm of Brooks Fitzgerald McKenna. This was worse than I could have ever imagined.

I missed the good old days, when Harper and I were in love, that long ago summer at Martha's Vineyard. We first met at the Global Food Safety Conference for food manufacturers. My father and her mother were co-chairs at the conference. Big Daddy and Elizabeth assigned Harper and me to be Business Evangelists for their respective brands. Our parents decided it would be good business marketing experience for Harper and me to work together on lead generation. Our job was to be responsible for mingling with the newbie food producers to identify potential leads among the food manufacturers. We mingled with each other instead.

Twenty-six-year-old Harper Montgomery was headed to graduate school at Columbia in the fall. I was thirty-one with degrees from the Naval Academy and Columbia Business School. I was headed for Wall Street.

We became friends and lovers. Our relationship was intense.

We quickly fell for each other—deep and hard. We got into each other's soul. I suspected our parents had high hopes for a future merger between us. They almost got their wish. Maybe it was time now for me to get mine.

"Tonight's all about pleasure Nicky. It's my wedding night. It's New Year's Eve. Try to enjoy yourself. Do it for Riley . . . and me," Mico said.

"I promise you I will be on my best behavior, Mico. I will do everything in my power to keep the peace with Harper tonight. Now as far as that wretched excuse for a woman, Mackenzie Rhodes, goes, if she runs her bullshit interference again tonight, all gloves are off," I said.

"She'll be too busy taking wedding photos of the bridal party and family. Mackenzie will be working, remember," Mico said reassuring me. "And if Harper shows up with Brooks on her arm, what could possibly send Mackenzie on the warpath?"

I could already tell this was going to turn out to be a long night. I had a lot to think about. Harper might be at the wedding with Brooks McKenna. Mackenzie the antichrist was going to be there taking pictures. This was supposed to be a good night. Instead, this was a lot to digest.

Our limousine came to a stop in front of the cathedral.

"Mr. Becker, Mr. Dunham, we've arrived, sirs. Mr. Parks has pulled up right behind us," Silas said, moving around the limousine now to open the door.

Stephen Parks was both my friend and much needed bodyguard. His protective skills were useful to have around when the paparazzi got out of control. He came in handy when I needed to keep the occasional woman-turned-stalker at bay. A few of the women I dated simply couldn't handle it when they realized they were being replaced. Especially the ones that needed "closure." When things got ugly, and they sometimes did, Stephen was very helpful to have around. Maybe I was going to need him tonight to keep me from killing that Fuckwad Brooks Fitzgerald McKenna. Game on.

"Okay Mico. Are you ready?"

"Man, I'm beyond ready. I've waited years for this moment," Mico said. "And don't forget Nicky, when the priest says "Noah, the ring," don't fall asleep at the switch. He'll be talking about me remember. We're not in school anymore," Mico laughed.

"You will always be Mico to me," I said. "Happy New Year,

24

man. Congratulations."

We stepped out of the limousine, bear hugging each other again one more time, topping our hug off with a fist bump.

CHAPTER TWO

Harper

"Harper, this cathedral is beautiful, baby. I can see you and me walking down this aisle together one day," Brooks said, grabbing my hand and tucking it inside his own.

"I've told you a hundred times Brooks, I'm not the marrying kind. I'm already married. The Montgomery Consulting Group is my husband."

God, I hope I don't have to listen to his drivel all night. Marrying Brooks Fitzgerald McKenna is the last thing I want to do. Why can't he take no for an answer?

"Oh baby, being married to a job is not the same as being married to me," he said.

"My business keeps me busy enough. I can't imagine having the time or emotional space for such a huge commitment like marriage. It's not in the cards. You should set your sights on someone else more suitable to your interests. I like my life just the way it is," I whispered as we entered the sanctuary.

"Oh, I can be very persuasive when I want to be, baby," Brooks said wickedly.

Ugh, the mere thought of ever being married to Brooks made me want to shoot myself for ever having wasted my time with him tonight. Why on God's green earth did I pick him to be my plus one this evening? *I don't know why I keep doing this to myself.* I would have much preferred to have come with the bride's brother Reese. It was a given that Reese would be in the bridal party, so I asked Brooks instead.

I opened my little black book and did the finger walk, and Brooks was it for tonight's plus one. All the rest of the eye-popping, jaw-dropping possibilities had gone to Europe for the holidays.

No doubt, Brooks was the poster boy for good breeding, fitting into most of the influential circles of the rich and famous. Handsome as hell, Brooks always made nice arm candy. If I had to suffer through an evening of dry conversation I wanted to at least be with someone visually appealing. Brooks was tall, gorgeous, and had perfectly straight teeth from years of orthodontic care. He flashed a lady-killer grin that typically got him most anything he wanted. Who could resist those penetrating baby blue eyes, that strong jaw, and chiseled features that came with a muscular physique to match? His sharkskin grey Armani suit made him look as if he stepped off the pages of *Gentleman's Quarterly*.

Brooks was CEO of McKenna Textiles, which meant he wore nothing but the finest of fabrics. He was six feet three inches of come-and-get-me, until you actually got there and reality set in, distorting the apparent fantasy. That beautiful specimen of a man was all talk and no walk. I suppose most women that wanted him were in it for his money. Why else be willing to put up with that limp libido?

Hmphf. But Harper Montgomery doesn't need a man for his money. Matter of fact, I didn't need him at all. He was what he was and nothing more. Blond-haired, blue-eyed arm candy. But what the hell. I doubt any of the other women in here knew about him but me. Thus, he served my purposes for the evening.

The reality was Brooks's personality bored me to death. Okay, so he wasn't great in bed. And he wasn't the worse either. But he sure as hell didn't knock my socks off. I might as well be in a coma. To me, he sucked balls. There would be no real fireworks between Brooks and me in that department. For some reason however, his oversized ego couldn't accommodate that little fact. Brooks carried on as if he turned every woman out sexually. Me, he bored completely to tears. I hated that he was constantly picking my brain in bed, asking me about the senator. The last thing I wanted to do in bed with any man was to talk about my father. I preferred you didn't talk at all and just do. No talk. Do. Thank you. Goodbye. Go home.

Maybe it was time for me to check myself. Perhaps I was

getting jaded. This business of my spending time with men that bored me was starting to get old. I was working too hard to fill a void that was left in my heart a long time ago.

"Well it's not like you're some spring chicken anymore Harper," Brooks whispered back. "What about kids? You're thirty-six. Don't you gals always have that whole biological ticking clock-thingy going on?" he said leaning into my ear as the usher directed us to the bride's side of the cathedral for seating.

"Well if I did, I certainly don't need a man to fulfill that objective," I hissed under my breath. "There are sperm donors and adoptions," I huffed. "Those options come without all the aggravation of having to deal with the antics and childish whims of a man. Why are we having this discussion here anyway?"

It was crass remarks like this from Brooks that turned me off.

"Listen baby, those other jokers you've been toying around with aren't me," Brooks said. "You need a real man to take care of you."

"Take care of me? Has somebody dropped you on your head?"

"Okay, so you can throw a hundred million out the cockpit of your Lear and never feel it. But look, baby, I am everything you could ever want in a man. I know how to tick tock that clock of yours," Brooks said tugging me under his armpit, placing his hand in the small of my back, helping me to the seat in the pew.

Jesus, Harper. Did you really do this to yourself tonight? So much for letting your fingers do the walking down your little black book. You need to get it together, girl. Now you're stuck putting up with this joker all night.

"Harper. We're both CEOs of our own businesses. We're both wealthy. I'm handsome as hell. And you're not too bad yourself. We make a great team sweetheart," Brooks spouted off with unflinching confidence.

The church organ music began playing softly in anticipation of the service to start. *God, I could just puke. Kill me now, Lord.* This man was so full of himself. Brooks Fitzgerald McKenna was the kind of guy that preferred most people refer to him by his full name, always introducing himself that way. He liked to think of himself as a blue blood from a very aristocratic bloodline, despite the fact his family lineage was anything but.

A small handful of people knew that Brooks grew up in an

Irish Catholic blue-collar family of hardworking fishermen from Boston, Massachusetts. He broke out of the old neighborhoods, excelling scholastically and earning himself a college scholarship to the University of Pennsylvania, later finishing his graduate studies at the Wharton School of Business. From there Brooks landed in Manhattan, in the garment district, where he worked his way up in the textile industry. Years later he would become highly successful in the industry, owning a slew of import/export garment distributorships, moving fabrics globally by air, land, and sea worldwide anywhere from Hong Kong to Australia. Brooks Fitzgerald McKenna had reinvented himself so successfully that very few people knew his blue-collar roots. Even I had to admit I admired his tenacity.

Most of the Manhattan socialites and wannabes saw him as a proper must-have on their charitable event's guest lists and summer themed parties in the Hamptons. Brooks had socially climbed his way onto some of the most sought-after guest lists in all of New York. None of that changed the fact that he was an overconfident arrogant jerk that thought way too highly of himself.

It was a good thing I was joyful about the happy marital union of Riley and Noah, or else I would dare not spend my New Year's Eve like this. If it weren't for the fact I promised my friend Reese that I would hang out with him later after the reception, I would have run out the cathedral doors kicking and screaming, asking for a bullet to put myself out of my own misery for being stuck with Brooks tonight.

At least Reese and I had tons of things in common both on a personal level and a business level. We took an instant liking to each other, having met years ago when I was a graduate student. He was my Adjunct Professor of Financial Forensics at Columbia University. Reese was the expert in the field, taking me under his wing, teaching me everything he knew. After graduation, Reese often called on my firm, The Montgomery Consulting Group, to do second-level reviews on many of his major financial forensic projects.

"We could light some fireworks of own tonight, sweetcakes," Brooks said, chiding me further and rubbing his hand on my knee.

I squirmed, trying to put some physical distance between Brooks and me. I was hopeful I'd be able to dump him after this wedding, hook up with Reese, and put myself out of this misery. I wanted to have some real fun tonight.

"Hush, the service is starting," I said, watching as the bridesmaids were making their way down the aisle. I moved his hand off my knee to back in his lap, throwing water on his plan for fireworks.

I admired the bridesmaid's elegant, beautiful cream-colored gowns that were tied at the breasts with black sequinned bows. They each shimmered as they glided towards their respective places at the front of the cathedral.

As the groomsmen stood in their appointed places, fury coiled in my gut as I laid eyes on the real *Mr. Fireworks* himself, Nicholas Miles Becker, bad boy CEO of the Milk Money Angel Investment Firm. There he was. Standing front and center at the end of the aisle. He was the pinnacle of dashing style and timeless sophistication. He looked dynamic in his impeccably tailored Italian-made tuxedo, looking like a shiny new penny. His tuxedo hung well on him in all the right places as he stood picture perfect and statuesque. Nicholas was best man to the groom, Captain Noah "Mico" Dunham. I wasn't sure if it were me or not, but I'd pretty much lay bets that half the bridesmaids' eyes were glued on Nicholas. Nicholas had an uncanny effect on women, always making them want to do the panty drop at his feet.

Yes. That was him. Mr. Cool, Calm, and Collected. God incarnate himself. Every woman's eyes in the church were fixated on him for the Greek god that he was. No one was immune.

Those piercing emerald eyes reflected that naughty glimmer, always looking as if he had contemplated a thousand different things he could do to you, and you knew you'd enjoy every one. His six-foot-tall muscular frame, his lush eyelashes, the five o'clock shadow accentuating his strong chin coupled with the dimple on the left side of his face when he smiled, did me in every time. His dark brown hair had no hints of grey, although I knew he would soon be turning forty-two. Nicholas was indeed aging well. His crisp white tuxedo shirt hid the physically fit body underneath. He was armed with a hard six pack any twenty-something man would die to have. With his usual confident ease and charm, his eyes widened as he caught a glimpse of me.

Most times I pretended like I wasn't affected by him. I tried to hide it, but the reality was I hadn't truly mastered the emotionless mask well. I knew him well enough to know that he too was struggling with the same problem. Hiding. We could not deny that years ago there was an eternal flame that had been lit between that had never been extinguished. Whenever we were in each other's space, it was almost as if we could both hear the igniting of a flame that radiated between us like a beacon, invisibly tying us together. All these years, I still hated that the memory of his body was branded in the recesses of my brain, igniting a need that I'd never encountered before. I was angry that he still had that effect on me years later. How dare he claim my body as if it belonged to him. There was way too much heat between us. I was determined to extinguish it. It was time I figured out how to put an end to his power over me. It was starting to feel like too much work against his constant magnetic pull.

The only thing a man could do for me now was to give me a baby and keep walking the other direction. The truth was, Nicholas wasn't even a viable candidate. Mostly because I didn't want to have to be responsible for killing my baby's daddy.

"The bride and groom must really be scraping the bottom of their friends list, if they let that womanizing fame whore, playboy money-grubbing, God-impostor Nicholas Becker in this wedding as best man tonight," Brooks said. "Who let the hound dogs out?" he said under his breath.

I tried to pretend like I didn't hear Brooks. I wanted to ignore him, the guests standing as the bride came down the aisle.

"I heard the two of you have history, but I still can't figure out what you could have possibly seen in him?" Brooks sneered.

"Since when is my past any concern of yours?" I asked. "I doubt very seriously that anyone would classify Nicholas as a 'money-grubber.' He's a lot of things, but money-grubber, he's not. He can't help the fact that everything he touches turns to gold like Midas."

"Whatever," Brooks said, disinterested.

"That's a bit short-sighted on your part don't you think," I said, working to keep my voice down.

Not that I had anything nice to say about Nicholas myself, but I sure didn't feel like I was going to sit here and listen to Brooks berate him in my presence. After all, my family and

Nicholas's families were close. Real close. I did have some loyalty to his family, if not for him.

"Not golden enough." Brooks spit back. "Nicholas Becker will never get another chance in life to steal one of my women again. Fool me once, shame on me. Fool me twice, shame on him. The next time he tries to get anywhere near what's mine, I'm going to reckon with him in the most serious way once and for all." Brooks hissed. "He's like a gnat that needs swatting."

I secretly wondered what woman Nicholas had snagged away from the great Brooks Fitzgerald McKenna that turned him into the green-eyed monster. The mere thought of that tickled me some. Nicholas changed women so fast it was hard for even me to keep up. Whoever she was, Nicholas didn't keep her around long. Nicholas wasn't the commitment type. I knew because I kept tabs on him.

"I now pronounce you man and wife," the priest said as we watched Noah kiss his bride at the stroke of midnight. My eyes glanced briefly towards Nicholas. He was staring back at me with the look of a panther, gazing at me as if I were his prey, good enough to eat. I noticed his jaw clench at the same moment Brooks whispered in my ear, his chest rising and falling in exasperation.

I gave Nicholas my best forget-about-it-never-in-your-next-life look, rolling my eyes at him and turning my head toward Brooks. I gave Brooks my best you're-the-greatest-guy smile.

Nicholas glared at Brooks with fiery eyes as if somebody had stolen his candy.

It didn't matter that I didn't give a hoot about Brooks Fitzgerald McKenna. Nicholas need not know that. All he needed to know was that I, Harper Montgomery, was out for financial revenge. I intended to keep forcing him to dig deep into his pockets. I was on a roll. This was gonna be like taking candy from a baby.

After all, you only get to crack and break my heart once in a lifetime. Then you have to pay up, because Momma is in it to win it.

JUDE E MCNAMARA

CHAPTER THREE

Nicholas

The wedding nuptials at St. Patrick's Cathedral were executed perfectly at midnight as planned. It was clear when I entered the wedding reception that this would indeed be the high point of the evening. The Marriott Marquis View Restaurant at Times Square was a perfect choice. The decor was a perfect reflection of the bride and groom's taste and sensibilities. It was a timeless mix of elegance and tradition. You couldn't help but feel the warmth and ambiance as soon as you entered. There were black sequinned touches here and there that accentuated the candlelit tables, a tasteful reminder of the bride's signature touch. I didn't doubt for one minute that Mico must have loved that the room rotated ever so slowly, revolving around on its axis, providing all the guests a magnificent panoramic view of the New York skyline after midnight. The holiday fireworks lighting up the sky on Times Square were spectacular. You could even see the Statue of Liberty just beyond Battery Park on the room's slow and easy rotation.

I sat to the left of Mico and his new wife Riley at the bridal party table. I gave myself a mental pat on the back having finished my best man duties making a celebratory toast wishing Mr. and Ms. Noah Dunham a Happy New Year with many more to come. After my well-applauded salute, the three-piece jazz combo began playing music in the background, compliments of the bride's sister-in-law who was a well-known jazz musician.

I'd managed to survive picture taking while putting on my

happy face as Harper's best friend, Mackenzie Rhodes, finished photographing those of us in the bridal party. The intimate gathering of family and friends mingling about wishing each other a Happy New Year, created a jovial atmosphere. Congratulatory remarks were extended to the bride and groom amid lots of hand shaking and dancing. Champagne was flowing freely in tulip-shaped flutes as restaurant servers hustled among the guests at warp speed.

It didn't take me long to realize I was going to have to fight off a couple of twenty-something beauties who were friends of some of the members of the bridal party. They had managed to plant themselves close to me, and my suspicions were soon confirmed. When I moved, they moved. I suffered through the small talk, but I must admit these gals were beyond chatty. It took a lot for me to get undone by beautiful women. Tempting as it was, the fact remained that I had no real interest in either of them. All that mattered to me tonight was that the newlyweds were happy, and that Harper wouldn't start World War III tonight.

I nursed my drink, pretending to pay attention to the two ladies that had me cornered, when I shifted my gaze across the room. My business partner Lucia was engaged in a conversation with Mico's new wife. I suspected she and Riley were trading stories about how the new Mrs. Riley Dunham was using the Milk Money cash infusion for her company Black Sequinned Bows and Champagne Nights. Mico's introduction of his wife's company to me had been a profitable investment. I gazed at his beautiful bride, pondering if she and Mico had discussed whether she'd be changing her name or leaving it as is for business purposes so as not to dilute her brand. I suppose at the end of the day it didn't much matter. Not my business. Not my woman. I sipped more of my drink, hoping it would drown out the background chatter rolling in my head from these two wannabe *Real Housewives of New York*.

Suddenly, I felt a change in the aura of the room. No doubt Harper had arrived. The head of her security entourage, Malcom Coles, had stepped inside the doorway, which meant Harper's father, Senator Clayton Lawrence Montgomery was not far behind. Harper never felt she needed a security detail, but the senator insisted. She typically took Malcom off his leash, letting him loose and on display in order to put up a front whenever the senator was around. Harper liked giving the appearance that she was adhering to the senator's wishes.

As far as I was concerned, Malcom wanted Harper for himself, along with all those other male wannabes who were forever sniffing around her. Malcom, an extremely handsome, articulate African American man, could have most any woman he desired. But like most of the men in Harper's orbit, he eyed her in a way that suggested there was more he wanted to do besides guard her.

Ugh. I needed to rid my mind off this notion. The mere thought of Malcom's hands on Harper left me feeling a rush of pissdom that coursed through my veins at high speed. So what if Malcom was an ex-Army Ranger who'd spent several years fighting the Taliban in the invasion of Afghanistan as a part of the War on Terror? I'd match my Navy Seal bodyguard Stephen's skills against his any day of the week. The fact Malcom did a pretty decent job of keeping Harper safe made me happy, so I forced myself to ignore the look of lust in his eyes. But still, his closeness to her bothered me immensely.

My mood shifted again as Lucia, moving like a gazelle, approached me. She was a perfect wingwoman. I needed her to cock block so I could ditch the *Young and the Restless* camped too close, boring me to tears with their constant chatter about the Twitterverse and Instagram. While I admired attractive women, I had no intention of robbing the cradle tonight. Lucia's arrival into my little circle of doom sent their smiling faces into a serious pout when I redirected my attention to Lucia.

"Nicky, there's a call for you," Lucia said, handing me my buzzing cell phone previously tucked in her clutch while I posed for pictures with the bridal party. "I think it's Three," she said, referring to my big brother Blake Ross Becker, III.

"Happy New Year, God speaking."
"Can you knock it off with the God shit, Nicky?"
"Fuck, Three, lighten up. It's New Year's. Don't you take a

break? What do you want?"

"What makes you think I want something?" Three quizzed.

"Three, whenever you call, you typically want something. I can't help it if my alter ego shows up and shows out," I laughed. "Your prayer is my command, my brother, what do you need?"

"It's not what *I* need. It's what Big Daddy needs," Three said, his voice clipped and professional.

Three had his family lawyer voice on, trying desperately to maintain a serious tone with me. I loved pushing his buttons, making him crack his legal armor.

"And that would be what?" I said, putting my defenses up, knowing the tables were getting ready to turn and I was being primed to get dragged into something I'd likely not want to be dragged into.

It was predictable whenever Big Daddy came into the equation. Big Daddy used Three against me whenever he could, simply because he knew Three and I got along well. Three could get things out of me that Big Daddy never could.

"Well this is a heads-up, Nicky. Two things: One, Big Daddy says it's time you settle down, get yourself a wife, make some babies, and start thinking about the family legacy. He respects what you've done with Milk Money, but he wants more grandkids, specifically some male grandkids."

"You call me on New Year's Eve with this agenda?" I said, feeling a tad agitated.

"I'm following orders, Nicky."

"So you give him some more kids, Three. You having trouble cloning yourself again or something?"

"I have girls, brother. Big Daddy's got this thing about having grandsons. Marcy has no interest in making any more babies with me. She claims she's made her contribution to the Becker clan punching out three kids. She doesn't intend to have any more. She claims babies are messing up her figure."

"You're the man, Three. Tell your wife to punch out one more and you'll buy her an island in the South Pacific or something."

"She's not having it, Nicky. She won't let me get anywhere near her now as it is," Three pleaded. "She claims if I so much as look at her, she'll get pregnant. She's threatened to cut Mr. Magic off and separate him from the boys."

"God, Three. T.M.I. Please don't tell me you let Marcy refer to your dick and balls as "Mr. Magic and the boys. I. Don't. Want. To. Know. This. Shit," I said, mentally shaking his words off, deciding this conversation was getting gross.

"Well, God knows all, now doesn't he?" Three snapped. "So if you aren't God, shut the fuck up claiming that you are. A bit of divine intervention would be in order right about now."

"Well Julianna can make some babies. Big Daddy just has to wait a few years."

Julianna was our younger sister. She was in Europe studying at Le Cordon Bleu, training to be world-class pastry chef. I doubted babies would be on her radar anytime soon.

"Knock it off Nicky. Julianna's still globe-trotting across Europe with her twenty-something girlfriends, still dancing to hip-hop and bubble gum pop. Doubt she'll be the source of Becker grandsons anytime soon. Besides, a man would have to come by you first."

Three was right. I'd be the first in line to kill any man that wanted to knock my baby sister up with child. I'd been the brother closest to her since we were kids. Her protector. The words *Julianna* and *babies* need not be said around me in the same sentence.

"Well I'm only the messenger, Nicky. Don't kill the messenger, brother."

Three, one. Nicky, zero.

"So, what else is new? You're forty-four man. You're a rock star attorney. You're going to one day run the Becker Foods empire. Grow a pair, man. Stand up to Big Daddy and your wife."

"Easy for you to say Nicky. You've never had a wife," Three groaned.

Three, two. Nicky, zero.

"So, fuck the shit out of her, make another baby and tell Big Daddy to leave me out of it. You've devoted your whole life to Becker Foods. Let Big Daddy deliver his own messages," I sighed, glaring across the room spotting Harper on the arms of that fuckwad Brooks Fitzgerald McKenna.

I felt my mood downshifting to funk mode and my left temple twitching, signaling a headache was forthcoming.

"What's the second thing?" I said, changing the subject, in hopes this discussion would fucking go away.

"Specifically Nicky, there's a plastics company called Joduku Plastics originating in Japan. The American division is located in

Princeton, New Jersey. It's up for sale. The parent company is spinning it off. Big Daddy wants you to buy it for Becker Foods."

"Buy it? For What?"

"We're in the food manufacturing business Nicky."

"So. Why plastics, Three?"

"Big Daddy's got this bright idea that Joduku Plastics has some innovative technology that Becker Foods can use for its poultry packaging. Big Daddy has good intuitions when it comes to shit like this. He's rarely ever wrong. As far as this acquisition is concerned, he insists you're the man for the job."

"Since fucking when?" I asked, unaware that I was beginning to raise my voice.

Lucia elbowed me in the side to lower my voice. She walked away, leaving me alone to my own devices.

"I'm giving you a heads up Nicky. You either get onboard or you'll be hearing from him directly, take it from me."

"I have my own shit to contend with, Three. It's not like I have a whole lot of time and money to be taking on acquisitions for Becker Foods," I hissed.

"Knock it off Nicky. Everybody knows you can buy whatever you want. It's one of the chief perks of being really rich, brother," Three said. "Just be you."

Three for Three. Nicky, zero.

I was beginning to get some black cat kind of feeling on this whole matter, but not knowing why. The one thing that served me well in my business was my gut. And my gut was turning backflips on this whole bullshit with Big Daddy. Babies, wives, plastics companies. Sadly nobody ever says no to Big Daddy and gets away with it. The good news was if I had to tangle with Big Daddy over a plastics company, a wife, babies, and a legacy, half the battle was won. Because I was laying eyes on my Becker baby-maker across the room. She was right here in front of me.

The bad news was, that first class shithead Brooks Fitzgerald McKenna was on the dance floor, coiled around my baby-maker. Not to mention Mr. Security himself, Malcom Coles, was gritting his teeth in anger, while popping Tums excessively. Who or what was giving him heartburn? Maybe it was Brooks. Maybe it'll be me. Far be for me to deny Malcom some heartburn.

"Fine, Three. I'll snag the plastics company for Becker Foods because that's business. Family business. But you tell Big Daddy for me, he doesn't get to control my personal life," I hissed back

40

at him.

"You tell him yourself Nicky. I'm only forewarning you as to what's coming down the slippery slope, little brother."

Three, four. Nicky zero.

"Yeah right, Three."

"After all Nicky, you're the omnipotent one, so you should know these things, remember? Part the Red Sea, Nicky, and make it happen," Three answered back in his serious lawyer voice.

"This really should be your project, Three."

"I've got bigger fish to fry right about now. Marcy wants to redecorate Becker Manor. She wants the girls in some new fancy-dancy private school in the fall that will practically cost me the price of a four-year stint at Harvard."

"You're starting to whine again, Three."

"I really don't like being the go-between Big Daddy and you. You get me, Nicky?"

Three, five. Nicky down on the mat.

I barely heard Three's last words as my thoughts were suddenly distracted. The band was playing *our song*.

"Gotta run, Three. Talk to you later."

Color me down for the count.

I slammed my phone shut. I could hear myself sighing heavily. Some freaking New Year's. Big Daddy sending messages about babies and plastic companies. I needed to get to a happy place. And if this new year had any chance of being a happy one, I was going to have to start with taming little Ms. Control Freak herself, Harper Montgomery.

"Are you okay, Nicky?" Lucia asked, walking back toward me again, noticing I had ended my call.

"Get me everything you can find on Joduku Plastics before next week, Lucia. We're going into the plastics business," I said, handing her my phone back.

Lucia shook her head, rolling her eyes up to the ceiling at the same time.

"Plastics," she muttered under her breath, slightly agitated.

I ignored Lucia, gliding across the dance floor to begin my mission. I wasn't the best dancer in the world, but one thing I did do well was slow dance. Mico had requested the band play Norah Jones's "The Nearness of You." He moved to dance with his bride. Mico requested this song for me. I knew his and Riley's song was "All the Way." Hell, I was the best man. I could slow dance to this. Mico taught me how to dance at the Academy, instructing me early on that black women liked their men well coordinated on the dance floor and in the bedroom. None of that two-left-feet shit. I glanced in Mico's direction. He gave me the go for it nod, confirming my suspicions. I was going to make a move on Harper and snatch her out of the arms of that fuckwad Brooks.

My eyes did a one-eighty of the room. Mackenzie Rhodes was on a picture-taking break. Mackenzie was Harper's BFF. A beautiful petite black woman with short black hair that typically hung in spiral wavy-looking curls, she was glammed to the max tonight, her hair pulled off her face, laying bone straight. She was gliding around elegantly in a yellow satin gown that moved with her in all the right places, accenting her shapely curves. She merged so easily with the wedding guests, one would hardly know she was working tonight. Mackenzie was engaged in conversation with Malcom. She was so easy on the eyes, I was certain she'd have Malcom's attention for however long she chose. This was my moment.

I honed in on Harper across the room on the dance floor like a radar-guided drone, ready to strike.

Harper was dazzling. Beautiful. She looked absolutely edible, taking my breath away. Her caramel-colored skin complimented the emerald-green oriental-inspired dress that hugged her curvaceous body tightly. Her dress was shiny with green trim, making her look like cool, lickable lime sherbet—good enough to eat on a hot day. Her long black hair was swirled in an updo with two emerald-and-black oriental chopsticks that were holding her hair in place. She had thick wide diamond cuffs on both arms, and some cotton-candy-colored stilettos that accented those sleek brown legs. Harper looked like a million dollars, the envy of every woman in the room, the lustful desire of every man. I strolled across the room tightening my tie, pulling the cuffs on my tuxedo for good measure, all while moving to take her hand, putting it in mine.

"Excuse me Brooks, I'd like to have this dance with Harper if I may," I said, my eyes narrowing thin, daring him not to step aside like a gentleman.

I knew I could count on the fact this his sense of aristocracy would compel him to step aside like a gentleman. I held my breath hoping I wouldn't have to threaten him. It was a question mark because Brooks held it against me that I enticed one of his women friends away from his harem a couple of years ago. It was my way of paying him back for crossing me in business, so I wasn't certain how he might respond.

I was gratified when he nodded reluctantly and walked away, edging his way towards some young tall lanky-looking blonde on the other side of the room who'd caught his attention. He sauntered her direction like the sly fox that he was.

"Hey, Kitten," I said, tugging her body close to mine, pulling her hard and tight against my chest. We weren't exactly indifferent to each other. Expectations between us hung in the air. I felt my gut knot.

"Nicky, I almost didn't recognize you tonight. Two of your limbs seem to be missing. You're minus the blonde and black-haired bimbos that seem to be your regular appendages every time I see you," Harper said.

I knew Harper was throwing daggers, referring to supermodels Mallory Morgan and Jessica Leonard. Unfortunately for me, I'd managed to be splashed across the pages of that rag of a blog, The New York Esquire, a few weeks ago. I was cuddled in a booth at Club Below Zero in Soho with Mallory and Jessica. Truthfully, I was by myself until the paparazzi started sniffing around the club, about the same time Ms. Hot and Ms. Bothered walked into the door. And of course those two sirens surrounded me on both sides, unwilling to miss an opportunity to be photographed with me. They both are gorgeous as hell and they know it. Long on beauty. Short on brains. But they loved being "seen" with the rich and famous. Far be for me to deny them my company.

"And for the record, I'm not your Kitten," she said rolling her eyes, falling right in step with the beat of the music.

"You scratch like a kitten, or better yet, a tigress," I said, putting my arm around her waist, gliding her slowly on the dance floor, now humming in her ear.

I couldn't help but drink in her big brown eyes with eyelids that were glittering under the dance floor lights. She smelled like a mix of vanilla, jasmine, and oriental spice. She was wearing Obsession. Her favorite. I loved it on her too. I needed to call Calvin Klein and make an angel investment in his next new cologne solely to pay homage.

"Can't you ever give it rest, even for a celebratory night like tonight?" I asked. "You're such the hard nut to crack. They're playing our song, honey."

"Have you had a lobotomy since I've seen you last? You and I no longer have a song."

"We'll forever have our song, Kitten."

"What's wrong Nicky? Can't get any attention from your other women tonight? You have to come haunt me? Not to mention if there's any nut cracking to be had, it won't be with you."

"You know you're the only woman that means anything to me," I said dismissively, twirling her around once to the beat of the music.

"Don't patronize me Nicky," Harper said, looking up at me, her voice breathless.

Her eyes were big, brown, intelligent, and leery. Suddenly I felt like she had all the power in the room. I could feel the back of my neck sweat.

"Honey, you do look dazzling tonight," I said, trying to change the subject, pulling her even closer to me.

"Save the crap. I don't need it." Harper was glaring at me with the utmost frustration. "You aren't dazzled now, and you weren't dazzled ten years ago," she snapped.

"Goddamn, Harper. Here we go again. Aren't you ever going to let that go?"

As soon as the words popped out of my mouth, I knew I'd said the wrong thing. I had to try to recover. "At some point we have to forgive each other for what happened. Even then, our relationship had more good than bad."

Harper moved her red luscious lips to say something but paused, her lower lip quivering. "We could have a re-do you know if it weren't for the fact that you fight me at every turn," I snapped. "Haven't we hurt each other enough?"

The band begin playing "Try a Little Tenderness." I held on to Harper even tighter. I wasn't letting her go. I could feel her heart pounding hard against my chest. I flashed a quick smile down on her, searching her soul, trying to burrow my way inside those cold dark places trying to reach her heart. I believed there was a spark still left there between us. I felt it whenever I touched her. I felt it whenever I was in her presence. I knew she could feel it too. At some point I had to knock down her defenses and that freaking stone wall that she puts up every time I come around.

"I think you have your facts wrong, Nicky. I don't recall being the one to have doled out the boatload of hurt and pain that summer," Harper growled.

"No, that was my fault," I said, whispering the words softly in her ear. "I own that. But you sure as hell have doled out your share of hurt, pain, and venom ever since. I think ten years later, it's time for you to cease with this war you've waged against me, Kitten."

I could feel myself losing my temper which was not the outcome I wanted to have. *Goddamn she brings out the worst in me.* This wasn't going so well.

"Venom? War?" Harper said, pushing back on me, her feet now coming to a halt on the dance floor.

"Heeeeey, Harper," Mackenzie said, shuffling across the dance floor in our direction as the song was coming to an end. "How long are you going to stay on this dance floor slumming with the asshole? The senator and your mother are on their way up, and Malcom wants you a bit closer to him right now," Mackenzie said, looking me up and down with undeniable annoyance.

"What's wrong Mac, you're short on folks to harass tonight?" I said, disgusted that she had appeared. I decided making me miserable was a part of her life's mission. "Shouldn't you be taking some photographs or something? Harper's a grown woman. I doubt that she needs a seeing-eye dog to get around on her own tonight," I said, peering down on her five-foot-two frame, our eyes colliding.

"Go to hell, Nicky. You're lucky she speaks to you at all," Mackenzie hissed.

"I'd like to think she and I can still be friends even though you don't."

"*Humpf.* Who needs enemies around with you on the prowl?" Mackenzie growled.

"Perhaps we can have a seat, Harper?" I pleaded, seriously

wanting to ditch Mackenzie. "Can I get you something to drink, a glass of champagne?"

"She doesn't need anything from you," Mackenzie said, shoving her champagne glass in Harper's hand and narrowing her eyes at me.

"Excuse me you two," Harper interrupted. "Last I checked I didn't realize I required either of you to speak for my interests," she snorted, ignoring Mackenzie and I staring each other down.

Harper directed her attention toward the arrival of her parents.

Almost immediately I could hear the familiar sounds of the senator's entourage arriving. The senator and his wife headed for the bridal party table, the senator shaking heads with the guests along the way, making his usual *Grand Poohbah* entrance. They quickly moved across the floor, headed toward the newlyweds to graciously extend their congratulatory wishes. It was hard not to notice the buzz that was suddenly filling the room.

I pulled Harper close to me. "Excuse us Mackenzie," I said, at the same moment Malcom was walking towards us. I quickly tucked Harper under my arm. I turned my back on both of them, guiding Harper towards the direction of her parents, my hand on the small of her back. I knew she'd want to see her folks, and I wanted to be at her side when she did. I was confident as I guided her across the room, she wouldn't put up an argument. She understood the history between our families.

"Daddy, Mother," Harper said, rushing to give them both a hug. "It's good to see you."

She smiled boldly, kissing them each on the cheek.

"How's my girl?" Senator Montgomery said.

Senator Clayton Lawrence Montgomery was a distinguished fair-skinned African American man. I was sure he had some native Indian in his lineage by the red undertones in his skin. He reminded me of General Colin Powell. A fit man, always well groomed. Dressed in a black silk-collared tuxedo, his silver grey hair, strong jawline, and face framed with clear rimless glasses, he had a regal-like air of authority. Whenever the senator was around, all heads turned. There was never a doubt who was in command.

"Nicolas, it's so good to see you again. How's the Deuce doing?" Senator Montgomery said, referring to my father, Blake Ross Becker II.

Only a handful of people from back in the day referred to my father as Deuce. Over the years, as my father grew in power and wealth, he somehow moved from being "Deuce" to "Big Daddy."

I grumbled to myself, my thoughts skittering through my brain at the mere mention of Big Daddy. He was making me buy a damn plastics company. Deuce might as well been labeled "Ass" tonight as far as I was concerned.

"He's well sir, thank you for asking," I said politely, trying to forget my own frustration with my father tonight.

"Oh Nicholas, it's been ages since we've seen you, darling," Harper's mother Elizabeth Carmichael Montgomery said, air kissing me on both cheeks, European style.

I flashed a huge smile back at her, still holding Harper's hand tightly. No one but Senator Montgomery would have a wife as lovely and beautiful as Elizabeth. It was obvious where Harper got her good looks. She came from a beautiful gene pool. I swear her mother grew better looking each year with age.

Elizabeth was the consummate political trophy wife. Her long sandy brown hair with streaks of blonde highlights hung bone straight on her shoulders. Her red off-the-shoulder gown complimented her voluptuous breasts, small waistline, and curvy hips. The woman looked hot. Her green eyes were unusual for an African American woman, making her all the more alluring. Her skin was a golden brown, making me wonder if she had been in a warmer part of the world recently and had gotten a tan.

"You're looking as beautiful as ever, Elizabeth," I said, bringing her hands to my lips, kissing her knuckles affectionately. "You get more gorgeous every day," I said.

"Watch it son," the senator laughed haughtily. "That one belongs to me last I checked."

"Oh Clayton," Elizabeth grinned. "Behave yourself and stop acting like a jealous old man." Harper's mother smiled politely, loving every bit of the attention. "Nicholas is practically family, Clayton. Come sit with us Nicholas. Come Harper," she said, directing her daughter to sit near her.

Elizabeth glanced over her shoulder, noticing that Malcom was easing himself closer on Harper's heels, perhaps letting the senator know he was on his job. "Oh Malcom dear, we'll be fine for now," Elizabeth waved him off with her hand to dismiss him. "Feel free to take a break," she said in a commanding voice.

Malcom looked miffed at having to take an order from

Harper's mother, but he distanced himself nonetheless. Harper didn't seem to mind though. She moved gracefully, sitting next to her mom. I held the chairs out for both of them. I took the seat to Harper's left, putting a protective arm around the back of her chair, crossing my leg, and marking my territory. Harper and Elizabeth seemed happy to have a mother and daughter moment without the fuss of the entourage that came with being in the senator's presence, grateful the senator had politely excused himself. The senator left, moving across the room to engage in conversation with other guests.

I watched out the corner of my eye as Mackenzie snapped multiple pictures of the newlyweds and their guests with the senator. Those pictures would draw a big sum in *New York Magazine* this month as the "Who's Who Wedding of the Year."

"Listen Harper," Elizabeth said, as Harper sat glaring across the room, not at her mother, but at Mico's new brother-in-law Reese Nelson. Reese was engaged in conversation with the jazz combo's pianist and vocalist that were on a set break. I started feeling paranoid again, wondering whether Harper and Reese were more than friends. Harper and Reese seemed to frequently land at all the same places at the same time.

"Do you see something you like?" I said, grabbing a couple of champagne glasses off the server's tray, and setting them both in front of Harper and Elizabeth.

Harper's eyes were still locked in on the jazz combo across the room.

"What's it to you?" she asked, turning her head slightly my direction, giving me her once-over look.

I glared back at her intensely, deciding whether to respond to her dig or not. She spoke before I could form a sentence.

"But I'll be sure to not let you know when I do," she said, turning her head back towards her mother's direction.

One of the red-coated servers was right on time, setting a vodka martini down in front of me. I took a huge much needed gulp. Man I so needed to get this train I called Kitten on track. I decided to shake off her words.

"Harper, I have a small matter that I'd like for you to handle darling," Elizabeth said, not paying attention to Harper and me.

"And what might that be, Mother?" Harper said, tapping her fingers on the table, signaling to me that she was annoyed.

Yeah baby. I'm equally as annoyed. But tonight I'm going to make peace, not war. With my arm still wrapped around the back of her chair, I placed my hand on shoulder. Her body stilled under my touch.

I listened passively to Elizabeth, noticing Brooks had made his way over to the senator, inserting himself into the picture-taking activities with the bride and groom. Brooks' chest was pumped up another level. He was eager to be in the same room with the senator. His head was so big, I wondered how he kept it on his neck.

"I know you're busy, love, but I need a favor, my darling," Elizabeth said. "There's a little plastics company in Princeton, New Jersey that's for sale that I'd like you to acquire for Carmichael Ketchup."

Plastics. Company. Did I hear the words plastics company?

"Given your high level of expertise in risk management, business consulting and turnaround services, I'd like it if The Montgomery Consulting Group could take the lead on the acquisition for us," Elizabeth said very casually. "Joduku Plastics, love. That's the company. That's what I need."

Holy shit. I started to choke on the vodka martini I was drinking. I could feel my own brows pull together. Did Elizabeth just say *Joduku Plastics*? Fuck. Shit. Fuck me.

Harper looked at me funny, as if she were wondering if she was going to have to do the Heimlich maneuver on me. I was spitting and choking all over myself.

"Nicky, are you okay, baby?" Elizabeth said, looking worried. I could feel my face turning red. Vodka had gone down the wrong way, making me feel like my windpipes were collapsing in on me. The words "plastics company" were stuck in my throat.

"Nothing a good smack across the back won't fix, Mother. Right, Nicky?" Harper glowered, whacking me hard across my back.

I winced. She looked pleased with herself, having knocked the living shit out of me. Air flowed inward. I forced an exhale, grunting loudly.

"No ma'am. Thank you I'm fine," I said catching my breath, coughing deeply a couple of times so as to clear my throat. I chugged some of Harper's champagne down rapidly.

No way in hell did I want to end up in an acquisition war with Harper over Joduku Plastics. How in the hell could this be possible? And worse, Harper was going to think I was going to want to buy the company to spurn her. She would never believe otherwise. No way. No how. It was bad timing that this conversation was coming up now. The fact that I was sitting right next to her during this discussion would create all kinds of problems. She would never believe or accept that my brother had beaten her to the punch with this information less than an hour ago. One thing's for sure, despite Elizabeth Montgomery's interests, Harper was *not* going to have this discussion with Elizabeth in front of me.

Immediately, I felt Harper's brain shift gears, moving into a state of defensiveness. This was information she did not want *me* to have. No sirree. As soon as Elizabeth pushed the conversation further to gain momentum, Reese Nelson walked over to greet Harper. That was both good and bad. Good because the conversation quickly changed directions. And bad, because now Reese was grabbing Harper out her chair, whisking her back on to the dance floor to dance to some fast number that was playing. Harper fell right into step with Reese, I'm sure taking advantage of the opportunity not to have to have the discussion about Joduku Plastics in front of me.

I was failing at pretending that my attention was directed elsewhere, as I listened to Elizabeth tell me how Reese was like a brother to Harper. I watched the two of them on the dance floor, Harper shaking those curvy hips of hers far too sexily to be anybody's sister. Harper is an only child. She doesn't know how to do sibling. I love Elizabeth dearly, but I wasn't buying what she was selling. I was pissed and jealous that it wasn't me out there with her on the dance floor. Fortunately, the senator and Brooks were making their way back over to where Elizabeth and I were sitting before my paranoia kicked up another notch.

"Nicholas my boy, I know better than to leave you too long with my beautiful wife," the senator said, chuckling heartily, slapping me on my back hard. Goddamn. He must have taught his daughter how to dole out that same slap on the back. It's true the apple doesn't fall far from the tree.

"Yeah senator, he's a regular modern-day gigolo," Brooks laughed, stirring the pot. "Every time I open the morning paper, Nicholas is plastered across the cover of Page Six," Brooks said cunningly. "You should watch your woman when he's around."

"Don't believe everything you read senator," I said, shooting Brooks a suspicious look. "One has to consider the source. Surely you can appreciate as well as I, sir, how the media outlets tend to distort truths." I bristled with anger at Brooks.

The senator stared directly at me a moment too long as if he were studying my expression, casting doubt, or perhaps wondering if my comment was somehow intended for him. "Of course Nicholas," Senator Montgomery said, unable to penetrate my poker face.

Brooks had forced me to put all my guards up now.

"You've never struck me as the settling down type," Brooks persisted. "You seem to be the honey that attracts all those beautiful beauties that flock around you." Now he was turning the knife he'd put in my back.

"You don't know me well Brooks. I hold no claim to those . . . what did you say? Beautiful beauties. But that which I do lay claim to as mine, is mine," I hissed back at him.

"Oh Clayton, you know Nicholas is saving himself for that special someone. Right Nicholas?" Elizabeth interrupted.

"Do you have a girlfriend Brooks?" Elizabeth said a little too innocently, taking up my cause.

"Well no ma'am, I . . . I . . . I can't say that I do," Brooks said, starting now to stutter and stumble, gulping his scotch. *Good shot at that fuckwad, Lizzy. I am saving myself for someone special, and she is right here in the room.*

Lucky for me, Reese and Harper were exiting the dance floor, both moving toward our table. The pianist was announcing in the background that it was time for the bride to throw the bouquet, and for the groom to go for the garter. Oh, man, it was definitely time for me to get the hell out of here. No way I was going to end up in the center of the room catching some freaking garter with that snap-happy camera-shooting Mackenzie around. Mico was my man, but this was where I drew the line. For me to land on the gossip pages again this month would be bad form.

Anticipating my every need, Lucia appeared out of nowhere, standing at my side as I stood for Harper who had not yet taken her seat.

"Nicky, you have an important call from the airport hanger," Lucia said. "You're needed to authorize release of one of the jets in the Milk Money fleet that's on standby for the newlywed's trip to the South of France."

"Thank you, Lucia."

"Senator, Elizabeth, it's good to see you both again. I hope to do it again soon. Harper, Brooks, if you will excuse me, I must attend to this call."

"Good seeing you again Nicholas. Happy New Year," Elizabeth said, grinning.

"Give my best to Deuce," Senator Montgomery said, reaching to shake my hand.

I reached out, pulling Harper close to me before she could take a seat. I kissed her softly on the cheek. She briefly closed her eyes, looking irritated and uneasy.

"Happy New Year, Kitten," I whispered, stroking my index finger and thumb along her chin.

Harper's eyes glossed over me, softening. She let out a breath she'd been holding. I felt her skin heat under my lips.

The realities were what they were. Harper and I were so not done.

CHAPTER FOUR

Harper

"Ms. Montgomery, Mackenzie Rhodes is here to see you," Charlotte Hall, my Administrative Assistant, said over the intercom.

Before I could respond, my best friend Mackenzie was busting through the double doors of my office.

"Hey Harper."

"Mackenzie, what a surprise."

"I thought I'd drop by and share photographs I developed from Riley and Noah's wedding a couple of weeks ago," Mackenzie said.

She opened a large black portfolio full of prints, pulling up a chair at my circular table. "Sorry I'm dropping in on you unannounced, but I figured you wouldn't mind. I've forwarded the newlyweds a digital copy of their proofs so I thought you might want some of the extra pictures I took of the senator and Elizabeth."

"No problem. It's been a slow morning anyway," I said, clicking the calendar on my Macbook Pro to see how the rest of my day was going to shape up.

"Well, I managed to get some great shots of your mom, the senator, and of course you and Brooks."

Mackenzie was trying to restrain her look. She was losing the battle, looking like the cat that had swallowed the mouse.

"Here's a couple of shots with you and Reese," she said. "Aaaannd, here's the one shot that killed me to take, of you and

Mister Sleezeball."

But of course it was a picture of me and Nicholas. Most of the time when Mackenzie spoke bad about a man, it was usually a reference to Nicholas. I wasn't at all surprised.

"You're never shy about how you really feel, Mac. Not much has changed these last ten years," I said, twisting my oversized plush leather chair around.

I walked over to the circular table to look at Mackenzie's photographs.

"These are really good," I said, flipping through the pictures of my parents at the wedding. I thumbed quickly through the pictures of me with Brooks and Reese. And then I stared at the picture of Nicholas and me.

"Really Mac, you took a picture of Nicholas whispering in my ear? That's interesting," I said, trying to smother a giggle.

"Yes," she said. "The look on your face is priceless."

I kept my head down hoping Mackenzie wouldn't catch the expression on my face. It would reveal more than I was ready to discuss. I was putting up a front to appear emotionless.

"Hard not to capture it, Harper. If I didn't know better, I'd say you look a little smitten. Ya damn sure don't have that same look on your face in this shot with the Fitzgerald," Mackenzie chuckled wickedly.

Mackenzie held up the photographs to the light, twisting her head from side to side studying the shot and the expression on my face. She even pulled her little photographer's magnifying glass out of her jeans pocket, plopping it right on my top of my face in the picture.

"Jesus, an entire night with Brooks Fitzgerald McKenna is about as close to a death sentence as I could get. Can you imagine what it was like to be stuck with the Fitz at a great wedding party given by Riley and Noah Dunham? You know what they say, Mac, 'a picture is worth a thousand words'."

"Well the fact is Harper, you're just not into the Fitz."

"Or any of the rest of those noodles out there," I said.

"Fitz is totally a hot-looking guy. You have to admit that, Harper," Mackenzie said, taking a moment to sift through the emotional landmine I was working overtime to conceal.

"Yup, and a really cold guy in the bedroom. He doesn't bring any heat in that department," I laughed.

"Yeah, So what did the Becker have to say for himself? Spill the beans. Give up the goods, girlfriend," Mackenzie said, swaying back and forth in her chair waiting patiently for my answer.

Mackenzie was going to get information out of me if it took all day. She was steely like that. She could wait me out. I knew it. She knew it.

"Oh you know, his usual stuff," I said, trying to sound nonchalant, admiring her outfit.

Mackenzie had a great sense of style. She was rocking some hot straight-leg denim jeans with a blue cashmere hooded poncho. She'd propped her feet up on the light beige leather swivel chair next to her, showing off a cute pair of four-inch Jimmy Choos. Her hair was back to her natural look in short spiral-like twists, a change from the short straight look she wore at the night of the wedding.

"Harper there is no such thing as saying *Nicholas* and *usual* in the same breath. There is nothing usual about the man."

"Okay, okay, okay. He may have mentioned how it was time for me to forgive him and how he and I needed to have a 'relationship re-do'," I said, moving my fingers in air quotes.

Casually still flipping through the photos, I made it a point not to look up at Mackenzie, despite the fact that I could feel the heat of her glare burning a hole through me. I could only imagine the look on her face.

Mackenzie didn't truly dislike Nicholas as much as people thought—although it was sometimes hard to tell since she treated him crappy whenever she saw him. It was her way of expressing her loyalty to me. Mackenzie knew my history with Nicholas. She knew how much he'd hurt me. Her outward anger towards him was the closest thing she could manage as a point of revenge for treating her best friend poorly. Mackenzie had had a front row seat to the pain Nicholas had caused me. Had it not been for experience of holding my hand through the months of pain, they might have ended up to be good friends. They were a lot alike, each being undeniably persistent and headstrong.

"Both the angles on the long shots and the close-ups are really very good, Mackenzie. Very creative."

"Mackenzie always does good work. They don't call me "Magical Mackenzie" for nothing," she said, amused and unrepentant for her ego now running amuck. "And, so what was your response, Harper? What did you tell Mr. Gazillionaire bad boy slug?"

"I essentially gave him the same response I always give him."

I kept flipping through the photographs. Mackenzie wasn't giving up. She waited me out, her arms folded across her breasts as I glared, discerning the look on my face.

"I told him to forget about it."

"Ummm," Mackenzie hummed.

"Hell will freeze over before I turn on the heart lights giving Nicholas Miles Becker any chance to be with me ever again in life." I cocked my head to the side, looking more closely at the pictures of Nicholas and myself.

"Well I can understand how you feel, Harper. Ten years ago in Martha's Vineyard, the relationship with you two started off really good. But by the end of the summer, things happened. Unfortunately he handled things really shittily."

"No one knows that better than me. Nicholas accused me of setting him up and backing him into a marriage that he wasn't ready for, but felt he needed to commit to out of obligation. Then when I lost the baby, he acted even worse."

"Only because by the time he came around to finding his right mind," Mackenzie said sarcastically, "you had miscarried. His accusations of you having had an abortion were so unfounded," she grumbled. "I still never understood why you never corrected his misunderstanding, Harper."

"I thought we were in love. I thought he knew me. I thought he knew who I was. He should have known better than to believe I would abort his child."

"But you didn't correct him."

"I know, Mac. I let him believe whatever he wanted to believe. At the end of the day I was hurt. I was done with him."

"You two were in love. He panicked, got scared, and ran for the hills. By the time he got it together, it was too late for you."

It was painful thinking back on what Nicholas and I had lost. A flood of conflicting emotions momentarily filled my body. My heart hurt in my chest every time I thought about how happy we were then. A couple of young lovers, freshly minted with new degrees. It was going to be us against the world. We had such huge dreams for our life together.

"Mackenzie, a couple of months in pregnancy time feels like a lifetime when you're figuring things out and your lover suddenly decides to bolt. I was in the middle of a crisis. Nicholas and I were having a crisis. It wasn't like we weren't old enough to get married. I was twenty-six and he was thirty-one, for Christ's sake."

"Yeah, well maybe Nicholas wanted to play the field and sow his oats."

"Uh huh, and he didn't feel like he wanted to be tied down to me and a baby," I snapped.

Mackenzie handed me more photographs of him. Damn, that man is fine. He walked the line between heartthrob and gorgeous. No, he was a fine, gorgeous, heartthrob. A fine, gorgeous, arrogant ass, rain-on-my-parade heartthrob. Just thinking about this all over again was causing my temperature to rise. It was a painful period in my life then and there was no way out but through.

"Thank God I had you to lean on Mackenzie. I don't know how I could have gotten through those days without you. I'm so blessed to have you as my friend."

"Which is exactly why you should tell that asshole to keep it moving and don't look back, Harper."

"Yeah, except now my biological clock is ticking. I wouldn't mind having a baby now. I look at your relationship with Gill, Jr. I love being his Godmother. I have so much fun with him. I kind of want my own son or daughter now. I just don't want the man it takes to make it," I chuckled, trying to keep the mood light after all this talk down memory lane.

"Well being a single parent is tougher than you think Harper. Ever since Gill died in Iraq, raising a baby on my own hasn't been a cakewalk," Mackenzie said. "I'm not sure it's a good idea to bite off a piece of that apple alone if you don't have to."

"Well, I have an appointment with my therapist Dr. Richards this afternoon. I plan to run the idea of my having a baby by myself by her. See if she agrees. I'm ready to do this now. I feel like I've got the moxie to raise a child on my own. My panic attacks have long since ended. My career is at a stage where it's the best it's ever been."

"And, you're filthy rich," Mackenzie said mockingly. "And, I could keep adding to the list. You hot, you're beautiful, you're smart. Whatcha need a man for, girl? Love 'em and leave 'em Momma," Mackenzie said supportively.

"Exactly. I'm ready for motherhood. It's now or never. I'm

thirty-six years old. I'm not getting any younger. Speaking of men, Mackenzie, when are YOU going to get back in those waters? When are you going to find a new man and a dad for little Gill? It's been several years now. It's time, don't you think?"

"Oh you're in my business now," she laughed, swiveling her chair around to face me.

"Yup. Gill left you financially comfortable. You're the go-to photographer for anything and everything important on the social scene in Manhattan. You're the same age as me. You still have a lot of kick left in you, girl. We can play the field together."

"Well I've kind of got my eye on someone special," Mackenzie said slyly.

"Who? Girlfriend, spill it like you tell me," I prodded.

"Well it's too early yet for me to say. I don't want to jinx things. But if I decide to jump into that pond again, you'll be the first to know. You can count on it."

Mackenzie was always the one to play her cards close to the vest. Why wasn't I surprised that she was holding out on me again. She was very overprotective of her son. If she made a decision to put herself out there with a man, he was well going to be worth it. Mackenzie didn't allow her son to bond with men that she felt held no possibility for a long-term future.

"So Harper, back to these pictures of you and Nicholas." She turned the pictures around again and tilted her head to the side a bit. "Are you absolutely sure you and Nicholas still don't have feelings for each other?" she asked, right as my assistant Charlotte buzzed my intercom again.

"Ms. Montgomery, I have your mother on the phone for you."

I looked at Mackenzie, picked the phone up, and mouthed that I had to take Mother's call. I was glad not to have to answer her question. I was going to have trouble denying that I had no feelings at all for Nicholas. Quite the opposite.

Mackenzie mouthed back that it was time for her to leave, tapping her finger on her watch. I nodded. Mackenzie grabbed her things, but left the pictures, signaling she'd call me later, blowing me air kisses.

"Good afternoon, Mother, how are you?"

"I'm well thank you. It was so good to see you at Riley and Noah's wedding, darling. You looked absolutely divine."

"Thanks Mother."

"I was tickled pink to see Nicholas, dear. He looked so handsome in his tuxedo."

"Yes Mother, he did," I said, still silently studying the picture of me and Nicholas.

"However, I was a bit surprised to see you with that Brooks McKenna fellow. I don't think Nicholas is too fond of him," Mother paused briefly.

"Nicholas doesn't get to pick my dates Mother," I said, hoping to keep my voice at a level that made me sound disinterested.

Mother was never one to get it out of her head that Nicholas and I belong together. She treated that man like he could do no wrong. She was downright obsessive compulsive about her affection for him. Of all the men I've dated this decade, Mother kept coming back to Nicholas like clockwork.

"Well for what it's worth dear, I think the two of you look cute together," Mother cooed. "Nicholas is a fine man with lots to offer. I see no reason why the two of you can't put the past behind you, Harper. You know, let bygones be bygones. You're not getting any younger, darling."

"Must we discuss this right now Mother? I'm busy."

"It's obvious the two of you still have feelings for each other, Harper," she said, ignoring me. "You need to start to thinking about settling down, dear."

I wondered how many more years was it going to take for my Mother to get it through her head that I was fine without a man. I imagined that when I told her I'm contemplating bringing her first grandchild into the world absent an identifiable father, she was seriously going to blow a fuse. But, I'd have to cross that bridge when I got to it. Today was not the day.

"Mother, surely you didn't call me to talk about Nicholas?" I closed my eyes, pinching the bridge of my nose, wishing this call was over.

"No dear. I'm calling to see how things are progressing with Joduku Plastics."

"Ah yes, plastics. Well, I've got the latest prospectus on them right here in front of me."

Thankfully, Charlotte had dropped the financials on my desk shortly after Mackenzie left. I relished the thought of being prepared whenever Mother and I did business together. We had a healthy respect for each other's business acumen. "Preliminarily, the financials look good. There are no real fires in the financial statements. I've assigned a couple of folks on my staff to do due diligence. I'm waiting for their feedback."

"Good to hear Harper. I take great comfort in the fact you're on top of things."

"I'll probably take the jet early next month to Princeton to meet with their CEO, Nobu. As best I can tell, there's a short list of three other potential buyers who may possibly be serious contenders. My team is doing intelligence now to identify our competition."

"Well it's still early in the game, Harper. I trust you'll keep a rein on things. Keep me informed. *Carmichael Ketchup* really wants this acquisition. If we can acquire this business, it will really be a coup for us."

"I understand Mother."

"We'll be able leave our competitors in the dust, Harper. I have a lot of faith that The Montgomery Group will come through for us. Make this happen."

"I still don't understand why you didn't keep this acquisition in-house with the Carmichael staff, Mother? Don't you think this project would be easier to control in-house?"

"Oh, not really. The staff here are far too comfortable. They're way too slow at getting out of the gate for my tastes. It's time for me to rock the boat. Perhaps roll a few heads around here."

"Interesting."

"But then again, I know of no one that loves to win more than you do, Harper. That's the kind of tenacity I need to have on this deal, sweetheart."

"Well I do what I can, Mother."

I did not quite believing my lying ears. I barely believed that crock of crap Mother was shoveling about her staff being too comfortable. Mother didn't build a ketchup empire surrounded by fools. Something was up with this acquisition. I didn't know what, but I was sure going to get to the bottom of it sooner or later.

"I need to run, Mother."

No problem sweetie. I'll check back with you next week. I must go now too," she said. "I promised your father I'd join him at Le Bernardin for a dinner. He's meeting with some politicos in the New York Democratic Delegation.

"Daddy's favorite place to politic," I said nonchalantly.

"Well it seems the New York delegation is gearing up to discuss the gubernatorial race. Your father and I are sponsoring a fundraiser to help pay off some of the campaign debts and to replenish the coffers from the mid-year elections. Expect a call from my secretary. She'll be contacting Charlotte soon to make sure the fundraiser is on your calendar."

"I'll be in touch mother."

I hung up wondering what else I was getting myself into again. Acquisitions. Politics. I was starting to feel like a dull gal with a dull life even by my own standards.

"A Mr. Brooks Fitzgerald McKenna is here to see you, Ms. Montgomery," Charlotte said over the intercom, startling me out of my thoughts.

I suddenly remembered I had Brooks on my calendar this afternoon. Poor Charlotte. Brooks had her calling him by his full name too. Some weird expectation of his. By now he probably heard about me going back out to the clubs after he'd escorted me home from the wedding reception. At the time I thought it was a coup, that as soon as he dropped me off, I ran right back out again. Unfortunately, I made the TMZ website the following morning. Reese Nelson and I were spotted exiting an after-hours club, our picture having been taken by one of those TMZ stalkers that prey on the rich and famous.

"Send him in Charlotte."

Brooks sauntered in my office as if he owned the place.

"Hey Brooks, good to see you," I said politely, extending my hand.

My effort at creating a bit of distance was wasted. Brooks pulled me into his arms, planting a wet slobbery kiss on my lips.

"You're on my calendar today, Brooks, what can I do for you?" I said, fighting off the urge to say "ugh" out loud.

"You've been a busy bee, Harper," Brooks said narrowing his eyes at me. You've been cheating on me behind my back again, baby."

"Cheating on you?" I said in disbelief. "Again?"

"Bad enough I had to watch you at the wedding, fawning, curled up in the arms of that "Sugar Daddy" Nicholas Becker. But then you went out behind my back after I took you home, sneaking around with Reese Nelson of all people." Brooks sulked.

Uh Oh. Time for me to stop relying on Brooks Fitzgerald McKenna as a future plus-one date option. He was talking as if he believed we were a couple or something.

"I told you at the wedding Brooks, I. Don't. Do. Relationships. You know this. There's nothing exclusive between you and me. *Cheating* is a strong, totally inappropriate word. We're not in relationship."

Talking to Brooks was equivalent to talking to a brick wall. Did the man ever listen to a word I said?

"And *I* told *you* that we make a great team baby," Brooks said, with some weird look of pride on his face.

"And *I* told *you* I had no interest in "teaming" with you—or anybody else for that matter." I could feel myself getting truly annoyed.

"How do you think it looks with you plastered across the Web on the arms of Reese Nelson? Not a good look, Harper. It's the appearance of things. Folks will start to think I'm losing my touch," Brooks snapped, his face completely solemn.

Harper this is exactly why you have to be careful with being too nice to these guys.

"I can't have this, Harper."

He can't have this? Was he kidding me? Give Brooks an inch and he freaking takes a mile. I should have never slept with this fool. It was time to withhold the booty. Brooks Fitzgerald

McKenna obviously didn't know the meaning of "friends with benefits."

"I remembered that you want to have a baby. We can make sweet baby music together, Harper."

"We are not making sweet anything together," I said fully stunned.

"Hell woman, I have a lot to offer. What woman in their right mind wouldn't want to be my wife?"

"Me. I don't," I answered sternly.

"You know you want me. You're just playing hard to get. And I get that. If it'll make you feel better to play that game, I'll go along with it for a beat. I know how you women liked to be chased."

Blaaaah! Puke fucking city. I was seeing red now. Crack a couple of eggs on my head and they would fry right about now.

"Now look here, Brooks," I said, swinging out of my chair so hard the Joduku Plastics folder hit the floor. All of the file's contents scattered to the floor at both our feet. I had lost my thought.

"Here let me help you with this," Brooks said squatting down on the floor at the same time as me. He was a whole lot faster than me, gathering the file papers. "You're buying a plastics company?" he said, with surprise. "What the hell for?"

"None of your business," I snapped, rushing frantically to scoop the papers out of his view. "It's confidential," I said, grasping the fallen papers that were out of his reach.

Not only was Brooks a social-climbing-get-on-my-nerves-pain-in-the-ass, he was predictably nosy as well.

"Listen, honey buns. We can turn this little plastics thing into "our" business. I've got a few connections in Japan at high places."

"No thanks. This is a private family matter."

"You know the Japanese have a tendency to manipulate their currency. I could help you with this. My textile business does import/export transactions with Japan all the time." Brooks spoke as if he was in charge of the world. He still hadn't let go of the folder as we both rose together from the floor.

"I'm very capable of managing a foreign acquisition all on my own, thank you. The Montgomery Consulting Group has a deep bench of executives capable of handling international transactions," I sputtered, snatching the folder out of his hands and pushing all the documents back in the folder haphazardly. "This is a private matter, Brooks," I reiterated.

I slipped the file out of his view, moving back to my swivel chair. I sat down behind my massive oak desk, sighing loudly.

"Baby you don't see my value yet," Brooks harped as he plopped down in the chair across from me. "I guess I'm going to have to step up to the plate and prove my worth to you, Harper," he said, winking. "We can marry our businesses as well as each other, baby."

"I believe we're done here Brooks. I've got other pressing matters to tend to today."

Brooks hadn't grasped that I had nothing more to say on this subject and that this visit was over.

"I don't mind chasing you, baby. I have no intention of letting you get away. You know you want me. But I'm only going to wait on you but for so long," he persisted.

Thank God, Charlotte knocked on the door and entered the room.

"You're going to be late for your next appointment Ms. Montgomery. Would you like for me to reschedule?"

"No thank you, Charlotte. Mr. McKenna is leaving. Aren't you Brooks?"

"Yes I am," Brooks said, rising out of his chair.

I could have kicked myself for dropping the Joduku Plastics file on the floor giving Brooks access to the data. I couldn't be sure that he wouldn't disclose confidential company information.

"You're looking quite lovely today Charlotte," Brooks said, flirtatiously. "I love your hair that way."

Brooks grabbed a fallen curl of Charlotte's hair, slipping it behind her ear as he sauntered out the double doors. Did he just flirt with Charlotte? God, this man knows no bounds. He must be out of his mind to think I would ever think of marrying his philandering ass.

"Ugh. God, I cannot believe this man," I said out loud to Charlotte with indignation.

I watched Brooks exit the office waiting area. Poor Charlotte. She was completely flushed, looking like she didn't know which way was up. I shook my head, heading back into my office to grab my things.

"Ms. Montgomery, before you go, Swann Galleries called," Charlotte said hurriedly, blowing her breath out in a rush.

"Another Ernie Barnes piece suddenly hit the market. It's a limited edition original. The gallery would like to know if you're interested in making a purchase. The piece is up for auction."

"Ummm not really. My last art purchase was a revenge purchase. You know like one of those things you don't really need, but you get so much satisfaction when you buy it. And for what I paid for it, I had a whole lot of revenge going on. You get me?"

"Not really. But I think I understand."

I was trying to tell Charlotte, as nicely as I could, that I only brought that my last piece of artwork to piss off Nicholas. I knew how badly he wanted it. I think Charlotte understood my unstated words. She's a smart young woman. But sometimes I'm wasn't sure how well she reads in between the lines.

"Charlotte, tell Winston to bring the car around please. Let Malcom know, I'm getting ready to go. I don't want to be late for my appointment with Dr. Richards."

I grabbed my purse. Part of me was still fuming from Brooks' visit.

I headed out the doors towards my limousine. I caught a glimpse of Malcom's expression as I moved to hop into the rear seat while he held the door.

"Where's Winston?"

"I told him to take a break. I'm taking you myself today," Malcom said. "We need to talk. You haven't made much time for me."

"What is it?" I asked, as Malcom pulled out into the traffic.

He was sulking. I suppose he was in some huge funk over seeing Brooks leave my office. Frankly, he'd been acting strange for a couple of weeks now, ever since the night of the wedding reception.

"This is getting hard to watch," Malcom said.

"What is *this*?"

"Him."

"Which one?" I asked.

"Both," he said.

I shook my head. I turned my attention towards the pedestrians walking briskly down the street. Here we go. What happened to the days when a guy just shagged a gal and never called back again? Jesus. I must be picking wrong.

"They don't deserve you. They can't take care of you like I can. I've told you how I feel," he said calmly.

"I've told you I don't need taking care of, Malcom. I'm not the relationship type. What happened between us, we agreed wasn't supposed to get serious. Now you want to get serious. This doesn't sound like your wanting to keep your end of the bargain," I continued. "Find someone else to focus on," I said getting pissed for a yet second time this afternoon.

What the hell is wrong with these guys? Don't they know how to kiss and move on? It must be something in the water around here. Nicholas wants a re-do. Brooks thinks he wants to be married to me. And now Malcom is behaving like a lovesick puppy dog. I could feel my frustration building again.

"I'm prepared to wait," Malcom continued.

"Don't," I said dryly.

There was a moment of silence between us. I figured he sensed my seething. I took a deep breath, exhaling slowly to calm myself. "Listen Malcom, I know you take good care of me, protecting me and all. I don't want to lose your services, but I can't have this talk with you every time you see me out with someone new. I don't need this drama in my life right now. If I wanted to settle down, you would know it."

"You don't know what you want."

"Yeah, well I've got on my big girl panties. And I damn sure don't need you to tell me what to do with my life. That's not your job. And, it's sure as hell beyond your job description," I huffed.

I glanced back out the window. What's with these guys today thinking they know what's best for me. This is *my* life.

"There's a lot going on between us, Harper, that's beyond my job description," Malcom snapped back. "What's your problem exactly? Have you been hurt by so many guys you can't find one to trust? Are you concerned about what the senator will think about us being together?" he said, his voice rising a notch.

"The senator has nothing to do with this." Now *I* was the one raising my voice several octaves. "It's about what I think. What I want. You don't get to make choices for me," I snarled through my clenched jaw.

"I'll have Winston waiting for you when you're done. I'll follow behind you in the Range Rover on your drive back. Call me if you need anything. Otherwise I don't want to talk about this anymore today."

"Good, that makes two of us," I snapped, pushing the privacy button forward to raise the window that was a barrier between us. It was just as well. I was ready to declare this day to be damn over anyway.

The marimba starting playing on my phone. For a minute I thought it was going to be a good thing to have a distraction from Malcom, until I looked down at my caller ID. *Nicholas Becker*. Could this day get any worse?

"What the hell do you want? Why are you calling me?" I snapped.

"Harper, Harper, Harper. Are we having a bad day, Kitten?"

"What is it Nicholas? Some of us have busy lives and don't have time to reach back in our pasts to dig up old lovers we kicked to the curb," I snarled.

"You've got the claws out today."

"Every time you make me have to stop what I'm doing to deal with you, Nicholas, I swear you're going to regret it," I hissed.

"Oh I love it when my little kitten turns into the feral cat. It's so damn hot and sexy when your claws come out."

"I told you before, I'm not your kitten."

"Dear, I was wondering if you'd be interested in selling me back the Sugar Shack piece? Some of Ernie Barne's work is coming on the market. I thought maybe you'd be a sweetheart and sell me that piece. I could avoid having to bid on his next piece."

"And why would I do that exactly?"

"Well, it's not like you didn't overpay for the piece. You and I both know that was very vengeful of you. I had a particular purpose for that piece."

"You should have thought about that when you purchased Global Gilliam out from under me. Two can play your game," I sneered.

"I see no reason to dig this up again, Harper. Let sleeping dogs lie. Will you sell me the piece or not? Can't we call a truce on this?"

"Nope and nope."

"Fine, I see you're going to stay on your tough-muffin seat today. Sooner or later you're going to have to come down off that high horse of yours and act like a decent human being," Nicholas shouted.

"Decent human being? Did you just say *decent human being*? I got your decent human being, Nicholas Miles Becker," I yelled.

Click.

He must be crazy out of that beautiful Adonis head of his, questioning whether or not I'm the decent human being. I swear Nicky acts like he's lost some brain matter. I am going to make that man pay through the nose every time he so much as thinks about me. Sooner or later he'll be forced to leave me the hell alone. Take my name off his lips.

I pulled my phone out of my purse to call Charlotte. I dialed the digits on my phone faster than usual. I was overflowing with anger.

"Charlotte. Call Swann Galleries please. Tell them I'm bidding on the artwork after all. Anonymously please. Have them check in with me on a price ceiling."

"Thank you Charlotte."

Malcom pulled up to the curb of Dr. Richards' office, opening the door.

"Malcom, please let Winston know I'll be ready in an hour."

Malcom nodded, saying nothing. I could tell by the look on his face he was still stewing. He looked like I felt.

Humpf. Whatever. People in hell want ice water, too.

CHAPTER FIVE

Nicholas

"Shit. Shit. Shit. She hung up on me. Harper burns my ass. How hard can it be for her to extend some shred of kindness and decency to me some of the damn time? It doesn't cost her anything to sell me that artwork. She only purchased it to spite me anyway," I fumed.

"Face it Nicky, women can be difficult," Stephen said.

"I can't reach back in time and change what was," I said breathing heavily, sweating harder, wondering why I was doing this to myself. "All I can do is go forward," I said, trying to duck my head out of the way.

It was a dumb idea to get into the boxing ring at my penthouse with Stephen. Surely there were better ways to work off steam then to get into a ring with my own bodyguard. Stephen was an ex-Navy Seal. This was a dumbass idea.

"Since seeing her at Mico's wedding, it's been harder than ever to put her out of my mind. She was looking so gorgeous, practically edible. Beautiful."

"She is a knockout, Nicky," *Wham. Wham.* "Very beautiful indeed," Stephen said plowing his fists into my mid-section.

"But that fiery attitude requires me to delve deep into my toolbox. She forces me to pull out attributes I'm not used to using," I said, breathing harder, ducking quicker, but still taking a flurry of punches upside my head.

"Yes Nicky, patience and fortitude are not your strong suits when it comes to Harper. I know. I've observed you. It's hard for you to be in her space without throwing a few of your own grenades, too." Stephen pounded on me.

Oh God, why did I get into the ring with this serial killer? He's killing me. I moved to the corner of the ring, dancing in circles to catch my breath, pumping my gloves together, hoping to appear more menacing.

"She wants to control me. It's bad enough Big Daddy thinks he can tell me what to do, how to do it, trying to control and plan out my life," I puffed, stepping back into Stephen's reach.

It was hard for me to admit out loud, but I believed I could see myself building a life with Harper. Assuming we didn't kill each other first. It just didn't need to be Big Daddy's idea.

"That hardcore veneer of hers is so difficult to crack. She never lets her guard down with me. And she's surrounded by that cast of impotent male clowns and that witch Mackenzie, making my job even harder," I said, double-pounding my fists into Stephen's six-pack.

Stephen might as well have been made of steel. He hardly moved. "Who?" Stephen asked quizzically.

"Mackenzie Rhodes," I repeated. "That wicked witch queen of ice who can't mind her own fucking business," I fumed.

Pow!

Stephen laid me out to the mat. *Bejesus. If I didn't know better, that blow felt personal.* It wasn't lost on me that Stephen had been pounding hard on my unprotected abs with a good deal of satisfaction. I rose slowly on bended knee trying to get to my feet. I forced myself to steady my legs as the room spun and tilted. I was starting to feel like the fly. And Stephen was the fly swatter.

I must be losing my mind over this woman. I'd managed to frustrate myself so much, I got this crazy idea of making Stephen put on boxing gloves today and get in the ring with me. Only an insane person would do this. Maybe I was insane. Harper was making me crazy.

"It's hard to stomach not being able to exert any kind of control or influence over her perception of me. I'm not a bad guy Stephen," I said, sweating profusely, breathing more heavily.

Stephen grinned, laughing harder with delight, all the while moving at lightning speed, throwing a flurry of punches directed at my head. I was tossed against the rope now, trying to protect my face from his stinging blows. Putting on boxing gloves with

Stephen was the dumbest idea I had today. He was giving me a royal ass whipping, bruising my ego in the process. I hated losing at anything.

"I'm the needle in the haystack, right? I'm not that damn bad of a catch."

"Not at all man. You're omnipotent, remember? It's not every day I get to punch and whup up on *God,*" Stephen said, bobbing, laughing, weaving, while he punched my lights out.

I didn't think Stephen would ever shut up talking about how priceless this moment was. He knocked me across the head, laid me out on the mat a second time, then skipped around the ring in circles like he was Muhammed Ali waiting for me to drag my sorry ass up again. Instead of this being the Thriller at Manilla, this was turning into the Thriller at Becker Towers featuring stupid ass Nicholas Becker. That was what *this* was.

"I love how she gets under your skin," Stephen mumbled. "I needed practice today at doling out a good beat down," he continued, still blabbing off at the mouth and skipping around even faster as if he were on some kind of high. "It keeps my skills sharp."

Pow. Pow.

"I can better protect you when I'm sharp, Nicky," he said, hardly even winded.

Protect me? Goddamn. Was he on something? Maybe I needed to start inspecting those protein shakes my housekeeper Ina liked to make for him that he drinks by the pitcher. Hell, maybe *I* needed to start drinking whatever that shit was he was drinking. Harper was punishing me day in and day out. And here I was abusing myself some more by getting into this fucking ass ring with Stephen.

"If Harper and I could at least graduate to "playing nice" that would be a huge breakthrough," I said, feeling my sense of resolve coming back.

Bam. Bam. Bam. Stephen knocked me to the mat. I fell flat on my back looking up, my heart pounding double-time.

This time I was determined to stay down. Hell no. I wasn't going to get up.

"No such thing as "playing nice" Nicky," Stephen said, standing over me with his fisted gloves on both hips. "You play to win."

The sound of Lucia's heels clicking on the marble floor

caught my attention as she headed into my gym. She'd been working in the home office tracking the stock ticker, following the price fluctuations in the Japanese yen. Lucia gazed down at me on the mat much like a mother bear would look at her wayward cub. She shook her head at me. All I could do was roll my eyes at her and moan. But not before I took note that she was blushing at the sight of Stephen. She didn't say a word but I was sure I heard her breath hitch as she glanced at Stephen's sweaty, ripped, V-cut six pack, her eyes taking in the entire package head to toe. Never saw her look at me that way. I tried to put on my wounded face hoping to solicit some element of sympathy but Lucia ignored me.

"It's time you to get back to work, Nicky. You should shower first. You smell." Lucia turned up her nose and frowned.

"Woman, it's a good thing you're my valued partner that I hold in the highest regard," I said, crawling up on my knees, slowly forcing myself to get on both feet. "Otherwise I would have thrown you across my knee and taken all my frustrations out on your sweet sassy butt," I said, digging deep within myself to exert what little of my manhood I had left here after Stephen's beat down. I was barely able to breathe.

"Save it for Harper, Nicky. Get moving. We've got work to do. Go shower. I've got news."

I let the water run down my back relishing the hot water from the shower jets soothingly massaging my body. I hated it whenever Lucia said she had news. That was code for good news and bad news. I was sure as shit not in the mood for any bad news.

It was bad enough that Harper had hung up on me today, refusing to sell me the artwork I wanted. I was getting nowhere in the mission of Harper and I working on a "relationship re-do." Re-do was looking more like a no-can-do. When Harper finds out that Milk Money is going to be a contender against The Montgomery Consulting Group for Joduku Plastics, it was going to be a regular little blood bath between us. I was going to have to do a novena. Maybe call on Saint Jude, the Patron Saint of Lost Causes just to be able to get through the experience.

I finished my shower, brushed my teeth, combed my hair, and slipped my David Yurman watch on my wrist. I grabbed my favorite grey sweat pants and a t-shirt. I figured I'd be comfortable if I was going to have to take on more bad news today.

Lucia was at the computer surrounded by my six new shiny Apple Thunderbolt display screens that I'd recently installed in my home office at Becker Towers. I walked to my desk, glancing briefly out the window—it was going to rain. I cherished being able to look at my office window and see the Empire State Building, even though the clouds were starting to turn dark and ominous, much like my mood.

"You smell so much better," Lucia remarked, looking me up and down. "You want the good news or the bad news?"

Bingo. Predictable.

"Good," I mumbled.

"Well the good news is that CEO Nobu of Joduku Plastics wants to see us. His assistant wants to know our availability to meet in Princeton. That means we've made their short list, which is good."

"Being short-listed is good," I said, thumbing through the folder she handed me.

"I've worked up the figures with the staff. I think we start this battle at around eight million. Nobu is asking for twenty. If at the end of the day we can land somewhere between fifteen and seventeen million, then Becker Foods has a good shot of averaging a twenty percent return five years from now."

Lucia handed me a spreadsheet.

"We've run the numbers twice. I think that's where the land should be," Lucia said, never looking away from the spreadsheet in front of her. "Once we acquire Joduku Plastics, you can transfer the assets over to Becker Foods, not that I'm completely clear on why your father is interested in this company," Lucia said, a bit puzzled.

That was the thing I loved about Lucia. We thought alike, almost as if we were cut from the same cloth. She was a shrewd businesswoman. Like me, this acquisition my father was engineering didn't quite make sense to her either.

"And what's the bad news?"

"There are three other bidders besides Milk Money and The Montgomery Consulting Group."

"And who might that be?" I asked, wondering how bad this shit project was going to be.

"Well there's a little plastics company from Georgia called Peachtree Plastics that's throwing its hat in the ring, but they are not a real serious threat. They see the business as synergy with their existing business but I don't see them having enough cash reserves to stay in the bidding game long. They're not a worry, as I see it," Lucia said, making eye contact with me now.

"Who else?"

"O'Donnell Plastics Company out of Massachusetts is bidding. It's a husband-and-wife-owned company that has lots of capital. But our competitive intelligence team says the couple's marriage is on the brink. Their existing company may even be up for sale."

"Talk about bad timing," I mumbled.

"Apparently it's all bad timing. The husband got caught cheating on the wife. They may drop out before the showdown is all over. They're trying to keep up a good front so that their shareholders don't get antsy," Lucia sighed.

"And the crowning blow that you've saved for last is who?"

I knew the real blow was coming next, telling myself to wait for it.

"McKenna Textiles," Lucia said solemnly

"McKenna Textiles? *McKenna Textiles*?" I said, sounding to myself like a broken record. "McKenna Textiles—as in Brooks Fitzgerald Fucking McKenna—McKenna Textiles?"

"Yes," Lucia said.

"What the fuck does that blowhard, social-climbing, pinhead Neanderthal have to do with this?" I bellowed. "Why would a CEO of a textile company be interested in buying some little Japanese plastics company in Princeton, New Jersey?!"

"Calm down. Get a hold of yourself, Nicky," Lucia snapped.

"Why is that exactly, Lucia?" I asked, intuitively knowing I wasn't going to like the answer.

"Word on the street is that Brooks intends the purchase to be used for purposes of gift giving," Lucia answered formally.

"Gift giving? Gift giving?"

"You're repeating yourself Nicky," Lucia said calmly, anticipating my building hysteria.

I supposed one of the two of us should be calm because I sure the hell wasn't. "Gift giving to whom?" I asked, right at the same time the light bulbs went on. "Oh hell no!" I yelled, slamming my fist down on my brand new steel grey desk. It was durable. Contemporary. The perfect purchase, meant to take a beating for both my current and future rants.

"I have it on good authority that he wants into Senator Montgomery's family. Apparently Brooks Fitzgerald McKenna has some political aspirations of his own," Lucia said calmly.

"No fucking way," I ranted.

"An acquisition such as this solves a couple of his problems," Lucia spoke stoically. "He wins the favor of the family for one."

"And the second?"

"He thinks a business merger will lead to a proper marital merger. A merger, business or otherwise, shores up his financial liquidity troubles. Brooks would improve his company's balance sheets overnight," Lucia said.

"Merger by necessity. He's such the slimeball."

"Rumor has it he's willing to take the twenty-million-dollar risk on Joduku Plastics hoping it will turn into a cash cow down the road."

"Who knew that fuckwad was having financial troubles?" I said sarcastically.

"I did," she said dismissively.

Goddamn, this day was rapidly going from bad to worse.

"Apparently McKenna has made some not so good investments in the Asian markets. He's gotten caught up in the Chinese currency fluctuations and that has stressed his company's liquidity, forcing him to overextend his business. He's taken out some not-so-smart business loans with some not-so-nice investors in order to stay afloat."

"Doesn't surprise me," I grunted.

"If you ask me, his business is a house of cards waiting to fall. But if he marries up, of course his financial problems quickly dissolve," Lucia said.

"In other words, he's looking to marry for money," I growled. "That social climbing slug never ceases to quit. Amazing."

This was why I loved having Lucia as my business partner. She was thorough, never leaving a stone uncovered. This was a truism about her—business, personal, or otherwise.

"Oh and here's the good part, Nicky. I'm not sure Harper knows who the other bidders are yet," Lucia continued.

"Well that's only a matter of time. She may not know it now, but she'll get around to it sooner or later. And likely more sooner than later," I said. "She has a competitive intelligence team that is second to none."

"Umm, that's debatable," Lucia said casually, not at all intending to sell Milk Money short.

"Well one thing for sure," when she finds out that Milk Money is her competition, I suggest everyone around better take cover from the fallout. It won't be a pretty picture. Harper's going to go nuclear."

Man, Lucia's "news" was more like a crap sandwich. Good news on top, bad news in the middle, more bad news, and bad news on the bottom. Either way I wasn't up for digesting any of it. I could feel myself vacillating between anger and panic. I was angry that on top of everything else I had to contend with Brooks. However, I was even more motivated at the same time to emerge the winner in this acquisition battle. But I was panicked, knowing that this was going to create a huge impediment to my working toward a do-over with Harper.

"One thing for sure, if we emerge the winner, there will be no Brooks Fitzgerald Shithead McKenna running off gifting any companies away."

Especially not to my woman.

"Big Daddy will be happy, remaining king of his food processing empire for generations to come," I huffed, moving over to the wet bar and pouring myself a vodka. I poured Lucia a Jack Daniels neat.

"Nobody is going to be getting what is mine. Not Brooks, not anybody," I said out loud, gulping down vodka, pouring myself another before walking back towards Lucia and setting her cocktail down.

"Getting what's yours? Interesting," Lucia cooed. She glanced at me with piercing eyes, taking a slow sip of her Jack Daniels.

I avoided eye contact, pondering where a win would leave me with Harper. That was a piece of this puzzle that I was going to have to resolve quickly throughout the bidding process.

"Everyone involved is going to have to face it. At the end of the day, I, Nicholas Becker, CEO of Milk Money, am going to end up with Joduku Plastics."

And the woman.

"I have no doubt, Nicholas, that you will get what is yours," Lucia said confidently, sipping her drink.

"Lucia, we are going to be on an adventurous roller coaster the next several weeks. But one thing is for sure—I am up for this ride."

"I love roller coaster rides," Lucia said, as she sat on the nearby loveseat and crossed her legs. She tossed her auburn hair back while throwing both hands straight up in the air, smiling wickedly.

"Oh and Nicky . . ." Lucia grinned, still sipping her Jack Daniels.

"Yeah what?" I said, turning my attention to the computer screen noticing that the Dow Jones and the S&P were up.

"Swann Galleries called. The new Ernie Barnes piece that you want that's up for auction . . . well there's an anonymous bidder in play signaling he or she may be planning to outbid you. The other bidders have dropped out at four hundred thousand," Lucia said with a sly look on her face.

"That piece can't be worth much more than three hundred and fifty thousand. Who in the hell is inflating the bid?"

"Well I'd take an educated guess if you insist," Lucia laughed.

"Jesus, won't that crazy woman let me have anything I want?" I shrieked. I stood up now, pacing the floor, walking in circles.

"What shall I tell the gallery?"

"Keep bidding."

"Nickkkkkkkky," Lucia said, sounding exasperated with me.

"Tell them to keep fucking bidding."

We both turned our attention to the speakerphone as we heard the Becker Towers concierge say I had a call.

"Milk Money, God speaking," I said.

"It's me, Three. Any chance you can part the Red Sea and let me in, motherfucker?"

I didn't even answer. I hit the entrance button. The fact that my brother was on his way up was telling. It would take him a few beats on the private elevator to reach the penthouse on the eighty-sixth floor.

"I wonder what he wants." I said, turning to Lucia.

"Don't know," she said shrugging her shoulders. "Your

brother, you tell me. I'll leave you alone. Give you Becker boys some space," Lucia chuckled. "Shall I go greet him?"

"No, let him use his key. This whole Becker Foods adventure Big Daddy has dragged me into has turned into a mind fuck, so let him work to get in here," I bristled.

I wondered what could possibly be up with Three that was so important he was gracing my presence today. No sooner had that thought crossed my mind, than Three busted through the penthouse doors joining us in my home office.

"Bellisima! Resting my eyes on you has made my day!" Three said, speaking in Italian. "I would have come by sooner had I known you'd be here to bless the view," he grabbed Lucia's hand and kissed it tenderly.

"If I didn't know better, I'd think you were trying to woo me, Three," Lucia answered back in Italian. "All you Becker men are just alike," Lucia laughed.

"What sane man in his right mind could resist your beauty, lovely?"

Lucia laughed heartily.

"I'll give you two some privacy," she said speaking now in English. "I'll be in the Great Room, if you need me, Nicholas."

"Leave my partner alone, Three. You've got a wife."

"I'm not dead Nicky. I've still got eyes," Three said calmly, grinning his sly fox grin ear to ear.

I studied Lucia as she grabbed her things, tucking her dog-eared copy of *The Heart of a Helmsman* by Jude E. McNamara inside her Tumi, and sauntering past Three much like the goddess she was as she left the room. Who would have thought the formidable Lucia Falco read romance? Our little secret.

"Ahhhhh man, to be a single again," Three said, his eyes still hungrily pinned on Lucia's rear and filled with unleashed desire.

Lucia was indeed a beautiful and clever woman. She possessed both beauty and brains. She was a Rhodes Scholar, and a world-traveled woman with a keen appreciation for the finer things in life. Her attributes were quite attractive. Lucia never failed to get a rise out of most men who were in her orbit. Except for me of course, which even I found strange. Harper Montgomery may have cracked my heart in two, but not my libido. But with Lucia, it was different. I didn't see her that way, which was a good thing. Otherwise we'd never get any work done around here.

"What brings you to these parts today, Three?" I said, turning my attention back in his direction.

"Big Daddy, brother. He wants to catch up with you. Senator Montgomery is having a fundraiser to retire some of the party's campaign debt. Big Daddy promised Elizabeth Montgomery, who by the way, has extended an invitation to you as well, that you would be there," Three said.

Three was grinning, knowing I was going to resist.

"Oh hell no. Big Daddy is planning out my social calendar now? What the fuck? Who does he think he is?"

"Certainly not God," Three snickered, raising his eyebrows and pulling his lips together while swiveling his chair around, kicking his feet up on my brand new desk.

"The Montgomery's are Democrats," I said. "We're Republicans." I moved back to the bar to pour myself another vodka.

"No *we're* Republicans," Three said, answering affirmatively to my quiet nod of the head to see if he wanted a drink. "You're a pretend, wishy-washy self-proclaimed Republican who's really an Independent at heart," he said, sipping his martini.

"And why on God's green earth does he want us to be there?"

"It's called bi-partisanship Nicky. Jesus, how did you get to be so rich and yet so stupid? It's a good thing you've got me to hold your damn hand, man."

Three liked the feeling of being the big brother that always had to take care of me and watch my back. So I let his stupid crack go by. He was known for his sarcasm. The one thing he knew for sure, stupid I was not. I was valedictorian of my class at the Naval Academy.

"It's hard to get a break around here with Big Daddy all up in my world," I grumbled. "Ever since mother died he's turned into a regular fucking control freak," I snapped.

"Yeah, well there's more," Three laughed.

"What?" I said, my emotions moving from pissdom to indignation.

"He would like for you to make a fat donation to the cause."

"Fuck that, Three. You tell Big Daddy I said, no . . . no . . . never mind. I'll go to Elizabeth's fundraiser because I like her, but I plan to tell Big Daddy to his face to stand the hell down with me," I growled.

79

Three laughed so hard I thought he was going to fall on the floor.

"Good luck with that one little brother. I'll buy a front row ticket to that show," Three laughed harder, throwing a hundred-dollar bill out of his pocket on my desk for effect.

"How much am I to give this time?" I asked, feeling like I might need to rethink my position. Three might be right.

Going up against Big Daddy over something as small as a donation might be a bad move on my part. I didn't want to win the battle and lose the war. I'd donate to this bullshit all right, but Big Daddy was going to get out of my personal life, ordering me to marry and make babies. Big Daddy could be a treacherous man. He was powerful, his reach was long.

"Fifty thousand," Three said, padding over to the wet bar and pouring himself a second drink.

"Fifty fucking thousand dollars? Is he shittin' me? To the Democrats? Really Three? Is this some kind of joke?" I asked, now a whole lot more serious.

"Milk Money, baby," Three said. "God doesn't run out of riches, little brother. Maybe if you stop answering your phone sometime like you're God, folks will stop expecting big things from you."

Oh wow, I was seriously aggravated now. And as for Three, he was enjoying every minute of the misery Big Daddy was putting me through. Now I knew why he came by personally to deliver this news. He wanted to see my face in person so I could fulfill his laughter quotient for the day.

"Oh and Nicky, I saw those two beautiful bombshells of yours, Mallory and Jessica, the other day. It appears they're going to be at this fundraiser."

"They're not mine, Three."

"I beg to differ, but that's neither here nor there. Apparently those two BFFs are going to be working the room, modeling lingerie that will be a part of the fundraiser's silent auction table."

"Who cares," I groaned.

"Those Page Six pictures they took with you were hot. Who wouldn't want to know what secrets those two angel beauties are keeping for Victoria. Yowsa."

"Just because they're Victoria's Secret models, doesn't mean you have to come to attention every time you see them, Three."

"Oh little brother you just don't know. A man can only dream. But then again, I'll bet money your lover boy ass has knocked boots with both those angels."

"I don't kiss and tell, Three," I said, not looking at him, trying to figure out why my life had suddenly gone to hell in a handbasket.

Things were definitely getting worse. I took inventory in my mind. Let's see. I was going to have to fight Harper for Joduku Plastics. Fuckwad Brooks McKenna was going to be bidding against us both so he could get a shot at trying to marry *my* woman who doesn't want to be *my* woman. And, on top of everything else I had to give fifty thousand dollars to some measly Democrats, all while fighting off two drop-dead gorgeous glam goddesses in the presence of *my* woman and her senator father. Life couldn't get any more fucked up.

"Hey Nicky," Lucia said. "Sorry to interrupt your brother bonding moment but the gallery called. You're up to six hundred thousand," Lucia said sternly. "Don't you think you should let this piece go?"

Lucia narrowed her eyes at me as if to say, *stop this stupidity, motherfucker.*

"Whatever it is, God's got it all under control, Lucia," Three laughed loudly.

Lucia ignored Three but kept her eyes pinned on me.

"Not yet Lucia," I said guiltily.

"Idioto stupido," Lucia barked.

She slammed the door behind her so loud and hard, even Three jumped.

Tell me how you really feel.

It didn't take a degree in rocket science to figure out what Lucia thought of my staying in this bidding war.

Fuck me.

CHAPTER SIX

Harper

"I believe having a baby right now will bring me a lot of joy."

"Oh, why is that?" Dr. Richards asked.

I knew she was taking note of my body language, watching me as I shifted uncomfortably in my chair. Dr. Jayne Richards had been my therapist for a few years now. She had helped me through some very stressful lonely periods in my life. She knew me well enough to recognize all of my nonverbal signals.

"I have too many reasons to count. But just offhand, I would say thanks to your helping me through some very difficult life moments, my days of panic attacks are long gone. My career is at a place where the business is going well, and I'm able to delegate to the staff without feeling like I have to watchdog my own business."

"That's so good to hear Harper."

"I really have a great team of people working with me," I went on. "I'm not getting any younger. My childbearing years are on the decline. I can afford it. So it's now or never," I shrugged.

"Well have you considered that this is a life-changing event and that you don't really have to choose to go it alone?" she said thoughtfully. "From what I can tell, you have plenty of suitors clamoring at your doors who'd be more than excited to share their world, and parent with you," Dr. Richards said, prodding me some more.

"Well none of the guys I've been dating the last few years really do it for me, not like . . ." I paused to reflect, rubbing my forehead.

"You mean not like Nicholas?" Dr. Richards added, finishing my sentence.

"Yeah, well, not like Nicholas," I reluctantly agreed.

"Harper, we all make choices every day. If a relationship with Nicholas still holds promise for you, perhaps you should consider opening yourself up to the idea of letting go of the past and creating the future that may be possible for you two. Pursuing motherhood alone is very do-able. But it's a big life-changing step."

"Well I was thinking I could go to one of those fertility clinics, pick a sperm donor, and have my own baby without all the headache of pleasing and catering to a husband," I said dismissively. I paused looking up to see if my words were registering any shock with Dr. Richards. But of course she showed little emotion. That wasn't a new revelation.

"People do it every day Harper. Some under difficult and challenging circumstances that you would never have to endure. Unlike many folks, you have the luxury to choose the marital and parental life you that want to have." She gazed at me thoughtfully for a moment. "I could recommend some good physicians at the more reputable fertility clinics in town, but I think you need to consider keeping your options open, Harper. You've been playing the field with some of the most sought-after men in Manhattan, and none of them have yet to meet your standards. Surely one of them makes the cut?"

"No, no one has stirred my heart the way . . . no . . . the answer is no."

"I'm surprised things haven't gotten more complicated by now since you've juggling multiple suitors," Dr. Richards said, pivoting on her last point.

"Well actually things have gotten incredibly complicated," I laughed. "I don't know why I'm laughing, because it's really not funny. I've been able to keep my own emotional distance, but things are starting to get messy with these guys. The men in my life seem to want to have a more serious relationship with me."

My mind floated back to today's misstep with Brooks and my conversation with Malcom. Juggling men was more trouble than it was worth.

"Brooks Fitzgerald McKenna has even suggested we consider marriage. Ugh. There mere thought of being married to

Brooks McKenna sends me over the edge."

"Well let's discuss this a little further. It's human nature that one party in a relationship would want more. Relationships don't stay static. They either grow or they end, but they don't stand still."

I nodded, signaling my understanding.

"And when you add sexual intimacy into the mix, relationships can really begin to get complicated."

"Yes, I'm finding that out Dr. Richards. Brooks and Malcom are both unhappy campers right now."

"Case in point," Dr. Richards said, taking a few notes on her notepad.

"A couple of weeks ago, even Nicholas opened the door to the possibility of our getting back into relationship. And he and I are not sleeping together. As a matter of fact we can hardly stand to be in each other's company for too long."

"Umm," Dr. Richards murmured, allowing me to ramble on.

"He had the nerve to suggest we start over. Have a 're-do'," I said, moving my fingers in air quotes. Nicholas wants us to put the past behind us and start over."

"How do you feel about the possibility of rekindling a relationship with Nicholas, Harper?"

"Well, the whole idea of it plain scares me," I said, hoping my voice didn't tremble. It's hard to forget the holes people leave in your heart. Betrayal is not an easy memory to shed."

"Indeed," Dr. Richards said, still taking a note here and there.

"Some days it only takes a word on a page, a song on the radio, a look in a person's eyes to trigger those memories you thought you had shed. It's not so much the loss of the person that you feel early on in the heartbreak process. It's the years of deep loneliness and loss that you discover down the road. It's the loss of the idea of what you thought you could have been as a couple."

"What are you afraid of Harper?" Dr. Richards delved deeper.

"Dr. Richards, ten years ago, I was madly in love with Nicholas Becker. I still love him," I said, pausing and catching my breath. "In some strange way, I guess. It's just that now, I've learned to save some of the love for myself. Nicolas can't hurt me like he once did. I love myself differently now."

"You have your boundaries back," Dr. Richards added.

"I must admit I've even been a little angry at myself for not having saved enough love for myself back then. I gave so much of it away not knowing if he even deserved it."

"That's good to hear, Harper. How do you love yourself differently now?" Dr. Richards asked.

"I suppose over time, I've learned to love myself first. Even if Nicholas and I gave it the old college try, and it didn't work out, my life wouldn't fall apart at the seams, because this time I'd be saving some of that love for me. Going forward, I will not ever put love on a pedestal with someone for which it has no place . . . or better yet is undeserved."

"I'm impressed, Harper. You've actually grown into your womanhood. That's very good, dear."

I gave Dr. Richards a huge smile. I was proud of myself too at how far I had grown the last several years. I was so much wiser now. I no longer wore my heart on my sleeve for folks to stomp on it.

"So when Nicholas asked for a re-do, why did you turn him down? It sounds like you feel stronger and confident enough to handle any outcome. You could in fact hit the reset button."

"I turned him down because I could," I said, blinking. "I don't intend to make his life any easier after all he's put me through. Nicholas wants instant forgiveness at the snap of a finger." I snapped my finger up in the air.

Dr. Richards' brow furrowed a bit.

She thinks I'm still carrying too much anger.

"He even had the balls to lose his temper with me, angry over my inability to come right out and forgive him." I feared my face had a ferocious scowl. I was getting angry again.

"A decade later is not asking for instant forgiveness Harper. Don't you think it's time to forgive? Forgiveness helps you as much as it helps him. You are holding on to quite a bit of anger."

Yup. That was pretty much how I thought Dr. Richards was going to perceive my slight outburst. *She thinks I'm holding on to too much anger still. Okay. So maybe I am.* I decided a long time ago, that if Nicholas and I ever got back together I was not going to make life easy for him. He could slip and slide with someone else, but he was not going to play that game with me. If he ever had any chance of getting me back, he was going to have to work for it.

"I'm not sure it's worth the time, energy, and effort to take a chance on Nicholas Becker again two times in a lifetime," I shot back. "I hate it when Nicholas thinks he can tell me what to do. I decide who, when, and how," I said, venting some more.

"Well that's true when it applies to your choices that only affect you. But a relationship is full of compromise. It has to be nurtured. Don't you believe you're capable of compromising in your relationships?" Dr. Richards asked, ignoring my momentary anger.

"I suppose I should give that some further thought," I said.

"Motherhood for example, is all about teaching children about compromise and sharing. You'll come to know this as a mother. But compromise works for the grown-ups too, Harper. Perhaps you should begin to work on being able to see yourself compromising with Nicholas, and others, for that matter," Dr. Richards added gently. "It's a good skill to have."

"If you say so, Dr. Richards. But Nicholas and I have been in such a tenacious competition these last ten years since our breakup, it's hard to imagine he and I ever working on the same team. He hurt me to the core back then when I got pregnant. He made it clear that he didn't want to be a husband or a father."

"Yes, it was hurtful."

"When he calmed down and acted like a normal person months later, he started saying that he loved me, he loved the baby, and wanted to be a family. I'd lost the baby by then. Then he bitched like a madman, accusing me of having had an abortion. He was all over the place. How dare he?"

"Yes, we can all agree, he did behave poorly."

"Why should I reward him now that he's decided to grow up and act like a mature person and wants to re-create the same picture again with me?" I huffed.

"Maybe because then he was young, inexperienced, and now you could choose to forgive him?" Dr. Richards said, raising her brows.

"So? I was young too. I was much younger than him."

"Yes but you were at a different place emotionally than he was. There's a lot of truth to the fact that women mature faster than men. People grow at different paces," Dr. Richards said, not really inviting me to respond.

I knew she was giving me a chance to think about my choices in this moment with a clear head without distraction.

"It sounds as if Nicholas has fully evolved into his manhood. The fact that he could see his way to forgiveness is very telling.

You should consider that he has felt hurt too on some level. His hurt drove his behavior for a long time too, but now he seems to want to let it go and grow," Dr. Richards reminded me.

Yes I knew Nicholas was hurt as much as I was, but I thought we were in love enough to weather any storm. Then when the stormy winds of relationship hit, he jumped ship. It damn near felt like mutiny. No part of him was going to help keep our ship afloat.

"Perhaps Nicholas can offer you what you need now. Give you that which you couldn't get from him then," Dr. Richards suggested.

I nodded my head so as to say that might be possible now, years later.

"Harper, you should try the idea on for size and answer the question for yourself whether Nicholas could be the partner, husband, father, you need for him to be now. Sometimes in life, time has a magical way of healing us and our circumstances," she said.

"Sure Dr. Richards, I could try the idea on for size, but that's all it is for now, an idea."

"I think you should give some thought to unpacking that suitcase of unpleasant memories between you and Nicholas and let the baggage from the past go."

Dr. Richards rose from her chair, moving to her desk grabbing her calendar.

"Even if you choose not to do a re-do with him, forgiveness will serve you in the long run. Think about it. We can discuss it some more in our next session," she said, smiling her beautiful warm smile while writing a note down in her appointment book, then handing me a card.

"I'll think about it Dr. Richards," I assured her.

"Here's a fertility clinic that you may want to consider. I'm personal friends with Dr. Francis Stone at Stone Fertility. You may want to make an appointment with him and familiarize yourself with the sperm donor process so that whatever you decide, pursuing motherhood alone or with a future partner, you'll at least be making an informed decision," Dr. Richards said, handing me the slip of paper with Dr. Stone's address and number.

As I exited Dr. Richard's office, I felt a twinge of guilt thinking maybe I had been too hard on Nicholas all these years. I was getting pretty good at making him pay. I made him pay in more ways than one. I had mastered the ability to hit him where it counted . . . in his pockets.

One thing for sure, Nicholas understood money. And, I had been making him dig deep for some time now. Whenever there was something that I knew he wanted, I snatched it right out of his little 'turn-everything-to-gold, moneymaking hands. I snatched everything he wanted, almost like he snatched my heart, making me pay to the gods of emotional pain, never ever looking back.

Every time Nicholas answers his phone saying, "God speaking," my mind automatically goes into overdrive saying *ca-ching, ca-ching. Time to pay up, Mr. Big.* I figured sooner or later, I'd get his attention and he'd have to come down off his personal little mountaintop and pay homage to the god of my heartbreak. It gave me great satisfaction, making it my mission in life to snuff out his little burning bush of bullshit.

Was it time for me to quit needling him? I suppose. Perhaps it was time for me to move on too, and stop giving Nicholas the one-two and at least trying to move to a place of friendship. How hard could that be, right?

But then again, he just seriously burns my ass.

Choices.

You are going to have yourself a baby all by yourself, Harper Montgomery.

I *can* choose to do this alone. I *am* the queen of payback. And everybody knows, payback is a bitch.

Thank God my limousine drive back from Dr. Richard's office to my home was peaceful without the added pressure from Malcom. My driver Winston was waiting for me, like Malcom said. I knew by the way Winston was driving that Malcom was trailing not too far behind. Malcom was a stickler about Winston not taking careless risks in traffic whenever I was in the car.

I was glad to be having some down time at my penthouse

suite in Soho. Winston's wife Nell was my housekeeper. She was a gem. She was good at anticipating my needs, having laid out my favorite denim jeans with the hole in the knee, a turquoise blue cashmere turtleneck, and my beige Ugg moccasins. I swear that woman could read my mind. It was almost as if she had sensed that I was overdue for some down time. I opened my refrigerator, noticing Nell had made me a huge pot of fettuccini alfredo this evening, one of my favorites.

The recessed ceiling track lights in my kitchen were dimmed softly. The lights were very soothing against the white marble floors and the white cabinetry. I found the soft mint-colored walls and the water-like rippled glass kitchen countertops very calming on those days when I was in a funky mood.

Living in Soho's most elite penthouse, an exclusive Sotheby's International property, my own urban oasis, afforded me floor to ceiling windows, ample sunlight, and staggering views of the city. It was everything that I wanted in a home, despite the fact that my travel schedule kept me away more than I wanted. It was rare moments like today that I really got a chance to enjoy my home.

Nell had put a large bowl of green apples on the dining room table along with service for twelve already set. The table was set with my favorite yellow Momma Ro china along with matching yellow tapers. The fireplace off the kitchen was already lit. The sheer curtains were semi-closed, allowing for some privacy but still giving me a peek at the New York skyline.

I turned on the Bang and Olufsen sound system deciding to calm my mind, listen to some music, and digest my session with Dr. Richards. Cassandra Wilson's "Time After Time" began to play. It was perfect for connecting me with my current mood. The song reminded me of days long gone with Nicholas. Nicholas used to say the "Nearness of You" by Norah Jones was "our song." I disagreed, saying Cassandra Wilson's rendition of Cyndi Lauper's "Time after Time" was "our song."

Gosh, we never agreed on anything even back then. So they both became "our songs." Hmmm. Compromise. Perhaps that was Dr. Richards's point. Maybe I did know how to do that a little bit, or did I?

I tossed the fettuccini in the microwave and moved toward my white mushroom shaped bar stools, picking up the style section of the *New York Times*. I cracked open a bottle of Opus

One from my wine cellar, pouring myself a large glass of the cabernet. I waited for the chime of the microwave to ring. Reflecting, I twirled around in a circle on my bar stool. The peace and quiet gave me a chance to think about how I wanted to pursue the Joduku acquisition.

I waited for my pasta to heat, grabbing my Macbook to check in to see if Charlotte had any word back from The Montgomery Consulting Group's competitive intelligence team on who was going to be my competition.

I flipped through my Gmail account looking for threads from Charlotte hoping there would be something in my mail by now letting me know who the competition would be. I had an email from Charlotte letting me know the artwork bid was up to six-hundred thousand dollars. I heard the ping of my microwave. Thank God my pasta was ready. I was famished.

Let's see. Just how far do I want to ride this artwork pony? Do I let him suffer some more or play nice? Do I let him have the piece? Do I practice compromising? I pondered the whole matter a bit just as my phone rang.

"Harper?

"Yes Mother, how are you?"

"I'm fine honey. I only have a minute. I was calling to remind you about Daddy's fundraiser. I expect you to be there. It's important that the family support him."

"Yes, well I have to check my calendar . . ." I mumbled through a mouthful of fettuccini.

"Not," Mother warned. "My girl has already contacted Charlotte and the fundraiser is already plugged into your schedule. This is your mommy reminder, dear," she said, in her busy voice. "It's at the Lincoln Center two weeks from tomorrow night at six p.m. I've already called Mackenzie. She'll be there to take photographs. Nothing special. Everyone looking beautiful and having fun," Mother said. "There will be a silent auction, so bring your checkbook, dear. I expect Mackenzie's picture's to make the Sunday style section."

Elizabeth was always one to dot the i's and cross the t's.

"Fine, Mother, I'll be there if it's on my calendar."

I twirled my pasta around on my folk, throwing my head back, practicing my sensual eating move in case I needed to pull out the big guns on my next dinner date.

"How's the acquisition coming, dear?" she said, pausing.

"As a matter of fact Mother, I was sitting here going through my email to see if we have a string on the competition yet. I'm pretty sure CEO Nobu is going to want to open bids around twenty million. I have no doubt we can make the buy at several million less."

"I know that Carmichael Ketchup is in good hands with you at the reins."

"Well I'm glad I have your support and confidence, Mother. After all, I'm doing this for you. This is your parade, remember?"

"Yes, sweetheart. I'm fully aware of what I'm doing. I don't anticipate any rain on my parade." She laughed. "If, anything, I'm hoping this will end in a really long overdue homecoming of sorts." Then she giggled.

"What exactly does that mean, Mother?" I said, recognizing that her comment awakened my spidey senses. And my intuitions were good. Something was brewing. I just didn't know what.

"Oh nothing dear, I'm thinking out loud. Don't mind me. So how was your session with Dr. Richards?" she asked , sounding a bit cagey.

"Oh it was fine."

Throw the grenade.

"I told Dr. Richards that I'm pretty sure I'm ready to have a baby, so I'm doing some research into some fertility clinics for the possibility of doing the whole sperm donor thing."

I put my fork down, closing my eyes waiting for my grenade to hit. Silence. A deep sigh.

Bingo. Direct hit.

"Harper Carmichael Montgomery. You do not need a baby made by some . . . some . . . some . . . freaking *stranger!*" Mother yelled through the phone. "Don't you think for one minute you're going to let some . . . some . . . some . . . *outsider* into the Carmichael Montgomery gene pool. The senator and I—Will. Not. Have. It," she snapped. "Besides, you have no problem with fertility. That's for women who can't make babies or find husbands. That's not your problem. That's not who you are."

I took a deep breath. This was exactly the response I expected Elizabeth Carmichael Montgomery was going to have.

"Well mother, you know it's not like there are *any* decent men out here," I said, raising my voice a couple of octaves.

I glanced at my computer, hearing the ping on my Gmail

account letting me know that Nicholas had pumped the artwork bid up two hundred thousand more. Eight hundred thousand dollars? *Oh so he's gonna play serious. Guess I have to snap that moneymaker's God-like dick off.* I emailed Charlotte back and ordered that my bid increase another hundred thousand.

"There are plenty of suitable men out there Harper."

"Don't you dare say Brooks Fitzgerald McKenna, Mother." I was hoping Mother didn't think for one minute that I would ever consider Brooks as marriageable solely because she saw me with him a couple of weeks ago.

"The thought never crossed my mind. That is not your husband," Mother said firmly. "That's beside the point Harper."

"And your point is . . . ?"

"My point is that I do not intend for my only grandchildren to be spawned by God knows who?" Mother argued, her voice getting more excited. "It would completely"—*okay, here comes the guilt*—"it would break my heart."

I called that right on time. Mother was sounding like she might be on the brink of tears.

"You have to think about the family legacy. Stop being childish Harper. Your grandfather did not build an empire to let it be inherited by some . . . some . . . some . . . *stranger*," she said again. "I simply will not sit for this"—*here she goes with all three names*—"Harper Carmichael Montgomery."

"My child would be half me Mother. That does not equal a stranger," I said, thinking it might be in my best interest to deescalate this discussion.

I cocked my head back again, tossing another fork of rolled up pasta, wondering if this was an inherited trait of the rich and famous to utilize the first, middle, and last names of their children all in one breath. I hoped I'd never do that to my baby. But then again, I did have my mother's genes.

"You know there's nothing wrong with stopping this war of yours and maybe giving him a chance to . . ."

"I gotta run, Mother."

I was not giving her a chance to finish that sentence, glad that the concierge was buzzing my intercom to let me know that I had a guest. I knew whose name she was going to call next. The good news was I was certain Mother could hear my buzzing intercom in the background. Reese Nelson was waiting for permission to enter. Apparently Malcom was insisting on an okay from me to let any guests enter the penthouse elevator. Geez, Malcom was really showing his behind these days. I couldn't imagine what was going through his mind. Malcom's known Reese Nelson for years. He knows that he's not a threat. At least not to me.

"Fine, but don't think for one minute"—*here we go again*— "Harper Carmichael Montgomery, that I'm through discussing this subject," Mother stated firmly. "Clayton will not be pleased. I know you think you're Daddy's little girl and it won't matter, but even the senator has boundaries when it comes to you, Harper. Especially if he plans to live with me," she hissed.

"Love you mother, we'll talk more later," I said, hanging up.

Mother was seriously pissed. But I expected it.

"Reese Nelson is here to see you Ms. Montgomery."

"Send him up," I said, wondering what was happening to my peaceful night at home, chilling. Reflecting. It was a good thing company was turning out to be Reese, otherwise I would have turned everyone else away so I could come down off this to-be-expected awkward phone conversation with my mother.

Sooner or later I was going to have to have had this discussion with her. It might as well have been sooner. I was giving her a chance to adjust to the idea, in case this turned out to be the path I would take.

Over the years, Reese had taught me how to think strategically in business. I found it worked well in my personal life, too. That's what made Reese good at being the most sought-after financial forensics executive in New York. Reese was a strategic thinker. He was cool, calm, and collected under most circumstances that didn't involve his family. In those moments he became Mr. Overprotective.

I heard Reese enter the foyer double doors and ran to meet him.

"Hey, babe. What's with Malcom today? He practically gave me his ass to kiss, screening me like I'm some stranger or something. Did he forget about the fact that he and I are both Army? Practically comrades," Reese said, with a curious look on his face.

"He's been in a funky mood all week. Ignore him. Can I offer you some pasta or wine? I was finishing up my dinner."

"I'll take a pass on the pasta. Gotta watch my figure," Reese said jokingly, patting his six pack. "But, I'll have some wine with you, beautiful."

Reese walked into the kitchen pretty much knowing his way around, grabbing a clean wine glass.

"You? Watch your figure? That's a joke right?" I laughed. "Everybody with eyes and any semblance of a brain knows that Reese Nelson is Vin Diesel incarnate," I replied, admiring his soulful eyes that were wrapping me in warmth.

"And you're the beautiful Zoe Saldana," he said, kissing me on my forehead, grabbing the wine bottle, and pulling us closer to the fireplace. He was tugging me in such a way that we both plopped down together on my oversized stuffed chair. Reese placed my feet and his on the ottoman, kicking my moccasins off and then shedding his driving slippers. His faded relaxed denim jeans hugged his buttocks as he moved with masculine grace. His skin-tight grey t-shirt with the word ARMY written on the front emphasized the chiseled muscles in his chest, shoulders, and arms as they swung around my shoulders cupping me under his chest. Reese Nelson was my male BFF. For a moment I wondered with curiosity if he'd be a suitable sperm donor for my baby project. That might make Elizabeth more comfortable with the idea of my making a baby sans man. I could roll with that idea of Reese being my baby's father. He was good stock. Smart. Intelligent. Good looking. Wealthy. All of the attributes you want for your child's father.

But then again, mother, Reese's sister Riley, and Nicholas would each surely pitch a fit and have a heart attack and a stroke—all in that order. Perhaps this wasn't a good idea. I kept my thoughts to myself. These significant decisions were best handled without the participation of known conspirators and best not said out loud.

"So how's the Joduku Plastics acquisition coming?" Reese said.

"Wow. Damn, Reese, how do you know about the acquisition already? This is the first time in a couple of weeks we've even had a chance to catch up. Isn't anything sacred in this town?" I cringed. "It's not like this is public information for Christ's sake."

"I got the news from my sister Riley, who got it from Lucia Falco at Milk Money. Don't you recall? Milk Money is an investor in Riley's company," Reese said. "Apparently Lucia let it accidentally slip that she had to move Riley's quarterly investor presentation to the next quarter. Claimed she and Nicholas Becker were tied up with the Joduku acquisition with you and three other companies," he said casually, sipping his cabernet.

"Well shut your mouth, Reese Nelson," I said, jumping up in a nanosecond, running to my Macbook and scrolling quickly through the hundreds of emails I had accumulated, looking for everything and anything from my competitive intelligence team. This was weird. It would be unlike Lucia to make accidental slips.

And there it was . . . an email from the head of my competitive intelligence team. I scrolled through the email quickly, my eyes speed reading through the email.

Harper, pursuant to your recent request, our intelligence efforts have revealed that our expected competition on the Joduku Acquisition are the following companies:

> *Peachtree Plastics*
> *O'Donnell Plastics*
> *Milk Money*

Financial profiles on each company are attached. I believe there may be one other competitor that we are yet to identify. Our team is still working that issue as we speak. I'm available to discuss this with you at your earliest convenience to answer any questions that you may have about each of the known companies in more detail.

Sincerely,
Joseph P. Lester.
Chief of Competitive Intelligence
The Montgomery Consulting Group

"Oh hell to the no!" I yelled out loud. "I can't believe this. Reese? Milk Money is *my* competitor," I shouted. "I am going to kill him! Just because *he* overheard the conversation with *my* mother at your sister's wedding reception, he thinks he can just pull the rug out from under me anytime he gets ready? Has he no dignity at all? No sense of fairness?" I fumed.

"What are you talking about Harper?"

"And to think he sat there at the reception at my side pretending like he wasn't even listening to my mother's conversation, like some Mr. Goody Two Shoes," I ranted. "He's doing this to me because I outbid him on that freaking Ernie Barnes artwork last year. He's trying to get back at *me*!" I shouted, pulling my scrunchie out of my ponytail and tossing my hair around wildly.

"Calm down honey," Reese said.

"Bad enough he stole Gilliam Global out from under me," I snapped. "That low-down dirty dog," I ranted. "And to think *he* asked *me* to think about our doing a relationship 'do-over.'"

"What are you talking about?" Reese pleaded, trying to make sense of my rant.

"Yeah, I've got his do-over!" I was pacing back and forth around the room in circles. "I'm going to do him over all right. I'm going to cut his blue balls off!" I shouted.

"Well, I vaguely remember you and Nicholas having words about Gilliam Global on New Year's Eve at his home a year ago," Reese said. "But you need to calm down, baby," Reese said, rising and grabbing me by the waist, tugging on my shirt and pulling my body closer to his. "I don't want you to bust a blood vessel. You're supposed to be chilling, remember?"

Reese was standing next to me, both of us hovering over my Macbook with me tucked under his arm. Malcom busted through the double doors looking alarmed.

"Are you okay?" he asked. "I heard yelling and shouting." He looked Reese up and down, his eyes cutting to our feet, noticing we were both barefoot.

"We're fine," I said, slamming the lid on the Macbook quickly, cocking my head to the side, looking at him like I wanted to pull out an invisible machete and take all my frustrations out on him.

"Yeah man. No problem," Reese said. "But thanks for checking. Our game of footsies got a little loud," Reese said boldly.

As soon Reese made that crack I knew it was the wrong thing to say to Malcom. Reese might as well have rubbed salt in the wound. This moment was turning into a downhill slide. Mr. Overprotective in a stare down with Mr. Possessive, both appearing as if they were each laying claim to me.

I sucked in my breath. I repeated, "We're fine, Malcom. Some business matters have come up, that's all," I said, hoping to quell the situation.

Malcom's eyes flicked to me and then to Reese. Malcom noticed that I looked a bit disheveled. My hair was practically standing up on top of my head from my pulling on it like a raving lunatic.

"Since when has a game of footsies turned into business, Harper?" Malcom growled.

I shot a look at him that said, "Oh no, you didn't just go there," pretty sure my eyes had turned red, now glaring into his green ones.

"Since business requires us to stomp out a few enemy game plans," Reese shot back at him, eyes narrowed, squeezing me a little tighter.

I hoped no one noticed Michael and Janet Jackson's "Scream" playing in the background. The moment was almost prophetic. Because that was what I wanted to do. Scream.

"Just doing my job," Malcom said. "The senator would have my ass if I let anything happened to you, Harper."

Malcom was practically nose-to-nose with Reese.

"Well your job is done for now," Reese snorted. "Because she's fine. It's not like *I'm* going to let anything happen to her."

"I don't answer to you, motherfucker, last I checked," Malcom said. "The job of not letting anything happen to her is mine. Mine. You don't want any of this, Reese," Malcom fumed.

Reese's face changed. He stepped in closer to Malcom, pushing me behind him, realizing Malcom's veiled threat. "And you don't want any of this," Reese fired back.

"Stop it. I've got more important things to deal with right now," I said, stepping back in front of Reese to get in between them.

"Thank you, Malcom, We're fine. Really. You can excuse us now." I tried to keep my voice polite, knowing Malcom was pissed to the high heavens. "Thank you for checking in on us."

"The check's on you only, Harper," Malcom fired back, his brow frowning, taking a minute to lob a threatening stare back at Reese.

We both watched as Malcom exited the penthouse. I exhaled deeply, moving to go grab more wine from the wine cellar. "I need another glass of wine," I said.

"I think I'm going to have something stronger," Reese replied, heading to my wet bar.

I knew Reese well enough to know that he needed a beat to calm down himself. I poured myself another glass of wine. I lifted my Macbook cover open again and then slammed it down. I had another message from Charlotte saying that Nicholas had won the bid at one million dollars.

"Shit," I said out loud. *Well at least I made him pay*. "I hate freaking losing."

"So you slept with him, huh?" Reese said, looking as if he had hit his reset button and composed himself. He was drinking Stoli now.

"What difference does it make?" I asked dismissively, knowing that he was talking about Malcom.

Reese crawled back into the overstuffed chair, pulling me next to him. He moved to put my bare feet back on the ottoman.

"Babe, it's never a good idea to sleep with the help," Reese said, taking big gulps of his vodka. "If he doesn't tamp his emotions down some over you, it's going to get in the way of his doing his job. Every man is a threat to Malcom right now," Reese said.

"Is it that obvious?" I sighed.

"He needs to be able to protect you. Part of that job means having the ability to perceive true threats from false ones. Your sleeping with him is blurring his lines," Reese said with all seriousness.

"I never thought things would get this out of control," I said, tapping my hand back on the chair for Reese to sit back and curl up next to me.

The day's events had made me weary. I needed some comfort and some strong arms around me for emotional support.

"You've been toying with Malcom, and with that geekster Brooks Fitzgerald McKenna. And god knows who else," Reese said.

"You tell me now," I moaned.

"Woman, everybody can't handle getting the booty and walking away from it," Reese said. "You love them, Harper, and then leave them in your wake."

"I thought this would be simple."

"No. For some guys, this business of you knocking boots

with them, then walking away can get dangerous. Trust me, I know," Reese exhaled, squeezing me hard. "I've had my fair share of women that I tapped that ass, trying to walk away afterwards. Those gals turned into stalkers with guns pointed to my head trying to walk me off a plank." He chuckled.

"Yeah like that nutty girl—Susan Whatshername," I said. "I had to call her up for you, I told her that we were married so she'd think you were a liar and a cheat and drop your ass," I chuckled.

"Susan St. James," Reese said. "She was a real prima donna, too. My dad, said," Boy I'm ordering you to drop that woman right this minute. Can't you see she's crazy?'" Reese lowered his voice by several octaves.

We both starting laughing until we had tears in our eyes. How I loved these moments.

"So why haven't you ever pursued *me*?" I asked. We both caught our breath. "You're practically the only guy I have around me that hasn't tried at least once to pursue me," I said curiously.

Reese looked surprised. I guess he never expected me to ask the obvious question.

"Don't get me wrong. I love being friends," I continued. "I like being able to have a good time with you and not have to worry about you making sexual demands. I'm completely comfortable in your space. But, I have had my days when I've been curious as to why you've never really tried. What's up with that?" I asked.

"You know the answer to that question, Harper."

"No I don't."

"Yes, you do," Reese said.

"Don't you see it?" he asked, keeping his voice calm and even. "Everyone else can."

"See what?" I asked.

"Babe, you're still in love with Nicholas Becker. And Nicholas Becker is still in love with you. The only people that don't know it are the two of you."

"You must have been smoking something on your way over here tonight, Reese," I laughed. "Nicholas Becker and I are archenemies. Do we *look* like we are in love with each other?"

"Yes. You do," Reese said, taking another swig of his vodka. "Love takes many forms, Harper. Sometimes it can even look like a little mini war," he said, arching his eyebrows.

"Yeah, Nicholas and I are at war all right."

"The battle is between who's going to put their guard down first and show the fuck up. Who's going to take the risk to appear most vulnerable. You two people need to bury the hatchet, kiss, make up, fuck each other like two wild animals, and whatever the else two idiots that can't admit they still love each other do," Reese laughed more heartily now.

I didn't know if he was laughing because I was looking at him as if someone had dropped him on his head or what.

"Think about this, Harper. Think about it long and hard because if you're that deep into denial and can't admit this to yourself, then you are definitely fucked."

Clearly I was definitely fucked. This was like the second time today this subject had come up.

I was laughing a bit too much now, practically hysterical. Maybe it was the wine. Maybe it was the lost art auction bid. Maybe it was Dr. Richards. Maybe it was Mother. Maybe it was fertility clinics and sperm donors. Maybe it was Malcom. Maybe it was the Joduku Plastics acquisition. Maybe it was that motherfucking Nicholas Miles Becker making me crazy. *Maybe I was in love?*

"Listen Harper," Reese said. "No matter how hard you laugh at what I said like I told some huge joke or something, the fact still remains you're in denial, babe. You're in love with Nicholas Becker. And . . . it's okay. Maybe if you stop fighting the feelings and knock this war off between the two of you, you could both see it for yourselves."

"Are you crazy, Reese? Nicky is my competition for anything and everything. And now he's my competition for Joduku Plastics. That company is going to end up being merged into the Carmichael Ketchup empire, and Nicky isn't going to stop me from getting it. What would he want with that company anyway?" I said. "Joduku doesn't need an angel investor."

"It's not for him. It's for *Becker Foods*," Reese said. "Apparently that plastics company holds some value for the family chicken processing company," Reese said.

"Yeah, like the same value it holds for Carmichael Ketchup," I said.

"Kind of interesting if you ask me, Harper. You want it for your mom, and Nicholas wants it for his dad?"

Hmm. Reese's point did raise my curiosity a tad, but this was business, and stranger things happened all the time in business.

"Nicholas Becker will not keep me from getting what I want. Those days are long since over."

"That's right, Harper. Those days are over. As in ten years' worth of days over," Reese said. "I'm your friend. Put that time in your life behind you. Call a cease-fire. You and Nicholas are made for each other. You guys are cut from the same cloth. And just think about it; you merge your empire with his and the world becomes your playground."

"You mean oyster, don't you Reese? Too much vodka for you."

"Yeah. So let's get drunk," Reese said, squeezing me, tickling me.

"You're already drunk."

"So let's do like we use to do in college, babe. Get drunk and have spin night," Reese said. "You remember, get so drunk the room spins!" Reese hollered.

We both fell out laughing all over again.

"Spin night, babe," Reese laughed again.

"I'm getting that company," I said sharply.

"Have it your way, babe. I'll still be here for you when reality sets in. I got your six either way, but I think a cease-fire is in order," Reese said calmly.

"Watch me," I hissed under my breath.

"Let's spin, woman, before I end up as collateral damage," Reese laughed.

"I'm getting that company," I laughed back at him.

And my baby.

Chapter Seven

Nicholas

"I'm sorry sir, but the traffic is pretty heavy tonight," Silas spoke softly.

"No problem Silas. Just get us as close to the red carpet rope as you can," I said, desperate to jump out of the limousine so I could stretch my legs.

"Are you ready, Lucia?"

"Of course, I'm ready. You act like you're walking down the plank to your own execution or something, Nicky."

"No, I'm just ready to get the hell out of here. And the night hasn't even begun. Spending a night in a room full of Democrats is not my idea of fun. Not to mention I have to contend with Big Daddy and Harper at the same time, on the same day, in the same space," I grumbled. "Big Daddy has really pushed the envelope this time."

"You should be used to Big Daddy's demands by now Nicky. Besides, it's merely a political fundraiser."

"But for the fact that this is Senator Montgomery's shindig, I wouldn't give a rat's ass. I wouldn't throw this kind of cash around for anyone else, especially the Democrats. I'm doing this for Elizabeth Montgomery," I grunted, pouring myself a vodka off the limousine bar.

It appeared the wait to arrive on the red carpet was going to be extra long since all the big shot politicos had to get out of their limos too tonight.

"I'm sure Big Daddy calls it *greasing the skids*, staying on

Elizabeth's good side," Lucia said glancing at her watch.

"Yeah, Big Daddy and Elizabeth go way back in the day to God knows when." I moaned. "No way that Big Daddy isn't going to do whatever it takes to stay on Elizabeth's good side. I've never been able to quite figure out their history, but this I know, they have some kind of mutual understanding."

"Interesting," Lucia said.

"Whatever Elizabeth wants, Big Daddy gets. And whatever Big Daddy needs, Elizabeth delivers. It's the strangest thing," I said shrugging my shoulders. "Been observing it for years and I still don't have a string on what makes the two of them tick."

"Well that's almost hilarious. Especially since you and Harper are oil and water," Lucia laughed. "Whatever you want, Harper opposes, and whatever she wants, you decimate her. It damn sure isn't like father like son, like mother like daughter."

"It's not the same with Harper and me, Lucia."

"Perhaps you and Harper should rip a page out of your parent's handbook and try getting along sometime," Lucia said, her glare fixed on me.

Lucia crossed those beautiful lean slender legs one over the other, tugging on her black pencil skirt and adjusting it, covering the edge of her knees.

I gave her my best hungry man look, eyeing her up and down for kicks. I didn't want her to assume that just because my head was all screwed up with this Harper stuff, that I had completely lost my grip. Fuck. I was a man. I did have eyeballs. Every now and then I turned my bad boy light on for Lucia for kicks. I enjoyed needling her, knowing full well she rarely took me seriously.

Lucia, being the professional business partner that she was, rolled her eyes, dismissing me, looking at me as if I were a wayward castoff. Lucia was smart. Somewhere along the way in our business relationship, she had completely figured me out. No matter how much I pretended, my Harper was the only woman that I truly cared about and desired. But hell I was going to at least put up a good front. I could still admire a beautiful woman when I saw one. Far be it from me to let the entire male race down. I did have eyeballs in my head and I *was* going to look, dammit.

Lucia looked at me as if the only person that I was fooling was myself. She was probably right. So I figured I'd go into overdrive. I practiced my best James Bond look on her next. Why the hell not? I was momentarily bored. She knew it. She knew me.

"Stop clowning around Nicky," Lucia said, looking me up and down. "Don't look at me like that. Tonight is not the night for games. You need to focus. There's a lot that could go wrong tonight," she hissed.

"What in the world could go wrong?" I said, sipping my vodka, leaning back against the cold leather seat as if I hadn't a care in the world. I wanted to practice my "Hello, Ms. Moneypenny" look on her, but thought better of it. Lucia wasn't enjoying my playful mood.

"Big Daddy will be here, for one. And two, if you have to go completely nuclear with Harper on this Joduku Plastics acquisition, you fucking better remember not to leave any missiles in the silo," Lucia said calmly. "CEO Nobu at Joduku Plastics is narrowing down to his short list of bidders and the word on the street is that Milk Money and Montgomery Consulting Group will likely make the cut.

It had been almost a month since I'd last seen Harper. By now, we both knew that the other was involved in this acquisition and would likely be the last competitors standing.

"And three, keep your ego in check and your dick in your pants with Vicky's Angels tonight."

"You know you need to lighten up Lucia," I said gulping down more of my vodka.

"There's twenty million dollars riding on the line tonight with Joduku Plastics in play," Lucia scolded. "You're a Republican getting ready to enter a Democratic fundraiser, so knock your shit the fuck off. Put that magical moneymaking brain of yours in high gear. This is business. You've got your *Pussy Galore* face on," Lucia continued, admonishing me.

"Okay. Okay. Cool your jets. "You're too damn serious, Lucia," I said, teasing her. "Put your fun house hat on some time, baby."

"One of us has to keep a cool head. I'm looking out for Milk Money's bottom line, Nicky."

"Which is exactly why I have you, lovely," I said, putting a wide smile on my face.

Lucia shook her head. She immediately dialed Stephen. Stephen was behind us in line.

"Stephen, Lucia. Nicholas needs an update," she said, staring me up and down with disgust.

I suppose Lucia thought I wasn't on top of my game tonight. Oh well. Perhaps I wasn't. Harper was going to be here. Big Daddy was going to be here. The bimbo twins were going to be running loose. There were lots of balls that had to be juggled tonight. And at the end of the end of the day, any balls subject to be cut off were likely going to be mine. Even I had to admit my nerves were starting to rattle. This was not a night that I was looking forward to frankly. As far as I was concerned, I was being dragged into this moment kicking and screaming. Last I recalled, this wasn't even my fight. If it weren't for Three lacking his own set of balls to tell Big Daddy to go shove it, I wouldn't be here at all.

Stephen tapped on the window of the limousine, as Lucia pushed the button to let the window down a bit.

"We're five cars away from the Lincoln Center entrance," Stephen said, looking at Lucia as if she was something good to eat.

What was with these two? You would have thought it was Christmas time and they were each other's presents.

"There's a ton of paparazzi out here, Nicky, so let me get out first," Stephen ordered. "I'll come around, open the door to let you and Lucia out. I'll be at your side to the left the whole time, okay?"

I nodded in silence.

"My team will cover Lucia," Stephen said, looking at her while flashing his million-dollar smile.

"Got it," Lucia said, swiftly rolling the window back up.

Lucia tapped the privacy window.

"Silas, follow Stephen's lead," She ordered.

"You've got your checkbook, right, Nicholas?" Lucia asked.

"Of course. No way Big Daddy is going to let me off the hook for fifty thousand dollars tonight."

"Don't start whining about the donation again tonight, Nicky."

"Milk Money, baby," I grinned, throwing back another vodka shot.

"We're entering Lincoln Center now, Nicholas. It's all red carpet and rope tonight," Lucia said. "Keep your wits about you. There are wall-to-wall cameras. Paparazzi, Nicky. Keep a clear head. Image is everything."

"Yeah, yeah, yeah. I know the drill," I said, disgruntled. "Senator Montgomery, Big Daddy, and New York's finest glitterati all in the same room, equals a big crap sandwich night."

I started to feel like Lucia was right. Maybe I had consumed too much to drink. My stomach was feeling queasy. Lucia must have sensed my unease and snatched the vodka glass from of my hand.

"Careful Lucia. You're about to splash vodka on my Armani, woman."

The last thing I needed was to show up in front of Big Daddy smelling like a distillery. Not to mention I happened to love this particular navy pinstriped suit that I had custom made in Italy. I'd paired it with a handmade white shirt monogrammed with my initials on the cuff. I wore my favorite red silk tie, so as to remind those big spending Democrats that a few charitable-minded Republicans still walked the planet.

"You've had too much to drink," Lucia barked. "Pull yourself together." She leaned over, straightening my collar and tightening my tie so tight I thought she was going to choke the life out of me.

"What the fuck Lucia? Kill me already," I grumbled.

"Nicholas. You're known for being pristine. This is not the time to come unglued. Pull yourself together," she said with an air of encouragement.

She was right. I was acting like a man that was rattled.

"You're right Lucia," I said kissing her sloppily on the lips.

Lucia slapped me across the face. Hard. Oh. My. God. I couldn't believe she did that. That slap sobered me up quick and fast. The woman slapped the buzz right out of me.

"Thank you, I needed that," I said, rolling my eyes at the bitch. "It takes a village, love," I said, laughing out loud.

Lucia and I walked the roped-off red carpet that wrapped around the iconic Revson Fountain leading into the Lincoln

Center. I felt the heat of the bright lights. Camera flashes were popping from the numerous paparazzi snapping pictures of the arriving guests, including Lucia and myself. The red carpet was a slow-moving process full of flashing camera lights, celebrities, Kodak moments, and poses. I paused for a minute, putting my hand in the small of Lucia's back, pulling her to my side as we posed for the cameras. Lucia was a pro at working a red carpet, falling right in step with me. Stephen stood a safe distance, off to the side, talking in his earpiece to someone on our security team. He remained in close proximity to us both with a conspicuous watchful eye.

There was a crowd of Tea Party protesters shouting lots of obscenities off to the right of the ropes. They were being pushed further back with guardrails from the incoming arrival of guests by New York's finest, NYPD. I was thankful that if Page Six or any of the other tabloids took pictures, I'd at least be seen with Lucia rather than my usual photographic history of being splashed across tomorrow morning's front tabloid pages with a starlet, heiress, or the latest flavor of the month supermodel. Lucia was beautiful, holding her own against any of the arm candy I was typically seen with on the pages of the tabloids.

After a ton of picture taking, Lucia and I entered the designated banquet area of the Lincoln Center. I laid eyes on the Senator and Elizabeth Montgomery far across the room. They were interacting with a crowd of dignitaries and other well-known political operatives. I was thankful those two piranhas, Mallory Morgan and Jessica Leonard, hadn't yet spotted my arrival. My brother had warned me that Mallory and Jessica would be working the event, modeling clothes for tonight's auction, raising money for the Democrats.

The banquet room was decorated in patriotic colors. An American flag hung from the tall ceiling, lit up against the glow of the crystal chandeliers. The tables were draped in blue tablecloths with red, white, and blue balloons anchored on each table. A full orchestra was playing "Happy Days Are Here Again" in the background. The male musicians were suited up in white tuxedoes. The female musicians adorned in long black gowns. This was another typical political fundraiser for the money magnets.

Oh Lord. I could see Mallory and Jessica strutting those perfectly honed bodies from across the room as every inquisitive hungry-eyed male politician eyed them stealthily, as if their next new mistress had revealed herself. Wait. My brother failed to mention that Mallory, Jessica, and several other beauties were modeling Victoria's Secret lingerie, prancing around the banquet hall half-naked. He'd only said they were modeling *clothes*.

They might as well have been naked, strutting like peacocks in a room full of glamourous, diamond studded, mink-wearing moneyed predators who were ripe for the picking.

Mallory and Jessica looked like two celestial angels sent down from heaven as gifts from above. The Greek gods of love must have been working overtime. Every man in the room wanted to pay homage. Victoria wasn't holding back on any of her secrets, that was for sure.

Mallory was wearing a skimpy, hot-pink, lacy bra and thong, and gold stilettos that laced around her calves like Cleopatra. She had on matching hot-pink angel wings that were wrapped behind her bodice, setting the room ablaze in her path. She looked like a gazelle, her long blond curls falling down her back in ringlets that swung from side to side at the same rhythm of her hips. Her luscious breasts were bursting out of that hot-pink bra held together with diamond-studded clasps and straps that glimmered across her creamy pale skin, reflecting off her deep ocean-blue eyes. Her curved mouth was laminated with a pinkish lip gloss.

Jessica strutted like a poised peacock in an all-white glittering bra and thong, and matching white angel wings. She was showing off that beautiful chocolate-brown skin, twirling around on four-inch crystal clear stilettoes, reminding me of a candy-coated M&M that could melt in my mouth and not in my hands. Her long black hair hung straight down, falling deliciously against those voluptuous breasts, her short wispy bangs framing her face as if she were readying for a carefully crafted Kodak moment. Together these two looked like coffee and cream. It was hard not to want to taste. Holy happy spirit, this was going to be an extremely long night.

I still hadn't spotted Harper yet, but I knew it would only be a matter of time. I didn't want her to see me with these two sirens curled around me. And I damn sure didn't want to have to look at her on the arms of that fuckwad McKenna. Either of those pictures would make the night practically unbearable.

"I hope I don't have to babysit you tonight, Nicky, with Hip and Hop running loose in here, do I?" Lucia muttered, her expression impassive.

Lucia was referring to Mallory and Jessica.

"Oh I'm definitely going to need a babysitter. Let's hope Big Daddy doesn't need one with these two gazelles igniting the room."

I grabbed two champagne flutes off a passing server's tray, handing one to Lucia. No sooner had I gotten the words out of my mouth, than Mallory and Jessica strutted over to me at the same time, holding hands.

"Bid on me Nicky," Jessica yelped.

"No Nicky, bid on me," Mallory whined, twirling around in a circle, rocking that beautiful ass to one side with her elbow on her hip, then quickly to the other side. She pirouetted back around to the front, winking at me.

I was at a loss for words as I seductively eyed them both. I sipped my champagne slowly, wondering how I was going to save myself from an impossible choice. I wanted to bow down to the Gods of I'm Willing and Able, pay homage, lay my cards on the table, and make love to these two damn beautiful bodies at the same time. Oh boy. I was going to have to write another big check with itty bitty zeros.

Before I could mouth a word, Lucia rolled her eyes at me, walking away headed toward Stephen's direction at the same time Big Daddy walked over, grabbing both girls by their waists.

"Now ladies, let's don't fight," Big Daddy said in his deep, husky, in-control voice. "Money is no object for the two most beautiful creatures in the room. I think I'll take them both," Big Daddy said, positioning himself in the middle of the both of them, kissing Mallory on the cheek first, then kissing Jessica on the cheek next.

"Hello Father," I said, straightening my back.

"Nicky, this is your father?" Mallory and Jessica asked, screaming, jumping up and down, clapping their hands like two starry-eyed kids in a candy store.

"Father, may I introduce Mallory Morgan and Jessica Leonard."

Big Daddy turned his natural charm on full force, all the way up the Richter scale, fat cigar and all.

"You ladies look so lovely. Perhaps my son will let me hold *The Julianna* so the three of us can make a hop, skip, and a jump to the French Rivera. We can sprawl out on the deck in St. Tropez, drink champagne, bubble and bathe."

Mallory and Jessica giggled like two school girls who had hit the jackpot.

"You lovelies are strikingly stunning. I feel like giving all my money away tonight. Good God, dollars, and Pradas. I think I might give away a million bucks," Big Daddy chuckled, looking both ladies up and down while admiring their striking figures.

Oh no he didn't say that. What the fuck was in that cigar Big Daddy was smoking? I know he did not say he wanted to take *my* two-hundred foot yacht, *The Julianna*, any-fucking-where to go on some enticing venture in St. Tropez with Mallory and Jessica. I could not believe my lying ears. I was going to be low man on the totem pole if Mallory and Jessica got pulled in by Big Daddy's shenanigans. It wouldn't take those gold diggers long to sniff out the fact that Big Daddy's green was as long as his reach.

"Oh Mr. Becker," the gals screamed. They were jumping up and down, shaking those luscious booties, their breasts desiring to escape those teeny weenie bras, all while eye-googling Big Daddy.

"My friends call me "Big Daddy," my father said huskily, yanking both of them closer to himself by their waists, grinning from ear to ear.

I rolled my eyes. I wasn't sure how long I could bear this scene. I scanned the room, hoping to pick Lucia out of the crowd. She was across the room with Stephen. Her eyes locked onto mine like radar. She shook her head at me as if I were losing my touch, lifting her glass up acknowledging that she had her eye on me. I wondered if she realized I was being out-manned by my own damn father. I lifted my glass back at her, nodding through clenched teeth in a fake smile.

Mallory and Jessica were flirting, kissing, and hugging my father, completely enamored. Mackenzie Rhodes moved our direction with her long-lensed Nikon camera in tow.

"How about a picture, Nicholas?" Mackenzie said with a wicked gleam in her eye.

"Come Nicky, let's all take a picture with Big Daddy," Mallory spouted, bubbling over with excitement.

"Yes, let's all take a picture," Jessica said, pulling me into the frame with her, Mallory, and Big Daddy.

Big Daddy and the ladies smiled ear to ear. I feigned

enjoyment for the camera, figuring MacKenzie was pulling this stunt, taking my picture on purpose so she could have some evidence against me to slide under Harper's nose. I had no idea how Big Daddy expected me to be able to meet his expectations of wooing a woman or a wife under these conditions.

When the fight for Joduku Plastics got underway with Harper, it was going to be rough going all around. It was bad enough Harper made me dig deep to win that piece of artwork I wanted, knowing all the time she was forcing me to overpay. I made a mental note to seriously school that woman. The mere thinking about that art bidding stunt she pulled made me vacillate between wanting to take her over my knee and spank her, and wanting to wrap her in my arms and kiss her. I was a ball of mixed emotions and confusion.

One thing for sure, Harper was going to be angry all over again when she saw tonight's pictures. I wondered what tabloid god I was going to have to pray to or pay to keep myself off the front pages with these two hot tens and Big Daddy.

"Well if you ladies will excuse me, I'd like to have a moment in private with my son Nicholas here," Big Daddy said. "Don't worry ladies, I'll be careful to make sure my boy here doesn't outbid me tonight," Big Daddy laughed heartily.

"Not at all, we still have more money to raise," Mallory purred in Big Daddy's ear, flashing her seductive smile, licking her tinted pink lips with her tongue. "C'mon Jessica."

Mallory grabbed Jessica's hand and off they swished to the other side of the room to shake down some of the other rich patrons into parting with their money.

"Bye Nicky, Bye Big Daddy," Jessica said, turning her back, flicking her hips, and burning a path of heat as she turned walked away, leaving me and Big Daddy in shreds in her wake.

"Good God, boy," Big Daddy said. "Let's go to the VIP area with the big dog donors and talk in private. It's time for you to stop your monkey business with these sirens and start thinking about your future," he said calmly, walking us into the VIP area, and propping us both in a red velvet–lined booth, raising his hand to get the server's attention.

"He'll have a vodka," Big Daddy growled, pointing his cigar laden hand at me. I'll have a Jack Daniels double, neat."

Big Daddy was all over Mallory and Jessica, yet he stood here accusing me of being the one engaged in monkey business tonight. He was souring what little good mood I had left.

"I want some grandsons Nicky. Your brother Three seems to only shoot gal sperm. We've got the girls and now we need the boys. Your mother and I talked about our having granddaughters and grandsons, God bless her soul. We need some boys, son," Big Daddy said.

I swigged my vodka down in one large gulp, forcing myself to sit through this conversation in peace.

"Your Mother had no doubt that you and Three would have some boys. Now I want some grandsons, Nicky."

"Maybe you should think about making your own," I said, knowing I was crazy to be challenging my father, maybe even taking my life in my own hands. Literally. As soon as I let those words roll off my tongue I knew that was the wrong thing to say to Big Daddy.

"I'm only going to have this conversation with you once Nicholas," Big Daddy said sternly, his eyes narrowing as he let out an exasperated sigh. "You get with the program. Becker Foods has a legacy to protect. Stop horsing around with these beauty queens. Dating, playing, and fucking are fine for a while, boy, but a man needs a family. Family keeps a man grounded," Big Daddy said in his husky voice. "You're running out of excuses to not settle down. You're getting too old to be running around like some overgrown playboy."

"I know this may surprise you, Father, but I actually spend most of my days and nights working, contrary to popular opinion."

I kept my gaze on Big Daddy intense just in case he thought I was going to back down from him.

"Okay. So you've done well with that little company of yours," Big Daddy growled back at me. "Milk Money—even your company name sounds like child's play, Nicholas. You, Julianna, and Three are heirs to Becker Foods. You're a well-educated graduate of Annapolis. You're handsome. You've got enough money to last through your kids *and* their kids."

"Child's play?" I interrupted, before asking the server for another drink. "That little company you call "child's play" has a net worth of six hundred million dollars," I frowned, thinking that this conversation was turning into a painful gut-wrenching experience.

Big Daddy shrugged his head, nodding in agreement like I

had a legitimate point.

"Six hundred million dollars hardly sounds like child's play, even by your standards, Father," I said. "Don't you think I'm getting a bit old for you to be telling me how to live my life? You're always trying to dictate my life," I shot back.

"I'm making a point here, Nicky."

"Bad enough you've got me all tangled up in buying a plastics company for Becker Foods," I said, shaking my head in disbelief. "I've done everything you've ever asked me to do. Enough is enough," I said, pounding my fist on the table.

I knew my words were going to be the shot heard around the world. I pondered how long it was going to take Big Daddy to spiral out of control on me.

"You are going to settle down and marry, son. You're a Becker. You're going to act like one. You're going to be the gift that keeps on giving, because *I* fucking said so," Big Daddy snapped hard back at me.

I wasn't surprised my words had unleashed the beast. This was going to escalate into a tirade. Big Daddy was the type of man that what he said, happened. There was no room for compromise. Three always gave into our father too easily as far as I was concerned. Julianna was a daddy's girl who never had to battle him. Me, I rarely won these battles with Big Daddy—but not for lack of putting up a good fight. He respected the fact that I pushed back on him. I refused to wimp out with him on matters I found to be compromising my principals. They were non-negotiable, but Big Daddy was the type of man who was going to turn the screws hard to test your mettle. He relished seeing if his gene pool could hold its own. This conversation was going to be tough, but oh well. Game on.

"I'm still the head of this family, and goddammit, I'm not dead yet. Until then, you'll do as you're told. I promised your mother on her deathbed that I would see to it that you would get married, have a family, and settle down. I plan to keep my promise if I have to hog-tie you down myself, Nicky."

"I'm a grown man, father. You're no longer in charge of me," I said, tempering my words, reining back my outburst so as not to make a scene.

"Are you trying to break your mother's heart, really?" Big Daddy said, registering curiosity on his face as he ordered another Jack Daniels. "I need to be able to sleep at night in peace, knowing I've kept my word to your mother, boy," Big Daddy growled.

Oh God. Big Daddy was pulling out all the stops. Playing the guilt card with my deceased mother was a low blow. I would never do anything to displease my mother, nor her memory. My mother, Julianna Becker, was my rock in a storm. She died giving birth to my little sister, her mid-life baby and namesake, Julianna. Big Daddy knew how much I loved pleasing my mother and making her happy. Big Daddy never ever played fair. He was pulling out his big guns. This was the same man that minutes ago was cuddling up with two hot twenty-something babes, talking about taking them in my yacht to fuck around on the French Rivera playground.

Take your own fucking yacht.

"Ever since you and Harper Montgomery broke up, you've been flitting around sulking like a lost puppy dog, Nicholas," Big Daddy glared at me. "You've sown your oats. Now it's time to man up. Get on with a more settled lifestyle."

For whatever reason, it was important to Big Daddy that he still felt in control of the family now that mother was gone. Mother insisted Big Daddy was the head of the family. She relied on him to run a tight ship when it came to her kids. She claimed she didn't want all the money and lifestyle to spoil us or wreck our values. I was going to have to either get with Big Daddy's program or this was going to turn into a long war that I would battle with every day, years from now.

I would never admit this. But I wasn't as opposed to the idea of marriage and settling down as Big Daddy might have imagined. Maybe on some level Big Daddy knew that about me. I have just never found anyone to love since the loss of my relationship with Harper. Hell, I'd slept with, wined, and dined many of the most beautiful women in the world. But none of them were Harper Montgomery. She was the queen of my heart. She was also the battle-royal-all-around-pain-in-my-ass. But I loved her. She owned me.

"Father, you need to understand that Harper Montgomery and I have a complicated relationship. This company you have me bidding on, Joduku Plastics, for Becker Foods—she's the competition," I snapped. "Fighting with each other over a company is not the greatest recipe for building a foundation for love and harmony, or don't you realize that?" I growled back at him.

Big Daddy looked at me and laughed in his chair, looking at me as if my words came out of the mouth of a juvenile. He drew heavily on his cigar.

What the fuck was his problem? He was annoying the hell out of me.

"Nicky, you've been running around with these brainless beauties so long, you're lost in knowing how to woo a strong-minded woman with an impeccable brain for business and body to die for," Big Daddy said with authority. "You need to come up to speed quick, son, because that is the kind of woman you will need to hold your attention for the long haul. One that can share your dreams, maintain your interests, and make you some babies. Some male babies," Big Daddy snapped.

Big Daddy was serious as a heart attack. No way I was going to win this round. Even I decided he was freaking me out a bit with his tenacity.

"And while I'm on the subject of business, make sure you get that plastics company, Nicky," Big Daddy said, leaning his body forward out of his chair to make his point.

Just as Big Daddy put the exclamation on his point to me, Elizabeth Montgomery strolled over to our table in the VIP area. Big Daddy and I both stood to acknowledge her.

"Blake, darling, it's so good to see you," she said, kissing Big Daddy on his cheek. "And Nicky, you're looking handsome as ever," Elizabeth smiled. "I'm so glad you both could make it."

"For you, Lizzy, we wouldn't miss this event for the world. You're looking lovely as ever," Big Daddy said, reaching up, grabbing her hand, and kissing it.

"Nicholas has a small donation for you tonight, isn't that right Nicholas?" Big Daddy bit out.

Since when is fifty thousand dollars to some damn Democrats a small donation? Not necessarily chump change. Okay so maybe it was chump change by my standards. But to give away good money to some Democrats? Seriously, Father?

I reached in my pocket and Elizabeth a check for fifty thousand dollars.

"Oh thank you, thank you, Nicholas. Clayton and I are most appreciative," Elizabeth sounded genuinely thankful.

"Our family is happy to contribute to yours. Isn't that right, Father?" I said, feigning happiness for having to make a political contribution to the Democrats.

"Yes indeed, Elizabeth. It's mere *milk money*," Big Daddy laughed heartily.

Oh no, my father did not just steal my line. He thought this was a joke. He always made sure he looked like the winner, despite the fact that this was my money and the joke was on me.

"Oh Blake you're such a character," Elizabeth smiled. She giggled, deciding to sit and join us.

"So how's that beautiful daughter of yours? I haven't seen her tonight," Big Daddy said, his eyes momentarily scanning the room.

My antennas went up listening passively to Big Daddy and Elizabeth's conversation while nursing my vodka. I grabbed a champagne for Elizabeth, minding my manners. Big Daddy and Elizabeth had been friends for ages, their alliance in the food manufacturing business as strong as ever. They chatted about almost everything, treating each other like family. There were times when Big Daddy was in the presence of women and he shoveled shit. But I never saw him do that with Elizabeth. With Elizabeth, He was different. He was . . . honest.

"She's as beautiful as her mother," Big Daddy said, looking at Elizabeth as if the sun rose and shined in her face.

"Oh she's close by. I expect her to arrive any moment now," Elizabeth said, smiling, looking at me with a reassuring smile much like a mother would for a son.

"We had such a huge crowd tonight. With those Tea Party protestors outside, the NYPD has had extra security tonight which has slowed the traffic. I understand from Malcom that her limousine should be arriving very soon," she said. "I'm so worried about Harper these days. Do you know, Blake, she's gone all 'modernist feminist woman' now, talking crazy. She claims her biological clock is ticking. That she wants to go to one of those fertility clinics and have a sperm donor baby? That's like having a baby with an unidentified father. I'm so beside myself. The mere thought of it is breaking my heart. Surely she can't be serious, Blake," Elizabeth said studying Big Daddy's face and searching for answers.

"Oh I'm sure this is just a phase, Liz. She's out of her element right now. She's not thinking clearly. She needs a good man in her life, and all that crazy talk will stop," Big Daddy said. "I don't want you worrying your pretty little head about such matters."

He grabbed her hand, holding it and tucking it inside of his own. "This will work out fine," Big Daddy said, comforting Elizabeth, and honing his glare on me.

Wait a minute. Wow. Did somebody say Harper, baby, and sperm donor in the same sentence? No way *my* baby maker was going to be making any deals with the devil, having a baby by some unknown seed-dropper-for-money stranger. Oh hell no. This was pure stupidity. She was taking matters way too far now. She was truly starting to spiral out of control. Harper was getting way out of my reach. I could feel my anger rising. Yup. She was definitely going to pay for this stupid idea of hers. This was so wrong on a lot of levels.

"Oh fuck no," I said, not realizing I had actually spoken out loud, cocking my head to the side, choking on my vodka.

"Nicholas?" Elizabeth said, concerned.

"Don't worry about him, Lizzy," Big Daddy said. "He needs a good whack on the back, or better yet, a whack on his head. Get a grip on yourself, Nicky," Big Daddy commanded. "There's a lady at the table."

I cleared my throat quickly in disbelief. Spit was coming out of my mouth and my nose at the same time. Maybe I would choke to death. This was way too much information for me to take in on one night. I was on emotional overload. Big Daddy, Mallory, Jessica, Democrats, fifty-thousand-dollar checks, Elizabeth, plastic companies, McKenna Textiles, art bidding wars, and now *this*? First Big Daddy's trying to run off in *The Julianna* with a couple of beyond-hot twenty-somethings and now *my* baby maker is trying run off to inseminate herself with unknown sperm.

"If you'll please excuse me, I need to go get some water. Air perhaps," I said, gasping for breath.

I promptly excused myself from their booth and that conversation. It was a good thing too because I could feel that she was here. I only needed to lay eyes on her and ask her directly if she had completely lost her ever-living mind.

My timing was good, too. Just as I turned the corner headed out of the VIP area, I spotted Harper across the room. Damn, she looked like a million dollars standing under the glittering chandelier. She was wearing a short, sparkly silver sequinned dress that hugged her body in all the right places, her beauty reflecting off the dancing light. That dress was too damn short.

Beautiful, but too damn short. She was drawing the attention of every man in the room. I wanted to toss her over my shoulder, take her to my bed, grab those beautiful brown legs, wrap them around my ass, and make our own baby. I needed to start figuring out how to take measures into my own hands. Drastic times called for drastic measures.

Harper was standing somewhat close to the senator but a lot closer to Mackenzie and Stephen. Lucia and Three were standing nearby. I headed in her direction, striding across the floor, quickening my resolve. I reminded myself not to get too distracted by whatever bullshit she was going to spill out of that cute little sassy pouty mouth of hers to throw me off my game. Not tonight. No, tonight I was in charge.

Damn, *my* baby maker was so darn cute and sexy. She was like a hot cocoa on a cold winter's day. All chocolate. All hot. All yummy.

CHAPTER EIGHT

Harper

"Girl, it's a good thing you're rocking that itty bitty dress looking like a rock star, because your face has funk written all over it," Mackenzie said, snapping my picture.

"It's been a rough day. I had to put Malcom in his place for the way he behaved when Reese came to visit. I don't want him speaking to my guests in the manner in which he was conducting himself. So he wasn't too happy with me," I said, glancing back over my shoulder noticing Malcom conversing with the senator and my mother.

"Yeah, well, sleeping with Malcom wasn't one of your brighter moments," Mackenzie whispered, still snapping pictures. "Hopefully you've cut him off. I don't think he can handle your sleeping with him and having to guard you at the same time. It's too confusing. But that's one fine man, so I forgive you," Mackenzie giggled.

"Well his actions with Reese were unacceptable. He needs to stay in his lane. Color him cut off," I said, grabbing a champagne flute. Recognizing the new freshman congressman at the bar who was making eye contact with me, I smiled shyly back at him, pressing my lips ever so gently and slowly against the lip of my glass.

"See that little move you're doing right there, Harper, eye-balling that fine-ass statesman, that's the kind of move that makes these guys go goo-goo gaga all over you. The next thing you know, you've got to pry them out of your life and out of your bed. You're only using them for their bodies." Mackenzie laughed. "I know you, girlfriend."

I ignored the fact that Mackenzie was making fun of me again. The way I figured it, I got dragged to this event by my mother. I didn't want to be here. Appreciating the eye candy couldn't really hurt a gal tonight.

"So have you taken any good shots tonight, Mackenzie?"

"Well I got some money shots of Nicholas with Big Daddy, Mallory, and Jessica." Mackenzie grinned. "Jesus girl, what took you so long to get here? You're unfashionably late."

"I thought I'd never ever make it inside Lincoln Center tonight with all the commotion going on with the Tea Partiers protesting outside. The whole scene was making Malcom edgy, not to mention he and I were having words. And to make matters worse, I tried to snatch some more artwork up for auction from Nicholas, but lost the bid."

"Sounds like you're having a rough start to tonight's festivities," Mackenzie said.

"What's worse, I find out from Reese a couple of weeks ago that Nicholas is also competing for the bid with the plastics company I'm looking to acquire. How dare he? I need to bring him to his knees once and for all. He's like the bad penny always turning up."

"Speak of the devil," Mackenzie said. He's headed this way. Ohhh . . . he's not looking too happy."

Mackenzie whistled out loud, snapping Nicky's picture.

I watched Nicholas stalk across the floor headed in my direction. He had his mad face on. His expression was stern. His face was flushed. My body stiffened in preparation for the fallout. I made sure I gave him my best murderous stare so he wouldn't think he could intimidate me. Then I gave him the "you're such a huge prick look" that I had been practicing all week just for him. I swear if he pissed me off any further tonight, I was going to take my stiletto off and whack him across his thick skull.

"Harper," Nicholas hissed. "We need to talk," he insisted, grabbing me by my arm and attempting to drag me out of Mackenzie's space.

"Who the hell do you think you are, shithead?" Mackenzie said. "Can't you see she's busy?"

Mackenzie snapped our picture. Both of us had to have looked like we were going to kill the other.

Suddenly Stephen moved quickly away from Lucia, grabbing Mackenzie's camera.

"And what the hell do you think you're doing?" Mackenzie said, turning her head towards Stephen, watching him as he deleted our pictures.

"I'm doing my job, babe. I work for Nicholas, remember," Stephen said calmly.

"Why's he calling you babe?" I asked, confused.

"Maybe because we're a couple?" Stephen says cocking his head to the side, handing Mackenzie her camera back, and glaring at me as if to underscore his point.

"I have a job to do here, too, Stephen," Mackenzie insisted, ignoring my inquiry. "Last I checked, you're not the only one working here tonight."

I could see she was starting to sizzle. At that moment, Lucia stepped over to our little huddle, looking perturbed.

"Stephen is everything alright here? What's going on Nicholas?"

"I'll tell you what's going on here," I snapped, stepping forward and closing the space between us. "Nicholas is going to get out of this competition with me immediately for Joduku Plastics. That's what's going on here, Lucia," I said, thinking I was going to have a hard time keeping my stiletto on my foot tonight lest I put it up someone's ass.

"No I'm not getting out the of Joduku Plastics competition. Not for you. And definitely not for that fuckwad Brooks Fitzgerald McKenna either," Nicholas fumed. "Don't think for one minute I'm going to get out of this competition to please the two of you piranhas. Fuck McKenna Textiles. And frankly, Harper, you should exercise more discretion as to who you decide to conspire with in business."

"What are you talking about Nicholas? McKenna Textiles and Montgomery Consulting are not business partners. What exactly is your problem?" I asked quizzically.

Clearly my competitive intelligence team missed that little tidbit. Things were slipping through the cracks.

Nicholas ignored me like I hadn't said a mumbling word.

"Brooks Fitzgerald McKenna? What's McKenna Textiles got to do with this acquisition? You've finally gone completely all out insane, Nicholas Miles Becker," I barked.

I was standing nose to nose with Nicholas, narrowing my

eyes that were blazing bullets at him. I noticed others in the room were sensing we were starting to make a scene.

"And while I'm at it, Harper, you're going to get your head out of your ass, and stop this shit about making babies at some goddamn fertility clinic with a goddamn sperm donor. That's just what the fuck you're going to do," Nicholas snapped.

Oh. My. God. I was certain my mouth dropped open to the floor as I gasped in shock. *No, Nicholas did not just spread my business out loud in public. I for sure am going to kill him right here and now where he stands and choke him into the next life. How dare he? Who told him?*

"Nicholas, what did you and I discuss earlier?" Lucia said, stepping next to Nicholas in sort of a protective mode. "Must I remind you?" she said sharply.

I had no doubt Lucia sensed I was going to string Nicholas's closet Republican ass up in a noose right in front of this room full of Democrats. Malcom wasn't even going to be able to stop me from whacking Nicholas across the head with my heel.

"Nicholas, you don't get to tell Harper what to do and when to do it," Mackenzie blasted out loud.

God this was getting so out of hand.

Before I could speak again, Nicholas's brother Three joined our group with those two gold diggers Mallory and Jessica twisted around his neck. Three was totally intoxicated, slurring "Can't we all get along?"

Those two fame whores were glued to Three like white on rice, rubbing those double Ds against his chest. Three's facial expression looked like he had died and gone to heaven. "I got a big fat check with lots of little zeros on it ladies," Three slurred, waving his checkbook in the air.

I rolled my eyes up in my head. I was going to slap Nicholas across his face for publicly spilling my business about wanting a baby.

Before I could mouth a word, a naked male Tea Partier protester ran across the room, yelling "Bomb Threat," with about ten New York police department officers on his heels. Stephen immediately un-holstered his Glock 45 and moved to grab Nicholas to protect him. *Oh Shit.* What was going on here?

Nicholas yelled back, "No Stephen, get Lucia out of here. I'll get Harper. Don't worry about me."

Everyone in the room began to panic, running in different

directions. Several drunk women and men were falling all over themselves. Security personnel for a room full of congressmen, senators, and statesmen were quickly moving to gather up their assigned protectees. Guns were flying out of holsters. People were yelling, screaming, and starting to stampede across the room. Someone pulled the fire alarm, which began blaring. I thought I caught a whiff of gasoline in the air.

Stephen grabbed Mackenzie in his arms with his free hand. Mackenzie was desperately clutching her camera, trying not to lose it, as some man yelling in what sounded like Russian, yanked it out of her hand.

"Motherfucker took my camera!" MacKenzie shouted.

"Forget about it," Stephen said, scooping Lucia up at the same time.

Several of the Tea Party protestors had broken through the police department ranks. Handcuffs were flying on the protestors, many of which were being pulled down on the ground, their wrists tied in little plastic ties. The protestors were yelling back at the swat team members. The well-heeled guests were screaming and shouting. The sounds of canisters rolling across the floor heightened my fears even further. I knew what was coming next. Blue smoke started to fill the air.

A scruffy looking protestor pulled on me from behind, but not before Nicholas kicked him in his side forcing him to release me. I fell to the ground. My Christian Loubintin stiletto broke in half, and I began free-falling to the ground, scraping my elbow and knee. Nicholas kneed another nearby protestor in his groin who had grabbed me by my ankle. Nicholas swept me up, throwing me over his shoulder, yelling words at Stephen that were inaudible to me as I was struggling to see and hear between the noise in the room and my dazed state of mind.

"Stephen. Call Silas. Have him to come to the back door exit," Nicholas hollered, setting me on my feet with the weight of my body leaned against his.

I could see Mallory and Jessica out the corner of my eye. They were stumbling and falling in those four-inch heels with their angel wings crushed. Both were bent over trying to hold Three up, trying to force themselves out the double doors amid the crowd.

"Oh God, we're going to die!" I hollered in a state of panic.

Big Daddy was rushing a few paces in front of us, guiding my mother over near Malcom's side. I could hear a voice over the Lincoln Center intercom asking the guests to remain calm and to leave the room in an orderly fashion. The wait staff looked flustered and confused.

Some people were screaming "fire," while others were yelling "bomb threat."

The room was anything but calm and orderly. I could hear sirens and whistles coming from outside the Lincoln Center from the police cars and fire trucks.

Oh my God. The last thing I wanted to do was to die inside the Lincoln Center like this. My only saving grace was that I was in the arms of Nicholas. I knew in this moment that Reese was right. Nicholas and I had both been wasting time these last ten years, holding onto our baggage of the past. I did love Nicholas. And now I was going to die in his arms in this godforsaken place. He would never know how I felt. We'd been fighting each other for so long, acting on our hurt and pain. Reese could see it, but I couldn't.

Oh my God, Reese. God knows I wanted to see my good friend Reese again. I could feel my heart starting to palpitate. My breathing was becoming erratic.

"I can't breathe, I can't breathe Nicky," I cried out in his arms.

I could feel myself starting to tremble. I was having a full-blown panic attack.

"Take deep breaths and try to stay calm, Kitten," Nicholas said. "I'm not going to let anything happen to you. We're going to make it out of here alive, I promise you, baby," Nicholas said, his voice calm and in command.

More canisters of tear gas were rolling across the floor. The room was starting to smoke up even more. My eyes were tearing. My ears were ringing. My body was trembling.

"Daddy? Mother? Where are my parents, Nicky? I can't see. I can't see!" I shouted.

"Don't worry about them," Nicky said. "They are going to be okay. Senator Carmichael is being flanked by his own security team. Malcom and Big Daddy are closest to Elizabeth and have her secured."

I looked past Nicky towards Malcom's direction. Malcom was waving his hand at me shouting "Stick with Nicholas."

"I've got you, baby," Nicholas said, reassuring me. "Don't

worry, Kitten. I'll get us out of here safely," Nicholas said, as he kept moving us through the crowd.

Nicholas moved us swiftly out through the back kitchen doors.

"Stephen has given me an alternative route out of this shit. Silas is going to get us all the fuck out of this motherfucker safely or else I'm going to fire everybody on my goddamn team tonight," Nicholas said sharply.

I knew Nicholas well enough to know that even though his voice sounded calm, his mind and body were on high alert. I suspected his Navy skills were coming forward and he would only get keener under pressure, the knowledge of which gave me reassurance. I was glad he was here with me tonight. In my heart and soul I felt that this moment in time was no coincidence. The universe unfolds properly as it should.

The alarm system started to go off. It was bloody ear-piercing loud. Suddenly, the exit door lights illuminated and doors began automatically opening.

"The backup generator must have kicked in," Nicholas said.

The sprinkler systems began to deploy. My heart was pounding rapidly. I wanted to get the hell out of this situation.

I was holding onto Nicholas for dear life. I wanted nothing more than to get out of this mire of insanity. People were shouting and screaming all while Nicholas was dragging me quickly through back corridors and a dimly lit exit area.

We reached the back exit doors in time to avoid the downpour of water. Like clockwork, Silas was waiting by the exit doors with Nicholas's limousine. Nicholas practically threw me in the back seat, he moved so quickly.

"Silas, get us the fuck out of here," Nicholas shouted.

"We're out of here, sir. Everyone hold tight," Silas said as the tires of the limousine began to screech.

My cell phone rang. My hands shook as I answered.

"Yes Malcom, I'm safe. I'm in Nicky's limousine. No. No please stay with Mother and Daddy's team. Don't worry about me," I shouted through the phone above the loud noises in the background, clearly feeling exasperated.

Nicholas reached for his cell phone in his inside jacket pocket. I could hear tires screeching to a sudden halt behind us. It was Stephen in the Suburban. Lots of horns were honking wildly. Guests were running out of all the exits in between the moving cars trying not to get hit by the hundreds of cars fleeing the scene. It was madness.

"Stephen, we're headed to Becker Towers," Nicholas said.

"I'm right behind you, Nicky," Stephen replied. "Lucia and Mackenzie are with me. I've got you in my sights. Our backup team is securing Big Daddy and Three. I've got this. I'm right behind you. Don't worry, Nicky."

"Get the fuck out the way!" I could hear Stephen yelling at a passerby, swearing loudly through the phone, honking his horn like a crazy man.

"Fine," Nicholas shouted, sighing heavily with exhaustion.

I looked down at my scraped knees that were slightly bleeding. Somehow I managed to hold onto my favorite little silver Judith Lieber clutch. My shoe heel was broken and my ankle was bruised from being manhandled by the protestor. Internally I was a mess. I burst out crying.

"Oh Nicholas, I am so scared," I whimpered.

"Don't be scared, baby. You're in shock. I'm not going to let anything happen to you. I'm going to take care of you."

Before I knew it, Nicholas leaned over and kissed me hard, hugging me with all his strength. I practically leapt in his lap, putting my arms around his neck, kissing him back hard like I never wanted to let him go. I was in a full-on adrenaline rush, succumbing to the insatiable heat of our attraction. Nicholas started kissing me profusely, his hands moving up to hold my face, allowing me passage to kiss him back. He kissed my forehead, my cheeks, my lips, burying his face in my neck, holding me as if his life depended on it.

Becker Towers was the home of Nicholas's eight-thousand-square-foot Presidential Penthouse Suite, nestled on the eighty-sixth floor of 15 Central Park West. The Becker family owned several key properties all over the world. Becker Towers graced the New York skyline in a most majestic way, second to none.

When the double doors of the penthouse opened, I was

reminded of how much I had missed his breathtaking views of Central Park and the glittering New York skyline. Nicholas truly owned New York's most wanted trophy property, second only to his One Hyde Park home in London.

The last time I was in Nicholas's home was a year ago. I was Reese's "plus one" for dinner at Nicholas's home last New Year's Eve. Reese's sister Riley was dating Nicholas's friend Mico. Riley was seeking an angel investor for her company Black Sequinned Bows and Champagne Nights and was presenting a pitch to Milk Money for funding that evening.

Nicholas's home was just as I remembered. I loved the oversized great room, the design and decor of which were impeccable. The full-wall floor-to-ceiling windows revealed three–hundred-sixty-degree breathtaking views of the New York skyline. Nicholas's home was equipped with a media room, an exercise room with a boxing ring, and a glass-enclosed swimming pool on a see-through roof. Nicky had spent hundreds of thousands of dollars to build a circular water slide into the pool. He never hesitated to spend his wealth in ways that always nurtured his inner child.

One only had to look up at the ceiling to see the swimming pool, which at night was lit with colored lights that created a warm dimmed aura in the room below.

As we entered the great room, Nicky moved to sit me down gently on the grey-and-white sofa, tucking a soft white baby alpaca throw over my body. A black baby grand piano positioned in the corner began to play soft classical music at his touch of a button. I immediately recognized the tune. It was one of Nicky's favorites, "L'Origine Nascosta" by Ludovico Einaudi.

"I need to get us into a calmer state of mind. I'll fix us both a cognac to warm us up," he said, hitting another switch that lit the fireplace.

The double doors to the penthouse flew open. Lucia, Stephen, and Mackenzie arrived, looking as frazzled as I was feeling. Mackenzie was trembling and cold. Stephen rubbed his hands up and down on her arms to warm her. Lucia headed to the wet bar pouring warm brown amber liquid half-filled to the top into a Baccarat brandy snifter that she immediately chugged down and began pouring herself a second. Mackenzie broke from Stephen's arms and ran over to hug me.

"What a fucking nightmare Nicky," Stephen said,

exasperated. "How are you doing?"

Stephen wrapped Nicky into a man-to-man bear hug.

Nicholas hugged Stephen back.

"Thank you for all your hard efforts and maintaining control under difficult circumstances. Good job."

"That why you pay me the big bucks," Stephen smiled, patting him hard on the back. "My job is to keep you and all that's precious to you alive and well," Stephen said, looking at me with a heartfelt smile.

I wasn't sure how to respond, knowing that Stephen knew all of the grief Nicholas and I had caused each other over the years. I wondered how he was able to still look at me with warmth and gentleness.

Stephen eyeballed Mackenzie, who had curled up under the blanket with me. Mackenzie was stressing over her overwhelming need to connect with her son, Gill Jr. Gill Jr. was asleep at this hour and she wasn't going to wake him. I could tell that her nerves were shot and that she was as shook up as I was.

Stephen reached over and handed Mackenzie a snifter of brandy. "Here take this. It will calm your nerves. I will get you delivered to your boy safely, babe," he said.

"Thank you," Mackenzie whispered softly.

It was weird watching Mackenzie interact with a man. She hadn't dated a man since her husband was killed in Iraq. Typically Mackenzie was fire and brimstone. This was a new look for her. Tonight's events had knocked all the spitfire right out of her. She was even treating Nicholas with kid gloves. How long would this last? Were we all in shock or was this change the calm before the storm? Either way, I felt the shift.

Lucia's cell phone rang and everyone turned their attention her direction.

"Yes. Yes. Okay. Thank you," Lucia said. "Stephen, that was your security guy Ross. Big Daddy and Three have arrived unharmed and are now back at the Becker mansion. Ross said his call dropped earlier and he lost connectivity with you. He wanted you to know Three and Big Daddy were safe. Mallory and Jessica were able to guide Three out of Lincoln Center to safety."

"Lucia, remind me to send Mallory and Jessica cupcakes from Magnolia's tomorrow. I want to thank them. Three was pretty wasted. He was having fun, but definitely wasted," Nicholas said calmly. "Thank God Mallory and Jessica were like

Three's appendages tonight. I'm not sure he would have made it out on his own," Nicholas said, shaking his head in disbelief.

Nicholas turned on his theatre-sized television in the corner. The news of the chaos at the Lincoln Center was playing on every channel. Nicholas quickly muted the sound while the television visual images continue to play in silence.

My iPhone buzzed with a text message. It was Reese asking me if I was okay. Reese had seen the news, but that was to be expected. Who hadn't heard the news by now? I turned to Mackenzie.

"Reese. Checking up."

Nicholas glared at me but said nothing.

I quickly tapped out a reply message to Reese to let him know that I was safe and would call with him tomorrow. I told him I was with Nicholas. Reese texted back a smiley face. I expressed a half grin that I'm sure didn't reach my eyes. Nicholas cocked his head to the side with a look of curiosity, never taking his eyes off me.

Mackenzie nodded in silence. I fought back the tears, so glad to know that I could see and talk to Reese again. I was overwhelmed with all sorts of mixed emotions. I gave Mackenzie another quick hug and looked back at Nicholas. His expression was completely impassive, giving nothing away in that poker face. Nicholas moved to put his arm around Lucia, who was still at the wet bar, chugging back her drink quickly and still re-pouring.

"What can I do for you Lucia?" Nicholas asked.

"I'm fine Nicky. Have Silas give me a lift home please. You and I can catch up tomorrow. It's time for me to head home and exhale."

Before Nicholas could respond, Stephen had already opened his phone, calling Silas, instructing him to bring the car around for Lucia.

"I'll walk you out Lucia," Stephen said, tossing his own drink back in one big gulp.

"Mackenzie, I'll take you home myself," Stephen ordered.

No wonder he and Nicky got along so well. They had a lot in common. Alpha males were bred to spit out commands.

"Are you ready? Or do you and Harper still need a moment, babe?" Stephen asked.

Jesus, this babe stuff was really killing me. Stephen and

Mackenzie, really? How weird was this? I wasn't used to Mackenzie having a man. I needed to adjust to this idea. And Stephen of all people. Was he her type?

"Yes, I'm ready," Mackenzie said. "This day is over for me. I've had about all I can take for one night. But gawd, I think I got some great pictures, Harper. I managed to upload some shots to my iCloud account before that jerk made off with my camera. I ought to be able to make a killing tomorrow with the news outlets. Some of the shots I think I got were pretty good," she said, starting to perk up a bit.

I heard Nicholas groan over at the wet bar, but I pretended not to hear him. I was exhausted and didn't want any conflict.

Stephen walked out the door to escort Lucia. My iPhone buzzed again on the cocktail table in front of me, the caller ID revealing Brooks Fitzgerald McKenna's name across the screen.

Maybe I won't be able to avoid more conflict tonight. I squirmed a bit in my seat, tugging at the hem of my skirt. My nerves were frazzled. It really wasn't the time to be pretty. My stiletto was broken, my hair was a mess, and my lips swollen from Nicky's kisses in the limousine.

"It's Brooks. I probably should take this," I said, watching Nicholas's face turn red. The mere mention of Brooks Fitzgerald McKenna's name was sending him into a slow burn. "He's probably checking on me to see if I'm okay. That's the proper thing to do between friends," I said, looking at Nicholas with pleading eyes, simultaneously taking the call and saying "Hello."

Mackenzie rolled her eyes up in her head and moved to gather her things to leave with Stephen.

Nicky loosened his tie and unbuttoned his shirt halfway, revealing a black roped chain necklace with a black cross hanging on the end. It was resting on top of the tight curls on his chest that were peeking out of his white shirt. His tie hung loose around his neck. He had rolled up his shirtsleeves. He looked sexy as hell.

"Yes Brooks, I'm fine. Thank you for calling. I appreciate your concern," I said, watching as Nicky set a plate of exotic cheeses and bread down, refilling his cognac and throwing himself into an overstuffed chair and plopping his feet on the ottoman.

Mackenzie waved a good-bye to me, kissing me silently on the cheek. Stephen had returned to pick her up.

"I'll talk to you tomorrow," Mackenzie said, quirking her eyebrows up, knowing her back was turned to Nicholas and that he couldn't see her expression.

I nodded and momentarily closed my eyes in exhaustion as Brooks continued babbling through the phone about how I needed to let him take care of me. Brooks was insisting that he come to my house and comfort me. Thank God I wasn't home. Brooks was foolish enough to show up at my home unannounced. I tried to put that thought out of my mind.

Nicholas clipped the end of a cigar and lit it. He was running his hands back through his hair again and glaring at me with a mix of seductive heat. His gaze was penetrating. I didn't doubt for one minute that he was holding his tongue at the mere thought that Brooks Fitzgerald McKenna was on my phone.

I was glad we were finally alone.

"No I don't need you to come comfort me, Brooks," I snapped. "And no, I don't need you come take care of me."

I could see the muscle in Nicholas's jaw twitching. He could hear the irritation in my voice.

I needed to get off this call knowing it was going to be the undoing of Nicholas.

Continuing to talk to Brooks was like playing with fire. It was the equivalent of taunting Nicholas straight out of his mind. Unless I wanted to watch him have an out-of-body experience up here on the eighty-sixth floor, I needed to end this call with Brooks right now.

"Goodbye Brooks," I said, hanging up.

I sighed out loud and exhaled. Nicholas and I stared at each other, neither of us saying a word. The piano music continued to play softly, although the verbal silence stretching out between us was deafening. Neither of us unlocked our eyes off the other. We both sipped our cognac. Neither of us gave away anything. I watched as his jaw tightened knowing that he was grinding on the back of his molars like he always did when he was under stress. Finally after a long pregnant pause, Nicholas spoke.

"I don't want to discuss business tonight," he muttered.

"I don't want to talk about babies tonight," I said softly.

"I don't want to discuss that fucknut McKenna,"

"I don't either."

"I don't want to discuss artwork, Harper."

"Then don't."

"I would move heaven and earth to keep you safe," he said.

"I know."

We both gazed at each other in silence. I took in his heat. He took in my need. We both wanted the same thing.

"Are you ready?" Nicholas said.

"Yes."

"Are you sure?" Nicholas asked, his voice husky.

"Yes, I'm sure," I said softly.

Nicholas stood up and wrapped me carefully in the alpaca throw. He carried me up the floating staircase to his bedroom. I nudged my head against the curve of his neck and took in his essence.

"Mine," Nicholas said.

No, mine.

CHAPTER NINE

Nicholas and Harper

I tucked the white duvet cover over her body to keep her warm, pulling my own body close against her back, spooning, while wrapping my arms around her in a protective mode. I loved watching her sleep. Her long black hair tumbling down in waves against the top of her breasts. The wavy strands draped loosely down her back, over her side, accenting the curve of her body. Harper's slightly parted curved thighs begged for my entrance again.

"Mmmmm." She moaned in her sleep, but didn't wake up.

I pulled several strands of her hair back over her shoulder. I kissed the nape of her neck, closing my eyes, and languishing in the memory of our night of heated passion and desire.

"Shhhh, rest," I whispered softly in her ear, wanting her to get as much sleep as she needed.

I glanced over her shoulder at my alarm clock, noticing it still wasn't daybreak as the minutes on the digital screen ticked down to four thirty a.m.

Last night's events were a revelation; a life-changing event. I was discovering that all this fighting between us was overrated. Unnecessary. Enough was enough. I had dated women that made a sane man drop to their knees, but none of them made me feel the way Harper did. I could never find it in my heart to love them. My ability to love other women was always overshadowed by my feelings for her. Harper held the key to my heart and my mind. There were no substitutes. She was the gold standard for everything I ever wanted in a woman. She was gorgeous. She was brilliant. She was independent. She was her own woman.

Nothing else mattered to me now but the two of us finding a way to be together. Last night, holding her in my arms, I realized I would give up everything I owned, throwing it all out the window if need be, in order to have a life with Harper. The possibility of coming so close to losing her last night only reinforced and deepened my feelings for her. There was no way I was giving her up. Not now. Not ever.

Joduku Plastics or no Joduku Plastics, I was keeping her. She was mine. Nothing and no one was going to stop me. She was worth more to me than everything I owned combined.

I snuggled closer to her, resting my naked body against hers. *My woman. My baby maker. My love.* I would dedicate myself to convincing her to take a chance on me. To forgive me our pasts.

Now, in this moment, our future held the promise of more nights of spending time moaning in each other's arms. Giggling in bed. Feeding each other delectables. Yes, we drove each other crazy in ways unimaginable, but I would never have it any other way. I wanted it to stay this way for the rest of my days. I'd be damned if I'd ever give up my happiness again. Okay . . . so there will be times that I might have to sleep with one eye open, but that's fine. That's who we are. One thing for sure, making love to her tonight made things click inside of me that I never fully understood that summer ten years ago. But I understood it better now. I was in love with her then, but too scared to admit it. When she got pregnant with our baby, I took flight like a scared jackrabbit, leaving her to deal with the repercussions of dealing with parenthood alone. I wasted too much time—a couple of months—drinking, partying, and carousing with other women acting out in a total state of denial of how I felt about her. By the time I came to my senses, she had aborted my baby. In my anger at myself, I blamed her for deliberately aborting our child and not talking with me first. Not giving me a choice. I wanted the baby. I wanted her. I acted like a certified fool. She walked away from me and never looked back, except only to cause me pain and to make my life miserable. The same pain I must have made her feel.

She has made me pay through my pockets, she has made me pay in my mind, and she has made me pay in my heart. Her trust in amorous love for me was gone. I knew how badly I had crushed her heart, because she showed me as much in her deeds and in her actions toward me these last ten years.

But tonight, faced with the possibility of the true loss of each other, I was clear that it must be true that forgiveness does indeed fly on the wings of angels. I knew in my heart that she has truly forgiven me. Now, I needed for her to love me again.

I want to marry her.

It was five thirty a.m. I slipped my hand outside of Nicholas's luscious white duvet and the warmth of his arms, turning over on my side to watch him sleep. I ran my fingertip down the front of his chest, tangling my leg with his. I could feel the twitch in his muscle answering to the call of my touch. Resting my eyes on his strong features robbed me of any desire that I had to get more sleep. I wanted to look at him. I wanted to take in his physique, his male scent, the soft stubble of his strong jaw. One thing that I knew for sure. I felt safe. I felt wanted. I felt desired. Protected.

The comparison of the Nicholas Becker from ten years ago who had made my life a living hell and the Nicholas Becker of today was striking. Perhaps it was from the blaze of a new path we were charting for ourselves to end our War of the Roses. We were trying to find a new middle ground that we could settle into anew.

Nicholas had always been so different from the many men I'd dated since our breakup. He was the most formidable man that I had ever known. Just as he did ten years ago and here now in our present moment, he was offering me his gifts of affection, selflessness, protection, and love.

Last night, I almost lost the only man that I've ever really wanted, needed, or loved. But could I trust him with my heart again? That was the untold story. A part of me within recognized that I had forgiven him tonight. I knew he too had forgiven me as well. But could we trust each other? Could we compromise? Could I? Could he?

Yes. I could stop making him pay through the nose for all the artwork, property, and deals he wanted that I snatched from him because I could. It wasn't because I really desired, needed, or shared his taste and sensibilities in his possessions. Could I give up the hard, expected fight for Joduku Plastics? Could I put my desires, my bubbling need for more of him above Carmichael Ketchup? Maybe so, maybe not. Could I give up my desire to have a baby and forego the fertility clinic regimen, not knowing whether we could make it or not, risking that my biological windows of opportunity might close? *Definitely not.* There were some boundaries that I had to maintain for myself lest my past lessons be in vain.

I sighed. Nicky snuggled closer, tucking me up under his chin. He moaned.

Yes our relationship was taking on a new level of complexity. But there was, in fact, one thing that I was certain of. Everything about last night felt perfect. Neither of us wanted to ruin it with talk of our businesses, personal issues, and long-standing grievances.

Yes, I wanted my Nicholas back. Because I love him.

"Good morning, baby," I said as she opened her eyes, noticing I was watching her.

"What time is it?" she yawned.

"It's almost nine a.m.," I said smiling, kissing the top of her forehead. "I wanted you to rest and recuperate from all the chaos and stress of last evening," I said, moving out of the bed, pulling the strings and closing the top of my drawstring pajamas.

"Thank you for saving me, Nicky."

"No need to thank me. I should be thanking you. My life holds no real meaning without you in it, Harper."

I'm not sure she believed me but I meant every word. I needed her in my life.

"Are you hungry?"

"Yes I am. What do you have a taste for?" She yawned again.

"Besides you? What taste could compare to the sweetness of

you?"

"Mmmm, maybe a hot stack of pancakes smothered in some warm Vermont syrup, with a big side of hash brown potatoes, and bacon," Harper smiled, grinning like a schoolgirl.

"I can make that happen," I said eagerly, grabbing the morning newspapers, flipping through them quickly, thankful that I hadn't made the tabloids.

"You can, can you?" Harper said raising one eyebrow.

"Yes it's like making magic, love. Snap your fingers and your wish is my command."

"And how might you make that magic happen, my dear? Do you have a genie in a bottle that you rub its belly?" She laughed, pulling the white sheet up close to her chin covering her breasts.

I walked to her side of the bed, kissing her softly on the lips.

"Just rub my belly, baby."

Kiss.

"I have omnipotent powers."

I kissed her again.

"I know how to part the waters baby."

I kissed her some more.

"And I have a jet," I cooed, pressing my lips against hers, probing for her mouth to give my tongue an entrance.

She grabbed my hair by both hands and pulled my lips to hers, gently kissing me back. I picked up the phone on the nightstand, calling Stephen letting him know we were going to be on the move.

"Let's get dressed. Breakfast in Vermont it is."

I specifically chose my favorite Lear jet out of the Milk Money fleet, the one that had a large double-sized bedroom suite. I told the flight crew not to disturb us until we landed. Stephen was busy arranging for our security and car service for when we touched down. By the time Harper and I landed on the airstrip in Vermont, we had taken out our official membership in the Mile High Club. We worked up a keen appetite for each other beyond our need for breakfast.

I shuttled us to the finest five-star location in all of Vermont, taking her to the Stowe Mountain Lodge, located at the base of Mount Mansfield within the Stone Mountain Resort.

Stowe Mountain Lodge was highly recognized for its classic beauty and pristine location. The Lodge reflected the very best of the quintessential New England town well known as a renowned destination for world travelers, offering the finest dining in all the Northeast.

I selected the Solstice, the intriguing artisan-inspired signature restaurant of Stowe Mountain Lodge for our dining enjoyment. I knew Harper would appreciate the restaurant's romantic ambiance with hand-carved Vermont crafted artistic woodwork and custom pottery. I had a fondness for their open kitchen with unsurpassed views of Spruce Peak Mountain.

Harper loved it. It was a true feast for our eyes and our senses. The best treat was that the restaurant prided itself on the finest natural local ingredients possible, preparing foods based on an ideology of farm-to-table local ingredients throughout the menu. Their food was not a just about a meal, but more of an experience.

The server sat us in a booth near the window. Stephen sat at another table across the dining room but maintained visual proximity to us.

True to her desire, Harper ordered a triple stack of buttermilk pancakes with maple syrup, Vermont butter, and fresh berries. She gorged herself on smoked ham, maple sausage, and Vermont bacon. I wondered where she put it all, thinking that whatever hunger I created for her in the Mile High Club, I was going to work it right back off of her on the flight back.

I settled on the poached eggs with lobster, tomato slices, English muffin, hollandaise, and farmers red potatoes, thinking I needed to be mindful of my rock-hard six-pack, otherwise Stephen would beat the shit out of me again, the next time we got in the ring together. Stephen had no tolerance for middle-aged men with flabby guts hanging over the side of their pants. Not an option as long as Stephen was in my world. He was an anal-retentive Navy Seal down to the bone.

"How are you this morning?" I asked.

"Well fed and well sated," Harper answered. "This place is so beautiful, Nicky. I love everything about it. The food is to die for."

"Well baby, I'm like that genie in the bottle. All you have to do is rub me, and magic appears. A rub-a-dub-dub, my love," I laughed heartily, savoring the clump of succulent lobster in my mouth, enticing Harper to take a taste.

Harper grinned and laughed at my jokes all while flashing her beautiful big brown eyes and a smile that made me melt. We were completely lost in our fantasy moment right up until the time that both of us began receiving email messages on our iPhones from Joduku Plastics. We both received the same exact emails.

Please be advised that your firm has been selected among our short list of contenders to compete in the bidding process for the sale of Joduku Plastics. CEO Nobu extends his invitation to your company to make bid presentations to its management team within thirty days from the date of this notice. We expect you to make your presentation in our Princeton, New Jersey headquarters on or about the first week of April. Enclosed is a packet of our company's financials, headcount, and quarterly 10K reports that you may find useful for preparation of your bids. Should you have any questions or require further assistance, our managerial staff is ready and available to assistance. We welcome your firm's continued confidentiality in these matters. Your firm will be expected to conform to all requirements for nondisclosure agreements that may need to be exacted for the confidential transmittal of trade secrets and any other confidential matter between our two firms. We welcome the opportunity to speak with you soon.

Sincerely,
CEO Nobu
Joduku Plastics

It was reality time.

"Did you get the same message I did?" Harper said, setting her fork down.

"Yes I did," I said, feeling as if someone had let the air out of my balloon.

"Let me see," she said.

Jesus, was there no real trust between us at all? I thought, peering at her intensely while handing her my phone.

"Show me yours," I said, thinking I was going to stay on her same level given this playground we had managed to find ourselves. One thing I admired about Harper, she damn sure was no pushover. She didn't know it yet, but she was going to one day have my sons, and they were going to have killer instincts in the business world, because their future mother was just an out-and-out downright fucking shark hidden inside a temptress body.

Quietly we checked one another's phones, looking at the email messages from Joduku Plastics, then looking at each other. We handed our phones back.

I sighed out loud, pushing my plate back feeling like I was losing my appetite. Harper hadn't raised those beautiful brown eyes to eye level yet. I searched her face and my heart trying to figure out what she must be thinking.

The server arrived at our table, "Is there something more I can get you sir, this morning?"

"Yes," I said. "We'd like two Bloody Marys please," I said, nodding at Harper, who nodded back at me in acquiescence.

We sat in silence for a beat, watching as the server brought our drinks to the table. I decided to man up and be the one to break our silence.

"Baby, what do you want to do with this information?"

"You know Nicky, I've given this a bit of thought. I'm doing this acquisition for Carmichael Ketchup. You're doing the acquisition for Becker Foods. At the end of the day it's not like it's *our* companies."

"Get to the point Harper," I grumbled, knowing I was starting to sound grumpy.

"It's not like you're doing this acquisition for Milk Money. I'm not doing this for mine. This isn't a Montgomery Consulting Group acquisition. It's not like we have to make this whole showdown of buying this plastics company for our parents personal to us, do we?" she asked, her eyes pleading for some sort of assurance.

"Well you do have a point. But we still have to manage Elizabeth's and Big Daddy's expectations. There's no way we're getting around that fact, which means this whole acquisition process puts your interest and my interests at odds with each other," I reminded her.

"Well for all we know, neither of us could win," Harper pondered. "Not that I'm very good at losing," she said sipping her

Bloody Mary through the straw.

See? That's the shark that I know. The devil is in the detail. All you have to do is listen and pay close attention. I cocked my head to the side looking and searching her face to read past her words.

"I'm a terribly sore loser, too, Harper, but then again you know that. I try not to make losing a word or action that I keep in my tool box," I said.

Fuck, somebody give me a gun now. Let me shoot myself and put myself out of my misery. I was just getting myself off the sidelines getting in the game to get my woman back and now I was stuck in the middle of this bullshit company acquisition for Big Daddy. *Why can't he buy his own damn company?* Fuck, he could goddamn go into the plastics business himself. Big Daddy was always dragging his crap into my world. And, Elizabeth, what was her game? Surely I was missing something here. I fucking didn't like this picture, feeling that the pout might have started to show on my face.

"Well we could tell them both to go kiss our asses," Harper said laughing, finishing her Bloody Mary.

"Yeah Kitten, we could leave the country, and leave them holding the bag," I laughed, ordering myself another Bloody Mary. "I could make Three take over the acquisition," I said, feeling a bit buzzed now, and thinking this might not be such a bad idea at all. "Del-a-fucking-gate this mess to Three."

I waved my hand high to get the server's attention and asked him to bring us a pitcher of Bloody Marys now. I was feeling inspired.

Stephen had finished his breakfast, was sipping on coffee and flipping through his iPad. I suspected we were starting to get a bit loud. Harper was giggly. I noticed Stephen had shifted uncomfortably a couple of times in his seat as he glanced our way through his Ray Bans.

"Yeah Nicky, I could have mother's in-house acquisition team take over the negotiations," Harper laughed with enthusiasm, starting to slur her words.

The thought of both of us getting out of our parent's business caused us to get super excited.

We both decided the pitcher of Bloody Marys was indeed inspirational and re-ordered more. Harper laughed and chuckled with the server, flipping her hair around causing the server to laugh with us. She was a natural born flirt.

She slid her body closer to mine resting her head on my shoulder and began looking at me with those doe eyes. Her body heat was radiating off of me.

"You're just such the smartest man, my Nicholas," she said stumbling over her words.

"Oh baby, it's not me, it's you," I slurred, kissing her on the top of her forehead.

"You always have had such good ideas," I said looking at her with hungry eyes.

"Nicky, I want you," Harper said smiling, looking like the seductress I knew her to be. "This fireplace is so warm. I'm starting to get sooooo hot," she said, drawing out her words while unbuttoning the top button of her crisp white blouse.

I could see her bosom starting to pop out, her eyes twinkling against the rays of the morning sun peeking through the window. She looked absolutely mouthwatering.

"Kitten, Kitten, Kitten." I rocked side to side, loosening my tie, and pulling off my suit jacket.

"Let me give you what you need baby," I whispered in her ear.

"Now," she whispered back, running her hand up my thigh under the table stroking my bulge.

"Yes now, my love."

"Mine," she said.

"Who needs me, baby?" I asked.

"I do," she said. *Certainly not Elizabeth!*

"Who needs me, baby?" she asked.

"I do," I replied. *Certainly not Big Daddy!*

"Nicholas, take me to the mountaintop baby," Harper said with the heat of the fireplace in her eyes, biting her lip and tipping her head to the side.

"Sweetheart, I've have a suite upstairs with our name on it," I grinned.

I motioned to Stephen to deal with our tab. Stephen nodded back at me peering at me with a perplexed look. I suppose he could tell we were high as kites, but I could care less. He sat his iPad down and picked up the local newspaper. I suppose we were boring Stephen. It didn't matter. I was happy. I had my Harper back.

I took Harper's hand and grabbed what was mine.

CHAPTER TEN

Harper

"You have a call from Mr. Becker, Ms. Montgomery," Charlotte said over the intercom.

"Put the call through."

"Hey Nicky, how are you today?"

"I'm fine Harper, but I'd be even better if you have dinner with me tonight."

"I really want to, but I've got all kinds of deadlines in order to be ready for the Joduku Plastics presentation. Plus I have early evening appointments," I said.

While I was still pursuing my original goal of trying to land the acquisition of Joduku Plastics for Carmichael Ketchup, my enthusiasm for the whole matter had waned. I was going through the motions absent the attack-dog persona that I typically employed when going in for the kill on a new acquisition.

"I'm surprised you aren't knee deep under tons of paperwork on this yourself, Nicky. Don't think Big Daddy is going to let you go all half-baked on this one," I chuckled.

"Who cares about what Big Daddy thinks? I only care about us, Harper. We promised each in Vermont three weeks ago that we weren't going to let this business stuff with our parents get in the way of our relationship. I hope that wasn't just the Bloody Marys talking?" Nicholas asked suspiciously.

"Bloody Marys or not Nicholas, I meant what I said. My relationship with you is more important than this deal. I intend to keep it that way," I said, hoping to quell any doubts Nicholas might be having about my intentions.

"That pleases me, baby, so let me please you. Have dinner with me. I'm wooing you, Kitten," Nicky pleaded. "Let me woo you, baby. You know, just like that Jeffrey Osborne song that you like to play over and over and over when I'm around. Can you woo, woo, woo," Nicholas laughed.

He started singing in my ear through the phone. I could just imagine the look on his face. I wondered if he could sense my grin and the eye roll that I was projecting on my face.

"You're so cute when you turn your nose up like that, Kitten."

"And what makes you think I have my nose turned up?" I said rather flirtatiously.

"I'm not sure you think us Anglo-Saxon Annapolis Navy boys know how to woo, woo, woo." He laughed. "I had a good teacher baby. Mico was the king of woo, woo, woo, and he taught me how to woo, woo, woo, too, sweetheart. I was a good student," Nicholas taunted.

"So you think you know how I liked to be wooed?" I asked, loving Nicholas's playful side.

"Charlotte should be arriving in your office right about now. A little something special from the woo-woo man," Nicholas laughed.

Just at the exact moment, Charlotte walked through my office door with six pounds of pink-iced Hello Kitty cookies wrapped in a huge pink basket with a large pink bow tied around the cellophane.

"These just came for you," Charlotte said, smiling from ear to ear.

I still had the phone up to my ear, knowing that Nicholas was awaiting my reaction.

"Cookies, Nicky!" I squealed into the phone. "How did you know I was hungry? I needed a pick-me-up this afternoon. I missed lunch working so hard."

I ripped the cellophane off and dove into the basket in a state of utter delight.

"Exactly," Nicholas said. "I'm here to anticipate your every need, Kitten. But don't you think it's time you rub the belly, baby, let the genie out of the bottle so he can work his magic?"

"No I think not. You're just trying to screw up my focus and concentration so you can beat me out of this acquisition,

Nicholas Becker," I said, putting my hand on my hip and squinting my eyes, wondering if he were pulling dirty tricks.

"Oh ye of little faith," Nicholas exclaimed. "Harper, you know you're the only thing that really matters to me," Nicholas's voice was sounding more serious now. "But I'm not losing sight of the fact that Brooks Fitzgerald McKenna's company is in play along with Peachtree Plastics. The fact remains, if your company or mine loses to either one of them, neither you nor I will be able to go to our parents' house for holiday dinners for years. We'll never live it down. I don't know about you, but I have a reputation here to protect."

"You do have a point, Nicholas. This whole thing is so confusing to me. Why would Brooks even want to be bothered with this business? I'm not sure of his motives, but I do plan to get to the bottom of what and who is driving what in this whole process," I said, treading lightly with this dialogue with Nicholas.

Too much talk about Brooks would send Nicholas into the ozone layer. He was insanely jealous of Brooks. Still, I was sure that he knew something about Brooks' motives that I did not. And let's face it. The keeper of the information is the keeper of the power. Nicky had information that I did not have. Nicholas had Lucia on his team, and God forbid if that woman ever, ever missed a beat. One might as well be Jonah inside the whale to be a force to contend with Lucia. Lucia was the whale and everyone else was the meal.

"I don't want to talk about it. Let's talk about dinner instead," Nicholas pleaded. "We agreed in Vermont not to mix business with pleasure."

"As if either of us can remember anything we did or said that morning in Vermont, Nicky. We were toasted," I shuddered. "Totally wasted."

"Yes and I loved every minute of our time together, darlin'."

"Thank you for the cookies, Nicky. You made my day. Can I call you back after my appointments?" I asked, crunching a cookie in his ear. I'll have a better sense of my schedule later today."

"Your wish is my command, babe. But if you keep me waiting too long, I'm going go into high gear and whip out my woo-woo card," Nicholas chided, laughing loudly. "And then I'll have to get down and dirty."

"Bye, Nicky. Busy, baby. Gotta run." I giggled through the

phone.

"The genie wants out of the bottle, Harper."

And just like that Nicholas hung up.

Ummm, the cookies were good, but maybe I had waited too long to eat this afternoon. I was starting to feel queasy.

"Charlotte, tell Winston to bring the car around please," I said over the intercom. "I don't want to miss my appointment. Tell the management team that I'm putting the forecasts on the plastics acquisitions in Dropbox for their review. I want mock presentations to begin tomorrow."

"Got it. I'm one step ahead of you," Charlotte replied.

"We're down to the final hours of perfecting our presentation materials. I want a full report in the morning," I said, clicking off the intercom and taking a moment to catch my breath.

"I have it under control, Harper. I'll have Winston bring the car around. You have an appointment with Dr. Richards at three and the fertility clinic at four-thirty. Mackenzie Rhodes is on your calendar for two-thirty, and Mr. McKenna has arrived. He's not on your calendar. He's walking through the lobby doors now."

Charlotte escorted Brooks into my office and closed the door quietly behind him. I took one look at him and realized Brooks was not in a good state of mind. If I didn't know better I would have thought he had been drinking.

"Why the hell haven't you been returning my calls, Harper?" Brooks snapped at me.

"I've been busy, Brooks," I snapped back, my eyes narrowing.

I hated the fact Brooks had shown up unannounced. That move never sits well with me from a man. I caught a whiff of alcohol on his breath as he moved closer to me.

"Last I checked, I don't recall having to answer to you. I'm my own woman and I do what I want to do when I want to do it," I sneered.

"Bitch, I tried to come to your aid, after hearing about you being caught in that bomb threat at your senator Daddy's little fundraiser," Brooks said, wobbling on his feet, and looking very reptilian. "You blew me off then and you've been blowing me off since. I don't appreciate you snubbing me. I told you once if I've told you twice, you're gonna be my woman, bitch. You're gonna belong to me," he said, stepping closer to me, slurring his words and waving his index finger back and forth at me.

"Bitch? Exactly who do you think you're talking to? You may as well turn right around now, discontinue this conversation, and come back another time when you're sober and in your right mind," I demanded.

"No I'm talking to you, you little bitch. You're going to hear what I have to say to you now," Brooks wobbled.

"Now you wait one minute, Brooks Fitzgerald McKenna. I'm *not* your woman, not now and not ever."

"Oh yes you are, baby, because I've jumped into the little acquisition bidding process game with you and Mr. Sneaky Nicky Picky Licky Becker," Brooks slurred. "I did it just so I can take that fucking plastics company away from him and you. And when I do, you're gonna need me for that fucking-ass ketchup company to stay on your momma and senator daddy's good side. Then I'm gonna give it to you as my wedding present to you, you cute little dick tease," he slurred, breathing his hot breath in my face and pumping his chest out as if he were a proud peacock.

I turned my head the other direction, repulsed at having Brooks's alcohol-laced breath being blown in my face.

"Then you're gonna marry me and we're going to be Manhattan's most respected power couple. You got me, bitch?" Brooks said staggering. "I'm even going to knock your little tight ass up."

"You must be out of your shitty little pea-brain mind, you asshole," I said, fingering rapidly to push the emergency alarm button under my desk for Malcom.

"And who the hell are those from?" Brooks said staring angrily at the large pink basket of Hello Kitty cookies from Nicholas on my desk.

"None of your business. Get out of my office right now, Brooks. We can talk another time when you're sober."

Brooks leaned all the way into my space, grabbing me by my waist. He put his lips on my mouth, kissing me sloppily, pushing his tongue in my mouth, his hot breath smelling like whiskey.

I started pushing him back off me, yelling, "Get off me, you asshole," just as Brooks began ripping the mother of pearl buttons off my blouse dipping his head low trying to kiss my breasts. He ran his hands up under my skirt, trying to make his way into my panties.

"Get out of here!" I screamed, scratching his arm and digging my nails in his biceps, forcing my legs closed, my feet kicking and flailing.

Brooks wrapped his hand around my hair forcing my lips against his, tugging hard on my panties.

"You know you want some of this," Brooks said, still attempting to kiss me while rubbing his erection against my leg. I was turning my head from side to side to avoid his touch and fighting to squirm out of his reach. He grabbed my face, squeezing it hard in his attempt to hold me in place while he tried to force his tongue in my mouth.

"Oh I love it when you fight, my little dick tease," Brooks slobbered.

I screamed loudly calling for help. Malcom burst through my office door. He grabbed Brooks with two hands, pulling him off me, hitting him hard in the jaw one time and then another blow to his midsection. My knees buckled and I fell to the floor forcing myself to crawl to the opposite corner of my office to get out of the way. Tears were streaming down my face.

Brooks bent over, yelling "motherfucker" at Malcom, and swung back at him wildly, staggering all over the office, his nose bleeding. Malcom punched him hard again, several times to the head and the body. I gasped, crawling back against the wall, watching as Brooks swung wildly. The two men fell across my worktable knocking over a couple of glasses and a pitcher of water that was in the center of the table. Glass began to fly everywhere. Nicholas's cookie basket hit the floor and smashed into several pieces. Brooks was no real match or threat to Malcom. Malcom had Brooks's neck in a chokehold, and was dragging him across the glass-covered floor.

"Malcom! Malcom!" I cried. "Please don't kill him, he's just drunk!"

Thank God I yelled at Malcom, because he was in some emotional place I'd never seen him go. I wasn't quite sure he was going to be able to come back from the kill zone his mind had gone to in at the heat of the moment. Charlotte ran into the room, stepping sideways to avoid the broken glass. She immediately dropped to her knees at my side. She was as pale as a ghost as Malcolm yelled at her.

"Call the police!"

Malcom pulled plastic ties out of his back pocket and locked Brooks' arms behind his back and cuffed him. Brooks spit in Malcom's face. Malcom knocked Brooks straight out with his fist.

I watched as Brooks hit the floor with Malcom dragging him across the room and out the door, his white shirt bloodied. Charlotte ran to my desk phone and called 911.

"Are you okay Harper?" Charlotte said, running around in a circle in a state of hysteria.

"I'm fine," I said, breathing heavily, my heart racing a mile a minute. "Can you bring me a cup of tea or something? Put something strong in it too, Charlotte. I can't believe this is happening to me," I said, moving over into my office bathroom to check my appearance and to pull my clothes back together.

Luckily I kept a spare change of clothes in my office. Despite the fact that my hands and knees were shaking, I wanted to be able to make myself presentable for my next appointment. I wanted my sense of normalcy back. I wanted to try to recoup fast and pull myself together. Except when I looked in the mirror to comb my hair back in place, I had large bruises on my arm, my thighs, and another bruise on the side of my face. I willed myself not to lose it.

Brooks Fitzgerald McKenna just brought himself a death wish from Nicky.

Charlotte returned with a spiked tea for me, and one for herself.

"Harper what do you need me to do?" Charlotte said, her voice trembling.

"I think I just need a moment to collect myself," I said.

I sat down for a minute and drank it to calm myself, grabbing another of one of Nicholas's Hello Kitty pink cookies, still wrapped in cellophane, off the floor. I munched down on the cookie hard, wondering what I was going to say to Nicholas. He wanted to have dinner with me tonight and now I had to explain these bruises all over me. This was not going to be good. I swallowed hard, holding back more tears. I needed to call Mackenzie. She would know what to do, I thought to myself, feeling totally out of control and flustered.

"Charlotte, can you get Mackenzie on the phone for me please?" I asked, brushing crumbs off the front of my fresh blouse and working hard to steel myself to keep my hands from trembling. I simply refused to lose it.

"Mackenzie," I whimpered through the phone. "I just need to talk to you right now and hear your voice," I said, holding back the tears. "Are you busy? Do you have a free moment?"

"Anything for you Harper," Mackenzie said. "I was just about to call you. I need a raincheck on our two-thirty appointment today. I overbooked."

I paused, sniffing hard to collect my thoughts.

"What's wrong Harper? You sound like you've been crying. Has that shithead Nicholas upset you again? What's wrong honey, tell me," Mackenzie begged.

I took a deep breath so as to calm my words so I wouldn't sound like a complete babbling idiot.

"Brooks Fitzgerald McKenna just showed up to my office totally drunk. He was hollering, screaming, and calling me a bitch, mad because I had not been returning his calls these last several weeks. He was slurring his words, staggering, and insisting that I was *his* woman and that we were going to be married," I said, talking fifty miles an hour, not even pausing to breathe between my sentences.

"Oh my God," Mackenzie gasped.

"Then he said that he had jumped into this acquisition process with Joduku Plastics because he was going to own the company and that it was going to be my wedding present from him," I sniffled.

"Has that fool completely lost his mind Harper? I think he's losing it. Seriously. I heard on the grapevine the other day when I was doing a photo shoot for some big wigs in the garment district that McKenna Textiles was having some financial trouble."

"You did?"

"Something about McKenna Textiles not being able to make their deliverables timely and that their creditors were all over them for overdue payables," Mackenzie babbled on.

"Wow. Do you think that was why he was so drunk in the middle of the afternoon? Mackenzie, Brooks was tearing my blouse off. He was trying to force his hands under my skirt. I had to call to get help from Malcom," I said, exasperated.

"That sorry piece of shit!" Mackenzie shrieked.

"I was so scared. Malcom beat the hell out of him, cuffed him, called the police, and dragged him out of here. I thought Malcom was going to kill him for sure."

"Jesus, what a mess," Mackenzie said. "Stupid asshole Brooks Fitzgerald McKenna."

"Yeah and now I've got bruises all over my body and face. I don't want Nicky to see me like this. He'll have a fit. It will be a race to see who's gonna kill Brooks first: Nicholas or Malcom," I said, shaking my own head now.

"Or me," Mackenzie said. "I'm going to kill him myself."

"I'm sure he didn't mean any of it, Mackenzie. You know Brooks is practically harmless. He wouldn't hurt a flea. He's a big overgrown arrogant baby at heart."

"Girl, don't even think about giving that slug a pass. Try to play this down with Nicholas if you can."

"I don't know what to do."

"You can either tell Nicky the truth, or avoid him until the bruises clear, which will take some time."

"Somehow the latter doesn't feel like the right answer."

"Or you could slap on some big designer sunglasses, makeup, and hope he won't notice," Mackenzie said, thoughtfully weighing out all my options.

"Oh this is so bad. Not to mention McKenna Textiles has made the short list which means I have to see Brooks again."

"No, bad is that Nicky has to see him again. You're not exactly the problem," Mackenzie said.

"What a stupid asinine idea for Brooks to involve himself in these matters for some silly purpose of winning me over. We were never like that, Mackenzie," I insisted.

"Honey whatever it is that you whip on these men, can you bottle it up and give some of it to me please, because I swear it's golden. You drive all these guys straight out of their mind right into insanity mode."

"More like I attract crazy, huh," I shuffled in my chair, grabbing another cookie. "I'm changing the subject, Mackenzie. How are things with you and Mr. Stephen Parks, "Miss I've-Got–a-Secret?" I teased her, looking through my cosmetic bag to find some lipstick and concealer.

"I should have told you earlier but I didn't know where things were headed between Stephen and me. I hate you had to find out about us that way at the fundraiser. That was such a crazy night with the bomb threat and all."

"Well the good news was he made sure you were safe."

"Safe yeah, but he forced me to leave my camera behind when that Russian asshole grabbed my Nikon. It was a good thing I had been uploading my shots all night into my iCloud account. This is business for me. I'm not sure Stephen respects that."

"Well it was also about your life, Mac. Stephen's trained to think about those things. You should cut him some slack. So tell me how are things going between you two?"

"I suppose things are moving along for us. It's hard to say. I'm not ready to bring him around Gill Jr. just yet. I never like to expose my son to a man unless I know the relationship is going to get serious and go somewhere. I don't want Gill Jr. to experience any more loss than is necessary. So I have Stephen on a long leash right now."

"Wow. You and Stephen. This is really going to get interesting. Are you looking to get serious?"

"Stephen's the kind of guy that is always playing his cards close to his vest. He's a hard nut to crack. He doesn't open himself up very easily. Ever since the bomb threat at the fundraiser, he's been acting like he's the great protector or something. All macho alpha male," Mackenzie teased.

"He's the consummate alpha male," I said, squinting through my pain, hoping Mackenzie wouldn't notice it in my voice.

I knew she wanted to kill Brooks.

"Some days I find myself looking over my shoulder wondering if he's watching me or something. We're both treading very lightly I think. Taking it one day at a time. I'm not sure where this is all going to go, but I'm going to enjoy the ride for a change and have some fun in the process."

"Are you suggesting he has stalker tendencies, or is your

imagination running away with you again, Mackenzie?"

"Well if he's a stalker, just remember I've got a camera and I see all kinds of things through this lens of mine. He's the one who should be careful. Maybe I'll stalk him."

We both giggled and laughed. I moaned out loud because it hurt my face to laugh. I so needed this moment with Mackenzie to bring me back down to Earth from all the excitement with Brooks.

"So Mackenzie, what shall I do about Nicky and this business with Brooks?" The thought of how Nicky would take this news was weighing heavily in the back of my mind. I knew I had to step into this. Unfortunately I wasn't going to be able to go over or under this mountain, but through.

"It's going to be bad either way," Mackenzie said, her words just confirming my own line of thinking.

"Might as well err on the side of truth, girlfriend. That's the best advice I can give. But when I see that shithead Brooks Fitzgerald McKenna I'm definitely going to kick him in his balls, Harper."

Now that's the Mackenzie I know. Forever loyal.

"Gotta run Mac. Got appointments. Thanks for letting me vent. Your turn next time."

"Anytime Harper. Feel better sweetie. Talk to you later."

As I headed out my office doors to go to my appointment with Dr. Richards, I knew this ride to her office was not going to be good. Malcom had dumped Winston again and was back in the driver's seat. Thank God I had freshened myself up, put on makeup, combed my hair, and thrown on my Bulgari sunglasses to cover the bruises near my eye. Hell, I couldn't seem to catch a break today. I just wanted some peace and quiet. Not to mention, I was feeling nauseated again. My stomach was turning backflips from the day's excitement. Maybe these fools were going to give me an ulcer.

"Are you okay, Harper?" Malcom asked, grabbing my hand

softly and pulling me closely into his chest.

My body stiffened and I stepped back from his hold reflexively. Malcom opened my door, his expression pained.

"Yes I am, thanks to you. Thank you for coming to my aid," I said, as he closed my door, then slid into the driver's seat.

"I always knew Brooks McKenna wanted you," Malcom said. "I just didn't know how bad."

I turned my head and looked out the window, not wanting to run up that flagpole again whatsoever and revisit these discussions about the men in my life.

"I turned him over to the police. They are going to want to take a statement from you. I have some friends on the force. I told them you weren't in any shape to talk, but I'd bring you in to give a statement."

"Thank you Malcom. I appreciate everything you've done for me."

"Listen, we need to talk," Malcom said honking the horn at the car in front of us.

"I can't do this today Malcom, please."

"You need to know that the senator has asked me to head up his security team," Malcom said, dismissing my pleas. "Your mother seems to think it's a good idea. It would be a promotion of sorts for me. I think it would make you and me and . . . well you know . . . I think it would make things less complicated. It's getting hard to watch you do what you're doing, knowing how I feel about you."

Oh thank heavens for my mother. There is a God.

I swear my mother must be psychic or something.

"Up until today, I didn't want to seriously consider the move. But now, with everything that's happened, I think it's a good idea," Malcom said.

"Well, I think it would be a good move for you, Malcom, promotion and all. I don't want to be the one to hold your career back. And Daddy values your skills."

"Umm," Malcom moaned.

"I don't think you should let this opportunity pass you by. It won't be like I won't get to see you and talk to your from time to time as long as you're on Daddy's detail," I said trying to hold back anything telling in my voice.

I was happy this was happening. But it was still bittersweet nonetheless. Malcom had protected me from Brooks. That wasn't lost on me.

I knew Malcom was taking this move harder than I was. So much for me and my friends with benefits. Friends with benefits was starting to turn into friends bringing on headaches. Furthermore, I'd have to hire someone new to head my security team and it was going to be bad timing to have to do security interviews in the middle of an acquisition.

"When do you plan to switch teams?" I asked solemnly.

"The end of the month, as soon as a replacement for me is secured. I will need to help the guys with the transition. I can set up some replacements for you to interview," Malcom said as the car pulled to the curb in front of Dr. Richards's office.

"That would be fine. Keep me posted."

I pulled out my phone and texted Mackenzie, *Malcom just quit.*

Malcom came around and opened my door. He waved to the suburban behind us.

"Winston will drive you back."

The universe must be in a bad mood; piling it on today, Mackenzie texted me back.

Malcom reached down and pulled my chin up to his lips and kissed me softly on the lips.

I waited for any electricity. Nothing. Not like Nicky.

"Good-bye, Malcom."

"My goodness Harper, are you okay? You look like you've been in an accident," Dr. Richards said, looking incredibly alarmed. She rushed to my side to help me to my chair, even though I didn't feel I needed help.

So much for hiding bruises under makeup.

"I'm okay Dr. Richards. Thank you for asking."

Dr. Richards waited patiently for me to speak.

"One of my friends with benefits showed up to my office today intoxicated and he got out of hand. I'm bruised from his drunken assault on me. Believe it or not my feelings are hurt worse than I look," I moaned.

"Well you're done with that one, right?" She frowned, searching my face for agreement.

"For sure. There was nothing really to that relationship for me anyway. It was just something to do. But I realize now that not everyone can manage a sexual relationship and keep emotional distance. Even my security chief quit on me today. Another one down," I sighed.

"How do you feel about all this, Harper?"

"Well it was time. My friend Reese kept telling me mixing my sex life and my business life with these guys was too difficult. Reese always says "never play where you get your pay." He's right. First it started off being fun, and over time it just became burdensome," I sighed, feeling totally exasperated.

I couldn't decide which was more sore, my body or my ego.

"Well you've had an emotionally charged month," Dr. Richards said. "I heard about the bomb threat, and the chaos and hysteria that it caused at Lincoln Center. I understand your company is in play for this big acquisition. It's all over the financial pages. How are you holding up, dear?"

"Yeah well the cat is pretty much out of the bag on the acquisition. Nothing is confidential anymore. I'm surprised the whole world doesn't know my own bid numbers," I shrugged. "I have Nicholas to thank for getting me out of Lincoln Center with my life," I smiled shyly.

"Ahhhh, Nicholas. So you decided to try the advice I offered the last time you were here," Dr. Richards said inquisitively.

"Well I kind of got thrown into his arms running for my life. It was a wake-up call for us both. He took good care of me. We both decided the least we could do was to try to work at forgiving each other for the things that have happened in our past. I feel good about it."

"That's good to hear," Dr. Richards said.

"It feels like a burden has been lifted off my shoulders. When faced with the potential of death, we all of a sudden discovered our worth to each other. I don't think so much anymore about how to hurt him."

"I'm glad to hear that, Harper."

"My own hurt is subsiding in the process now, because he's working really hard to build new memories between us and I'm letting him," I said, keeping my face stoic and my hands folded neatly across my lap.

I watched as Dr. Richards kept her poker face on as usual, searching my body language and honing in on the intonations of my words.

"I see," Dr. Richards nodded. "So have you decided how this new beginning of mending fences is going to proceed with Nicholas in light of the fact that you're both in business competition with each other?"

"Well we try not to talk about it too much. It is what it is. One thing we for sure agree on is that the acquisition is not for our own companies, but for our parents' companies. So we're kind of treating the whole matter as if it's not us. You know, just our families . . . our parents . . ." I said softly.

"Interesting," Dr. Richards said.

I wondered what she was thinking. I cocked my head to the side and squinted. We both paused. I squirmed in my chair and looked up at the ceiling for a bit. When I broke the silence, I forced myself to sound a tad more upbeat.

"I've arranged to meet your associate, Dr. Stone at the Stone Fertility Clinic," I said, trying to sound more cheery.

"Oh so you've decided to proceed along the parenthood path alone?" Dr. Richards said.

"Well I'm keeping my options open. The fact is, my biological clock is ticking. I want this for me. Relationally, I don't know where things are going to be end up for me with a man in my future . . ."

"You mean Nicholas," she said.

"Okay . . . Nicholas," I agreed, nodding my head. "I can at least make an informed decision in the meantime just so I know all the facts. I really am making an effort to try to clean up my act and get to forgiveness with Nicholas. I'm learning to be more compromising in my relationship with him and others. Although, others," I said with air quotes, "are exiting stage left very rapidly it seems."

"As in your friends with benefits?" Dr. Richards asked.

"Yes."

Dr. Richards nodded her head slowly as if to suggest that was the right thing that needed to happen now in this stage of my life.

"But my *not* having a baby is not negotiable," I said firmly. "I need this for me. In more ways than one."

"And those ways are what?" Dr. Richards asked.

"I need to heal from the baby I lost ten years ago. I know I said I've grieved that loss, and I have. I've gone through my five stages of grief and completed the cycle. But it's just kind of nice to know that if I make another baby now, that there will always be a guardian angel sister or brother watching over him or her. That gives me some peace of mind," I said.

"And do you plan to involve Nicholas in this process? How do you think he would feel about this choice just as you are opening the doors to a new relationship with him? Would he be joining you in the rearing of a new baby that's not his? Is that something you think he can handle? Does Nicholas want a baby?" she asked.

"Nicholas doesn't get to have a say in any of this."

"Oh?" Dr. Richard said with an element of surprise.

"I want to have a baby regardless of whether Nicholas and I succeed at our newfound relationship or not. I don't know what he wants."

"Remember, Harper, a healthy relationship is all about openness. Compromise. Trust. This is a decision that is not to be taken lightly. The two of you should discuss this together. We'll talk in our next session about how things go at the fertility clinic," Dr. Richards said, moving to hand me an appointment card for my next visit. "I'd like to explore this with you further."

"Thank you Dr. Richards. I'll see you soon."

I headed out the door to my waiting limousine thinking about the words Dr. Richards spoke. I guess she wanted me to go slow. Think things out. My mind was in a fog and on overload after today's events. I pulled my sunglasses down on my face to shield the bruises. Malcom had disappeared and Winston was back.

The Marimba played on my phone. It was a text message from Nicholas.

Kitten. Dinner. Genie in a bottle rub. Making Magic.

I called Charlotte back at the office.

"Charlotte, can you reschedule my appointment with Dr. Stone at the Stone Fertility Clinic? I'm pooped. I'm going to join Nicholas for a quiet dinner tonight. Cancel everything else on my calendar. You can take off early too. You've had a hard day as well. I'll talk to you tomorrow." I said.

Charlotte thanked me and hung up. I texted Nicholas back,

Your place or mine?

Mine, Nicholas texted back.

Might as well get this over with. Bruises and all.

Drama time for you, Harper.

CHAPTER ELEVEN

Nicholas

"Do you mind, Lucia, if we wrap up all this work on the plastics presentation this evening? I know you've been working hard on this, but I need a break. I promised Harper she and I would do a quiet dinner this evening."

"Not at all Nicky. I'm pretty worn out myself. By the way, Three called an hour ago. Big Daddy is looking for an update from you on how things are progressing with the acquisition. It's been over a month since he's chatted with you about it at the fundraiser."

"Yeah, I'll be sure to give Big Daddy an update when I get a free moment," I grumbled.

"Oh, Mallory and Jessica sent a thank you card with smiley faces, thanking you for the cupcakes you sent them from Magnolia's for helping Three at the fundraiser. They want to know when you're 'coming out to play on *The Julianna*'," Lucia said, flipping their thank you card at me. "They want to know if you'll bring Big Daddy along." Lucia bit her lip while making air quotes with her fingers, trying to hold back her laughter.

"For the record Lucia, no Mallory, no Jessica, no Big Daddy, and definitely not *The Julianna*," I demanded, arching my brow with a frown. "Those gals would give Big Daddy a heart attack," I said as I stalked over to my wet bar.

"I seriously doubt that," Lucia said, reaching over our worktable to gather up all of our working PowerPoint presentation layouts.

"Look Nicky, I'm getting out of your hair. I'm beyond tired today and need a mental health holiday right about now," Lucia said, answering the call from the Becker Towers Penthouse concierge.

"Yes, let her in please," Lucia said.

"Nicky, Harper's on her way up. So, what are you feeding her for dinner tonight?" Lucia said curiously, shuffling papers and not paying very much attention.

"Me," I chuckled. "I'm going to be the meal."

"Jesus, Nicky. I swear. I wonder sometimes what she even sees in you," Lucia said, looking me up and down, rolling her eyes at me.

"You know I'm all that and a bag of chips, Lucia," I laughed, grabbing her by the waist, lifting her off the floor, and swinging her around.

"Put me down Nicky," Lucia said, slapping her hands against my chest.

It felt good getting Lucia's goat. I lived for these moments.

"You know ever since you and Harper starting working on putting your relationship back together, I've noticed the change in your demeanor, Nicky. You seem to be so much more relaxed and at peace these days. Calmer. I'm happy for you."

We both flinched before I could respond, hearing the doorbell ring. Lucia buzzed Harper inside.

I ran past Lucia to greet Harper myself. Lucia was practically grabbing the side of my desk to balance herself. I'd almost knocked her over in my excitement. Although Harper and I had talked several times a day since we left Vermont, it had been three weeks since I had seen her. I was taking things slow. I didn't want to come on to her too hard, too fast and risk losing her again. We had trust issues to work through.

"Hey Kitt, how are you? What the fuck? . . . Oh my God . . . What the *hell* happened to you, Harper Carmichael Montgomery?" I said, looking at her in a state of shock.

She pulled the big dark sunglasses off her face.

"Have you been in an accident or something, Kitten? Jesus, Mary, Mother of God," I exclaimed in shock, noticing the bruises on her face and arms.

"The only accident I've been in has the name Brooks Fitzgerald McKenna's name on it," Harper said, gliding slowly past me.

Lucia was completely silent, wide-eyed. She was looking at Harper and then looking back at me. I suspected like me, she couldn't believe what she was hearing.

"What does that mean Kitten?" I asked softly.

I was forcing myself to try to maintain my cool for Harper's sake. Inwardly I had begun counting to ten. I started praying to the Gods of Cool, Calm, and Collected to keep me in their care. There was no way I was going to be able to keep it together. My anger was building. Surely I was going to lose it. I closed my eyes for a beat and tried to slow my breathing in order to calm myself down. That wasn't working too well, because all I could do was see that fuckwad's face and imagine that shit-eating smirk. I could just see it on his face. Hurting and assaulting *my* baby maker.

"Well specifically, Nicholas," Harper said, clearing her throat and coughing. "You see it's like this . . . Nicky," Harper muttered, taking way too fucking long to get her words out.

I waited.

"You see . . . Brooks . . . Brooks . . . well you see Brooks . . ." Harper closed her eyes and exhaled loudly.

"Brooks what?" I said as gently as I could, running both my hands through my hair. I was starting to lose what little control I had. "Out with it, Kitten," I said, firmly willing myself to remain calm.

I watched intently as Harper took another deep breath and sighed.

"Let me get you glass of wine," Lucia said. "Sit down, sweetie. White or red?"

"White, please," Harper answered.

Lucia moved slowly to the wet bar and poured Harper a glass of Riesling, handing it to her. Lucia poured two shots of 80 Proof Stolichnaya vodka neat for both her and me. We waited. I felt like time was frozen. Harper was twiddling her sunglasses in her hands, fidgeting and sipping her wine slowly.

At last she spoke. "Brooks showed up in my office today. He was drunk, Nicholas." She sighed heavily again. "I'm sure that if he had not been drunk things would have turned out differently,"

She started speeding up the pace of her words as if she had to say it all in one breath just to get it out. "He was babbling about how I was *his* woman. He ripped my blouse. We struggled. But nothing bad happened, I assure you. Except he put his hand under my skirt," she said, twirling the strands of her long black hair nervously. "But you know what I mean, Nicky."

"No, I fucking do not know what you mean, Harper," I said through clenched teeth. I could feel the heat flushing my face. Oh almighty Gods of Cool, Calm, and Collected, have mercy on my soul tonight, lest I kill that social climbing motherfucker Brooks Fitzgerald McKenna. I bit my bottom lip hard so hard I thought it might bleed.

"Brooks claimed he was competing for Joduku Plastics so he could win it and give it to me as a wedding present," Harper said, trying to sound nonchalant. "I have no idea how he got that stupid idea in his head. I have no plans to marry him," she said, shaking her head in exasperation.

I'm sure I must have been staring at Harper as if she were speaking in tongues. I could not believe my lying ears.

"He was angry that I had not been returning his calls. I guess I've been so busy with the presentation that I hadn't gotten around to telling him that you and I were together now. I had planned to tell him. He was just so drunk and out of control, Nicholas. That's all."

"That's all"? I said trying to speak calmly. "That's all?" I raised my voice. "That's all?" I shouted.

"Nicky, you're repeating yourself again," Lucia said softly.

Lucia knew me well enough that my brain going on automatic was never a good sign of where I was emotionally. That was always the first surefire clue that I was on my way to losing it. I suppose she pointed that fact out to me just in case I had any sliver of control left to reel myself back in before all my gaskets blew.

"I will kill that social-climbing fuckwad Brooks Fitzgerald McKenna," I yelled and threw my cocktail glass into the fireplace, relishing the sound of it smashing in a thousand pieces.

I growled like an angry grizzly and pounded my hands against the mantel.

"Well so much for what I said earlier about your being calmer, Nicky," Lucia said. "I take it all back," she stammered, picking up the phone, anticipating that I was going to ask her to call Stephen.

"Goddammit, Lucia, get Stephen on the phone. Tell him I need to see him now," I shrieked.

Lucia was already dialing. God that woman could read me.

"It's all been taken care of now, Nicholas," Harper said, just as I moved to contain my rage and put my arms around Harper to comfort her.

"Oh baby, oh baby," I said kissing the top of her forehead. "Let me get you another glass of wine."

I poured Harper another glass of Riesling and poured myself and Lucia another Stoli's.

As I handed Harper the glass of wine, I said, "So baby, where was Malcom in all this?"

I hoped that whatever was coming out her mouth next about Malcom was going to be the right thing, otherwise Malcom's ass was grass, and I was going to be the lawnmower.

"Well I hit the emergency aid button under my desk, and Malcom came very quickly. He pretty much beat the shit out of Brooks. He secured him and turned him over to the police," Harper said, sipping her wine, her eyes filling with tears.

"Oh Harper, I so sorry you had to endure this," Lucia said, trying to comfort her.

"I have to give a statement to the police. Malcom made arrangements so that I didn't have to deal with that right away. We both agreed it was best to keep this incident out of the public eye."

"You're giving the police a statement when?

"Tomorrow perhaps," she sighed.

I knew this was hard on Harper. She's just way too tough for her own good. I didn't want her to have to carry the weight of this assault all alone. I wanted to help her shoulder it, but all I could think about was getting my hands around Brooks's throat.

"Malcom should have never let that fuckwad get in your office space or anywhere near you if he was drunk," I shouted. "What kind of bodyguard does that? The bodyguard is supposed to guard your fucking body. You're surrounded by a bunch of incompetent fucks," I growled, pacing about, gesticulating wildly.

"Well it's water under the bridge now anyway, Nicholas. Malcom quit today," Harper said, sounding a bit calmer and taking another sip of her wine.

I looked at Harper as if the whole world had gone mad and I was the only sane person left on the planet Earth.

"Quit!? Quit? Quit?" I said, repeating myself like a broken record.

"Yes Nicky, she said he quit," Lucia snapped.

I knew Lucia was working double time helping me to stay on track.

Smash. I threw a second cocktail glass in the fireplace. This time the fire in the fireplace roared and blazed high from the alcohol. There was a loud swoosh sound in the air. Lucia and Harper both practically jumped out of their skin at the same time.

Lucia said, "Okay Nicholas. Fuck it. That's it. I'm taking your gold stars back, and I take back everything I said today about your being calm." She gulped hard on her drink before slamming her glass down on the cocktail table.

"He needs time to process this information, Lucia," Harper said calmly, crossing her legs as if nothing about my temperament was surprising her. *That woman really does know me.*

"Yeah like when he starts repeating himself. That's a sure sign he's about to lose it. He needs to calm down," Lucia said. "He's going to have a stroke."

"He's going to need a moment to roar first. It's in his DNA," Harper said.

They both were ignoring me, talking around me as if I were freaking invisible.

"I'm fucking in this room, ladies. I hear what you're saying and I don't intend to calm down for a very long fucking time. I swear on everything I own, this shit with McKenna is not over, do you hear me? Not the fuck over," I stomped.

Lucia moved closer to Harper and tucked her arm around her, ignoring me.

"The good news is that you're okay, Harper. At the end of the day this was a decent outcome," Lucia said supportively, nodding her head up and down.

"Oh Lucia, he was just so drunk. I really think he didn't know what he was doing. I don't think Brooks would have been carrying on like that sober," Harper said.

Smash. Swoosh. Smash. Another glass hit the fireplace.

"Nicky, those are limited edition Riedel's you're smashing," Lucia grunted loudly.

"Order some new ones tomorrow," I pouted. "Because this is exactly what I'm going to do to Brooks's face when I see him."

Stephen entered the room dressed in sweatpants, still sweaty from working out. He moved across the room like a panther, a monogrammed towel with my initials *NMB* still wrapped around his neck.

"What's up Nicholas? What can I do for you, sir?" Stephen said wiping his brow, and drying the beads of sweat off his brow and chest.

"Harper's going to need a new head of security for her protective detail," I said.

"Oh Jesus, Harper, are you okay?" Stephen said, his breath hitching, catching a glimpse of Harper's appearance.

"Hell no she's not okay. Just look at her," I snapped at Stephen. "Does she look fucking okay to you, Stephen?"

"Now wait just a minute Nicholas," Harper said. "Malcom is going to have me interview some of his recommended security people for my detail over the next couple of weeks," she exclaimed, straightening in her chair. I watched as her body moved to attention.

"I'm not going to like his choices," I spit back. "I don't even like him, which means I'm not going to like his choices," I gritted through my teeth back at her, trying to keep my voice firm and calm.

"Well, Malcom is going to be joining Daddy's security detail, so if he's good enough for a U.S. senator, then he should be good enough to pick a slate of folks for me," she said, rising up off the couch and walking toward me.

Well, why aren't I surprised that this was going to turn into a real hoedown showdown. Harper Carmichael Montgomery is like a smooth cream, always rising to the occasion. Never to be pushed around. Never letting anyone tell her what to do. But this time I was determined to hold a strong hand on this point. This was *my* goddamn baby maker and I was not going to have some weak-ass wussy security detail watching over her, letting a bunch of drunk fuckwads toss her around.

We were nose to nose now, practically invading each other's space.

"I can fix this myself," she said, narrowing her eyes at me. She straightened her spine, armed with the battle look she puts on just before she lobs the grenade.

"Like I said, Kitten, I can and I will fix this," I spoke in almost a hushed whisper.

Just looking at the bruises on Harper was making me even more determined to stand my ground.

"That's right Nicholas," Stephen said interceding. "We can fix this right now. I've got just the right man for the job," Stephen swiped his phone, dialed, and said, "Scott, do me a favor and haul your ass up here right now to the penthouse, please. Got a matter that needs handling. Yeah, man, I know you're in a middle of a workout, but this won't take but a minute. C'mon man. I've got some folks waiting to meet you."

Thank God, Stephen cut off our confrontation. I looked at Harper, daring her to challenge me on this one. Harper was staring me down. I momentarily wondered if she was trying to decide whether to kiss me or slap my face. I couldn't tell which, so I put on my best hangdog face, just in case she wanted to slap me, but that only made her madder. That, I could tell. So I changed my expression and gave her my "woo-woo" face, but she gritted her teeth even harder like a pit bull about to eat up the Heinz 57 hangdog.

So I readily changed my expression, putting on my "I'm not to be fucked with on this matter, woman" face. Jesus, she looked so pissed I thought for sure I might need to start thinking about ducking. She and I were headed down the road of collateral damage and everyone in the room was subject to our wrath. We were a lot of things and knew it. We were walking down our path together on eggshells. But we were slowly approaching one of those intersections, where she was about to pull out her Uzi and I was already mentally strapping to lock and load. Harper and I really didn't do power plays well. We were seriously going to have to work on this in our relationship. Maybe we could go do meditation or yoga together. Find our Zen.

The doorbell rang. Thank God. Saved by the bell. And the man walking through my door was who I intended to be Malcom Cole's replacement. I grinned with a smirk.

"Everybody, this is my twin brother Scott Parks," Stephen said.

"There's two of you?" I heard Lucia gasp in disbelief.

"Oh hell yeah, there's two of them," I said, my smile reaching ear to ear.

I placed my hand on Lucia's back to brace her and to keep her from falling. She was acting like she'd never seen a hot sweaty man without a shirt on before. What exactly was Lucia's malfunction? Okay, so he has a nice six-pack with an awesome v-cut. It was just like looking at Stephen for Christ sakes. You've seen one, you've seen the other. Identical Twins. Except. These weren't any old run-of-the-mill twins. This was Scott Parks. Brother to Stephen Parks. This was a mean green fighting Navy Seal machine. Just like Stephen. A goddamn duplicate. Another Annapolis well-trained, "not going to let some drunk fuckwad get in and accost *my* baby maker" man. And I'll be dammed if I wasn't going to have the last say on this shit. I was going to rip those big girl panties right off her cute little ass if necessary. I intended to win this battle.

"Harper, Scott is an owner and partner in our security company," Stephen said. "Parks and Parks Security Group. Scott's available to take on additional clients, and would be the perfect man for your security detail replacement."

I didn't know whose mouth I was going to have to walk over and close first. Lucia's or Harper's. I cocked my head to the side and decided I needed to replace my smashed drink, before my mind ran away with me wondering when the last time Harper looked at me that way. She and Lucia were gawking like he was a double chocolate cake with extra icing.

Scott pulled his business card out of the back pocket of his sweatpants and handed it to Harper. I grabbed my drink and moved to Harper's side, pulling her close to me, kissing her temple, claiming what was mine, marking my territory.

"Scott, I'm sure Harper can put you on her calendar later this week and you guys can chat, right, baby?" I said.

"Ahem," she said. "Sure, that will be fine," Harper stared like she couldn't believe her lying eyes.

"Stephen you've never mentioned you had a twin brother," Lucia said, still eyeing Scott up and down like he was a vanilla ice cream cone she wanted to lick.

"Yeah darlin', double the trouble." Scott winked at Lucia.

"But I'm the oldest," Stephen said.

"Oh the difference three minutes can make," Scott laughed, and gave a backhanded slap against Stephen's six-pack. Stephen never budged.

Scott was looking starstruck at Lucia, never taking his eyes off her.

"Okay, so, you people need to go home right?" I said, thinking I was now on emotional overload. My ego couldn't take anymore tonight. I fiercely needed some alone time with Harper. There was starting to be too much heat and sexual tension in the room, and none of it was directed at me. This was getting too mushy even for my tastes.

"No problem," Stephen said. "You want to catch a lift, Lucia? Scott and I would be happy to drop you off at your home," he said, nodding at his brother.

"Oh yes indeed," Lucia said, grabbing her things so quickly you would have thought she had been struck by lightning and that someone had lit a hot fire under her. She was moving like she was in a NASCAR race. Lucia was looking at Scott like she was in the desert and he was a cool drink of water. I just shook my head and closed my eyes momentarily in disgust.

Moments later I had managed to clear the penthouse. It was just me and mine now.

"I promised you dinner, Kitten, let me feed you," I said noticing that Harper was looking a little peaked and fatigued around the eyes. It was paining me to look at the bruises without going ballistic on Brooks. He had punched above his weight this time and I was going to see to it that he paid. I focused my attention back on Harper.

I needed to nurture and comfort her. No doubt her mind and body were in a state of shock from tussling with Brooks. *Oh god, I can't think about him or else I'll get angry all over again. She and I need to wind down.*

"Baby, Ina made us some food earlier. I've got some salmon, small red potatoes, and asparagus. Would you like to eat? It's light and nourishing."

"That's fine Nicky. I need to eat. I've been feeling squeamish all day."

"I'm sorry to hear it," Nicholas said.

"I don't know if I'm coming down with the flu or something. I've just been feeling like I've been running on half a tank all day today. I'm sure I'm just tired from the day's events."

I set two plates full of food on my dining table off the great room and sat Harper down in front of her place setting, pouring her a glass of cabernet to have with her meal. I sat across the table opposite her so I could keep a close eye on her mood.

"Gee baby, it didn't sound like anything good happened to you today," I said, stuffing my face with the salmon. "Lucia and I spent the whole day doing PowerPoint workups on the Joduku Plastics presentation. I hear Big Daddy wants an update from me on the status. What about Elizabeth? Has she been riding you about the acquisition?" I asked curiously, making conversation.

"Not today. But I'm sure she'll be blowing up my phone soon about it any day now. She's not one to be kept out of the loop for too long," Harper said, picking over her food with her fork. "I hate that our parents have dragged us into this plastics mess," Harper said. "We've got to find a way out this nightmare, Nicky, especially since Brooks is now involved. The three of us in competition is not good."

"You need to eat."

Harper had always been a healthy eater so I knew she was under stress for sure. Or maybe preoccupied. Worried.

"What else is bothering you besides the obvious?" I asked.

"I had an appointment scheduled with Stone Fertility Clinic today, but I had to cancel. I was just too wiped out from the day's events."

"Good," I said, not holding my emotions back. I felt vulnerable for stating my position.

"Well, I didn't cancel because I don't intend to go, Nicholas, I just wasn't up to it today. I do intend to go," she said, pushing back on me.

"Please Harper, must we do this now?" I pleaded.

"I know you can't appreciate this, Nicholas, but I want a baby," she said, setting her fork down. I'm not getting any younger. I'm thirty-six years old and the window of opportunity is closing in on me fast," she huffed. "I want a baby."

"You don't have to have a baby with a goddamn stranger, Harper," I said, feeling the angst coming across in my voice.

"You know that I am my own woman, Nicholas. I want to be fully aware of all of my options," Harper said. "It doesn't hurt for me to be informed. And, there's something else that I think it's time you should take under consideration, Nicholas."

"Yes?" I asked inquisitively, knowing she was getting ready to toss one of her little grenades at me.

She had that grenade-throwing look on her face.

"And that would be what, Harper?" I asked, steeling myself.

Harper paused for a minute and took a sip of wine. Tears welled in her eyes. "It's not like I could foresee that I was going to have a miscarriage back then. No woman can predict that kind of thing," Harper said, looking at me like I had grown two heads.

"Miscarriage? You mean abortion, don't you?" I asked, gritting my teeth, and chomping on my back molars just having to regurgitate this memory all over again.

Why must we have this discussion now? Hadn't we both been through enough tonight? Right about now, Lucia would tell me to breathe. In an effort not to lose control, I tried to talk Lucia into my head.

"God you can be so pig-headed sometime, Nicholas," Harper said, shaking her head.

Surely, she isn't talking about me? Moi?

"Abortion? You idiot. I did not have an abortion, Nicholas. I had a miscarriage," Harper said, glaring at me. "I know ten years ago you thought I had an abortion. Well I did not. I did not abort your baby, Nicholas. I could never do that. I had a miscarriage. Are you listening to me? I miscarried our baby!" Harper said, gasping.

Argh! Too much information.

I dropped my napkin and shook my head, running my fingers through my hair. *What the hell is this woman saying to me?* Surely I had the deer in the headlights look on my face.

"Why on earth would you let me believe this about you all these years?" I pleaded. "Why, Harper?"

"You believed what you chose to believe, Nicholas," Harper sneered.

"The hell I did," I dropped my fork, not able to finish my food. I'd lost my appetite. "I would have gone through the miscarriage experience with you. That was not something you should have had to go through alone. You *let* me believe you aborted our baby."

"Oh really? You would have gone through this with me, when? My third trimester when you decided you might just consider making a cameo appearance or something?" she squealed. "No sir, buddy. You let yourself believe I aborted the baby. That was *your* choice. I just didn't correct you. How could you even think I would do such a thing anyway?" Harper snapped, the tears starting now to stream down her cheeks.

"Didn't you know who I was? Didn't you know who *we* were?" she said through the muffled tears, dropping her head down toward her plate and not giving me eye contact.

Harper had folded her hands across her chest. I considered her body language and knew this was not the dinner conversation that I wanted to have.

I stood up, walking across the room, loosening my tie, and pacing in circles.

"Are you seriously trying to tell me ten years later, that you've let me believe you had an abortion when you didn't? I've been guilty all these ten goddamn years? Seriously, woman?" I was already starting to lose the battle, hearing the sound of my own voice escalating.

"Last I checked, you left me holding the bag, Nicholas Miles Becker," Harper snarled. "It was you who couldn't handle the information. Not me. You got what you got. A girl's got to get in where she fits in, and, clearly that was not with *you.*"

We were headed down a dark path. This was a sensitive subject. We had to clear it now. But we both wanted to avoid discussing it as well. How could I be sorry for what I didn't know about ten years ago, really? She let me believe that she aborted my child. She didn't try to correct me or change my opinion. I had held on to my anger for so long for something that wasn't even true or real.

Harper got up from her chair and I pulled her into my arms to keep her from storming out of the room. I held her close and I held her tight. We must have been the epitome of the young, gifted, and stupid back then.

"It's okay baby," I said. "We can't go back, but we can move forward, together."

I wiped the tears from her cheeks. I decided a long time ago that a strong man gets cool points when he is able to comfort a woman through the tears. I needed all the help I could get now that the tears were flowing.

"It's all right, Kitten. Sit back down and eat. Okay, baby?"

"Okay, Nicky," she said, sitting back down and wiping the tears from her face with her white cotton napkin.

Silence stretched out between us.

"Harper, baby . . ."

"Yes Nicky?"

"You're not going to the fertility clinic," I said, just as I saw her mentally pull her Uzi out. I could almost hear the *click clack* going on inside her head.

"And you're not the boss of me," Harper said softly, her face stern and her eyes squinting.

I locked and loaded. War was near.

We stared at each other for what felt like a lifetime. This was a dance we had perfected over time. Which one of us was going to blow up our fragile new beginning of a relationship first?

I grabbed a biscuit off my plate. I jumped out of my chair, and grabbed her up in my arms, swung her around in a circle, and kissed her passionately, then stuffed the biscuit in her mouth. Harper laughed, chewed the biscuit down and wrapped her arms around my neck, planting a thousand kisses on my face, wrapping those beautiful caramel legs around my waist as she jumped into my arms. We both had crumbs all over our face. I was careful to hold her gently and not aggravate the tender places on her body.

We laughed and fell back on the sofa, kissing, hugging, moaning, and groaning. I had no idea what Harper might have been thinking at this exact moment, but one thing for sure, this was *my* baby maker, *my* woman, and the only babies coming out of that womb were going to be mine. I could still see the reluctance and hesitancy in her face. I was just going to have to work harder to convince her to step down off that freaking "no one can tell me what to do" rock of hers. She was not buying any of the hype from me regarding my dislike for her trolling through some fertility clinic. I knew that nothing was settled between us on this point. It was going to be a challenge, but I was definitely up to the task. I considered that we were just going to agree to disagree tonight and call a temporary truce on the matter.

And then I ripped those big girl, black silky lace come-hither-more-like-a-thong panties right off her.

Mine.

CHAPTER TWELVE

Harper

"Oh Harper honey, Malcom told the senator and I everything that happened between you and Brooks Fitzgerald McKenna. I've been so worried about you, darling. Daddy's been calling all over town to see if charges have been pressed against him."

"Yes mother, I know."

"Brooks is only getting a slight slap on the wrist since he was intoxicated. His lawyer argued that his state of mind was compromised and that he didn't intend any real harm; good lawyers and all," Elizabeth sighed.

"I don't want you to worry Mother."

I reached in my dresser drawer to find some warm socks to put on my feet before heading out in the cold. I grabbed my black suede over-the-knee boots out of my closet, and reached for a turtleneck and my oversized angora poncho.

"Brooks has been sending me flowers every other day, calling me daily, and desperately trying to apologize for his behavior," I said, hopping up and down on one foot. "It's been two weeks now. I'm pretty sure he's ashamed and embarrassed by his actions. I've refused to accept the flowers, returning them upon delivery. He and I can't be friends."

"Well of course you can't be friends dear. With friends like that, who needs enemies? There's no excuse for that kind of conduct, coming from a grown thirty-eight-year-old man," she said.

"It is what it is Mother."

"Thank God Malcom was there to help you. Who's heading your security detail now?" she asked.

"Well Nicholas's bodyguard has a twin brother. They both are in the security business together. His name is Scott Parks, Mother, and he'll be heading up my security detail, so tell Daddy not to worry," I said, noticing my jeans were starting to feel a bit more snug than usual. "I'll be sure to send him around so that you and Daddy can be introduced. So far, he's working out pretty well. He's a real heartbreaker though, and to think there are two of them," I giggled.

God, I need to get to the gym.

"Oh that Nicholas always has had your best interests at heart. He takes such good care of you, Harper. I just love Nicholas."

"It's not like you hide your affection for Nicholas, Mother."

"Do you think you need to get a restraining order against Brooks, dear?"

"I doubt it. Nicholas will not let that man get anywhere near me in this lifetime. He actually makes my new security chief report in to him as if the man doesn't work for me."

"That's a good thing, yes?"

"That's debatable. Nicky is starting to behave like a stalker regarding my safety. He just thinks I don't know what he's doing behind my back."

I could just imagine Mother beaming through the phone.

"Nicholas is such a good man. He wants only the best for you, Harper. He's just like his father," Mother said. "He takes care of what he holds dear."

"Listen Mother, I have to run. I've got an appointment at Stone Fertility Clinic today and I'm about to be late," I said, closing my eyes.

Wait for it . . . wait for it . . .

"You know Harper, I'm going to go along with this little fertility clinic project of yours for just about a few more days. But it's time you grow up, dear, and put these silly notions out of your head. You're just trying to make me gray-headed before my time."

"I told you I wanted a baby, Mother."

"Don't break your mother's heart, with this foolishness with fertility clinic's stranger . . . what do they call that? Stranger baby daddies. Yes that's it . . . stranger baby daddies. There will absolutely be no such goings-on in this family."

"It's not as bad as it seems, Mother."

"The senator and I will not stand for it, Harper. It's just not the ladylike thing to do. That's for those other women who have trouble. It's not for you," Mother fumed.

"You should try to get used to the idea, Mother."

"You have choices beyond the ones you're focused on. If you just want me to get down and dirty with you on this, I will if I have to. The fact remains, you need to look at what's right in front of your face, if you get my drift."

"What exactly does that mean?"

"I need to go now, Harper. I can't have this conversation with you. I refuse to entertain this foolishness and give it any more of my attention or energy."

"My plans to have a baby is foolishness to you?" I said, challenging her.

"You need to focus on the plastics acquisition and get your mind off fertility clinics and babies. I expect an update on Joduku Plastics by the end of the week," she huffed.

And just like that, she hung up and was gone.

Okay, now that went well, I pondered to myself. *Right according to my expectations.*

The Marimba played on my phone and I looked at my caller ID. It was Brooks Fitzgerald McKenna. He just wasn't going to give up no matter how much I avoided him. I supposed he needed to hear the words come out of my mouth directly.

"Hello."

"Oh Harper honey, I'm so sorry, I don't know what got into me. I lost my head. I had too much to drink. I'm so sorry, baby. Please let me make this up to you," he begged.

I sighed. "There's nothing more we have to say to each other, Brooks. I think you've done quite enough. I'm seeing Nicholas now. You should move on. Don't call me again."

"I promise you, darling, I'll make this up to you. This is not who I am. I was just so out of my head. I've been under stress. I just—"

Click. Done. Next...

"Are you ready Harper?" Reese texted me. *"I'm downstairs waiting. Shall I come up?"*

"No I'm coming down," I texted back.

I grabbed my sunglasses, tote, hat, and scarf. I buzzed Winston and told him that I was headed down.

"You know you're really wrecking my reputation, dragging me to some fertility clinic with you. I'd only do this for you, sweetie. If any of my women see me out here like this, they may think I'm having some fertility issues or something. This could seriously mess up my game, baby," Reese texted back.

"And what game is that?" I typed. *"As far as I can tell, the only game you're focused on is basketball with your nieces and nephew."*

"Woman, don't underestimate me," Reese texted.

"No really, Reese. I need the emotional support. I didn't know who else to ask. I really appreciate your coming with me today," I replied, before hitting the Send button.

"You could have asked Nicholas," Reese texted. "It's *not like the two of you aren't knocking boots right about now."*

I would have bet money that Reese was laughing out loud as I looked at my iPhone screen.

I hit the elevator button, laughing on my way down, still holding my phone and smiling. As I reached the ground floor, I clicked my phone off. I flew out the double doors and pulled myself close to Reese, who was standing by Winston, waiting for me like the good friend that he was. We both jumped in the car together.

"Nicholas is not at all happy with this idea, Reese," I said. "He and I can't even talk about this, really. I told him I was planning to see what my options were, but I didn't tell him I was coming today."

"Can you blame him? He sees you as his woman, and you going in a fertility clinic to make a baby without him is as if he doesn't count or exist. It feels like you're still punishing him on some level," Reese said. "People will start to think he's the one with fertility woes. The great Nicholas, a.k.a. God, Becker can't make a baby? Are you kidding me?"

"It's not that, Reese. It's just that I've had to learn to depend only on myself these last few years. I don't want to be dependent upon anyone. I can only count on myself," I said.

"You know I'm your friend, Harper. I'm going to tell you like it is. You need to get over all that old baggage with Nicholas and lean into it, babe. You are seriously taking this independence thing way too far. You and Nicholas love each other. Nothing stopping you from making a baby with him, you know," Reese said.

"The subject of our making a baby hasn't come up," I said. "I think we're both avoiding it. It's a sensitive subject."

"You two shouldn't have to avoid it. It's just what people in love do. It just happens, and it's okay honey. Some things in life ought not to be forced. Baby making is less about science, Harper, and more about human nature," Reese said. "Trust me on this one."

"Oh you're going to give me advice on babies now? Mr. Never Stay With the Same Woman Twice?"

"Sometimes you have to let a man be a man. It's okay for you to drop the reins, Harper. Everyone knows that you know how to take care of yourself. You've proven that to yourself and to the world twenty-five times over. The world won't come to an end just because you let Nicholas do for you sometime. Unstrap those gold balls you're wearing down there," Reese laughed.

"Oh you're really having fun at my expense today, Reese," I said jokingly.

"Nicholas is man enough for you, baby. Lean into him, Harper."

Reese grabbed my hand, held it next to his lips, and kissed it just as my driver pulled up to the doors of the Stone Fertility Clinic.

I knew Reese was right. Nicholas was more than enough man for me. Matter of fact he was exactly my kind of man. Gorgeous. Alpha. Smart. Passionate. Hot. Rich. But could we last the long haul?

"It's hard for me to take a chance on Nicholas, Reese. He left me standing on my own years ago. I don't know if I can or should count on him. I'm really trying this time."

"Yes, sweetheart, but think about what you're saying. That was ten years ago. Nicholas has changed. You've changed. That's not who he is now, any more than you are the woman now that you were then. You two have grown," Reese said.

Reese was always the voice of reason in my life. Mr. Practicality. Always.

I looked at Reese and he looked at me.

"You know you could be the donor, Reese. I would let you father my baby," I said, raising an eyebrow.

"Okayyyyyyyyy now. Temporary lapse in sanity. Reese Nelson loves his life. Nicholas Becker will not be taking my life anytime soon," Reese laughed. "Hell no. That's a killing waiting to happen," Reese chuckled.

"Just a thought," I said, not taking any of my own words seriously.

"You ready, Harper?"

"Yes, let's go."

"Dr. Stone, thank you so much for seeing me. Dr. Richards has spoken so highly of you," I said.

Dr. Stone was very young too. Somehow I expected someone older.

"This is my friend Reese Nelson," I said, introducing Reese.

"Oh so are you the expectant donor to be?" Dr. Stone said.

"Oh no I'm not a donor," Reese said looking much more wide-eyed. "I'm here for emotional support. Harper will have to pick a donor from your pool of . . . of . . . donors," Reese said, looking embarrassed.

"No problem. Ms. Montgomery, we've been expecting you. We will need to begin with a few preliminary diagnostic tests. We'll be taking some urine and blood. Then we'll do an ultrasound to get a three-dimensional view of your reproductive system. I'll explain the medical procedures along the way, and then we'll talk about how to get your process for motherhood under way," Dr. Stone said, smiling.

I liked him. I liked the fertility clinic. Dr. Stone's clinic was fresh and clean. His staff was warm. I felt comfortable. *I can do this. I am my own woman.* Women make babies as single parents every day.

So maybe I wouldn't be in a relationship with my baby's father. I wouldn't know him per se. But I could pick him. I could pick the best of all the attributes that I would want in my child. But then again, it wasn't like the men I had been involved with over the last few years had been the kind of guys that I wanted to get to know better anyway. They weren't father material, so this couldn't be so bad after all, except if you were . . . maybe . . . Nicholas.

But Nicholas never wanted a baby before. I doubted that he wanted a baby now. Maybe he thinks he wants me now, but me with a baby, now that's a whole new discussion, yet to be had. If our past was a guidepost, we pretty much failed years ago on that level.

Yes, I could rise to this occasion. I could do this. I could seriously consider having a baby all on my own. Elizabeth and the senator would just have to get used to the idea. From now on, it would be me and my baby. I would insist with my parents, Nicholas, or anyone else for that matter, that I was a package deal. You take one. You take the other. They would just have to get used to the idea. Love it or leave it.

I might down the road regret the fact that I would never have Nicholas's baby in my future. But this baby would be the next best thing. It really would. This could work.

As I laid on the examination table, Dr. Stone's staff shuttled in and out of the exam room, poking, prodding, and taking samples, tests, and blood work from me. The only thing I wanted to do was get to those books of bios and backgrounds on the potential donors and pick the father of my baby. Reese could help me with that. Reese has good judgment and wouldn't let me make a wrong selection. If I applied enough pressure, I could maybe even convince Reese to be the donor if I could not find a donor suitable to my standards. But that would create the possibility of a whole lot of other complications down the line. God, I'm all over the place.

Yes, I needed to relax and quiet my mind.

A couple of hours later, I was tired of being poked on and having needles stuck in my arms. Dr. Stone had moved Reese and me into his office for a consultation. Reese was nervous and jittery knowing my moment of truth was getting closer. My goal of motherhood was becoming more of a reality.

"How are you holding up, Harper?" Reese asked, squeezing my hand. "I'm here for you, sweetie."

"Thank you," I said, pulling my body close to his and embracing his hug.

"Ms. Montgomery, aren't you the lucky one?" Dr. Stone said.

"Oh yes I am, Dr. Stone. I came here to get informed. I can't wait to proceed. I'm looking forward to this. I'm feeling really good about the prospects of being a mother," I said, grabbing Reese's hand and holding it tightly.

"Well, I'm glad to hear that, Ms. Montgomery, because you're going to be getting your wish, indeed," Dr. Stone said. "I'm so glad you have a positive outlook, because there's something I need to tell you," Dr. Stone smiled.

"Yes Dr. Stone." I said. "I am very much looking forward to going through the fertility process."

"You're a very blessed woman. I have a million mothers that would love to walk in your shoes right now," he said. "The fact of the matter is that my job is done. Mother nature has a way of laughing at people in my profession."

"I'm sorry, Dr. Stone, I guess I'm not following you," I said, a bit confused and squeezing Reese's hand.

"Ms. Montgomery, you're already pregnant. You don't need the services of my clinic. You're well under way into your first trimester," Dr. Stone said. "The way I figure it, you're right about six weeks along," Dr. Stone beamed. "You should plan on giving birth early fall."

Reese looked like he had seen a ghost and had turned pale white.

"I'm sorry Dr. Stone," I said. "What do you mean, exactly?"

"I mean you're going to have a baby, Ms. Montgomery. You don't need my services," he stood, shaking my hand. "But thank you again for considering my fertility clinic."

I was flabbergasted. Floored.

"Although we can't help you, we appreciate your potential business," Dr. Stone said. "You need to start a treatment plan with your regular obstetrician and get on a regimen of pre-natal vitamins. I've checked you over. You're in good health and should have no problem. I expect you to sail right through this pregnancy." Another big smile from the good doctor.

My mouth was still hanging open as I watched Dr. Stone fold my medical folder closed. "Here's my card, should your obstetrician need to speak with me directly. You'll need to sign some exit papers and then I'll have you on your way."

And just like that, Dr. Stone ushered Reese and I out of his office. As we passed by an empty waiting room, I moved to grab a chair and sit down. I was feeling dizzy.

"I need to pause for a minute and collect my thoughts," I said, feeling like my head was spinning.

"You're pregnant? By Nicholas?" Reese said turning his head towards me in disbelief, not sure how to respond to me.

"I guess so," I said in shock.

Reese moved to sit in the chair next to me.

"Congratulations, Harper." He kissed me on my cheek. "This is good news, right?"

I was speechless.

"Those damn Bloody Marys in Vermont," I said. "I'm shocked. Nicholas and I had marathon sex, no condoms. High on . . . the good life . . . and each other . . ."

I started getting up very slowly. I felt like I was walking out of Dr. Stone's office in a daze and feeling like I had been hit by a sledgehammer.

"No wonder I had been feeling under the weather lately. I thought I was getting the flu or just running myself down from working too hard," I said, walking towards the exit doors of the clinic slowly. I looked at Reese, in disbelief. I still couldn't believe what I was hearing. I was going to have a baby. Nicholas's baby.

"You're going to be a mother, Harper. Just what you said you wanted. And you did it the old-fashioned way," Reese said. "Shall we celebrate?"

"Oh my God, I'm pregnant," I said. "I'm going to have a baby. Nicholas's baby. Oh my God."

Should I tell Nicholas? How would he handle this news? Would he stay or run like he did ten years ago? This was unbelievable news. I thought for sure once I went to the fertility clinic it would take several months to get pregnant. Maybe even a year. I wasn't sure I was ready for this. This was soon. If Nicholas denied me and my baby this time, maybe I really was going to have to really kill him, once and for all.

"Oh Reese, what do I do?" I asked, feeling like my emotions had climbed up the top of a roller coaster and then slid downward at high speed and back up again.

"Do? I tell you what you are going to do. You have a baby, little momma," Reese said, starting now to get excited. "I'm going to be a godfather," he said, pumping his chest out, picking me up, and twirling me around.

"And I'm going to be a mother."

CHAPTER THIRTEEN

Nicholas

"Nicky I know you're feeling bad but you need to snap out of it," Lucia scolded. "You've been moping now for a couple of weeks."

"Frankly, if it weren't for this Joduku Plastic's acquisition being on my work schedule I'd head to the Mediterranean on the *Julianna* and not come back until this time next year," I said, watching the snow fall silently out of my penthouse window.

"Harper's been calling again today. Why don't you take the call, Nicky? I've been making all kinds of excuses for you," Lucia sighed. "I can't do this too much longer. She's smart enough to put two and two together."

"What's there to say? Everyone but me knows she's pregnant—Big Daddy, Mackenzie, Reese, and even his sister Riley knows. Maybe it's Reese's baby. I hear he went to the fertility clinic with her."

"Now you're being ridiculous, Nicky," Lucia said.

"Really? It's not like Harper picked up the phone and told me that she was actually having a baby through some unidentified sperm donor," I grumbled. "I thought she and I were working on re-building a future together and now she goes off and does this!"

"Honestly, Nicky," Lucia interrupted.

"It's like my feelings mean nothing to her. *I* mean nothing to her. She didn't even give us a chance. She just can't find it in her heart to let go of all of our old baggage."

"Well, not talking to her isn't going to help, Nicholas. Perhaps there's a way for the two of you to build a bridge across these troubled waters. If you would just talk to her," Lucia pleaded. "Avoiding Harper isn't going to help this situation. It's been two weeks now, Nicky."

I stared out the window watching the snowflakes fall, never turning around to face Lucia. My heart was broken. *My* baby maker had gone off and made a baby without me. She truly didn't want me. Perhaps her dislike for me was deeper than I thought. All I felt now was dread. Dread that I was really going to have to go forward and live my life without her. I didn't want to take care of someone else's baby when I was perfectly capable of making my own. Why didn't she want *my* baby? Why didn't she want me? She had to know this would be a deal breaker between us. I've never wanted any woman like I've wanted her. It hurt too much just to think about the loss of her. If I should lose this love, the pain would be too great.

"There is no situation Lucia," I said turning to face Lucia and looking at her pitifully. "She's made her choice."

"You're in love with Harper," Lucia said. "You always have been. Love can overcome incredible odds, Nicky. For once, try to follow your heart on this one."

I stared at Lucia, at a loss of words. My anger with Harper was mixed with my deep love for her. "I have been following my heart, Lucia. Harper needed to do the same. But no. No sir. What did she do? She went and got herself fucking knocked up at some freaking fertility clinic," I said. I knew my voice was revealing the deep agony and pain that I was feeling in my heart and soul.

I was a mess. Images of Harper and me making love haunted my brain like a bad memory on constant replay. Falling in love with Harper had created an ache in my heart as big as the Grand Canyon. My desire and need for her burned inside of me. How was I ever going to get myself through life without her? Why did I set myself up for failure a second time like an idiot?

I watched with disinterest as Lucia headed towards the fax machine to pull a document out of the feeder that was coming through.

"What is it?" I mumbled, swirling around in my chair to look back at the snow falling in Central Park. It was like a piece of heaven carved out in the middle of a Metropolis. How exactly did that come to be? So strange that we were in the month of March and snow was falling on Central Park. The climate was messed up with all this global warming madness. Just like my heart was messed up. Cold where it should have been warm.

"It's about the Joduku Plastics acquisition. We're on their agenda to make our presentation, Lucia said, reading the details of the agenda out loud.

"Fine," I said. "Game on. Let's acquire this fucking company for Becker Foods so I can get the hell out of Dodge," I grumbled. "I prefer to be on the other side of the world right now rather than dealing with some little plastics company out of Tokyo for Big Daddy. I just want all this mess behind me. I want it all to go away," I growled. "I need to go fucking play."

I closed my eyes and breathed in deep. Lucia nodded at me in agreement in the way that she had mastered her communications with me, giving me a look of acquiescence.

"I suppose when Becker Foods wins this acquisition, then that will just be another nail that Harper can put in my coffin. Just one more reason for her to shut me out of her life. It was already bad enough that we were in competition with each, but now this. A baby," I said, running my fingers through my hair.

"Nicky, you've taken this pity party way too far. It's not like Harper's not trying to reach out to you to communicate. She's the one that has been working to reach out to you. And frankly, that's more than I would have expected her to do given the fact that you're constantly avoiding her. This does not have to go down this way," Lucia said, her pleas starting to feel like nagging irritation.

Lucia's phone buzzed. She was getting a text message. I looked at her expectantly.

"It's Three. He wants an update on Joduku Plastics. He says Big Daddy wants a status report on the acquisition and you're not returning his calls."

"Handle it Lucia," I said, grabbing an unopened bottle of Stoli off my wet bar. "Just handle it. Just fucking handle it, Lucia."

"Nicky, you're repeating yourself. Perhaps you need to get in the ring with Stephen for a bit. Work out some of your frustrations. Exercise is good for you," Lucia begged.

"I'm going to bed," I said, twisting the top off the bottle and taking a huge swig.

I felt the heat of the vodka warm my insides. I needed to feel something. I'd been numb for so long now. I could feel the warmth of the vodka slide down my esophagus. It meant I wasn't dead yet. Too bad. I felt dead inside. Why wasn't I dead yet? I needed to drink some more.

"The answer to your problems is not in that bottle you know," Lucia said, looking at me with disdain.

"Who the hell cares," I said, headed up the floating staircase to my master bedroom suite.

"I do," she said.

"How long has he been like this?" I could hear Three say amidst the fogginess going on in my head.

"About three days now," Lucia said. "He's not eating but he sure as hell is drinking. He's been binging on the Stoli's ever since he got the news about the pregnancy," Lucia said. "I've tried to get through to him, but he's not listening to me right now. You're welcome to have at it," Lucia said. "The calls from Harper have even stopped, not that he's been taking her calls anyway," Lucia said.

"Lucia, he's got to get his head back in the game or he won't ever forgive himself. Not to mention that Big Daddy's gonna have my ass right along with his. This is a replay from the last time Harper broke his heart," Three said.

"It's time to pull out all the stops," Lucia said.

"I'll handle this from here, my sweet Bella. This is a mano-to-mano matter," Three said with all confidence.

"I suppose," Lucia shrugged. "See what you can do with him, but if you fail, I'm going to go to plan B and deal with him myself."

"God you scare the hell out of me, my sweet Bella," Three said.

"Just giving you fair warning, Three."

"You're a whole lot of woman Lucia. You require a whole lot of man, love," Three said, his eyebrows raised. "Wherever did Nicky find you?"

"1-800-Hell-To-The-No," I heard Lucia said dismissively.

Lucia and Three's voices dropped to a whisper. I could hear his footsteps heading my direction. I wondered briefly if the two of them were keeping secrets. Yes. They were keeping secrets. Ahhh, perhaps that was just my alcohol-infused brain operating on paranoia. No. They were fucking keeping secrets.

My head was pounding. I could hear Three coming up my floating stairs. I wanted to stay in my fog and nurse my pain. I didn't want to be disturbed. I wanted to lay right here with my vodka on my one-thousand-count Egyptian cotton sheets and goose down pillows. I did not want to contend with Three right now.

I wanted my woman to want *my* baby, not some stranger donor's from some bullshit fucking fertility clinic. Harper and I were destined to make our own babies. She put a bullet in my plans to make Big Daddy happy by making him a grandson. I couldn't deny my deep-seated desires to fulfill my dead mother's dreams for me. Jesus, it was too early in the morning for me to listen to Three's bullshit.

What the hell. I turned my bottle of Stoli up and took a huge swig. I might as well bite the dog that bit me. My pain was too great. I wanted to numb myself from the whole damn matter. Three was a good brother, but he couldn't possibly help me endure the pain from watching my own woman having a stranger's baby. Oh Lord, the mere thought of it all is just too much to bear. My mind hurts, my body hurts, my heart hurts. I turned the bottle of Stoli up again and took another swig.

"Jesus Nicky, you smell," Three said as he entered my bedroom. "When's the last time you've had a bath, brother? And you need to shave," Three gazed at me and shook his head.

He began picking my dirty clothes up off the floor and tossing them down the laundry chute. I was naked except for my pair of Hanro boxer briefs. I had a case of empty vodka bottles scattered around on my plush white carpet. I raised my head briefly only to peer into my fish tank. I must be seeing double. It looked like I had two of every fish I owned. That couldn't be right.

"This is so unlike you, Nicky," Three said. "What happened to Mr. Immaculate? God? Look at you," Three said in shock. "You look a mess. Look at this place."

"I've been nailed to the cross," I moaned taking another swig. "Didn't you get the memo?"

Even my five o'clock shadow was on its way to looking more like a beard. I felt crucified, so I was sure I was starting to look the part of being crucified.

"Last I checked I don't have to answer to you," I grumbled, my head pounding worse. "Leave me alone."

Three pressed the button on my electronic blinds letting the sunlight hit me in the face. He opened the drawer in my nightstand and pulled out some ibuprofen. Then he reached into the mini fridge and handed me some Evian water.

"Take these," he said, handing me four of the little pills. "Let me help you to the shower. You can't let this business with Harper get you down. You've got to get back in the game here with Joduku Plastics, man. Are you actually going to let that asshole Brooks Fitzgerald McKenna assault your woman and then walk off with the company that should belong to Becker Foods on top of that? Really Nicky?"

"Who fucking cares, Three?"

"You do, motherfucker. And so do I."

"No I really don't. I'm over this shit with her. She doesn't want a life with me. She only wants what she wants when she wants it. She's punishing me," I groaned.

"Maybe so, maybe not," Three said. "But you'll never know for sure drowning yourself in this vodka. The only way you're going to know for sure is to get in the game and find out. Otherwise you'll never forgive yourself for not finding out firsthand. What you're doing is speculating. She's not a prospectus. You're avoiding."

"Her stock value has gone down. She's no longer a Blue Chip."

"To hell she is, Nicky. Your eyes are too red to see blue, brother."

"What's it to you, Three? Why the hell do you care?" I bitched.

"You're giving the Becker name a bad rap with all this wallowing. We don't punk out like this. Get your ass moving," Three ordered.

"Ugh," I moaned.

"Trust me. You'll thank me later and owe me one," Three huffed. "Remember Nicky, we're Beckers first. You shoot our dog, we'll kill your cat," Three said.

"Yeah man," I grumbled sitting now up on the side of the bed and holding my head in my hands, my elbows propped against my knees. I swallowed the ibuprofen down with my vodka.

Lord, I can't stand this pain. If I should lose this love . . .

"We made a pact, Nicky. Have you forgotten? Or has this vodka-binge-laced-pity-party clouded your brain?" Three said, interrupting my thoughts.

"Nope I haven't forgotten. You put one of ours in the hospital, we put one of yours in the morgue," I said, reciting out the mantra my brother Three and I have lived by since we were little kids.

"That's right, motherfucker," Three said, knocking me off my ass and pushing me toward my bathroom door, opening the shower door and turning on the jets. "It's time for you to go get what's yours," Three insisted.

Three threw me into the hot shower and held me under the hot water. The beads of water felt good cascading off my body. I let the pulsating liquid beat down the back of my neck. My mind was starting to clear and I was starting to sober up . . . not that I was ready to get back in the game and deal. But the truth was, I knew on some level that Three was right. It was bad enough that I had lost *my* baby maker. But I damn sure didn't have to settle for losing the Joduku Plastics acquisition to that asshat Brooks. Between Brooks and me, I was the better businessman. Three and I had a philosophy that in business the best revenge was being successful. And Three and I were bred to take no prisoners.

"Look, Nicky," Three said, talking to me through the shower door. "You might be down, but you're not out, brother. We need you. Big Daddy's got a lot riding on you. And, Lucia can't run Milk Money alone. Pity parties don't become you," Three said, pulling my shaving kit out of the bathroom drawer and setting it on top of the marbled sink.

"Yeah, well you try dealing with that fuckwad Brooks McKenna tossing your woman around and you not being there to protect her; your woman saying she's "contemplating a sperm donor," and before you know it she's pregnant; and on top of everything else your father wants you to bid on a plastics company that he's perfectly capable of buying himself, and such business has absolutely nothing to do with your own company's business. Then father pulls out his trump card, reminding me that my deceased mother wants me to have grandsons. Hell I may drink for three more days," I growled, continuing to run my head under the hot water.

"I know it's a tough hand you've been dealt Nicky, but it's not like you to go down without a fight," Three said. "The family is counting on you. I'm counting on you. Everyone knows you're the best at what you do."

I turned the water off and took the white fluffy monogramed towel Three handed me out of the towel warmer, patting it through my hair first and then wrapping it around my waist. I looked at myself in the mirror, sighing loudly and taking a deep breath. I made every effort to steel myself. I stared at my reflection. *And what is the best that you do Nicholas Miles Becker?* I asked myself in the mirror. *You fucking take no prisoners,* I answered.

"Get your shit together and get back in the game," Three said, looking at me sternly. "Nothing is the only game in town, Nicky," he assured me, slapping me on the back. "Get dressed. I'll have Ina fix you some hot food. I'll have a barber sent up to you. You need some food and a haircut," Three said shaking his head. "Time to play ball, brother. We Beckers never let the fish get away nor leave millions on the table."

"Must you remind me?" I asked.

"You're just hung over Nicky," Three said. "Your head hurts right now. Go close this deal and then go get your woman. You and Harper can work this baby shit out later down the road. Hell, make another baby, Nicky," Three said. "It's not like this is the end of the world. She can have more kids you know," he said throwing his hands up like it was all no big deal. "I should know. I've got three of them," he grunted. "Three for Three."

Oh God this is a big pill to swallow. I guess I hadn't thought about the fact that there was still an opportunity for Harper and me to have our own baby. Could I learn to love a stranger's baby? It wasn't like this baby would know who its father was. I could raise a stranger's baby as my own and love it, couldn't I? I could learn to love Harper's baby. Who was I fooling? I exist for her. I suppose I could do this. Couldn't I?

I began to shave, looking in the mirror making sure that the conversation I was having in my head made sense. God, Harper made me so crazy with her shit.

"She hasn't asked me to share her world, Three. She went to a fucking fertility clinic and made a baby with some stranger's sperm," I grumbled. "She told me she was just being informed about her options. She said nothing about making a baby. She excluded me."

"So you say," Three said. "You haven't spoken to her, Nicky. You're operating on hearsay. You need to hear the words directly. You know, from her lips to God's ears, remember. Or has that vodka made you forget who you claim you to be?" Three chuckled.

It would be just like Three to make fun of me at a time like this. I was having a fucking crisis. Oh God, just saying the words out loud was killing me. Yes killing me. That was what the fuck Harper was doing to me. *Killing me softly*. I gazed in the mirror, wiping the shaving cream off my face. I contemplated how awful my future was looking. I needed to shake this off.

Three's phone buzzed. "Yes, my sweet Bella."

I knew Three was on the phone flirting again with Lucia. I shook my head.

"Yes send him up . . . Steak and eggs are fine. Good."

"You need to stop flirting with my partner," I said solemnly to Three. "You're married."

"I may be married, but I'm not dead, brother. Ina is sending your food up. Franco is here to cut your hair. You're starting to look like a shaggy dog, Nicky. An inch more and you could wear a ponytail."

I nodded my head in acquiescence, moving toward the walk-in closet to find a pair of sweat pants to put on. I looked for my favorite grey ones. I needed to get in the ring and beat the shit out of Stephen.

"I feel like boxing," I caught myself talking out loud to myself in front of Three, as I stood bare-chested in a fresh pair of briefs. I found a pair of jeans instead and a t-shirt. I put them on before Franco arrived to cut my hair.

"Shadow box or with Stephen?" Three said. "You're not in the best of shape right now to be fucking around with Stephen. Trust me. You need to eat."

"Uh huh," I said, completely ignoring Three. I had things I needed to work out.

Nope, I couldn't do this donor-baby business with Harper. But I could win Joduku Plastics. Maybe I wasn't any good at this relationship stuff, but I had a keen eye for identifying profitable businesses. I was good at acquiring companies. That was why Big Daddy picked me for this job. I knew it. Three knew it. Big Daddy knew it, and Harper sure as hell knew it. If I couldn't have her or my own baby, I could at least have this company. *I'll take my win where I can find it.*

I balled my fists up, moved them quickly in a one-two pattern, my feet doing the Ali shuffle, shadow boxing with myself in the mirror.

All is fair in love and war. . . and business.

"Call Stephen. Tell him I'm coming down to the ring."

"Not a good idea, Nicky."

"I shall fear no evil, Three."

"Idiot." Three just shook his head.

CHAPTER FOURTEEN

Harper

"I swear to God, Mackenzie, this whole situation has really gotten out of hand."

"Well I don't know why? You wanted to get pregnant. Now you're pregnant. What's the big deal?" Mackenzie said. "So what everyone thinks you're having unknown baby daddy when really you're having Nicholas's baby."

"Well this is really bad. I called my mother to tell her the news. I said that I was standing outside the fertility clinic and that I was pregnant. She hung up on me before I could get in a word."

"You knew she couldn't handle the fertility clinic stuff, Harper."

"It's not like I went down the sperm donor path."

"She doesn't know this yet Harper."

"I heard she was so distraught, she called up Big Daddy to cry on his shoulder about the whole matter."

"Oh my God," Mackenzie said.

"So now there's even more confusion. I'm pretty sure Big Daddy has made mention of my pregnancy to Nicky because now, he's not returning my calls."

"Yeah, I would say this has gotten pretty ugly," Mackenzie responded.

"And what's worse, Reese mentioned to his sister Riley that I was pregnant and that he went along with me to the fertility clinic with me. Apparently, Riley casually mentioned it to her husband Mico, who mentioned it to Lucia, who mentioned it to Nicholas. I think Nicky thinks the baby is Reese's. This is so messed up," I said.

"Fucked up to the ninth degree would be more like it," Mackenzie said.

None of her comments made me feel any better.

"Word is, Big Daddy mentioned to Three that I was pregnant, who I'm sure has also said something to Nicholas. Now this whole thing is a complete mess and out of control."

This whole thing had gotten so messy. I wasn't sure how to even begin to untangle it all with Nicholas. This had to be killing him. I knew Nicholas. I knew he had the wrong ideas floating around in that pea brain of his. None of this was going to make sense to him. This was not the kind of information that he was going to handle well at all. This time, this wasn't his fault. This was just a matter of bad information floating around without the right narration.

"Which is exactly why you need to talk to him," Mackenzie said. "According to Stephen, Nicholas has cut all social ties. He's not exercising. He's moping. He's bitchy. Besides throwing himself into his work, no one has seen him. If it weren't for this plastics thing, Stephen thinks he would have left the country by now." Mackenzie shrugged.

"Knowing him, I'm not surprised," I said.

"There's been no sign of him on the entertainment pages either. Always Mallory Morgan and Jessica Leonard on the gossip pages, but no Nicholas."

"And that's important, why?"

"It means Nicholas has taken himself off the market."

"I feel like I'm in the middle of some huge circle jerk with Nicky." I moaned. "He's thinking that I'm artificially inseminated with a baby by a sperm donor."

"Oh this is scary," Mackenzie said. "You're carrying God's baby, and he thinks you've done the do with a no-name stranger," Mackenzie laughed.

"Mackenzie there is nothing funny about this. Nicholas isn't speaking to me. When I call his office, Lucia just says that he's thrown himself into the Joduku Plastics acquisition presentation and is not taking calls."

"Well that would seem plausible," Mackenzie replied.

"I haven't had an opportunity to share the good news about

the baby with Nicholas or my mother properly. I can't even have my time of joy, Mackenzie," I said, starting to feel tearful for the third time today. I'm just a basket case," I said, tears rolling down my face.

"No, baby, your hormones are just swinging," Mackenzie exclaimed. "Everything feels worse than it is when a woman is pregnant. This too shall pass."

"I sure hope so, Mackenzie, because if it doesn't, I'm going to slice and dice some balls off a few people if you know what I mean."

"Yeah, girl. Let's don't get all crazy hormonal now."

"You know the least Nicholas could do is to discuss this with me. It's been a couple of weeks. That's a long time to ignore me. Maybe this is just a repeat of what happened between us ten years ago and the universe is trying to teach me a lesson. If I didn't get the lesson then, the objective is to make sure I get the lesson now," I exclaimed.

"I think you're reading way too much in to all of this," Mackenzie said.

"It's not like I think for one minute that Nicholas deserves the benefit of the doubt, but in this instance, I think before we can start judging his actions, you should at least let him know the baby is his," Mackenzie said, throwing a Cheeto in her mouth from the crystal bowl sitting on my end table.

Mackenzie was addicted to Cheetos. Whenever I needed to act out and climb the walls, I called her over for Cheeto night at my place. It was what we both did when we were upset. Tonight was my turn.

"Well one thing for sure, next week is the presentation at Joduku Plastics. I will for sure see Nicholas then. He will be there, and so will Brooks Fitzgerald McKenna."

"I'm not sure that's the best setting for you to have such a delicate conversation with Nicholas, Harper. Breaking baby daddy news and the 'Fitz' don't go so well together. That's not the best of circumstances under which Nicholas should hear this."

"I plan to tell him to his face that this baby is his. And I plan to do it when I see him. If he would take my calls, he wouldn't have to be in that position of finding out this way, so I really don't care."

"This seems kind of risky Harper."

"He'll just have to suck it all up and deal with it. I want this acquisition to be over and done. After Montgomery Consulting Group wins this acquisition for Carmichael Ketchup, Nicholas probably won't be speaking to me anyway. Nicholas doesn't take to losing well," I said stuffing my face with more Cheetos and grabbing a sparkling water off my wet bar. "If Nicholas wants to act like he did ten years ago, then this time he might as well tell me to my face instead of disappearing off the face of the Earth for a couple of months," I ranted.

"Are you going to be able to manage this on your own? What if he decides to take flight and run for the hills?" Mackenzie said. "I'm not sure you should be alone. I could come with you."

"Thanks but that won't be necessary. This is business and I have to be able to have a baby on my own and conduct my business."

"True," Mackenzie interjected.

"The world won't stop turning on its axis just because Nicholas Miles Becker decides he wants to act like a child and take flight again. Besides, Charlotte will be with me so I won't be completely alone. And, I'll have Scott at my side for protection. I'll be in good company," I said, feeling tearful again. "I just need to get this whole business straightened out with my mother first. I figure she's calmed down enough now to hang on the phone long enough for me to get out the facts." I sighed. "To think she's freaking out all on the wrong information."

"Whatever made you think that Elizabeth Carmichael Montgomery would handle you having a baby with a sperm donor well?" Mackenzie laughed. "Were you trying to send your mother reeling? Even I could have told you Elizabeth was not going to take to that idea very well at all. Seriously Harper, were you shooting to get disinherited or something?" Mackenzie said, shaking her head.

"Oh, mother would eventually get over the idea of it sooner or later. Once she finds out that this is Nicholas's baby, she's going to be tickled pink. Mother thinks Nicholas walks on water," I said rolling my eyes up in my head.

"That she does," Mackenzie said stuffing another Cheeto in her mouth.

"I'll give her a call tomorrow after my appointment with Dr. Richards and let her know the real truth. I'm due to update her on the status of the Joduku acquisition anyway. The presentation is next week and so I need to bring her up to speed," I said. "It's not like she's going to let this whole business of a baby get in the way of her own business for too long," I said.

"Well just remember, I'm here for you, girlfriend. At the end of the day, you still have me." Mackenzie smiled.

It was so nice to have Mackenzie as a best friend. She was loyal to the end.

"So let's figure out baby names . . . What shall we name him if the baby's a boy?" Mackenzie squealed.

Juniorrrrrrrrr, the panicked voice in my head said in a very high-pitched, glass-shattering operatic voice.

Perhaps, it will be a girl . . .

"It's good to see you again, Harper," Dr. Richards said. "Dr. Stone called to thank me for your referral. I see you went to the fertility clinic. How did things go? Did you feel you want to proceed down that path now that you've visited the clinic?"

"Well actually Dr. Richards, my visit to the fertility clinic revealed that I am already pregnant. Apparently I'm not in need of a sperm donor. Nicholas Becker has already donated. I'm having Nicholas's baby," I said.

"Well I guess congratulations are in order."

"Thank you," I said, smiling shyly.

"So you and Nicholas decided to have a baby together? That's interesting news."

"Well not exactly."

"What do you mean?" Dr. Richards said, looking a bit perplexed.

"I haven't had a chance to share the news with Nicholas," I said solemnly. "He doesn't know."

"Oh really?" Dr. Richards said, raising her eyebrow.

"Well he does and he doesn't," I said, knowing I wasn't making sense. "Everything was happening so fast. You see, I went to the fertility clinic to explore my options. While I was there, they ran the usual routine tests on me and in the process, they discovered I was already pregnant."

"Well, I bet that was a bit of a surprise," Dr. Richards said.

"Everything happened so quickly. Before I knew it, I tried to share the information with my mother and all hell broke loose."

"How so?

"Mother got the wrong impression. She hung up on me before I could explain that I hadn't gone through with sperm donor process," I said, shifting uncomfortably in my chair.

"Go on," Dr. Richards said patiently.

"Later, I discovered Mother had shared my pregnancy news with Nicholas's father. Before I could explain to anyone the real truth, word got around with Nicholas's family and staff that I had gone to the fertility clinic and that I was impregnated."

"Oh my," Dr. Richard exclaimed.

"Now I believe Nicholas has the wrong impression as well. He's not been taking my calls these days," I said, exasperated.

"Oh goodness. You really have had a tough go of it dear. How have you been feeling?" Dr. Harper asked sympathetically.

"Well, I'm having morning sickness and a few tearful moments that I guess comes with any routine pregnancy, or so my obstetrician says. Physically I'm holding up pretty good, to be nine weeks pregnant, but emotionally I feel like a basket case."

"Well that's to be understood in light of the circumstances," Dr. Richards said. "I don't want you to get your spirits down now dear. There's every good reason that all of this miscommunication can be readily cleared up. This should be your happy time."

"I just feel so alone, not having been able to share this information with Nicholas or my family yet."

"Well do you have a plan to for clearing this up with them?" Dr. Richards asked.

"Well, as a matter of fact, I plan to let my mother know tomorrow. She's had enough time now to calm down. Certainly long enough to hear me," I said.

"And Nicholas?" Dr. Richards asked.

"I plan to talk to him face to face next week. Our companies are competing against each other in an acquisition purchase so we'll both be in Princeton, New Jersey together. After we make our presentations at Joduku, I plan to let him know about the baby then," I sighed.

"I get the sense that you expect this matter of your having a baby may turn out badly like it did between the two of you ten years ago," Dr. Richards said.

"Well of course that's a concern I have, yes. I just can't bear to re-live that experience again with Nicholas. If Nicholas takes flight again like he did ten years ago, I'll be done with him and I won't look back. And what's even more threatening, I plan to win this acquisition."

"Ten years is a long time Harper," Dr. Richards said. "People grow and change in a decade. Try not to play to your old behaviors, old fears, and old expectations," Dr. Richards continued.

I nodded my head in agreement. I knew she was right. I had already factored in her concerns in my mind over and over.

"You both are grown up now with someone else to consider beyond yourselves," she continued. "Try to expect the best from Nicholas. I know you're afraid of history repeating itself, but remember it doesn't have to be a repeat."

"Yes I know," I said softly, still listening.

"You and Nicholas can create whatever future the two of you want to have. This business of the acquisition is another story. You're treading on difficult waters with this acquisition and competition between the two of you."

"And your point is, Dr. Richards?"

"Try not to let business get in the way of what's true for you, Harper. Business is one thing and a baby is quite another."

"I know. It's complicated. But then again Nicholas and I thrive on complications," I said.

"Just remember to show up and be yourself when you speak with him. "We'll revisit the matter again in your next session," Dr. Richard said.

"Thank you Dr. Richards," I said. "I plan to do exactly that. Show up and be myself," I said, thinking it was just about time for me to go nuclear. To the victor, goes the spoils.

"Why didn't you tell me this sooner, Harper?" Elizabeth asked, picking the anchovies off her salad.

I'd met mother for lunch at the Café Bella not too far from my penthouse in Soho. It was the first Saturday in April. Last week's snow hadn't completely melted, so things were still wet, chilly, and mushy.

Whenever we could, Mother and I tried to maintain a standing lunch date for the first Saturday of every month. This month we picked Café Bella because we both had a desire for pasta. Café Bella was considered a bit off the beaten path for some. I, on the other hand, found it to be a quaint intimate spot that had a great chef who was a real master at regional Italian cuisine. The foodie in me was in the mood for a really hot plate of spaghetti and meatballs now that I was eating for two.

"Goodness Mother, I've been trying to tell you this news for weeks now. You were just so mad about the fact that you thought I had gone the sperm-donor route that I couldn't seem to get you to hear a word I was saying," I sighed, stuffing a huge slice of focaccia in my mouth and reaching for the dipping oil.

"Of course dear, I understand. I was so distraught at the mere thought of your having a baby by some stranger," Elizabeth huffed while shaking her head in disbelief. "It was more than I could comprehend."

"I know," I said, hating how badly our wires had gotten crossed.

"A Carmichael having a stranger's baby was unacceptable coming from my only daughter who's quite capable of making her own baby without the help of a sperm donor," Mother said, motioning to the waiter to pour her another glass of pinot grigio.

"It's not like you were returning my calls," I said, reminding her that she was responsible for putting herself out of the loop. "I knew you just needed some time to calm down so you could hear me," I said.

"Well that's behind us now, dear," she said.

"Well what's not behind me, Mother, is the fact that Nicholas hasn't been returning my calls. I haven't been able to tell him that this is his baby that I'm carrying," I huffed, just as the server placed the huge plate of spaghetti in front of me and winked.

I was glad to know that even though I was starting to lose my waistline I at least wasn't losing my appeal to the male species. Even if Nicky didn't want me, all was not entirely lost if my man-catcher radar still worked.

"Well you surely could have saved me a few gray hairs had you told me you were having Nicholas's baby. This is such wonderful news, dear. I'm going to be one of those *glammothers*." Elizabeth laughed, clapping her hands together. "The senator is going to be so overjoyed. I can't wait to tell him the news."

"Well mother, before you go off telling anyone past Daddy, I'd like to be able to tell Nicholas the news first. He, like you and the rest of the world, seems to believe that this baby is a result of a sperm donor."

"Oh thank God it's not," Mother said, sipping her wine.

"I've been trying to reach out to Nicholas every day to explain, but he's avoiding me like the plague and not taking my calls. I don't expect this to go on too much longer. I plan to see him in Princeton on Monday at the Joduku Presentation. And, I plan to speak with him face to face then," I said, stabbing my fork into another meatball while catching the drips of gravy on my chin with my index finger.

"Oh I just know Nicholas is going to be so overjoyed. This is such good news," mother said, practically unable to contain herself.

"Maybe so, maybe not," I said reaching for my Pellegrino. "I hardly know what Nicholas is capable of under these circumstances. We both know how he behaved ten years ago."

"Honey, that was so long ago. You should get over that. I really don't believe Nicholas has ever stopped loving you," Mother said. "This will work out with him just fine. I'm almost certain."

"I'm not as optimistic as you at this point, Mother."

"Big Daddy, I'm sure, will demand Nicholas make an honest woman out of you," mother squealed. This will be such a wonderful merger."

"Mergers, marriage, acquisitions," I spouted between mouthfuls of meatballs. "Mother, I think you and Big Daddy need to just stay focused on your own companies and not worry about what goes on between me and Nicholas."

"Now, Harper, don't be bull-headed about this."

"These are modern times we live in, Mother. Because I'm pregnant does not mean that Nicholas and I are required to get married. Perhaps I don't want or need a husband. After all I have given a lot of thought and contemplation for some time now to my doing parenthood alone, you know."

"Oh Harper, don't be foolish." Mother waved her hand in the air dismissively. "I'm sure Nicholas wouldn't have it any other way. This is just your hormones talking, dear."

I just shook my head, realizing this was not a battle that I was going to win with Mother. At least not today. She could be quite relentless when she wanted to be. I would cross these bridges when I get to them. No need for me to argue with her about a baby, Nicholas, and marriage now.

"How are you feeling Harper? We need to go shopping. We need to have a mother-daughter outing, just as soon as you finish this acquisition and tell Nicholas the truth about this baby," she said, with absolute glee.

"I'm feeling fine mother. I have an appointment with the ob-gyn again soon. So far things are good. Finishing up this acquisition soon will take some of the stress off me too," I said. "Mostly I'm just hungry all the time."

"As I can see," Mother said, taking another sip of her wine. "And how are the presentation plans and acquisition bid coming dear?" she asked, looking at me with her serious face.

"I expect us to win, Mother. I'm not in the mood to lose this bid this month with all I've been through" I said, with all fierceness. "I plan to leave all the competition in the dust, including my baby's daddy."

"Oh my," Mother said. "Complications, complications. What would we do without them?" she said with a slight chuckle.

Mother was hardly being forthright. Something was definitely up with her. Complications my ass.

CHAPTER FIFTEEN

Nicholas

As I looked out the window of the Milk Money jet silently watching the rainfall, I knew I was watching my own life pass me by just as it was taking a major turn for the worse. Harper Carmichael Montgomery and I would have to face each other today. I would no longer be able to avoid her. We each were scheduled to make our corporate presentations before the Joduku Plastics Board of Directors with the goal of outbidding each other. This had been a long time coming with hours of work. Today would represent the culmination of tons of efforts by both our companies toward an outcome for which one of us would be unhappy.

I was vying on Big Daddy's behalf for Becker Foods. Harper was vying on behalf of Elizabeth for Carmichael Ketchup. I expected everything to come to a head today. At the end of the day, I'd be over and done with this madness. Win or lose, I'd be out of Big Daddy's business and out of her life. After the winning bidder was announced, my plan was to head to the Mediterranean on the *Julianna* for some much-deserved rest and recuperation. Maybe I would find myself settling in Spain for a few months. Perhaps I would rethink my life's purpose. Time off would be good for me to heal my broken heart. It wasn't every day that I had to accept the fact that *my* baby maker was proceeding down the path of motherhood with someone else's baby. The whole idea made me sick and depressed.

As I heard the wheels of the Milk Money jet skid across the

wet runway, I reached over next to me to nudge Lucia out of her sleep. She was nestled in the chair next to me. I looked behind me at Stephen. He was asleep in his chair in the back of the plane. Wheels down hadn't startled or moved Stephen to open an eye yet.

"Wake up Lucia. Time to take this jet's occupants to the gunfight."

"Well we are as ready as we are ever going to get Nicky," Lucia said, rubbing her eyes and tossing back what was left of her Pellegrino with lime.

"Sir, we've arrived at Mercer County Airport," my pilot Cameron said over the intercom.

"Silas should be on the tarmac right now to take us to Princeton," I said, turning toward Lucia who was fingering the text messenger on her phone.

I always insisted that Silas travel ahead of us on short trips. I hated traveling with unknown drivers. I stretched my arms out in front of me and cracked my knuckles as I waited for Cameron to shut the plane's engines down.

I watched as Lucia shuffled in her seat, wiping her lips with her napkin and gathering our things in preparation for our brief drive to Princeton.

"I see we have company," Lucia said as she turned her head to look out the plane's window.

I swiveled my chair around towards Lucia with a look of curiosity. "Yeah who's on the tarmac with us today?"

"I see McKenna Textiles' jet not too far from our gate, and if I didn't know better I think that's Harper's driver Winston nearby. Scott is helping Harper down the steps of Carmichael Ketchup's private jet," Lucia said. "And he's escorting her to her awaiting limousine. Looks like the gang's all here," Lucia grumbled.

"So it appears," I said.

"Game on," Lucia said, grabbing our things and putting on her game face.

"Well, well, well. Desperate times calls for desperate measures. Who would have guessed, *my* baby maker is on the tarmac at the same time with us and that social-climbing, piece-of-shit motherfucker Brooks Fitzgerald McKenna. This is truly my lucky day," I gleamed, wild-eyed.

I fingered my cell phone to call Scott. "You make sure that fucknut doesn't get anywhere near her," I said when Scott answered the phone, and then I hung up.

"Now look, Nicky, we have a presentation to give." Lucia glared at me sternly. This is not the time or the place for you to go all-out ballistic. Pull yourself together and focus," she said, rightfully sensing that my temper was flaring again.

I would have bet last year's portfolio that Lucia knew on some level that this was the beginning of a battle she was going to surely lose, trying to get me to tamp down my emotions about Brooks.

I can't tell you how many times over the past several weeks since Harper came to my home bruised and banged up that I've longed for this moment to deal face to face with Brooks Fitzgerald McKenna. You don't get to rough up and assault *my* baby maker and live to talk about it.

"Not in this life you don't," I said mumbling to myself, and swearing under my breath.

Lucia headed to the back up the plane and tossed a pillow at Stephen who was sleeping in a chair in the back of the plane.

"Wake up Stephen. Showtime. We've arrived and we've got company."

Stephen nodded, jumping to a state of attention faster than I could toss back the rest of my drink. I swear those Navy Seal guys never really sleep. They just give the appearance of sleeping. They always keep one eye open. God, I loved that about Stephen. He was always at the top of his game.

I stepped down the stairs of the jet into the pouring rain that seemed to be getting rapidly more intense. I could see Brooks Fitzgerald McKenna walking down the steps of his jet, stepping onto the tarmac the same time as me. Yep, it was fucking showtime alright. Lucia was right behind me, shaking her head. She looked back over her shoulder to tell Stephen to hurry off the plane to tend to me. Lucia's dark brown hair was blowing wildly in the wet rain. She really was truly beautiful even wet. Not only was Lucia my business partner, but she was also my best friend.

"Let me hand you an umbrella, Nicky," Lucia shouted out to me.

I ignored Lucia's umbrella suggestion. My mind was focused like a laser beam on one thing and one thing only.

Stephen's phone began ringing. I immediately recognized the ringtone as Scott, listening as it played the James Bond 007 theme song. I knew Scott was with Harper. He probably got a glance at me and Brooks hitting the tarmac at just about the same time. Or maybe he was putting Stephen on notice that I had called him and was on the warpath. Nevertheless, I was glad Scott was with Harper. Even though we weren't together, I still felt protective of her.

"Nope I've got this under control, but do keep an eye out in case I need some backup. Nicky's been in a constant funk ever since this plane took off," Stephen said, breathing wind and rain in his lungs just as a gust of wind and hail began to beat down on top of us.

It really didn't matter, because Stephen couldn't stop me now if he wanted to at this point. I had made up my mind that that asswipe Brooks McKenna was mine and only mine. I had been waiting for weeks to confront him. Now I was going to get my chance.

"McKenna, you shithead!" I yelled across the tarmac. "You've got a huge problem, motherfucker. You don't get to toss *my* woman around without having to answer to me for it, you shithead asswipe."

"Fuck off, Nicholas," Brooks hollered back on the rainy tarmac, still looking to be about twenty feet out of my grasp. "I don't recall having to take orders from you. What's wrong, asshole? You trust fund babies having a problem being a real man and making your own babies, motherfucker?"

Now I knew I was going to beat the shit out of him for certain.

"Go fuck yourself, Brooks," I sneered.

"Harper needs a real man to fuck and make a baby, you little bitch. If you ask me, you're not a member of the millionaire's boys club, but rather the millionaire's bitches club, you fucking wussy."

Goddamn. I couldn't believe Brooks had said that shit to me. I was going to put my foot in his ass. I could feel the heat of my own blood rush to my face. My brain seemed to implode and go into overdrive just as my mind started throwing off all of my civility switches, going on fucking kill mode.

"You go fuck yourself, McKenna," I shouted, stepping up my pace tenfold as the rain, wind, and hail began to whip against my cheeks. "Your bitch ass likes to manhandle a woman instead of going toe to toe with a real man! You want to manhandle somebody? I'm right here in front of you now. Try manhandling me, McKenna!"

I stepped my pace up to a run until I got close enough to lunge toward Brooks. I started beating the shit out of him right there on the tarmac. Stephen flew down the stairs of the Milk Money jet just as Brooks's security people were flying equally as fast off the McKenna private jet. This had turned into an all-out war on the rain-slick tarmac between McKenna's team and mine.

McKenna's people stepped toward me just as Stephen opened his coat and flashed his holstered weapon, saying, "I don't think so, assholes."

McKenna's security people began holding each other back behind some imaginary line just as Scott ran up to Stephen's side with another one of his men, joining a line that formed behind Stephen. McKenna's security began dropping their briefcases and flashing their weapons back at us.

I grabbed Brooks by his collar. Before I could speak again, he and I were rolling in the wet puddle-filled ground in our suits and overcoats. I knew I was getting the best of him, when my fist bloodied his nose. I wasn't sure but I guessed I may have taken out one of his teeth.

Brooks and I continued to swing at each other as I tried to land every blow I could to penetrate that motherfucker's face and mouth. Brooks got a couple of good hits into my rib section. I rolled on top of Brooks on the ground, pounding on his chest, yelling at him that he better ever never touch my woman again in this lifetime. I started kicking and stomping him so hard and beating him into the ground such that his security detail broke rank, rushing towards me rapidly. Somebody big jumped on top of my neck and began choking me from behind, putting my head in a chokehold. I began sputtering and spitting thinking I was going to lose consciousness. Stephen and Scott rushed to my aid and began dropping Brook's security detail like flies, starting with the gorilla on top of my back that was trying to choke the life out of me. Even though I was choking and spitting, I refused to let go of Brooks.

I looked out the corner of my eye and could see that Lucia was rushing towards Harper. Harper had jumped out of her limousine. She was screaming my name in the near distance. "Nicky, stop! Nicky, stop!"

I was too far gone, stomping Brooks on the ground, kicking him in his balls, swearing like a madman. I continued stomping on him until Stephen pulled me off of him saying "He's had enough Nicky. I think you made your point."

I could see the flashing amber lights of the airport security in the distance at the end of the tarmac headed our way.

I backed off from Brooks who was mumbling in the mud-filled puddles in the rain on the ground. I gave him one last kick before backing off him. My breathing was hard and labored. I pulled my trench coat back upon me in an effort to start pulling myself together. I was getting too old for this shit.

Harper ran up to me, yelling "Nicholas Miles Becker!" at the top of her lungs.

"Yeah, so you at least know my name. Congratulations, you can graduate to the next round," I shouted back at her. I ran my cold, numbed, blood-scraped fingers through my wet hair. I could feel the beads of rain against my skin mixed with the blood coming out of my nose.

"You . . . you . . . you," and just like that she projectile vomited all over me like she was in *The Exorcist* or something.

I jumped back in shock, yelling "Ugh . . . Good God, woman!" looking down at myself with her puke all over me.

Harper looked startled and wide-eyed. She looked to be in shock. She rolled her eyes at me, sobbing and mumbling something to herself that sounded a whole lot like "green-eyed jackass."

Lucia grabbed Harper's hand, offered her a handkerchief out of her purse, and began pulling Harper toward her own limousine. Harper jumped into it with the aid of her driver Winston. Her assistant, Charlotte, and Scott followed closely behind her.

I pulled my puke-drenched trench coat off me, balled it up and threw it in the air across the tarmac in a fit of anger, watching as it floated to the ground in the downpour. Thunder and lightning flashed all around me.

"Good lord, Kitten!" I yelled indignantly at the top of my lungs.

Silas sped my direction, pulling the car up quickly behind me, the tires screeching loudly. One thing for sure, I felt so much better now.

Even if Harper didn't want me or didn't love me, at the end of the day I wasn't going to have *my* baby maker, *my* woman, disrespected from the likes of *any* man, let alone Brooks

Fitzgerald asswipe McKenna. Not now. Not ever. There were just some lines that weren't going to be crossed. Today was the day that asshole got the message.

I began pulling myself together. Lucia had somehow made her way inside in our car having already dealt with the airport security's staff with Stephen. Thank God this airport was small and I had enough money to quell any fallout that might come from the Chief of Aviation. Perhaps Lucia told them I'd pave that puddle-ridden runway, just to keep this whole scene quiet. I was sure some of my scrapes and bruises came from those damn holes in the ground. Lucia was efficient like that.

"You feel better now?" Lucia barked, handing me a fifty-year-old Macallen neat from of the wet bar. I downed the scotch quickly, moaning loudly while rubbing my hands across the side of my ribs wondering if I had any bones broken.

"I damn well sure do," I hissed, running my fingers through my hair and ripping my bloodied soiled shirt off, thankful that Lucia had already pulled a fresh shirt out of her Tumi bag to hand me. Lucia reached in the car's first aid kit and tended to the cut that was oozing blood right above my left eye, shaking her head at me the whole time. I opened the wet bar. Hastily, I poured myself another shot of scotch to knock the dampness and cold chill off my body now that I was absent a coat.

"Stephen's following behind us," Lucia said looking down at her text messenger. "He wants to know if you're okay."

"Tell him I'm fine," I mumbled. "His training in the ring has served me well, tell him."

"Do you need a doctor? You're holding your rib cage like something might be broken," she barked.

I watched as Lucia's manicured fingers clicked the keys of her iPhone quickly.

"He says to tell you that he can still whip your ass," Lucia said scrunching her nose up tapping the phone's keyboard. "He says I should tape up your rib cage."

"I'll be fine I told you," snapping at her out of my own irritation.

"I've just about had enough of all this alpha male crap today," Lucia said. "We've got to get you a whole set of new clothes Nicky. You look a mess," she said noticing the hole in my pants leg and the mound of dirt all over my shoes. "You guys give a whole new meaning to the word testosterone," Lucia exclaimed.

"Tell Stephen we have to make a quick detour Lucia. We need to stop in Princeton on our way to Joduku Plastics' headquarters. There's a Ralph Lauren store at Palmer Square near the University. We can stop there on the way. I can buy a change of clothes," I said, rubbing my hand across my rib cage trying to forget my agonizing pain.

Lucia tapped on her text messenger for Stephen to head to Ralph Lauren. Then she tapped on the privacy window and barked at Silas to head towards Palmer Square.

"We'll tape your ribs up when we get there," Lucia said calmly.

Beethoven's Fifth Symphony ringtone began playing on my phone. Lucia and I both knew what that sound meant. The monitor screen built into the seat of the car, revealed that Harper was on the phone. Of course, we knew that already. Lucia looked at me with narrowed eyes. I gazed back with a look of disdain.

"Nicky, you need to take the call this time," she said. "Stop putting this off."

"God speaking," I hissed through the speakerphone, throwing back my three fingers of scotch, closing my eyes and running my fingers through my wet hair again. I left the call on speaker so Lucia could tend to the cuts on my knuckles with antibiotic cream from the first aid kit.

"Ouch, Lucia. What's wrong with you, woman?" I scolded her.

"Nicholas, have you completely lost your mind?" Harper said sternly through the phone, ignoring my wails at Lucia.

"Yes, I believe I lost it the day I found out you betrayed me and ran off to have someone else's baby," I snapped through the phone. "Not to mention, you puked on me!" I yelled.

Lucia kicked me. She was rolling her eyes at me, shaking her head reminding me that I needed to dig deep and try to remain civil throughout this conversation. I knew Lucia was right. This is not the way I wanted this conversation to go. Losing my temper with Harper would do nothing but force her to pull her Uzi's out again and tear me a new asshole. I knew Harper inside out so I paused. I waited for the sound of her locking and loading on me.

"Nicky, you need to get a grip on yourself. Beating Brooks to a pulp and damn near getting yourself killed is not the solution to our problems," Harper said.

214

"Problems? Problems?" I said, knowing it would only be a minute before Lucia would take note of the fact that I was starting to repeat myself again. That was her sure-fire sign that my stress level was up. "Since when am I the one with a problem, Harper?" I gritted through clench teeth. "*We* don't have a problem. *You* may have a problem. *Brooks Fitzgerald McKenna* may have a problem, but based on my recollection, *we* don't have a problem."

"Oh yes *we* do too, you simple minded, overgrown, control-freak action junkie extraordinaire," Harper shouted back.

"Last I checked, *you* were the one that flitted off with Reese Cook to some fertility clinic to make a baby with either him or some stranger. I doubt very seriously, that I am the one here with the problem," I hissed, emphasizing my words, my heart breaking in two at the mere thought of Harper having someone else's baby. "If anyone here has a *problem,* it certainly doesn't look like it's me!" I shouted.

I looked out the corner of my eye noticing that Lucia was now pouring herself a drink. If this kept up, both of us were at risk for being far too ripped by the time we get to the Joduku presentation to do Big Daddy's interest any good.

"Well if you weren't so bullheaded not returning my calls, and damn near trying to kill Brooks out there on the tarmac, perhaps you would come to know that my interests are your interests and vice versa," Harper said, sighing. "I've been trying to tell you for weeks, Nicky that—"

"Brooks had that coming," I said, cutting her off. "You know it and I know it. It was bad enough he assaulted you, but then that fuckwad added fuel to the fire by insulting my manhood, Harper. He actually thinks that *I* can't fucking make a baby because my woman has run off to a fertility clinic to make one without me!" I yelled through the phone.

Oops. Now I could hear the rattle of the lock and load sounds going around in that pretty little head of hers. War was near.

"You're a pig-headed asinine fool, closer to the devil incarnate than you are to a God, Nicholas Miles Becker," Harper hissed through the phone. "You know, I called you for something else, but never mind."

Yep that was it. Fucking war has been declared again.

"Never mind? Never mind?" I shouted through the phone. "I don't have a fucking mind, remember, Kitten?" I yelled.

"Like I saaaaaaaid Nicholas, my interests are your interests," Harper dragging out her words with all kinds of pissdom and venom. "When you decide to find your right mind again, the one you've seemed to have lost, you call me. And by the way Nicky . . . try looking up your ass for it!" Harper shouted at the top of her lungs.

"Well, if and when I do decide to find my right mind again," I said in a low stern voice, "I'll be sure to notify lost and found not to let you anywhere near it! You . . . you . . ."

"You what, Nicholas?" Harper said with all fierceness, her voice taking on a tone that I wasn't sure I had heard before.

Lord Jesus, I was treading on some very dangerous ground. All hell was getting ready to break loose and I was at the center of it. I starting fingering under my shirt looking for my St. Michael necklace to kiss. Right about now I knew I could use a guardian angel.

"You . . . you . . . Kitten . . . you," I said fumbling for the right words.

This was so not how I wanted our conversation to go. *I swear on everything I hold dear, my Harper makes me a crazy man.* I was asking for it. She was going to put my balls in a vice now and turn it until I begged for mercy. This woman was a force to be reckoned with and I had just lit the match to a huge stick of dynamite. Whatever truce we had called between us, *détente* was now over.

"Meanwhile, I think I'll snatch Joduku Plastics from you today, just because you're a pig-headed fool, Nicholas Miles Becker. No mercy for you, you . . . you . . . idiot."

Click. She hung up.

"Now, that's the Harper I know." I exhaled, grabbing the presentation brief and taking one last review of the numbers. "Things are starting to feel like we're getting back to normal, now Lucia," I grinned.

Damn. I think that woman really loves me.

"Let's just go buy this fucking little company for Big Daddy and get the hell out of Dodge."

"What am I going to do with you Nicky? In all your brilliance in the financial world, you still can't see what's right under your nose when it comes to women."

Our car had come to a stop in front of the Ralph Lauren store. A fresh set of clothes would help me get a fresh perspective because I sure as hell didn't know what the fuck Lucia was talking about.

"Who am I to understand *that* women and her escapades after all these years," I said, looking out the window. "So what am I missing that's right under my nose? Tell me, Obi Wan," I said, acting facetious. "Exactly what am I missing?"

"Has it ever occurred to you, that maybe *you* could be the father of Harper's baby, Nicholas?"

And just like that my brain came to a screeching halt. I was speechless. Not only at that moment did I feel like the deer in the headlights, I was sure that I looked like the deer in the headlights. Had I just pissed in the wind on any hopes of a future together with Harper? A baby? Mine?

Lucia just shook her head. "Oh Nicky, what are we going to do with you."

I shook my head and burst out laughing. Lucia was playing games with me. This was her way of getting back at me for fighting Brooks on the tarmac and embarrassing her. No way was Harper having *my* baby. This was some kind of joke. And, no way was I going to fucking fall for this crock of crap today.

CHAPTER SIXTEEN

Harper

I entered the Carnegie Center in Princeton. Joduku Plastics was located in this prestigious building. I took the elevator up to the top floor. As the elevator doors opened, I headed into the Joduku Plastics offices asking the receptionist to direct me to the boardroom in anticipation of making my presentation. I couldn't help but think about how crazy this day had gotten with Nicholas and Brooks fighting on the airport tarmac and me vomiting all over Nicholas's Burberry trench coat. I guess it was poetic justice that I had baptized him in that most-deserved manner. I couldn't have planned that picture better myself. I didn't mean to throw up on Nicky, but as luck would have it, I got totally excited amidst the state of events, and nausea followed. Far be it from Nicky to know I had been suffering from morning sickness, afternoon sickness, evening sickness and all things Nicholas sickness. My poor assistant Charlotte was beside herself during our whole ride to Princeton. She was worried about me potentially slipping on the wet pavement and falling on the tarmac while yelling at Nicky to stop. Although the thought never occurred to me in all of the excitement, I was glad to know that Charlotte had my best interests at heart.

Scott jumped into the mayhem to help his twin brother Stephen out. He was hardly winded from the whole ordeal, which spoke well of his skills, as well as his desire to keep me and his brother unharmed. Scott kept checking in with me every five minutes to see if I was okay, almost like an overprotective big brother. He was acting so nervous you would have thought I might be giving birth any minute now the way he was behaving. I suppose he didn't want to have to answer to his brother Stephen or Nicholas if something happened to me.

Lucia had been texting me behind Nicholas's back letting me know that he was a complete basket case at seeing me on the tarmac and speaking with me on the phone. Lucia and I had decided that at the end of the day, girl power needed to prevail and that we had to make Nicholas face certain realities faster than maybe he was ready. Nicholas had to hear the news that he was the father of my baby.

Lucia and I mutually understood the meaning of keeping your friends close and your enemies closer. We both agreed to set aside our professional differences for the time being in favor of the greater good. The greater good being Nicholas Miles Becker accepting reality about our baby and finally having to make a conscious choice about fatherhood and what role he wanted to play. Things were very different than they were ten years ago. This time I was in my third month of pregnancy. My doctors positively believed that I would have no problem with carrying *this* baby to term. If Nicholas was planning to take flight, he was going to have to do it right in front of my face this time and right now. There was going to be no disappearing acts for months and crawling back on his knees like a scared rabbit. If I had anything to do with it, Nicholas was going to fish or cut bait. I just needed to get through this presentation and then I could focus more on having this discussion with him.

"Ms. Montgomery, I'd like to seat you now if I may," the female representative from the Joduku Plastics team said. She was a beautiful petite Japanese woman with creamy skin and jet-black hair that was pulled back in a ponytail. She had bangs that looked to have been cut with exact precision. "Peachtree Plastics will present first. McKenna Textiles will be presenting second. Montgomery Consulting will be third in our list of presenters, and Milk Money will be presenting last," she said, as she moved to escort me to my seat. "O'Donnell Plastics has been eliminated from this final round."

The Joduku Plastics representative escorted me to my seat to what appeared to be the presenter's table. Brooks and Nicholas had already been seated. Lucia was sitting next to Nicholas. Nicholas was looking like a puffed up peacock with a small Band-Aid over his eye and his knuckles were red and scraped. He had changed out of his blood- and puke-covered clothing and looked like Mr. GQ himself, fresh and ready for battle in a dark grey silk sharkskin suit with cuffed pants, a crisp white shirt, a skinny grey silk tie, and gold Bulgari diamond-studded watch. He was wearing two-tone, buttery-soft Napa leather Ferragamo lace-up shoes with no socks. Nobody but Nicholas would do that. Except for his furrowed brow, bumps, and bruises, Nicholas was looking his usual regal self. Lucia looked completely unfazed and pristine as always dressed in a bright red knit dress with a sarong front tied at the waist. Like Nicky, Lucia too was immaculately dressed.

Brooks Fitzgerald McKenna was tapping his thumbs nervously on the long mahogany table that each of us were seated. Brooks had apparently made a change of clothes as well. He had changed from a brown suit previously worn on the tarmac and was now wearing pinstripes. While his clothing did not reveal he had been in a tussle, his physical appearance spoke volumes.

Brooks' left eye was black and he was sucking down pills that his assistant was handing him for apparent pain. Brooks was particularly fidgety, and he kept glaring toward the back of the room at tall well-dressed blonde-haired woman in a grey suit. The woman looked fairly ominous. Her hair was pulled back neatly in a bun so as to make her look nondescript, but I knew better. Underneath the facade was a thoroughbred beauty with brains that would likely slice and dice you up into a thousand little pieces and take everything you owned before you knew you were even bleeding.

I knew her type. She was the type of woman that reeked of means, who wielded a lot of power, and took no prisoners. I had done business with her type, and trust me, she was nothing to sneeze at, frankly.

As a woman that had to deal with nothing but powerful men in the circles I ran in, I had gotten pretty keen on identifying the sharks in stilettos in the room. She stared at Brooks like he was something good to eat, and he looked at her as if he were in a complete state of agitation. I wondered what her association could possibly be with Brooks. I momentarily dismissed my intuitions. Perhaps my pregnancy hormones were just making me neurotic.

Thank god the CEO of Peachtree Plastics and his firm's Senior Strategy Officer were seating in between Brooks and Nicholas. The last thing I needed was the two of them finishing right here what they'd started on the tarmac.

I, on the other hand, had broken out into a sweat just from having to sit at the same table with both Brooks and Nicholas. I was starting to have anxiety at the mere thought of how long the two of them would be able to behave themselves before they would start physically fighting again. Charlotte was seated on my left, ready to assist. One look at Charlotte and I knew that she was completely beside herself over today's events. Brooks looked as if he was trying to get Charlotte's attention, but Charlotte kept her eyes glued to the presentation packet, as she nervously flipped through the materials in front of her.

CEO Nobu spoke first on behalf of Joduku Plastics to give his welcome statement and overview of his company, as well as the company profiles for the remaining bidders.

"Ladies and Gentlemen, each bidder will be allowed to make their presentation on their company objectives prior to the opening of the sealed bids. We welcome you and wish each of you good luck today." He bowed and walked across to our table and shook each bidder's hand.

As I sat waiting patiently for CEO Nobu to finish, I knew from my competitive intelligence team that he wanted twenty million dollars out of the deal from the winning bidder. My team had discovered from the term sheets that the opening bid came in at eight million dollars in the first round of competition. I figured that was Nicholas's bid, because the rumor was the Brooks Fitzgerald McKenna was busy raising capital from somewhere in Asia, so I knew he was no match for me or Nicholas in the first round. My first round bid was ten million dollars. To my surprise, Peachtree Plastics had bid eleven million. I had initially understood them not to be a serious contender.

By the time we each proceeded through to the second round of bidding, Nicholas and I were tied in our bids at fifteen million. Peachtree Plastics was behind us at twelve million and Brooks had taken the lead at sixteen million.

Today, we were each down to our final bids. I looked at my watch waiting patiently listening to the Peachtree Plastics bidders chat tirelessly about the pros of their company acquiring

Joduku Plastics. I knew they were no real match for Montgomery Consulting Group so I remained confident despite the day's chaotic beginning. Brooks Fitzgerald McKenna was beginning to shuffle around in his seat a bit before he stood to make his way to the podium. His voice was horse and haggard as he began his presentation.

"Ladies and gentlemen, I'd like to thank you for this wonderful opportunity today to bid on behalf of my firm McKenna Textiles," Brooks stammered. "I am completely confident that before the day is over McKenna Textiles will emerge the winner and Joduku Plastics and our group will be a team."

His eyes darted at mine giving me a look of guilt and self-pity. I turned my eyes away from his, hoping he had abandoned his desire to try to grab this company on my behalf in an effort to win me and my family over. I had no intentions of having anything else to do with him.

Nicholas glanced my direction with gritted teeth and then turned his head back at Brooks, giving him a death look and then looked back at me, shaking his head. I could see Nicholas rubbing the tops of his knuckles and I knew he was under immense pressure despite the fact he looked incredibly together under the circumstances.

I was starting to feel nauseated again, rubbing my stomach a tad. Forty minutes later, the McKenna Textile presentation was over, and I was next up to bat, but not before CEO Nobu headed back to the podium to introduce me. I walked towards the podium not looking at Nicky or Brooks. The last thing I needed was to make eye contact with either of those two. The one thing that I was sure about was the fact that I was nauseated, I was emotionally spent, I was heartbroken, but I was determined to win this bid.

I walked to the podium which as much ease and confidence I could muster under the circumstances.

"Ladies and Gentlemen, Montgomery Consulting is pleased to have this opportunity to present why we are, in fact, hands down the best choice among all of today's competitors," I stated firmly. I immediately began with my PowerPoint presentation, alternately speaking in English and Japanese. I could see the smiles on the faces of the Joduku Board of Directors faces. I glanced over briefly to look at Nicky, whom I was sure didn't expect me to present in Japanese, although he knew I could speak the language. I suppose through the years that little fact had gotten by him. I couldn't say for sure, but his facial expression had traces of shock and awe, though his body language didn't betray his thoughts as he physically remained completely still.

Brooks looked down right angry and was squirming in his chair uncomfortably. His minions were shuffling to keep up with what was being said, thumbing through their presentation materials quickly as if they had lost their way. The blonde woman in the grey suit had changed her expression looking at Brooks now as with a great deal of disdain. She looked at me with such coldness I was even starting to get annoyed and pissed. The last thing I needed was an unnecessary threat from a woman who wanted Brooks. Brooks was one step away from me getting a restraining order as far as I was concerned.

Lucia had a look of keen interest on her face appearing to fully comprehend everything being said. She must speak Japanese. But of course. Lucia was one never to be underestimated. Whatever the case, my presentation was the shot heard around the world today, catching both Nicholas and Brooks off guard. Thirty minutes later, I wrapped up my presentation leaving a smile on CEO Nobu's face. The room broke out in thunderous applause. CEO Nobu made his way back to the podium bowing twice with his hands together in total excitement.

"Ladies and gentlemen we are now going to take a sixty-minute break before our last presenter," CEO Nobu said, while tapping the microphone to get the room's attention.

Inwardly I was pleased and proud of the presentation advantage I brought to the competition, speaking in their native language giving my firm a welcomed advantage.

"Please join us in the Joduku Plastics dining room for food and refreshments," CEO Nobu stated eagerly.

Yeah. My part was over and the thought of food sounded like a good idea. As I stood to head for the dining room, Nicholas walked briskly towards me.

"Harper, we need to talk," Nicholas said, his green eyes darkening with intensity and the muscles in his jaw flexing.

"No we don't," I said. "What's there to talk about? This just isn't going to work out," I said. "You'll have an easier time accepting this, Nicky, once I win this bid."

"Well you're certainly full of surprises sweetheart. Who knew you would make your presentation in Japanese? That's what I always love about you, Kitten, you're always forcing me to step up my game," he said, nodding his head in amazement.

"I'm not your *kitten*," I pouted, crossing my arms protectively in front of my breasts and pursing my lips.

Nicholas and I glared at each other each like two stubborn fools wondering which of us was going to speak next. I could feel the pull between us, drawing us together. It was hard standing toe to toe with Nicholas because he was just so goddamn sexy. I was sure he knew how he affected me. He was beyond perfect for me. And I was carrying his baby. *Our baby.* I drank in his bad boy looks knowing this conversation was not necessarily going to end on good note. Nicholas was born to win. But, I sensed he knew he was on the ropes, a bit unsure of what to do with me in this moment.

His emerald eyes bore straight into my soul giving me butterflies. Nicholas grabbed my hand, pulling me towards him and my feet followed him without my permission.

"I've missed you, Harper," Nicholas whispered weaving us in an erratic path through the room until we had reached an exit door and were now standing in a corner of the lobby area of the Joduku headquarters.

"*Missed me?* You? You haven't returned my calls in weeks and now you pull that stunt on the tarmac acting like a caveman who cares about my well-being. Save it for someone else, Nicky. I'm not that naive little girl from ten years ago. I'm a grown-ass woman now and I don't need an on-again off-again relationship with you for when you get ready," I grumbled.

"That's not what's going on here, Harper. Why must you compete with me all the time? I thought we agreed in Vermont we weren't going to turn this competition into a personal war between us," Nicholas questioned. "You seem to me to be pulling out all the stops on this one."

"Surely you didn't think I came here to lose, Nicholas? You know that's not who I am."

"And it's not who I am Harper. But we had an agreement. We had a plan, remember? We weren't going to let this be about us."

Before I could answer a familiar voice echoed across the room. One I didn't want to have to deal with today.

"What the fuck was that little stunt, Harper?" Brooks yelled, looking at me harshly, walking towards me double time with a seriously angry look on his face. "You're delivering your presentation in Japanese now? Exactly, who the hell do you think you are?" Brooks growled. "Are you trying to make me look bad?"

I momentarily flinched, caught a bit off guard by the physical intrusion and verbal assault. I'm sure Nicholas noticed me flinch too just from his sheer proximity to me and my look of alarm. I could sense the rise in Nicholas's anger.

Nicholas stepped in front of me, pushing me back behind him in a protective mode.

"Motherfucker, you better step off," Nicholas said to Brooks, furious. "Haven't you had enough, or do you need another reminder to stay away from my woman?" Nicky growled. "I know you don't want more of this, but I'll be happy to oblige you."

"Get out of my way, Becker. This is between me and Harper," Brooks hissed, stepping up in Nicholas's face with threatening eyes.

I watched Nicholas ball his fist. I could feel myself getting more nauseated as my anxiety levels shot up. I needed to get away from both Nicholas and Brooks. Jesus, what was this obsession with Brooks? He never quits. I needed to eat. I felt weak and famished. We were all making a scene. I didn't need this aggravation.

"Harper, is everything okay?" Charlotte squealed at me as she passed through the double doors looking my direction. Lucia was right on Charlotte's heels taking in the war stance between Nicholas and Brooks.

"Nothing that can't be handled," I answered Charlotte from behind Nicholas's grasp, trying to maintain my sense of professionalism and decorum.

Lucia was texting quickly into her phone and within minutes Stephen and Scott were flying around different corners in the lobby, both headed our direction. This was getting way out of control. Nicky gave both Stephen and Scott a menacing look as both appeared to quickly evaluate the situation.

"You know what? I've had enough of this foolishness for one day," I said. "Scott, I'm ready to leave please," I said, stepping out from behind Nicky who was still locked in a stare-down with Brooks. Lucia nodded at Scott so as to affirm that she thought it a good idea that Scott get me out of here. Stephen positioned himself next to Nicky so as to signal to Brooks that he had a double threat to contend with now.

"To hell with listening to any more of these presentations," I said, looking back over my shoulder at Nicky.

"C'mon Nicky," Lucia said, trying to coax Nicky away from Brooks.

"Charlotte, please get my things," I said as I headed towards the other end of the lobby. "We're leaving."

Scott continued to walk behind me keeping a safe distance positioning himself between me and the huddle that included Brooks, Nicky, and Stephen. Lucia was a safe distance between both groups rapidly working her smartphone.

To our surprise, the petite Japanese woman from Joduku walked past me, her eyes focused on Brooks.

"Mr. McKenna, Mr. McKenna, you're needed in the conference room to answer additional questions with the board please," she said with all authority.

"Don't think I'm done with you Becker," Brooks hissed at Nicholas.

Brooks moved to leave Nicky's space.

"I'll be right here waiting for you anytime you think you want some more of this McKenna," Nicholas hissed back at him. "Consider yourself a dead man walking!" Nicky yelled across the lobby.

I could hear Brooks phoning his assistant, telling him to leave the dining hall and to meet him in the conference room. This business between Brooks and Nicholas had gotten way out of control. Stupid me and my friends-with-benefits move. Not to mention, I couldn't put the genie back in the bottle either on this one.

My phone buzzed briefly letting me know I was getting a text message. It was from my mother.

"Withdraw the bid," Elizabeth had texted.

"What the hell?" I said out loud. I stopped in my tracks just as Nicholas was catching up to me, grabbing me and pulling me to his side.

"Just one minute, Harper," he said pausing briefly to answer his phone. "Please sweetheart, give me minute," he said with pleading eyes. "Hold on. This is my brother calling," Nicholas said, looking annoyed.

"You're shitting me," Nicholas said into the phone. "Big Daddy said what?" Nicholas frowned.

I moved to leave Nicholas's space so as to give him some privacy, but he held on to my hand and would not let me go. I needed to get away from him so I could call my mother and find out what in the world was happening that would make her want me to withdraw this bid. Mother had some explaining to do.

Nicholas closed his phone and said "You won't believe this Harper, but Big Daddy wants Milk Money to withdraw its bid," he said looking rather perplexed.

"I don't understand," I said. "My mother just texted me and told me to withdraw our bid, too. What in the hell is going on?"

"I have no idea what's going on." Nicholas ran his fingers through his hair quickly.

"Why in the world would both our parents tell us at the same time to withdraw our bids? This makes no sense, Nicky." My frustration level was increasing rapidly with my hunger. "All of these weeks' worth of work just to withdraw?" I said.

I was starting to get angry. I wanted off this acquisition roller coaster.

"Who in the hell cares. This is our out. Let's take it. Forget about the why and let's run the hell out of here," Nicky said.

"I'm not doing any such thing until I have more answers than this. This could be part of some game *you're* playing, Nicholas Miles Becker," I said, feeling somewhat out of control and a bit skeptical.

"Jesus, Harper I know you don't trust me, but don't you think you're carrying this a bit too far?" he asked, looking himself like he, too, was starting to get annoyed. "If you and I have any chance whatsoever of putting a life together you've got to start trusting me sometime, woman. Let's get out from under the grasp of Big Daddy and Elizabeth and make a break for it. Trust me. I have nothing to do with this bullshit, baby," he argued.

"Yeah, well speaking of babies Nicholas, I've been trying to communicate with you for weeks now to let you know that this baby I'm carrying is *yours*. But *you* haven't had any interest in returning my calls, otherwise you would know this by now," I said, poking my index finger in his chest hard and narrowing my eyes. "Why haven't you returned my calls Nicky?"

I was standing nose to nose with him now. I couldn't decide if I wanted to slap his face or kiss him. My hormones were way out of control and I could feel the tears welling up in the back of my eyes. I was mixed up and confused.

"Baby? *My* baby? *Our* baby?" Nicholas was incredulous.

"Yes Nicky. Your baby. Our baby," I responded.

"I'm having a baby?" Nicholas asked.

"No, *I'm* having a baby, Nicky," I said, with tear-filled eyes.

Nicholas all of a sudden burst out laughing. "This is some joke you and Lucia have cooked up, right? I already heard you went to the fertility clinic and got yourself knocked up by some unknown donor. You're trying to get back at me for not returning your calls for weeks. This is punishment right? C'mon, Kitten. I knew you would do anything to win this bid, but I had no idea you would stoop to this level," he laughed. "You're trying to wind me up before I make my presentation. This is good, Kitten. I'm impressed," Nicholas smirked. "You're trying to throw me off my game. This is your best performance yet."

In that moment, Nicky helped me to decide.

I slapped him hard across his face.

"Idiot," I hissed. "You're impossible."

Nicky glared back at me, a bit unsure of himself.

Just then the Joduku female representative approached. "Mr. Becker, you're up next to present. The board is waiting for you."

I rolled my eyes at Nicky, too famished to think any further. My head hurt. I needed to take care of myself before I collapsed. I didn't need all of this craziness. I stomped off in the opposite direction as far as I could to get away from Nicholas.

As far as I was concerned my job was done. I made it through the presentation. I made it through telling Nicky he was the father of my baby. And now I was going to make my way right out of this entire scene before the floodgate of tears that were building opened up on me.

I turned quickly, exciting the Joduku office doors, not looking back. But not before calling CEO Nobu, telling him Montgomery Consulting was withdrawing its bid. Fuck it.

CHAPTER SEVENTEEN

Nicholas

It was hard having to watch *my* baby maker make a quick dash out of the Joduku offices without me, but I needed to get Milk Money out of this bidding war first. Business was business and there were just too many millions at stake. I figured I could set things right with Harper and make peace later.

"Ladies, Gentlemen, and Board of Directors, this is going to come as a surprise to you, but at this time, Milk Money is officially withdrawing its bid. We thank you again for your careful consideration of our firm. However, extenuating circumstances requires us to forego our planned presentation," I stated calmly.

I heard a few voices in the room gasp. I quickly left the podium. I know I must have looked like a fool. I certainly felt like one. But I didn't care. As far as I was concerned, this was a stupid idea from the beginning that Big Daddy had drummed up.

CEO Nobu had his phone up to his ear and his face was in shock. I couldn't tell if it was the phone call he was on, or Milk Money's troubling news. What a fiasco. Brooks had a shit grin on his face, and Harper had conveniently left the building. Lucia was moving expeditiously, quickly gathering our things. I had mixed emotions. I was happy not to have to compete with Harper. I was pissed that this meant that Brooks was likely going to win the bid. Big Daddy seriously had shit up with him. Never in a million years had I ever been put in this position. Note to self. This is exactly why you stay the hell out of any matters having to do with Becker Foods. Next time, just say no.

"Tell Cameron to fuel the jet and let's get the hell out of Dodge," I said to Lucia.

"Fine with me," Lucia responded. "Stephen's waiting outside with Silas in the car to take us to the airport. It's raining cats and dogs, so we need to get out of town."

"Good. I've had about all I can handle for one day," I said wiping the back of my hand across my brow. "About Harper. How in the hell was I supposed to know that she was serious that the baby was mine, Lucia?" I asked shaking my head, walking and talking at the same time, exiting the Joduku headquarters.

"Because I told you," Lucia said shaking her head in disgust. "I gave you a heads-up Nicky."

"How is this even possible?"

"Ah . . . maybe you need to think back to you little soiree in Vermont, perhaps?"

"Oh . . . yes . . . that . . ." I grinned at the memory of our trip to Vermont. "The Mile High Club, among other things." I smiled as we entered the limo. "Bloody Mary mornings." I opened the privacy window long enough to say, "Get us the hell out of here Silas."

"Yeah well now you're in the Mile High Doo-Doo Club, Nicky," Lucia said. "Your skull is so thick. I tried to warn you, but you and Harper . . . it's this thing the two of you do," Lucia said with exasperation. "You two a have a thin line between love and evisceration that exceeds all bounds," she said. "I'm scared to think what your kids will be like," Lucia cringed.

"Well if it's a boy, he'll be beautiful like his mother and a shark like me, and if it's a girl, she'll be a beautiful piranha like her mother." I laughed loudly.

Lucia rolled her eyes at me, shook her head and went back to fumbling with her phone.

Thirty minutes later we were back at Mercer Airport ready to board the Milk Money jet. Silas let us out. He was traveling by car back to Manhattan.

"Have a safe trip Silas," I said.

"Thank you. See you in the Apple, sir."

The rainstorm was much fiercer now. It felt like we were in the middle of a monsoon. Lucia was completely engrossed in whatever she had going on that damn smartphone, not listening to much of anything that I was saying. It was always hard to make small talk with Lucia. If you're weren't talking multimillion-dollar deals, her attention span was short. I was used to it, but it still irked me from time to time when I needed somebody to talk to, wanting to forget about business. I might as well have been talking to a brick wall. I had to give Lucia credit for trying, however. Every twenty words she looked up at me, nodding and feigning that she was giving me her undivided attention. We both knew better. If I really wanted her ear, all I had to do was to start repeating myself. That was her signal I was under stress and that she needed to engage. Yes, Lucia was indeed the Yin to my Yang.

Stephen was back on board, annoyed for some reason about the fact that Scott wasn't answering his calls.

"This is your Captain," Cameron said. "Prepare for takeoff. We have about a three-minute window to get this baby up and out of here, otherwise we're grounded for the night. Most of the airports on the eastern seaboard are rapidly closing due to the worsening thunderstorms. "We're going to rock and roll, sir."

"That suits me just fine," I said to Lucia, who was fastening her seatbelt and looking concerned.

"Not to worry, Lucia. Cameron is an excellent pilot," I said, hoping to quell her concerns.

"No, it's not that," Lucia said. "It appears that between Peachtree Plastics and McKenna Textiles, the bid's going to go to Brooks after all. I know how you hate to lose, Nicky."

"Well we didn't really lose. We withdrew. And, as soon as we get back to Manhattan I'll be able to talk to Big Daddy and find out what the hell is going on with him, and Elizabeth too for that matter. At least Harper and I didn't have to shed more blood over which one of us was going to end up the loser," I said.

"Yeah I guess that at least was a blessing in disguise. I don't think I could have stood watching the two of you fight over companies and artwork for the rest of the year. Or will I?" Lucia said, not looking too confident that Harper and I were through lobbing grenades at each other.

"Nope, she's carrying my child," I said with all assurance. "Baby's mine. She's mine. To everything there is a season, and a time and purpose under the heavens," I said.

"I sure hope so, Nicky."

"Harper and I both know this is our time. She and I are going to learn how to make love, not war," I said. "It will be a new experience for us both. She just doesn't know it yet."

"You know, Nicky, you have a good heart underneath all that ... stuff," Lucia said waving her hand in the air.

"Thank you Lucia. I love you, too."

She blushed. I knew she knew I meant what I said. She was the best friend and business partner anyone could ever have. Devoted. I was getting sentimental now and she was getting embarrassed.

"Thank God this is a short flight. The turbulence is awful tonight," Lucia said after a long period of silence between us.

I raised my head from the *Wall Street Journal*. I wondered what was really bothering Lucia. She had good instincts. I relied on them often. I knew her well. My instincts were good, too and one thing that I knew, Lucia was a bit off balance.

I glanced back at Stephen. He was still looking anxious. I supposed it was due to the fact that he still hadn't connected with Scott. I suppose it had more to do with the fact that we were up in the air and his Wi-Fi was off. We all needed to get off this plane, out of this storm, and back on ground, solidly on our home turf.

My team had morphed into technology junkies, unable to function for a few hours when they were forced to disconnect. It was like watching them go through withdrawal. Me, I relished the technology break, brief as it was. It gave me time to think about how I was going to get my woman back. I was going to have a baby with Harper. I needed to make plans to create some differences in my life. I was getting a second chance. Things would be different for us than they were ten years ago. I was elated. I was looking forward to the change that was upon me. Big Daddy was going to be so happy. Three was going to get to be an uncle. I was going to be a daddy. A daddy . . . I rolled that word around in my mind. Just think, a little person looking up to me and saying "Daddy." It was like a prayer to my ears.

I would marry Harper before the baby was born and we would finally get our happily-ever-after. Harper and the baby would want for nothing. I would lay the world at her feet. I needed remember to call Mico when I landed. I want him to be my best man. It had been awhile since I had caught up with him and Riley.

What was I saying? I know I hadn't asked Harper to marry me yet, but I was not going to take a no for an answer. She was going to be my wife once and for all. Nobody was going to deny me my baby. I was going to have a presence in my son or daughter's life. Surely Harper wouldn't deny me. Surely she wouldn't deny me the very air I need to breathe. I loved that woman more than anything. It was impossible for me to live without her. Not getting a plastics company was one thing, but Kitten not being my wife was something entirely different. This was non-negotiable. And as icing on the cake, Big Daddy and Elizabeth would get a grandchild. Life's puzzle pieces were starting to fall into place.

I decided to grab a few winks.

I awakened to the realization that our plane had touched down in what appeared to be a major tropical storm. Thank God we hadn't gotten stranded in New Jersey. Fortunately we each had our Wi-Fi back. Now I could call Big Daddy and Three. Not that it mattered because I noticed my phone was buzzing out of control. I had messages from Big Daddy, Three, and Scott. *Scott? Messages from Scott, this can't be good.*

Stephen was on his feet, pacing up and down the plane's aisle, yelling at the steward to get the plane's "fucking door" open.

Lucia's face looked pained.

"What's wrong?" I said turning to Stephen.

"Harper's plane left New Jersey before us, but she and Scott weren't on it. Harper and Scott are unaccounted for, Nicky," Stephen said.

"Exactly what the fuck are you saying?" I shouted.

No way, *my* baby maker was—what did he say?—"unaccounted for."

"They are missing, Nicholas," Stephen said.

"Scott?" Lucia asked.

"Missing? As in their plane is missing?" I asked, seriously confused.

"No their plane is not missing," Stephen said. "*They* are missing. Harper and Scott are missing," Stephen said again, just as he punched his fist into the side of the plane's wall. "I fucking told Scott I didn't trust that Brooks fella."

"Brooks? What's Brooks got to do with this?" I asked.

"Their plane has landed at LaGuardia, but they're aren't on it," Stephen said. "I got a text on my phone from Charlotte. She was worried. Apparently Charlotte boarded the plane early ahead of them to do some work while Scott planned to take Harper to grab something to eat before boarding the plane. Harper was feeling hungry after the commotion at the presentation and was starting to feel ill. Their flight crew waited as long as they could. They had to leave without them to beat the storm. Harper and Scott never made it to the plane."

"Never made it to the plane," I mumbled out loud.

Lucia momentarily put her hand over her mouth and gasped.

"Charlotte said Harper told her to go on without them. Charlotte thought that perhaps Harper and Scott would catch a later commercial flight," Stephen went on. "When the Carmichael Ketchup plane landed in New York with Charlotte and the flight crew, Charlotte powered up her phone and noticed she had received a puzzling text message from Brooks."

"What did the message say Stephen?"

"The message said 'Today is the day that everything changes'. I have no idea what it means, Nicky, but I sure as hell don't like it," Stephen said. "Nicky, what do your messages from Scott say?"

"It says 'don't worry, Nicky. I mean to catch them'," I said, thumbing rapidly through my messages to see if I missed any more messages. "Them who?" I said out loud.

"We need to get back to Becker Towers as quick as possible," Stephen said. "It's time to marshal our resources. The quicker we move, the better." One thing for sure, Stephen was an aficionado in the art of war. His twin brother Scott was equally as lethal. If Brooks or someone else was involved in Harper's disappearance, it could only mean one thing.

I needed to do to find *my* baby maker and my baby as soon as possible or else somebody was going to die.

CHAPTER EIGHTEEN

Harper

"God that was a painful phone call. CEO Nobu was definitely not happy about my withdrawing our bid," I said, shaking my head at Charlotte who was ending her phone call.

"Harper, the flight crew just called. We need to get back to the plane as soon as possible. There's a major tropical storm headed our way. I was hoping to make my sister's bridal shower tomorrow," Charlotte said.

"No problem Charlotte," I mumbled. "Why don't you head back to the plane and call your sister. I haven't forgotten you've got maid of honor duties. I just need to get Scott to take me to get something to eat first."

"Are you sure?" Charlotte asked with a look of concern.

"Yes. You can work on the plane until we get there. We're done here. I'm going to run to the ladies room first. Tell Scott to have Winston bring the car around. I need to eat something before we board."

I was anxiously looking for the restroom doors inside the Carnegie Center. I was a bundle of nerves. God, I needed to relieve myself in more ways than one. My bladder felt like it was going to burst, I'd been holding back a flood of tears, and I was starving. My mood was rapidly turning sour.

I was long overdue for calling Mackenzie. She must be worried about me. I swore I'd keep her abreast of everything going on today. My mind was operating on several different tracks at once. I needed to call my mother and find out why in the hell this bid was canceled. This was turning out to be a really shitty day. As a matter of fact, the day was starting to get downright insane.

I watched Scott as he was finishing up his conversation with Charlotte and approached me.

"Scott, I need to go to the ladies room before we leave and then I'd like to get something to eat."

"No problem Ms. Montgomery. Winston will bring the car around for us. I'll just stand outside here in the lobby and wait for you," he said looking stoic.

"I'm not a baby Scott. I'm completely capable of going to the ladies room on my own. You can go ahead and wait for me with Winston," I said.

"I prefer not Ms. Montgomery. Mr. McKenna is still in the building and things have been tense today. I wouldn't want you to have to deal with him getting you upset, your being pregnant and all," he said with his eyebrows raised.

Damn, nothing is ever sacred around here. I just bet a pair of my favorite Louboutins that Nicky has already told Stephen, who has already told Scott that I'm pregnant. They are just starting to get to be a regular good ole boy's club.

"I doubt that Mr. McKenna has time to be concerned with me right about now. He has bigger fish to fry. Besides I'll be fine. Perhaps you should use the opportunity to relieve your own self before we hit the road. I'll be fine."

Scott glared at me hard. I could tell he wasn't too comfortable with the idea of leaving my side. I hope Nicky didn't think he was going to have my own security detail smother me like this.

"You work for me Scott. Go. I insist."

Scott nodded but headed for the men's room reluctantly. I eyeballed the ladies room, reflecting on the day's events. A fight on the tarmac, a bid withdrawal, and my baby's daddy thought I was pulling some joke on him. I could just slap him all over again just for the hell of it. I knew in my heart of hearts that I deeply loved Nicholas but it didn't negate the fact that he made me crazy. I was reminded of Beyoncé's song, "Crazy in Love." That song took on a whole new meaning today. Yep. That was me. Crazy in Love. I reached down on my phone and downloaded the Dangerously In Love CD. I immediately changed my ringtone for Nicholas. Yep. Crazy In Love. Every time Nicholas rings my phone, this little ringtone would make me think twice about whether or not I wanted to answer my phone and do crazy. I giggled briefly to myself.

As I exited the bathroom stall I looked in the mirror at myself. My body was changing. I turned to the side and peered at my stomach. I was losing my waistline. Nicholas's child was growing inside of me. I rubbed my belly.

Yeah, honey. You're getting fat. This is what happens when you do the panty drop at thirty thousand feet. Nicholas has invaded the gene pool and you've got the big belly to prove it.

I rolled my eyes up in my head, looking in the mirror and shaking off the voice in my head. I needed to talk to Reese. Mackenzie and Reese were going to have to help me get through this pregnancy. I tapped my phone changing my ringback tone to Beyoncé's "Me, Myself and I." Nicholas would hear that whenever he dialed my number. There was more than one way for me to deliver my message to him. If Nicholas didn't want to commit to me and this baby, we'd make it together alone. I thumbed through the rest of the album. Yes, I was "Crazy in Love." This music was very fitting for this moment in time.

As I moved through the Carnegie Center main building toward the lobby doors, I tapped the keypad on my phone hoping to be able to reach my mother. I hung up, briefly deciding that I needed to call Mackenzie first. I ended up in her voicemail instead.

"Hey Mackenzie, this is Harper. I've probably caught you right when you're picking up Gill Jr. at basketball practice. Give me a call, babe. I desperately need to talk to you."

My phone rang. It was Charlotte calling from the plane.

"Yes Charlotte I'm aware there is a major storm coming but I need to eat. Scott and I will be there to catch the plane as soon as we can. If we're too late, go on ahead of us. We'll charter a plane to get back if need be."

I paused and looked around to see if I saw Scott anywhere. I supposed he had already headed outside to join Winston.

I dialed Reese's number next. Reese's voicemail came on just as I was exiting the Carnegie Center lobby doors. I saw my SUV pull up so I hung up without leaving a message thinking I'd call Reese again when I got settled. I was thankful that Winston and Scott were waiting. Not wanting to wait for Scott to come open the door for me in the heavy rain, I bolted towards the door and jumped in with both feet. I was famished now. Food couldn't come quick enough. "Let's get some food, Scott," I said not looking up. The SUV took off at full speed just as I got in and fastened my seat belt.

"I can't say that food is on our list of priorities today, Ms. Montgomery," a strange female voice said just as the SUV doors automatically locked. I turned with a look of shock, wondering whose SUV had I gotten into. I swung around in my seat, desperately looking for Scott.

"We're going to take a short ride," she said, my eyes now peering at the blonde woman in the grey suit that I had seen earlier.

"Who the hell are you and what are you doing in my car? Where is Scott?"

"Excuse me. I believe you're in my car, Ms. Montgomery. I'm sure you're a bit confused since our vehicles are similar. There's no reason for you to be alarmed. Your driver is momentarily tied up right now. Your security chief is likely to be in quite a bit of a stir right now." The ice queen laughed. "I expect they'll be along shortly," she said smugly.

She poured herself some amber liquid in a glass.

"May I offer you something?" she said as she waved her hand across her car's minibar.

"No. And I don't appreciate your detaining me. What exactly do you want?" I asked.

"Well let me take a moment to enlighten you Ms. Montgomery. My name is Tatiana. I represent the interests of certain individuals whose interests shall we say . . . conflict with yours."

"Stop this car right now and let me out of here!" I shouted.

"I would try to calm down now, Ms. Montgomery, if I were you. You see, your dear friend Mr. Fitzgerald owes our organization quite a bit of money, and well, you seem to be today's answer to our organization's little problem."

"Listen lady, you may have a problem with Brooks, but I don't have a problem or any interests with either or you."

"Well we shall see now, won't we," she said.

"You don't actually think you're going to get away with kidnapping me, do you?" I hissed at the bitch.

"Kidnapping. What a strong word Ms. Montgomery. As I recall, you jumped into this vehicle on your own accord. Your timing couldn't have been better. You quite saved us from having to employ coercion tactics." Her laugh was positively evil.

"If you don't stop this car and let me out, you're going to have real problems beyond whatever your issue is with Brooks," I snapped.

"I like to think of this moment as a problem resolution session," she sneered. "Mr. McKenna has a problem and you are the resolution."

"Right now you're keeping me against my will, bitch. Let me out of this car right this minute."

"Yes I realize I am detaining you, but keep you? Nooooooo . . . I doubt that will be necessary in the long run. Think of this moment as our accelerating the pace at which we plan to recoup our money."

"Recoup your money? That's none of my business. That's between you and Brooks."

"Well it appears Mr. McKenna's plans to marry you in order to merge his business interests with yours have backfired. I understand your marriage was intended to be the means by which he planned to repay his little debt to us," she said, sipping her drink slowly.

"Marry Brooks?" I laughed hysterically. "You must be a psychotic bitch. I wouldn't marry Brooks Fitzgerald McKenna on a good day. Actually, I'm not even the marrying kind, or hasn't he enlightened you? And, if I were, he's the last man on earth that I would marry."

I moved to open the locks on the doors, jiggling both sides of the SUV doors to no avail. The ice queen looked at me quizzically. Brooks must have really convinced this cast of characters into believing that I would marry him. Certainly they must be amateurs. If Nicholas gets wind of this he is surely going to kill Brooks and this whole band of rogues.

"I don't think that will be necessary. A waste of your time actually," the ice queen said. "You can't get out until I say so."

"What exactly do you want with me now, Tatiana, or whoever the hell you are?"

"Well it appears that Mr. McKenna's indebtedness to us remains unresolved. Mr. McKenna convinced members of our organization that there was to be a marital merger with you and him, thereby ending his financial woes. It has come to our attention that he has failed to achieve those plans. I'm here to collect," she said.

"Collect? Surely you don't think I have any intention of paying you people, Brooks, or anyone else for that matter any money do you?"

I couldn't believe this was happening. I looked past her shoulder to see if I could see Scott and Winston following our SUV. It was hard to see anything through the tinted windows. The big burly man in the front passenger seat looking like Bluto was blocking my view of where we might be headed. He had unusually broad shoulders and looked strong as an ox. His bald head looked super shiny reflecting off the thick black mustache connected to thick-as-a-forest black goatee. I was sure he readily could crush a person on a whim. I couldn't see his eyes through the black-rimmed aviator sunglasses he had on his face. I was starting to get panicky. How in the hell could I have gotten mixed up with anything to do with Brooks Fitzgerald McKenna's mess? My stomach began to rumble. I was incredibly nauseated and pissed.

"You must not know who I am, bitch. You're going to pay for this move for sure," I scowled.

"Oh don't think for one minute we aren't aware of who you are Ms. Montgomery. Or, better yet, your worth to us. We are well aware that you're the daughter of a U.S. senator, heir to the Carmichael Ketchup empire, and lover to that very wealthy fine specimen of a man, Nicholas Becker," she said, licking her lips.

I wanted to smack this bitch's face for even taunting me about Nicholas.

Don't go all Ike and Tina on this bitch, Harper. You've got a baby to think about here.

I wasn't done with her yet, but I did have the baby to think about. Otherwise I'd take matters into my own hands right now and leap across the seat and choke her to death. I was hormonal too. Oh yeah. The visions of my hands around her neck were already starting to swirl around in my head.

Jesus, where was Scott? I hated that I couldn't see out these windows. All I could see was the back of the driver's head. Not as big as Bluto there, but he looked like the kind of man you didn't want to mess with, frankly. I felt physically close to really throwing up on the ice queen.

"And just how much to you expect to extort my family for with this little trick of yours and Brooks McKenna?" I questioned her.

"Twenty-two million," she said coolly.

"Twenty-two million, huh. Perhaps you've forgotten you're kidnapping a senator's daughter, you bitch. The FBI will be on top of you before you can count to three."

These clowns hadn't done their homework. Twenty-two million was chump change to both my family and Nicky's. Nicky was known to blow that kind of money in a few hours in Vegas at the Baccarat tables. Hell, my mother's credit line on her American Express Black Card was higher than that. What was wrong with these fools?

"Apparently you don't know how things work here in the United States. You'll never get away with this. You'll be hunted down with nowhere to hide," I said.

"I'll be well on my way and out of the country by then Ms. Montgomery. I'll lay odds ten to one that Mr. Becker will see to it that this matter goes away long before the FBI has time to ever get involved. I'm counting on his distaste for a media circus in this matter to get things resolved very quickly. How do you say it here in America? Pay to play?"

At the same moment she finished her sentence, the car stopped in front of a large red brick manor that looked to be located in a secluded area. We passed through some gates and turned up a very long driveway. One couldn't see the manor from the road. The place looked old, regal, and appeared to be well kept. We hadn't driven long enough to leave town so I knew we were still somewhere in the Princeton area. It was raining so much heavier now and the temperature felt like it was dropping. I was starting to get chilled. If I could just get away from these clowns and back to my plane.

As the car stopped, the large burly Bluto-looking man opened my door. He grabbed my arm hard, dragging me out of the vehicle. I struggled but it was no use. He was way too big.

"Take her purse and her phone, Ivann," the ice queen said as she headed up the walkway, opening the double doors to the dwelling ahead of me.

It was starting to turn to dusk now. We were a long way away from the locked gate at the entrance of the driveway. I looked back over my shoulder to see if I could see another vehicle or anything that resembled Scott and my security detail. There was a man-made pond to the right of the driveway with a wooded area with lots of foliage on the other side of the pond. The rain beat down on me a lot harder and the wind had picked up dramatically.

As we entered the manor, the foyer led to a very large dining room to the left and a sitting area to the right that had a large fireplace that was lit. The ice queen and Ivann led me into a sitting area.

"Leave us," the ice queen said to Ivann.

Ivann reminded me of Curly of the Three Stooges. He looked big and stupid. A yes-man with no brains. All muscle and brawn. He must have read my thoughts too. He left the front room rolling his eyes at me just as another older woman in a maid's uniform entered with a tray of food. Breads, cheeses, fresh fruit, and hot chicken noodle soup. A pot of hot water and tea bags with lemon were on the tray.

"You must be hungry. Eat," Tatiana said.

My emotions were swinging now between anger and fear. I was hungry, so I didn't turn down the food. I could feel the tears welling up in the back of my eyes. I took a seat and began to eat quietly. I needed to think about how the hell I was going to get out of this situation.

The ice queen walked towards the fireplace and stood with her back to me, her hands held out in front of her as if to warm them. I used the opportunity to observe my surroundings and to figure out if there were any windows and exits out of this old mansion.

"No need to try to take flight, Ms. Montgomery. That would be a waste of time. You're well guarded here. Besides, there's a major tropical storm coming."

Jesus is everybody psychic around here? I could have sworn she knew just what I was thinking.

"You're not going to keep me here against my will," I said, feeling a bit more fortified now that I had food in my belly.

The ominous-looking driver arrived.

"Is there anything else you need Tatiana?"

"Not now. Go back to your post," she mumbled. "I know it doesn't feel like it, but I want to make your stay here as comfortable as possible here. I've asked the guards to remain out of sight as much as possible. Trust me. I expect your visit with us to be brief. But don't make the mistake of thinking you're not being watched," she said.

"You're keeping me against my will and you have the nerve to suggest that I be comfortable? I'm not comfortable. I will never be comfortable being held against my will. And the day will come you will regret that you ever made me feel uncomfortable. For the record, you should consider me beyond uncomfortable," I hissed.

The ice queen handed me a cell phone.

"Make the call," she said, as if I knew specifically who she wanted me to call. I mulled the matter over in my mind for a moment.

"Now," she huffed.

I dialed the number.

"Nicky, help me."

CHAPTER NINETEEN

Nicholas

Lucia, Stephen, and I made it back to Becker Towers in record time, having arranged for one of the Milk Money helicopters to shuttle us from the airport to the rooftop of my building. We were the last ones to get clearance before all flights were canceled. The helipad on top of my building was one of the many conveniences that I loved about Becker Towers. In my business, time was money. The helipad saved me a ton of travel time. Once we got back to the Towers we connected with all of our GPS locater systems and began a search for Scott and Harper.

Lucia immediately went into overdrive, scanning all of our computers and emails for any information she could find that might lead us to their whereabouts. She had even hacked into Harper's Facebook account to see if there was any strange activity.

"Who knew you had hacker skills Lucia," I said with a raised eyebrow.

"When it comes to my knowing the depth of my skills, Nicholas, less is more," she said without raising her eyes from the computer screens, her fingers tapping at warp speed.

Lucia never ceased to amaze me.

I dialed Harpers phone for the umpteenth time. She had a new ringback tone on her phone that was playing Beyoncé's "Me, Myself, and I." I knew that song because Harper loved R&B and Hip Hop. Mico always kept me up-to-date on what radio stations played the best R&B and Hip Hop sounds. I made myself playlists of music I knew she would like, so that whenever we were together, I would play music she liked. She in turn would tolerate my love for Chick Corea doing the classics and violinist Lucia Micarelli, whose song "Oblivion" I use to play when I wanted to make love to her. I called her phone again. Still no answer.

I shook my head and paced the floor wondering if Harper was trying to send me a message that she was going to go it alone with having our baby and not even give me a chance to weigh in on the fact that I wanted to have a life with them. No way Harper would do such a thing as sending me a message via her ring tone, other than to annoy me. I suppose she wanted me to hear how she was feeling, but I knew that she knew in her heart of hearts that I loved her. I believed she loved me, too. Talking with her at the Joduku Presentation wasn't the time or place to have such a serious discussion. I figured that ringtone was her way of letting me know she was pissed with me.

Just as that thought raced across my mind, Lucia looked up at me saying, "Nicky I have something you need to see."

I moved towards Lucia's direction and peeked over her shoulder. Someone had sent me an email with photos of Harper and me dancing together at Mico and Riley's wedding, images of me carrying Harper in my arms at the Lincoln Center in the middle of the bomb scare, and photos of the Harper and me arguing in the lobby at the Joduku Headquarters. There was another photo of Harper exiting the Carnegie Center where our presentations were held. She was getting into the wrong SUV. That particular image had a text overlay written across the bottom in Russian. The words said Она будет нужна ваша помощь "What the hell?" I said out loud.

"What the fuck does that mean?" I asked out loud. "What the he—"

"Nicky please," Lucia squawked. "Give me a second," she said, still tapping her fingers at warp speed.

I waited patiently as best I could, noticing that Lucia was entering the words from the photo in a Google Russian-to-English translator.

Lucia swiveled her chair around slightly to face me.

"It says, *she will need your help.*"

All of a sudden it was clear to me that Harper hadn't just run off with my baby. Someone was up to no good and had taken *my* baby maker and my baby.

"Nicky," Stephen snapped at me, now entering the great room hurriedly. "I have some new information!" he shouted.

"Well that's a start," I replied worriedly. "It's been five hours since I spoke with Harper."

I knew time was of the essence in these matters. It didn't take long for Stephen to connect with his twin brother Scott but the news wasn't good. The little information we had was disjointed in that there was a major tropical storm that was hitting the east coast that was compromising all the cell phone coverage. Stephen had managed to get bits and pieces of information from Scott in between a host of dropped cellphone calls. The two of them had resorted to texting instead. Fortunately, Scott had loaded a GPS app on Harper's phone and had planted GPS devices in her belongings shortly after Brooks's assault on her at the office. Tracking devices were on all her vehicles as well. Stephen had a GPS system locator on Scott. Scott had GPS locators on Harper and Stephen. Everybody was looking at everybody. I momentarily wondered who was looking at me.

Ring . . . Ring . . .

I jumped. Startled.

It was the Becker Towers concierge. Lucia answered on the speakerphone so we could all hear.

"Mr. Becker, Senator Montgomery and his security are here. Shall I let them through?"

"Yes, let them through."

Stephen and I looked at each other, knowing what was coming next, just as Lucia went to the door to let them through. It was going to be hard for me to control events. If the senator knew, this thing was going to get out of control fast and that was the last thing I needed to have happen. I didn't want a bunch of government muckety-mucks to take over this matter because the media attention would be unprecedented.

Senator Montgomery walked in with Malcom Cole at his side and two agents posted outside my penthouse doors. Scott had placed two of his own guards outside the door long before the senator arrived so now we had two of the senator's guards watching two of our guards.

"Senator, welcome," I said, moving to him and shaking his hand. "Hello Malcom," I said.

"Becker," Malcom grunted.

Malcom and I gave each other the once over but neither of us said anything more than that to the other. Malcom shifted his weight from one foot to another as he took in Lucia's gaze as she extended her hand. He was affected. It wasn't a surprise to me. Lucia was an extremely beautiful woman and she had that effect on men. I heard Stephen make a growling sound deep in his throat. I wondered if he had spoken with MacKenzie regarding any word from Harper. I rarely heard Stephen growl and was wondering why was his protective nature showing itself over Lucia.

"Nicholas my boy," the senator said. "It appears somebody's got their hands on my baby girl."

The senator handed me an envelope with the same photos in it that Lucia had pulled off my email.

"The note inside is written in Russian. I'm instructed to come to your home immediately and to wait for further instructions. If anyone lays a single hand on my baby girl, I swear I'm going to bring the weight of the entire country down on them," he said in the iciest tone I had ever heard him speak.

Now I better understood how the senator had gotten so far politically. The politicos were on his heels for him to run for president and it was clear why. Like them, I saw his ruthless side with my own eyes. It was a quality that most politicians possessed and why I despised politics.

"Your baby girl and your grandchild. Harper is pregnant with my child."

Malcom looked at me as if he had seen a ghost. His expression towards me changed immediately as he looked at me with narrowed eyes. *Oh, if looks could kill.* I didn't want to make myself think any further about why Malcom was reacting that way or I was going to lose it entirely and tear him a new asshole. I pushed the thoughts that were being driven by my intuitions down.

"So I hear," the senator responded. "Elizabeth has read me in fully. She wasn't supposed to tell anyone until Harper had a chance to speak with you, but of course these are exigent circumstances that call for full disclosure. Elizabeth is beside herself right now. If anything happens to our daughter and grandchild, Elizabeth will personally cut my balls off and serve them up to my political enemies. So you see this matter has to be resolved quickly and quietly."

"What do we know so far?" Malcom interrupted. "I need to be brought up to speed."

Lucia put her hand on my arm and quickly began speaking so as to silence me.

"Stephen was just updating us right before you arrived. Go ahead, Stephen. Tell us what you have so far," she said.

I began running my fingers through my hair, heading for my bar to get a drink.

"What we knew for sure is that neither Scott nor Harper made it to their plane. They were separated. The photos you received confirmed Harper getting into a vehicle alone," Stephen said.

That was the worse news of all. My Kitten and my baby were out there somewhere without Scott's protection. "Apparently, before Harper left the Carnegie Center where the Joduku Plastics Presentation was being held, she was delayed getting into her SUV," Stephen continued. "Scott and Harper had agreed to both use the restrooms first and to meet out in front of the Carnegie Center. Scott radioed for Winston to bring the car up to the lobby door. Before Scott could exit the men's room, Harper was gone."

"You mean Scott lost her," Malcom said, staring at Stephen with an evil eye.

"No, Scott has not *lost* Harper," Stephen said with emphasis. "He's just not with her."

"Scott's first instinct was that Brooks Fitzgerald McKenna had made off with Harper. When he didn't see Harper, Scott called Charlotte, who was on board the plane in pre-flight mode and asked if she had heard from Harper."

Malcom stepped closer to Stephen so as to invade his space. I moved to pour myself and Lucia each a vodka, nodding at the senator to see if he wanted something.

"I'll have a Macallen neat," the senator said, walking over to the window to take in the view of Central Park, but still listening attentively. The senator seemed not to notice the snit Malcom and Stephen were in throughout the discussion. Maybe he didn't care. We both knew we had bigger fish to fry.

"Charlotte was alarmed that Scott wasn't with Harper but said she had received a puzzling text message from Brooks. It was at that moment that Scott got a visual on Brooks, who was exiting the Carnegie Center alone. Brooks was distracted with texting," Stephen continued.

Lucia gulped her drink down looking at Stephen and then at Malcom, both of whom were eyeball to eyeball now and practically nose to nose in each other's space.

"One of Brook's security men grabbed Scott from behind, still angry about the fight on the tarmac earlier and they tussled," Stephen continued.

"Fight on the tarmac?" Malcom asked.

"Another time," Lucia said pouring herself a second drink and topping off my highball glass.

"Scott knocked the man out and grabbed Brooks, binding his wrists with plastic ties and quietly tucking him in Harper's SUV that was being driven by Winston. Before the rest of Brooks's entourage could catch up to him, Scott took off with a tied-up Brooks."

"Elizabeth spoke with both Mackenzie and Reese today. Harper left a voicemail for Mackenzie," the senator interjected. "Reese had a missed call, but no voicemail."

"I listened to Mackenzie's," Malcom said. "The voicemail revealed nothing of interest. Harper sounded collected and fine. Girl stuff," Malcom said.

Stephen flinched upon hearing Mackenzie's name.

That felt weird, I thought.

"What time was that?" Stephen growled.

"Before she left Carnegie Center," Malcom hissed back.

I wondered what that crazy ass Mackenzie was up to with both these guys. I was certain Malcom had a thing for Harper, but now I wasn't so sure. Was his interest in Mackenzie? I wondered if Mackenzie had anything to do with these pictures of me and Kitten. She was the only photographer I saw at the wedding and the only photographer I saw at the fundraiser for that matter. But she wasn't at the Joduku Plastics Headquarters so this just didn't make any sense to me at all. When, how, and by whom were these pictures taken?

"Scott and I both wear GPS sensors in our belts," Stephen said. "My team says he's positioned outside a secluded mansion north of Nassau Street in Princeton, New Jersey."

"So we know where she is?" I asked.

"Scott hasn't moved for the last hour. Our satellite view of the area reveals an old manor located about two miles north of the governor's mansion. Because he hasn't moved from that location for the last forty minutes, I suspect that is where Harper is being held," he said.

"I can call the governor," the senator said, "and have the State Highway Patrol raid the place."

"No. No. No," both Stephen, Malcom, and I all said at the exact same time, sounding like a chorus.

"This is my daughter you're talking about Nicholas!" the senator yelled at me.

"This is my woman and my baby!" I yelled back at him.

"I'm going to get her!" Malcom yelled.

"Over my dead body," Stephen said.

"I guess you'll be dead then," Malcom retorted.

"No, I will kill you both if you don't shut up and focus on getting my woman and my baby back."

"Stop it," Lucia demanded. "We need to work together if we're going to get her back. Knock it the fuck off, all of you."

"We need to come up with a plan."

"Who do we think has her and what do they want?" Lucia said, staring at the senator, Stephen, Malcom, and myself.

None of us could answer that question.

All of a sudden, Beethoven's Fifth Symphony began playing on my cellphone. We all knew what that meant.

Stephen raised his hand for me to pause as he walked near the computers he had set up. Stephen docked my cellphone. Then he turned on several kinds of recording applications. He put the phone on speaker than nodded for me to answer.

"Hello," I said.

"Nicky. Help me."

"Harper? Baby?"

A new voice came on the phone. A woman with a Russian accent. "Mister Becker. I've been looking forward to speaking with you. I understand you're the man that has the ability to, eh . . . how do you say it in your country? . . . part the Red Sea." She laughed with all evilness.

"Who are you and what do you want?" I asked, trying to control my temper.

"I shall keep this short. You see, Mr. Brooks Fitzgerald McKenna owes my organization a great deal of money. Twenty million to be exact. Bring the money he owes us to me, and you can have your beautiful prized possession back," she said. "I trust you and the senator have the photos by now."

"We do. Who is *us*?"

"Us is . . . let's just say I represent the interests of some members of a corporation."

Lucia and I shrugged our shoulders. We were clueless about who we were dealing with at this point.

"I'm sure you'll figure it out. Just know that I'm extremely serious and don't wish to play games. I'll get back to you with where to find her. Just come with the money when you do."

She paused. I held my tongue, not giving anything away.

"Do not involve the authorities. Abide by my demands and you'll get your beauty back safely. Otherwise perhaps I'll keep her for myself." That evil laugh coming out of her mouth made my brows furrow.

It was starting to be a toss-up who to kill first. Brooks or this bitch. I was starting to see red.

Stephen was signaling his hand moving it in circles letting me know to me to keep her talking.

"How shall I address you? What's your name?"

"Tatiana to you, Mr. Becker. You have twenty-four hours to get here with the money. Otherwise, I leave for Russia. I'll take her to a place you shall never find. I suggest you and your people get a move on," she gloated.

"If you harm a single hair on her head I swear I'll—"

Click.

The call disconnected.

"Lucia!" I barked. "How fast can we convert our assets and chattel paper to cash?"

"We can pull cash out of our accounts in Asia," she said. "The banks are still open there and we can convert from yen to dollars if we hurry," she said.

"Let me help you with this Nicholas," the senator said. "I can have twelve million here within the hour."

"That won't be necessary senator. This is my woman and my baby," I insisted.

"This is my daughter we're talking about. She was mine long before you ever contemplated that she was yours," he squawked.

"Fine. We don't have time to argue over this," I said.

"Convert twelve million, Lucia," I said. "The senator will come up with the rest."

Senator Montgomery was already on his phone talking to Elizabeth and barking out orders.

Malcom was engrossed in replays of the recording of my phone call with the Russian woman and running her voice patterns through some kind of identification system to see if they could get a handle on who we were dealing with at this point. Stephen was working tirelessly to communicate with Scott, especially since he knew he had possession of Brooks. Lucia was going back over the photos at the Lincoln Center looking for any clues she could find. She was running facial recognition software.

That Tatiana bitch wanted us to pay McKenna's tab. How was I not going to kill McKenna first for dragging my woman and my baby into this madness? I didn't mind giving up a mere twenty-two million for Harper. She was worth so much more to me than that, but turning over money for Brooks was another matter. I would give up everything I owned for Harper, but that piece of shit Brooks . . . I just wanted to take him out.

"The transaction is already underway, Nicholas," Lucia said, letting me know the wheels were turning on raising the twelve million dollars. "The money is on its way."

I thought about the fact that I had two million in cash in my home safe, but I kept that little tidbit to myself. I wasn't sure what might come up down the road that we wouldn't be able to foresee. Lucia walked over to Stephen and touched him lightly on his shoulder.

"Scott?" she asked.

"He'll be fine Lucia. He's trained all of his life for experiences like this. He's the best," Stephen assured her.

Lucia nodded and headed back to the computer to check on the bank transfers. I knew she was worried about me, about

Harper, and Scott. She was tough as nails, but moments like these tested the mettle of all of us.

I sat down for a moment and put my head in my hands, running my fingers through my head. I needed Harper and my baby to be safe. I couldn't sit here any longer. I couldn't take it. I needed to get to my Kitten.

"Lucia, call Cameron and see if we can fly back to Princeton," I said.

"We can't. I've already checked. All the airports are closed, Nicky. There's a freaking storm."

It was two a.m. now. The clock was ticking. I shook my head and paced the floor. The good news was if we couldn't fly, then neither could that Tatiana bitch. But as soon as the airports opened again, it would be a new game plan. We had to move quickly.

Ring . . . Ring . . .

We each paused again and looked up. It was my concierge again. Lucia put the call on speaker. The silence was deafening.

"Mr. Becker, Ms. Montgomery and your father are here sir."

I exhaled. Damn. The rescue entourage was growing and maybe going to be a bit harder to control. Big Daddy and Elizabeth were here, both accompanied by their own security. Now we had four more security outside my penthouse doors. It was starting to look like a special ops team was outside my door, the presence of which was sure to draw unnecessary attention with the neighbors in my building.

"Let them through please."

Lucia opened the doors. Things were really starting to get crazy.

"Oh Nicholas dear," Elizabeth said. "Don't worry baby, things are going to work out," she said, putting her arms around me and hugging me tightly. "Harper's a strong woman."

"I know."

I hugged her back tightly. Elizabeth was my best ally. She

had always wanted Harper and me together. We both knew it, even though we never discussed it.

Elizabeth handed the senator a titanium briefcase with his ten million inside. Cold hard cash. The one thing I loved about Elizabeth. She was a no-nonsense, get-to-the-point kind of woman. I suppose that was why I loved Harper. She was a chip off the old block.

Big Daddy walked over and acknowledged the senator.

"We'll get your gal back, Clayton," Big Daddy said in a loud husky voice. "Don't worry. I will see to it that Nicky sees to it," he said.

Big Daddy turned to me to give me a bear hug. I made myself ignore his crack. I knew he couldn't help himself. It was important to him to always feel he was the one in control. Managing his ego was not on my to-do list tonight.

"Listen, son. I know how much you love Harper."

I looked at my father with an element of surprise. I didn't realize my father had any clue or knew how much I loved Harper. I always figured his interests were of a business nature.

"Really?" I said.

"Yes Nicholas. It's all over your face and hers so much that I need to share something with you, son."

"What, father?"

Big Daddy pulled me over off into the balcony area of my penthouse where our conversation was not in earshot of the others in the room. It was fucking rainy and windy outside, but Big Daddy was acting like it was summertime and that we were in Florida somewhere exchanging barbs. It was fucking storming. Did this man not realize there was damn near a hurricane outside? Surely I had my mother's DNA because Big Daddy was certifiably crazy.

"You see, Elizabeth and I set up this arrangement for you and Harper to compete for the Joduku Plastics acquisition. We knew that we needed to figure out a way for the two of you to get back in each other's space so that you could recognize how much you really cared for each other. You two people are the stubbornest mules that I know, and I've been in business a long time."

"You mean you've been behind this acquisition all the time?" I asked.

"Of course son. You and Harper just needed a nudge. You

two have spent the last decade cutting each other off at the knees. It's pretty obvious that you love each other."

"Of course we love each other!" I shouted. "But don't you think pitting us against each other is going a bit far, Dad?"

Whoa. That had to be real for him. I rarely called my father "Dad." I either referred to him as Big Daddy, father, or asshole, but never "Dad." It felt too loose to use on a man with such dignified formality.

"Our plan worked too, Nicky. Once we figured out that the two of you were "with child," we called the whole thing off. Elizabeth and I don't care about some Japanese plastics company," he said, looking at his watch and checking out Elizabeth through the glass patio doors. I could see Elizabeth was across the room talking to the senator.

"How could you set us up like this?" I said questioning him.

"Well goddamn, boy. You should be thanking us. I hear you're going to be a father with the woman that's been the love of your life for a fucking decade. Wake up and smell the roses, boy," Big Daddy grumbled, slapping me on my back and practically knocking the wind out of me.

He had that same look on his face that he had when I was twelve when he tried to set me down and explain the facts of life, specifically the birds and the bees. I acted like I was clueless not understanding a word he was saying. It was that look that said, "Boy, don't toy with me because I'm serious."

Back then I didn't want to play my hand and give away the fact that my brother Three had already educated me on every fact that was seemingly important to a young man that age because I knew it would burst his bubble. Big Daddy never like to be undermined. He always wanted to be the one to get there first, so to speak, so that when time went by, and you had to reflect on what you knew and how you knew it, Big Daddy would be the only person to come to mind.

"Thanking you?" I said, still surprised and apparently looking clueless. "Harper and I practically pulverized each other over this."

"Yes but you didn't," Big Daddy said with all assurance. "Lizzy and I knew that you two wouldn't take each other down. Anybody with eyes can see you two are in love, son. "Now, I don't want you to let this ransom situation to get out of hand," he said changing the subject before I could work myself up into a frenzy.

"This is Lizzy's only child, and first grandchild. Potentially my grandson's at stake here. Tell me how I can help you Nicky. I'm here to support you, son."

"I've got this under control father," I said, still in a bit of a state of disbelief and trying to pull my wits together.

Motherfucker. Damn. Is nothing sacred around here? Big Daddy and Elizabeth *planned* this bullshit of pitting Harper and I against each other? I knew Big Daddy had the capacity to reach all kinds of lows, but Elizabeth? She was more of a shark than I gave her credit. No wonder Kitten knew how to cut me off at the pass most times. She was trained by a female ninja bottom feeder. Worse, everybody and their brother knew that Harper and I were going to be having a baby.

Jesus. I wasn't sure what Harper was going to do when she found out this little tidbit of information but I knew what position I was going to take. Nothing was going to change. Nobody, not even my father, the senator, or Elizabeth was going to prevent me from keeping my woman and my baby safe.

Lucia opened the balcony sliding door. "Nicholas. We have her. We know who, we know why, and we know where," she said. "Jesus, Nicky, you'll catch pneumonia out here. It's a freaking thunderstorm," She looked at me and Big Daddy as if we were crazy to still be out here. She watched us move back inside. We were both soaking wet.

I nodded at Lucia as I trailed Big Daddy back into the great room of my penthouse. Lucia handed us towels. I hugged her and held on for a beat. I wanted her to know how much she meant to me.

"I know Nicky," she said. "We'll get her back. Stephen has promised me we'll get her back. Otherwise I will cut his balls off and then feed them to him."

Lucia was serious as a heart attack. I would not want to be Stephen. But then again Stephen was never one to fail.

"What's the deal? Who are we dealing with?" I asked.

"Try the Moskovski Group," Lucia said, looking extremely concerned. "Tatiana Gukovu is the go-to person for the Group."

"Fuck me. How in the hell did Brooks Fitzgerald McKenna get himself mixed up with the Moskovski Group?" I asked.

"Word on the street is that they are known for international money laundering. While it's never been fully proven, the belief is that they are entangled with the Russian mob," Lucia said, for the benefit of the others in the room.

"They *are* the Russian mob," I said, letting out a breath of exasperation through my nostrils.

Lucia had mentioned several weeks ago that McKenna Textiles was having some financial problems. But fooling around with this group was beyond the pale. These were some dirty players.

They were the front group and face for a lot of shell and dummy corporations. If you dug deep another level, you'd find there was nothing there but air. The group was on several federal agencies' and the SEC's watch lists. One of its corporate members was on the CIA's no fly list. Rumor was that particular individual was a family member who was well connected to a suspected terrorist imprisoned at Guantanamo Bay. Brooks would have been better off going bankrupt than to connect his business interests with this group of lowlifes. And now they had both my babies. This news drove my anxiety level up another notch.

"So now that we know who we're dealing with, what's the plan?" I said.

I was tired, exhausted, and hungry. I felt sleep deprived. But there wasn't a motherfucker alive that was going to keep me away from Kitten and my baby. Nobody. This group was going to go down.

Lucia grabbed my hand and we all headed for my dining room. There were plenty of seats, as my dining area sat twelve. We each took a seat with me at the head of the table.

"What's the plan?" I repeated.

"We give them the money," Elizabeth said.

"We trade her for Brooks," Malcom said.

"We kill them all," the senator said.

"This doesn't sound much like a plan people," Big Daddy said.

"We don't need media attention on this," Stephen said, "so

here's the plan. Based on where Scott is positioned, we have the GPS coordinates, schematics, and satellite photographs of the property. There are security cameras on all corners of the property, so they'll see us coming"

"Scott says there are two watchdogs on the front door," Malcom interjected. "They are a formidable enemy."

"Yes, their security system is upscale but it's not impenetrable," Stephen said. "Scott can disconnect the cameras and monitors pretty rapidly."

"How will we know where she's located?" the senator said. "If we go storming in there, won't we put her life at risk?"

"We can wait until everyone is asleep and go in with a surprise attack," Malcom said. "Stephen has infrared scans that can read the heat signatures of anybody inside."

"You people are not going to get my daughter killed," Elizabeth snapped back. She was directing her words right at the senator.

"I can give them an extra five million, Lizzy," Big Daddy added, hoping to console her.

"Make a call," Stephen said. "I say you let me have at this, Nicholas. We can open up the gates of hell on these rogues."

"What do you want to do Nicholas?" Lucia said.

Images filled my mind of a broken and hurt Harper. I'd almost lost her once ten years ago. I wasn't going to lose her again. I let out a deep exhale. I could hear my own heaviness in my voice. "They expect us to have intel and a proper plan. They aren't even making a real effort to conceal who and where they are located. They want to ambush us."

"They don't know that we have Brooks in our custody. I say we use him to our full advantage," Stephen said.

"Good point," Malcom added.

I got up from the table and began pacing the floor. No one said anything to me, but everyone at the table stared in my direction. I was seriously worried if we could pull this off. There were ten thousand things that could go wrong and failure was not an option. We didn't say it, but we all felt it and we all knew it. I moved across the other side of the room and pressed a code into my security panel. Doors began to open up to my safe room that was hidden from view. Another wall opened with all the manner of weaponry and gear that one could imagine for every kind of scenario. It was where Stephen's special weaponry was kept. Stephen and I were the only ones that had knowledge of this room.

Malcom was the first to walk forward into the room. He looked like he'd died and gone to heaven. Lizzy's mouth fell open. Big Daddy rose from his seat shrugging his shoulders and moving to pour himself a drink.

"Nicky always did like to play soldier when he was a little boy."

"Nice going Nicholas," the senator said, fully impressed. I've got to get me one of these," he said.

"Obviously you have your own plan Nicky," Lucia said, completely unfazed.

"Yes I do. I suggest we walk right through the front door and remind them never ever to fuck with me and what's mine."

CHAPTER TWENTY

Harper and Nicholas

I could hear the wind howling and rain beating hard outside when the heaviness of my eyelids gave way to my being able to open my eyes. I found myself in a strange house. *Ugh.* This wasn't some nightmarish dream that I prayed for when I could no longer keep my lids open. No, this wasn't a dream. This was real. My heart sank.

The ice queen was still in the room, her glare seemingly even more intense. I wondered what was wrong. Did Nicky not agree to give her the money when she spoke with him? Surely that wasn't the case. Why had her demeanor changed? She had gone from somewhat amenable to downright hostile in just a few hours. How many hours had passed? Maybe several. I could see daylight peeking through the windows now.

"Ah . . . Sleeping Beauty awakens . . ." she said with all iciness. "I've been staring at you most of the night," she said. "You talk in your sleep about a baby. You're pregnant, no?"

"I am," I said, squirming in the chair that I had fallen asleep in upright. My mouth was dry. My back and legs throbbed. I felt like I had cottonmouth. I looked down at my hands and noticed that I was now bound at the wrists with plastic ties. Things were starting to get even scarier.

I could see that the sun had risen. It was early morning. My stomach was starting to cramp from the stress of sitting upright sleep in a chair most of the night. Lord knows I needed real food and rest. I didn't want to re-live the events of my miscarriage a decade ago and lose this baby this time. I knew I needed to take care of myself if I was going to get through this pregnancy. Dr. Richards had explained that to me more than once. Taking care of myself and the baby was of the utmost priority. This experience didn't come anywhere close to my being careful. I remembered that I was ten weeks pregnant today. I felt like I was going to throw up. I forced the bile back down my throat. This was no time to be weak and helpless.

"Ummm. You're having his baby. Two for the price of one," Tatiana said coldly.

My mind drifted back to my call last evening to Nicky. I could hear his breath catch when I told him I needed help. I was as heartbroken as he sounded. I was well aware that Nicky would move heaven and earth to save me. That much I was sure. And now that he knew I was carrying his baby, there was no way Nicky was going to stand for any of this ransom bullshit.

Nicky wasn't the typical trust fund baby. He was very good at what he did. Over the years he had multiplied his own personal wealth beyond his family's wealth tenfold. While he had a keen sense of integrity, that character trait didn't overshadow the fact that Nicky could be ruthless if you crossed him and messed with his family or friends. His enemies rarely stood a chance.

Brooks had really dragged the both of us into some kind of nasty game. What the ice queen failed to understand was the depth of the shit storm that Nicholas would rain down upon her and her little friends. The enemy of my enemy was my friend . . . or in this case my lover and the father of my child.

Okay, so I had my moments in the past where I thought Nicky was a first class wrecking ball, a ruin-er of things. But, there was no way that Nicky was going to let this Russian bitch make off with me and his baby. Nicky loved us. That much I knew for sure. If I had to place bets, my money would always be on Nicky. He was a worthy adversary by my own standards and I knew him better than anyone. The ice queen was going to be in for a rude awakening.

I tussled with my hands to try and squirm out of the plastic ties with no success.

"I'm sorry I had to restrain you, but I suspect things to get a bit tenser today so I had Ivann tie you."

Ivann was in the corner of the room looking out the window.

"As if Ivann isn't a big enough skinhead disguised as a bloated dumbbell to restrain a woman like me without handcuffing me," I squawked.

"Don't you fuck with me, you little cunt!" Ivann turned and shouted at me.

"Or what? You'll squat on me? You moronic son of a goat," I said.

Wham . . . Ivann smacked me hard across my face practically knocking me out of the chair.

The tears filled my eyes as I pulled my tied wrists up to caress the side of my face. I spit on him.

Wham . . . he smacked me again harder. I flew out of the chair this time and hit the floor with no way to catch myself and break the fall. Ivann stood over me yelling at me in Russian. Words I didn't understand.

"Стоп! Стоп! Stop it right now!" the ice queen demanded, alternating between Russian and English.

"We won't get a dime for her if she's hurt," she said, speaking another flurry of words to him in Russian.

Ivann picked me up off the floor and sat me back onto the chair. I was glad that I had landed on my side and not on my stomach. I prayed my baby wasn't injured. Thank God the fall to the floor wasn't so far. My face hurt. I knew I was bruised. If anybody in this group was going to kill me, it was going to be Ivann.

The woman in the uniform that came last night was back again with food. She sat the tray in front of me but I turned my head so as to suggest I wasn't interested.

"Eat," Tatiana demanded.

I turned my head and rolled my eyes at her. My feelings were hurt. I was angry. I wanted out of here. I wanted no more of her pretend kindness. She didn't have my interests at heart. That whole business of wanting me to be comfortable was just some bullshit. She and Ivann were playing good cop bad cop and I was the pawn here.

I wanted no more of her fake hospitality. I wanted out of here.

"The rain storm is predicted to end soon," Tatiana said. "If the money does not arrive, we'll be planning to leave when the rain ends," she said.

I said nothing. I was through talking to her. This whole

business of holding me hostage for the likes of Brooks Fitzgerald McKenna was just so wrong on many levels. Unfortunately my captors didn't care about what I thought or what I was feeling. This was all about their greedy desires. The need to use me as a scapegoat for Brooks' liabilities was just plain appalling.

I swung my tied-up hands and swiped all the food off the small table and watched as it went flying across the floor.

The dishes cracked into a thousand pieces, startling everyone in the room. Food flew everywhere. It was just as well too, because the sausage looked greasy and the eggs were undercooked. While I wondered which one of them would have to clean up the messy floor, I could hear the sounds of helicopters outside the manor. The noise level was so pronounced, it sounded as if someone was making a landing on the front lawn.

Ivann ran out of the room yelling in Russian, simultaneously pulling a gun out of the back of his waistband and heading for what seemed to be the rear kitchen area. Two men that I hadn't seen before came running out of the same place Ivann had just disappeared to. One man crouched down near the window and the other by the front door. Someone from the outside kicked the front door open. The Russian man whom I recognized as the driver of the SUV fell through the front door, beat up and bloodied. He'd been shot in the shoulder.

"Snipers," he said, spitting up blood. "Silencers." He coughed and shouted more words in Russian.

Cold gusts of wind and rain filled the room. The woman in the uniform ran past me, leaning over the man on the floor, crying over him and talking rapidly in Russian. One of the men I hadn't seen before began speaking in broken English, saying something about the monitors being down and that they had been caught by surprise.

Tatiana came towards me and dragged my chair across the room away from the sight line of the window. She put a gun to my head.

"Say nothing, pretty lady."

Tatiana shouted for someone to close the door. The uniformed woman dragged the man she had been crying over into the foyer and slammed the door closed.

Ivann waved at the other two guys, giving them hand signals for one to go out front and the other to go out back.

It was hard to tell if those men were more afraid of Ivann or of what was outside. There was silence for several minutes before I heard a moan and the sound of something heavy hitting the concrete outside. I could hear branches crackling and what sounded like people moving about. The tension in the room went up several levels. Tatiana and her gang were under attack and they knew it.

"Somebody help me!" I yelled at the top of my lungs.

Tatiana immediately grabbed a roll of grey electrical tape nearby, ripped a piece off angrily, and covered my mouth, pushing the tape hard enough over my lips to cause my head to snap backwards.

The door flew open again, and another man fell through it, pleading, "Please don't shoot me. Please don't shoot me."

Ivann shouted out some more Russian words and waved his hands, appearing to give orders. The man near the window grabbed the fallen man and dragged him to Ivann's feet. Ivann kicked him over on his side with his boot so that he was facing up. I gasped and moaned behind the tape over my mouth and I could feel my eyes get wider as I realized that it was Brooks Fitzgerald McKenna.

Brooks was still dressed in the clothes he'd worn at the Joduku Presentation. His wrists had plastic ties around them much like the ones I had on mine. Tatiana ran to his side and knelt. She ordered Ivann to cut his ties. Ivann spoke a flurry of Russian words, rapidly mumbling the whole time he was cutting Brooks loose. I figured he was cursing him in Russian and didn't really want to cut him loose. Ivann seemed to dislike Brooks as much as he disliked me. Ivann helped to pull Brooks to his feet.

"I told you I would get you the money Tatiana," Brooks pleaded, rubbing his hands against his wrists. "None of this was kidnapping business of yours was necessary," Brooks hissed. "You needed to let me handle this my way."

"We have no more time for your empty promises," Tatiana said, pointing the gun at him now, rubbing it against his lips.

"You've kept us waiting much too long," she said. "We doubt you can deliver."

A Marimba ringtone began to play out loud. It was Brooks's phone. She nodded and Brooks answered it.

"Hello? Yes. It's that shithead Nicholas Becker," he growled, handing the phone clumsily to Tatiana. "He wants to speak with you."

"Mmm, mmm," I moaned, unable to speak through the tape on my mouth. I started stomping my feet loudly on the floor.

"Shut up bitch," Brooks said to me. "You're the reason I've got all of these problems."

Oh my god. Nicky wasn't going to have to worry about killing Brooks, because I was going to do it myself if I ever got free of these people.

"Mr. Becker," Tatiana said. "I've been expecting you. Although I must say I've clearly underestimated your ability to create such a ruckus."

Nicholas

Stephen, Malcom, Lucia, and I arrived by helicopter at the location Scott had been hunkered down at in Princeton, NJ. Stephen had flown all of us at the break of dawn. We got clearance at LaGuardia as the tropical storm was starting to lift. Lucia insisted on coming with us. I begged her to stay behind with the Senator, Big Daddy, and Elizabeth but she was having none of it. She insisted that Harper would need a woman nearby when we rescued her. She wanted to help her with any female needs. I mumbled at the whole idea, but agreed to let Lucia come anyway. If anybody was going to give my Kitten what she needed, it was going to be me.

Lucia had dressed herself in a jumpsuit-looking outfit made of black leather. She reminded me of the Catwoman. I insisted that Lucia stay inside the helicopter for safekeeping.

"Lucia. If anything ugly happens to us, use this weapon," Stephen said right before we landed. "Do what I taught you and then get out of here."

Lucia nodded.

Jesus, what had Stephen taught Lucia? Everybody around me had goddamn secrets, but I didn't have time to get into it with them now. I would ask Stephen and Lucia later when all of this was over.

It was early morning and the sun had risen. Stephen landed the helicopter right on the front lawn as if we were storming the beaches of Normandy. Scott had assembled a team that had surrounded the house. Scott and Stephen made hand signals with each other communicating silently. The fact that we employed the element of surprise was to our tactical advantage. Too, with Scott already on the ground, we were able to disable their cameras and monitors moments before our arrival. The heat scans revealed how many people were inside the manor, so we pretty much knew what we were up against man-to-man.

Scott and Malcom had managed to injure and disable several of the Russian lookouts posted outside the manor. Stephen's men threw a tied-up Brooks inside the front door of the manor as our calling card. We were deliberately letting Tatiana know of our arrival.

Stephen had a small army of men strategically located around the entire property. If Tatiana didn't give me my woman back, I was going to take down everyone in that manor down with no mercy. Torture wasn't at all beneath Stephen and Scott, so things would get ugly fast. I wanted my woman back.

We put a phone inside Brooks's suit jacket and programmed the number so that I could call and make the trade. My woman and child in exchange for twenty-two million dollars, which I was now carrying in a thick titanium case.

"You have something that belongs to me," I said to Tatiana.

"And you have something I want," she replied. "What I don't need or want is Mr. McKenna," she said rather haughtily.

"You have Brooks McKenna walk her out the front door and I'll give him the money. He can give it to you and you can do what you want with him," I said coolly.

"I have no use for him," Tatiana said.

"Not my problem," I answered.

"Give me a minute please," she said.

I could hear Tatiana, Brooks, and some other man with a Russian accent arguing among themselves in the background.

"You either walk my woman out here right now, or I come in and get her," I said interrupting their discussion.

A few moments passed and the front door opened. Brooks was dragging Harper by her hair. Her mouth was taped and her wrists were bound. She had a huge bruise across her face and tears were streaming down her face.

My heart starting beating overtime and all I could think about was killing Brooks and everyone inside that house for doing this to my Kitten.

Brooks stepped down four steps on the porch of the Manor with Harper in his clutches.

"Stop right there, asshole," Brooks said to me as I began approaching Harper rapidly. He pulled a gun out of his backside and aimed it at her neck.

I could feel my blood begin to boil now.

"Give me my woman!" I yelled at Brooks.

"Throw the money down in front of you," he said.

"Step back away from her and let her walk toward me," I shouted.

"We've got a lot of guns on you asshole. Throw the money over here," Brooks shouted again.

Brooks still hadn't let go of Harper. I was starting to feel like we might be headed towards a major standoff. Things were getting incredibly tense. My baby was shaking and was beginning to shiver. I knew this had to end quickly.

I kicked the silver case on the ground as close to Brooks's feet as I could get it. I swore under my breath that I would make him pay for what he'd put her through.

"Now let her go!" I shouted.

Brooks pushed Harper forward out of his reach and bent down to pick up the silver case full of money.

Brooks dropped to his knees to open the case.

"Come to me baby," I yelled at Harper.

Harper broke free from Brook's grasp and ran my direction. I ran to her as fast as I could to reach her and pulled her into my arms.

"Get down, Nicky," Stephen yelled.

Harper and I had barely reached each other's arms. I rotated Harper around the back of my body and pulled her behind me. Brooks had picked up the silver case of money and raised his gun toward us just as a big huge man opened the front door.

"Ivann no," Brooks shouted.

Ivann let loose several rounds of fire on Stephen who was to my left. Brooks turned to face me and Harper. I watched as his finger pulled on the gun's trigger. A swoosh of air passed my right temple and a flash of light illuminated in my peripheral vision.

"Son of a bitch," I barked at Brooks.

A second burst of air whizzed past me again from behind. I heard a loud thud hit the ground coupled with a loud groan. Brooks had taken a hit to the skull. Pink flesh and blood oozed from the middle of his forehead. I heard a loud female scream from inside the manor.

Scott and Stephen both simultaneously fired on Ivann, killing him dead.

I ripped the tape off Harper's mouth.

"Kitten, are you okay, baby?"

"Yes Nicky!"

That was all I needed to hear. We could talk the rest of this out later. I just needed to get her out of here. I shielded my body against her to protect her as frustration consumed me.

Sounds of gunshots filled the air. There was a tangled mess of bodies around us and bullets were flying across our heads. I pulled myself up, grabbed Harper off the ground, and pulled her towards our helicopter. Who had fired on Brooks to save us?

"Good going Lucia," Scott said, running up to hug her.

"Get out of the way Scott," Stephen said.

"Lucia are you okay, sweetie?" Stephen asked, looking her up and down to be sure.

"I'll be the judge of that," Scott said, pulling Lucia to his side and following quickly behind us to the helicopter.

Stephen removed the Glock 45 from Lucia's hand.

"Let's get out of here," Stephen barked, but not before taking a swipe at the back of Scott's head with his hand.

Fucking high strung alpha twins with egos. Were these two really going to use this particular moment to fight over Lucia?

"Guys, I'm fine," Lucia said.

I looked at Lucia in total disbelief. I couldn't believe what I had just witnessed. Lucia had shot Brooks to death. I looked at Lucia intently, grateful that she had my back.

"Lucia?" I said, not finding the words.

"Marksman classes," she said. "Happy to help Nicky."

"Lucia . . . I . . . I . . ."

"You're repeating yourself again Nicky. Knock it off," she said.

I shook my head again in disbelief thinking how much Lucia never ceased to amaze me. I was proud to call her my partner and friend. I owed her my life, Kitten's life, and the life of our little-one-to-be.

Stephen pulled a huge knife out of his waistband as big as Crocodile Dundee's. He immediately cut the ties off Harper's wrists.

"In about two minutes this place is going to be crawling with Secret Service, State police, FBI, a whole bunch of media, and God knows who else," he barked while revving up the helicopter's engine.

No sooner than Stephen had gotten those words out than the place was crawling with red and white flashing lights illuminating the morning sky. Police were surrounding the area from all directions.

This was part of the senator's contribution to our "big plan." He would have the authorities secure the scene once we had his daughter in hand. He didn't want any of these Russian hoodlums to get away and neither did I. Once I had what was precious to me back in my arms I didn't care what they did to the rest of those people.

Scott and Malcom remained on the ground directing the authorities on who was left in the house. Tatiana and the uniformed woman came out in handcuffs escorted by the FBI. Ivann and Brooks were dead along with several other of their minions.

Malcom was picking up the briefcase full of cash and heading to an unmarked car that I suspected contained the senator's people, just as we were taking off.

I held Kitten close to me not ever wanting to let her go.

"Let's get her to a doctor, Nicky," Lucia said. "We need to make sure she and the baby are okay."

"Good idea," I said to her and Stephen.

"I'm hungry," Harper said. "I need a bathroom and I want to lay down." She forced a smile but winced when I ran my finger down the side of her face.

I kissed the tips of her cold fingers. I knew Harper was weak. Her skin was turning ashy and her lips were looking a little blue.

"Okay Kitten. I'll take care of you."

The love of my life was safe in my arms. I was pretty sure I wasn't going to like any doctors poking on her and kicking me out of some hospital room to examine her. I needed to be right where she was, wherever that is.

"Hospital, right?" Lucia asked Harper.

Before Harper could respond, I said "Home. We can bring the hospital to us."

"And just how do you plan to do that Nicky?" Lucia resisted.

"I'll build a fucking wing if necessary and make it happen that's how. My Kitten is going home with me now."

"No, she's going to the hospital, Nicky. If you want to buy a new obstetrics wing for New York Presbyterian Hospital that's your business, but she needs an ultrasound, so knock it off."

Well that's my Lucia. She was back to her old self. Giving me orders again.

Harper looked at Lucia and tapped her hand on Lucia's knee so as to suggest she wanted to go to the hospital.

"I feel like I'm spotting," Harper said to Lucia.

"Don't worry, Harper. Hospital it is," Lucia commanded.

I could tell Harper was exhausted and weak. She had been through an incredible ordeal. Lucia just shook her head at me. She was used to putting up with me. I'm sure she thought I was being overly possessive. So what? I might be acting a bit ridiculous, but I didn't care.

I opened my phone to call my brother. He had kids so he'd know how to make things happen quickly. It helped that he was a lawyer and a Becker.

"Three, it's me Nicky. Call Elizabeth Montgomery and get Harper's doctors to meet us at the emergency room at the Presbyterian Hospital, Columbia University Campus. We'll be landing at the hospital's helipad within the hour. Harper urgently needs medical attention."

"Don't worry Nicky. I'll make it happen. If I run into any roadblocks Big Daddy can call the Chief of Staff. Nothing's going to get in the way of Big Daddy and the future of his grandkid," Three said. "Consider it done."

CHAPTER TWENTY-ONE

Nicholas

Three had delivered on his word, because an hour later a team of doctors, nurses, and numerous medical personnel were waiting on top of the helipad with a gurney. It was a good thing too, because Harper was starting to experience some cramping and was beginning to moan in pain. It was clear she wasn't doing well. It was killing me to hear her moan. I was going to tear this hospital down and build a new one if somebody didn't help my Kitten real quick.

Thankfully, the medical staff was pushing IVs in Harper's arms and rushing her off to an examination room. I held her hand tightly telling her how much I loved her and our baby. A tear rolled down the side of her face. I knew she was scared she might lose the baby. I was too.

Hell, things had happened so fast I wasn't even sure how far along Harper was in her pregnancy. Our conversation hadn't gotten that far in all the commotion.

"I want you and I want our baby," I whispered in her ear. "We're going to make it through this together, Kitten."

It was the first time I had ever seen vulnerability register on Harper's face. She was always so tough. So strong. For the first time in our relationship I knew exactly how much she needed me and how much I needed her.

"Mr. Becker, we need to move your wife into radiology for some tests," the nurse said. "You'll have to wait in the waiting room, sir."

Harper looked up at me through tear-filled eyes and smiled weakly. We both could read each other's minds. Yes, we were damn sure going to be husband and wife so we didn't correct her.

"C'mon Nicky," Lucia said. "Let's go to the waiting room with the others. Family and friends are starting to arrive," she said, looking at the text messages on her phone.

I looked at Lucia somewhat puzzled.

"What? How long did you think this was going to stay a secret?" Lucia said.

"Who's here already?" I asked.

"Everybody. When Nicholas Becker is involved, the whole world shows up. Paparazzi are being held off under guard at the hospital doors."

"Jesus," I squawked.

"We let Reese and Mackenzie through," Lucia said. "They went to the cafeteria for food and coffee."

I ran my fingers through my hair but said nothing out loud. Reese and Mackenzie were Harper's friends and I had to consider that now that I planned to be her husband.

Big Daddy, Elizabeth, Three, and the senator are in the family waiting room," she said.

"Let's go in then," I mumbled.

I wanted a moment alone, but I had argued with myself to put that desire off for now.

I had been pacing for what felt like several hours when Harper's obstetrician arrived.

"Mr. Becker I'm Dr. Elliot Fischer, Harper's obstetrician."

"How is she, Dr.?" I asked, praying that the news would be good.

Dr. Fischer was an extremely good-looking African American man. His gaze dropped from mine as he did a double take at Lucia. I gave Lucia the snake eye to let her know I noticed, but she just shrugged her shoulders dismissing me. I grinned at her and shook my head. I was pretty much used to men googling over Lucia. Lucia had that effect on most men. I almost always gave her a hard time about it. I just wasn't sure how I felt about the handsome Dr. Fischer poking in between my Kitten's legs.

It was also a good thing that I was surrounded by family and friends, because the next bit of news that Dr. Fischer delivered practically knocked me to the floor.

"She and the babies are good," Dr. Fischer said. "Harper's exhausted famished, and pretty dehydrated. She's in pain and her body is badly bruised from the assault she took. Thank God her fall to the floor wasn't injurious to the babies. Harper will need to be on bed rest for a bit, but otherwise I'm pleased to tell you they are all going to be okay."

"Babies? All okay? They? What?" I asked.

"You're having twins, Mr. Becker. You and Harper are having twins."

"Oh my Lord, twins!" Elizabeth exclaimed loudly.

Big Daddy walked over to me and slapped me on the back hard.

"Two shots at some grandsons. You did good Nicky," he said proudly.

"Thank God. Takes the heat off me, Nicky," Three laughed and came over to congratulate me.

"Senator, I'm required to make a statement with the large number of press waiting outside on behalf of the hospital and on your behalf," Dr. Fischer said. "The word has pretty much leaked out that your daughter has been admitted. It would be helpful if a family member would join me to make a brief statement."

The senator looked at Elizabeth who shook her head implying that she had no intention of going.

"I'll go," Three volunteered. "I'm a lawyer. I know how to handle these matters."

"Good idea," I said very quickly, knowing that there was no way on God's green Earth that I was going to do it.

"Besides, it will give me chance to talk to Mallory and Jessica," Three said. "I hear they both are outside taking advantage of the paparazzi moment."

"You're married," I said to Three.

"Yes married, but not yet dead, Nicky. I can still look even though I can't touch. Besides, those two beauties saved me. I owe them," Three grinned like a frat boy.

"If it's fine with Nicholas, than it's fine with me," the senator said, looking somewhat relieved not to have to be the one to go.

"Nicholas, you can go see Harper now, but not for long. She needs her rest," Dr. Fischer said. "She knows family and friends are here. We don't want to overwhelm her and tire her out any more than she already is, please."

"Dr. Fischer I'm ready whenever you are," Three said excitedly.

"Thank you, Blake. Give me a minute to give the nursing staff some direction and then we can go outside and feed the mainstream media among the bright lights," Dr. Fischer quipped.

I was still in shock as I watched Dr. Fisher and Three exit the family waiting room.

The senator marched over to me and shook my hand.

"I expect you to make an honest woman out of Harper. I'm an old-fashioned guy, Nicholas, when it comes to these matters. Of course it may take some convincing on your part as far as Harper is concerned. Might be hard to get her on the same page," the senator said.

I hardly heard anything the senator was saying. Twins. Twins. *Harper and I are having twins?*

"My Harper is like her mother. Got a mind of her own," the senator went on further.

"Oh Clayton, don't be silly," Elizabeth said, waving her hand at him, casually blowing him off. Elizabeth moved toward Big Daddy. She gave him a big hug and kissed him on the cheek.

"I'm just tickled pink," she said to my father.

"Yeah Lizzy, we're going to have double trouble, woman," Big Daddy laughed with her. They both grinned like a couple of kids. "C'mon Clayton, let's you, Lizzy, and I go pop some champagne."

It took Lucia to snap me out of my stupor.

Reese and Mackenzie walked into the waiting room.

"We're having twins, guys!" Elizabeth exclaimed out loud to the both of them. Reese and Mackenzie huddled around Elizabeth who was bursting with excitement.

I moved to sit down to calm myself.

"Oh no you don't," Lucia said, turning her focus on me.

"I'm having twins, Lucia."

"Yes and you heard Dr. Fischer. What are you waiting for Nicky? Go see her, Daddy."

Harper

I took one look at Nicholas's face and knew he'd heard the news that we were having twins. Just yesterday I had hit him with the news that he and I were having a baby, but how was I to know I was having twins? It was as much of a shock to my system as the news must have been to Nicky. I was completely floored when Dr. Fischer informed me that not only was I have one baby, but I was having two.

Even though Nicky had a gentle smile on his face, he still looked like he had seen a ghost. Yes he had heard the news. That much I was sure. He looked scared. So this conversation was just going to be a matter of what we were going to do with this information.

I watched as Nicholas gently closed the door behind him. He looked deeply into my eyes, moving slowing towards me. He flashed that megawatt smile at me that always melted my heart. He was so damn handsome. To not stare at him wasn't even an option. Nicholas bent down, slowly leaning into me, and kissed me softly on the lips. My lips still stung from when the tape was removed off my mouth, but I smiled at him as he kissed me. I didn't say a word, watching as he sat on the edge of my bed. Nicholas fingered my hair through his hands, twisting the strands slowly, staring at me. Not only did he look scared, I knew he was worried.

"Please don't worry, Nicky. I'm okay. We're okay, baby."

Nicholas took a deep breath and swallowed hard.

"Kitten, loving you has been the only thing I've ever wanted to fully dedicate my life to. You are the only thing that matters to me. Losing you . . . losing them"—he looked down at my baby bump and rubbed his hand across my belly—"I was scared out of my mind these last forty eight hours. I can't imagine my life without you. If you'll let me love you for the rest of your life, I swear on everything I own, you'll never regret it."

I put my hand on the side of Nicholas's cheek and ran my fingertips down the back of his ear, pulling a loose strand of his hair behind it. He closed his eyes, tilted his head and moved his lips to kiss my knuckles.

"I love you too, Nicholas," I said softly.

I could feel myself tearing up again. I loved Nicholas with every cell in my body. The thought of never seeing him again only reinforced for me how much I really did love him. He and I had wasted a lot of years fighting each other. Fighting our feelings.

"Marry me, please," he whispered.

I closed my eyes briefly and nodded. I was overwhelmed with a flood of emotions. The emotional gulf that existed for years between Nicholas and I was long gone. We had built our own bridge over our troubled waters.

"Is that a yes?" he pleaded, his eyes searching mine.

"You're mine Nicholas. Make me yours," I whispered.

I watched as Nicholas breathed a sigh of relief.

"Good. Because I wasn't going to take no for an answer," he grinned.

His green eyes shone brighter and his smile widened. Nicholas bent over and kissed my belly bump.

"Mine too," he said, talking to our babies.

He had the look of a man with paternal joy. I ran my fingers through his hair and held Nicholas in my arms close to my heart.

"Finally something we can agree on," I laughed.

"I wouldn't have it any other way," Nicholas laughed back at me.

EPILOGUE

Nicholas

"What shall we toast to, Kitten?"

"That you still have your sanity?" Mackenzie laughed, snapping pictures of the twins.

"How about to grandkids?" Big Daddy joked out loud in a husky voice grabbing both my daughter Milania and my son Miles. They were dripping wet, having just exited the blue water of the yacht's pool. Big Daddy was tickling them both simultaneously.

"Sounds good to me," the senator agreed.

The senator's skin was much browner now that he was tanned from laying out on the ship's deck all afternoon. His Cherokee heritage was much more pronounced in the light of the golden sun of the Italian Rivera.

"Pop," the twins both screamed, kicking and giggling out loud. They both had been swimming on deck with each of their nannies who were now trying to urge them from my father's arms. They seemed to be failing at their attempts to usher them in the opposite direction so as to towel dry each of them off.

Like their mother, Miles and Milania had their own minds. I was convinced they both controlled their nannies versus the other way around, despite what their mother thought. Kitten and the nannies functioned like a team despite my wondering who was really in control.

The twins each had their own security guards, so Stephen had more people under his command. Harper thought I was going overboard putting the twins under guard, but I was not about to have some nutcase run off with my twins, the way Tatiana and her gang of thieves had run off with everything I loved.

I was still in awe every time I laid eyes on my beautiful son and daughter. Miles was a spitting image of his mother, with big brown eyes and curly brown locks that framed his small face. According to Harper, he had a huge heartbreaker smile like his father. I thought Milania favored me more. She had piercing green eyes, long sun-drenched light brown curls, and long eyelashes. She knew how to use them too, because when she blinked them at me, all I wanted to do was to give her the world. Both twins had caramel-colored olive-toned complexions that were a blend of both me and Harper.

I glanced their way, recalling the day of their births vividly. Harper had delivered them by Caesarian section two months after we were married. I was a nervous wreck holding her hand in the delivery room. She wanted to push them out naturally, but the doctors felt her labor had gotten too prolonged. I couldn't stand the thought of losing her again, or them for that matter, so I spent a whole evening begging and pleading with her to get on with it. She put on her 'don't tell me what to do' face that I knew so well and loved. It took Reese and Mackenzie to convince Kitten that she would be doing the right thing to deliver by C-section. I had to sway Mackenzie with new camera equipment just to get her on my team and to move Harper off her rock. One thing about Mackenzie, she was a loyal and devoted friend to Harper to the end. She still had her bitchy ways but had softened a ton towards me after I rescued her BFF from the kidnappers. Reese took my side with ease. I was his sister's Angel Investor, so he wasn't going to get on my bad side over the safety of my babies.

I immediately put an eight-caret diamond in a platinum setting on Harper's finger at the hospital the day following the press conference about her rescue. By the time we were married, I'd added a ten-caret wedding band to match. I wanted everyone in the world to know that she was mine.

Kitten cried when I slipped the ring on her finger. She was a mess of emotions throughout the entire pregnancy. But, even I had to admit that her ring was indeed the most brilliant Harry Winston ever seen on anyone's hand. Kitten was in love with my choice. She fingered her ring a lot, always teasing me by saying "Talk to me Nicholas." I would just laugh knowing she was mocking me by repeating the Harry Winston "Talk to me, Harry" brand marketing scheme.

"The best for the best," I would answer her.

As soon as Dr. Fischer allowed Harper a reprieve from weeks of bedrest, I scurried her to the Martha's Vineyard. It was the place where we began our relationship a decade ago. Only this time going forward we were going to associate it with the happy ending we long deserved. Several million dollars later, Harper and I tied the knot.

We married at Martha's Vineyard in the hot summer month of August at the senator's compound. By the time Elizabeth was done with the wedding planning the event had turned into a huge ordeal. Harper gave up the reins of the planning to her mother, not wanting to be bothered with too many of the details. She was eating for three and was pretty much miserable carrying an extra load. Elizabeth's stamp on the event showed too. She made Kim Kardashian's wedding look like a high school prom. Our marriage made all the major newspapers and celebrity rags. Mackenzie got exclusives on the photos, so she and I rapidly became friends.

Our first year anniversary was total chaos, filled with bottles, diapers, nannies, and grandparents. Harper and I practically fell asleep on each other during our private anniversary celebration. I was determined that for our second anniversary celebration we would get out of the country and have some much needed down time and peace. A bit of wishful thinking on my part.

"To grandparents," Elizabeth said, interrupting my thoughts and lifting her glass towards Big Daddy and the senator.

"To godfathers, ahem . . . me," Reese laughed, tugging on his sister Riley's hand, pulling her away from her husband and my best friend, Mico.

"To love at first sight," Mico said, looking at his wife Riley with fond affection.

"To the fact you still have your sanity," Mackenzie said, snapping pictures of Big Daddy with Miles Carmichael Becker and Milania Carmichael Becker.

"To love, family, and good friends," Lucia suggested, clinking her glass of champagne first to Stephen and then turning to Scott, both of whom stood on either side of her.

"To wedded bliss," Harper said, kissing my lips and clinking her glass next to mine.

Harper and I were celebrating our second wedding anniversary with our children, close family, and friends. Everyone had flown to Italy to join us in our intimate celebration. Family and friends joined us this weekend on our two-hundred-foot yacht, *The Julianna.*

Prior to their arrival, Harper and I had spent several weeks sailing the Mediterranean coast. We were just outside the half-moon-shaped harbor of Portofino in the Italian Riviera watching the dolphins play at sunset. We were on course to head to the Becker Villa at the San Remo seaside close to the French border. We'd would be arriving just in time to take in the San Remo Music Festival that Kitten insisted we all attend as a group. I was begging to get out of the music festival, voting for the casino tables instead. Harper had dug in on the point, even though I was confident I could persuade her to give me a get-out-of-jail card and head to the casinos with the guys.

My daughter Milania began pointing up at the sky, noticing the loud sound of the helicopter approaching the landing pad on the deck of *The Julianna.* As the familiar man de-boarded the helicopter, the twins started jumping up and down and screaming.

"Uncle Thweee!" they began squealing, hopping up and down, jostling for attention.

Three stood tall in a linen white shirt, khaki shorts, and a six-gauge cigar hanging out of the side of his mouth. He had on aviator sunglasses and his New York Yankees baseball cap.

"You're late," I said to Three.

"I left Marcy and the kids in San Remo shopping. I told her we could meet up there. Make if a family affair. Better late than never, brother."

Three grabbed both the twins, tossing them each up in the air and then reaching in his messenger bag, handing them giant Tootsie Pops that were bigger than the both of them.

The twins began clapping their hands as if Three was Santa Claus.

"I brought you kids a surprise," Three said to the twins, their eyes now getting big.

Before Three could continue, three bikini-clad beauties on

jet skis flanked with two bodyguards in a speedboat buzzed the yacht. I knew without even asking that it was my sister Julianna and her girlfriends Maya and Logan. Or should I say three twenty-five-year-old partners in crime. It was going to be a real family affair now. It'd been months since I'd seen my little sister.

Julianna, Maya, and Logan boarded, all three looking beautiful, tanned, and soaking wet. Both the twins sped past Three like gangbusters and headed for the arms of their Auntie Jules.

"Hey family, the gang's all here now," Julianna said joyfully, breaking free from the twins and heading into my arms.

"Time to get this party started," Logan said, as she and Maya moved to hug Harper, Three, and Big Daddy.

"I'm so glad you made it, Julianna." I said, embracing her in a big hug, kissing the top of her forehead. "Now I can beg out of this music festival in favor of hitting the casinos with Three instead," I laughed with joy.

Three laughed too, handing the twins each miniature remote controlled helicopters.

"You're spoiling my kids, Three. And you're aiding and abetting Nicky by trying to get him out of this music festival," Harper said, moving close to me, but not before hugging Three.

"Old habits die hard, sister-in-law. We'll be back in time for the fireworks."

Three and I lifted our glasses together. I kissed my Kitten on the top of her head.

"I love you."

"I love you too," Kitten said, sipping her champagne. "Perhaps I'll light some fireworks of my own with you Nicky, once the twins are put to bed."

Her eyes were setting me on fire as she gave me her "I need you Nicky" look that drove me crazy with desire.

"Ugh. Too much information," Three said, walking off, leaving us both laughing at him.

"What's his issue exactly, Nicky?"

"Oh Three is just scared that fireworks leads to the production of babies. His wife has threatened to cut his balls off if she has any more children. She's done."

"I hope you don't feel that way, Nicky?"

I swiftly honed my eyes in the direction of her gaze.

"Not at all Kitten. I love making love to you. We can make an army of babies if you want," I said with a silly smile on my face.

"Well I won't go so far as to say all that," Kitten grinned. "An army of babies and I might have to cut your balls off too," she laughed.

Her eyes were full of love. But I didn't doubt for one minute that she wasn't kidding. She was one tough woman.

But she was mine.

THE END

A WORD ABOUT THE AUTHOR

I am Jude E. McNamara. Virtual adventurer. Keyboard ninja. Guardian of sassy romantic encounters. I am the alter ego of that other woman, Jude. You know, the one that loves snowy nights, is in a relationship with love, and looking for her own hero. While by day she's off being the disciplined scrappy businesswoman with the mind of a shark, I gallivant her keyboard by night, running wild and free on the down-low. I figure she'll have to catch up to me. Because once that blue power button turns on, I'm far too busy breathing life into those colorful characters that run around in her head, incessantly telling me their stories even if it's at the break of dawn.

You can find me and my merry band of jet-setting girlfriends running from the paparazzi at the high-end cocktail bars in Manhattan, drinking Patron Silver. I'm the flashy one wearing the sparkly tiara on my head. Like clockwork, when she faithfully dons her track shoes to catch up with me, I usually have to listen to her lecture me about my behavior over a glass of champagne. She loves champagne. Actually I love champagne too—except I like mine with a side of tall, handsome hunk begging me to stop at the intersection of heartbreak hotel and romantic encounter road, demanding a happily-ever-after.

It's an arduous race to "The End" before her blue button goes dark and I cease to exist. But once the blue light appears, the race is on, right up to the point when we two Judes meet on the same page, often in a book like this one.

For more about the author, visit:
http://www.judeemcmara.com/

Two Judes Publishing
668 Stony Hill Road Suite 339
Yardley, Pa 19067

STAY CONNECTED WITH JUDE

Thank you again for your readership and support. If you enjoyed this book, please leave a review on Amazon, Barnes and Noble, and Goodreads. If you would like to learn more about my next book, below is an excerpt for my soon to be released novel. Also, you may wish to sign up for my Newsletter to be notified when my new novels are released.

Visit me online at judeemcnamara.com where you can learn more about me, find book trailers, my blog posts, and other new upcoming work.

Best Regards

Jude E. McNamara
judeemcnamara.com

Email Jude: jude@judeemcnamara.com
Follow me on Twitter @judeemcnamara
Follow me on Instagram: iamtwojudes
Follow me on Facebook: Jude.E. McNamara

AN EXCERPT FROM *SUGAR MOMMY ON TOP*

For more about Nicholas and Harper, read
Sugar Mommy On Top *from Jude E. McNamara.*

CHAPTER ONE

Julianna

"Are you sitting down?"

I sensed in my gut that those words meant nothing good would follow.

"I wanted to let you know I got married."

And there it was. Three godawful words: "I got married." Was he kidding me? Okay, so it was Halloween, and this felt like he was playing a bad trick; but it wasn't even time to hand out treats, and this was worse than any trick I'd ever gotten.

My heart sank in disbelief. I swear that I felt a physical blow to my gut; it was as if a giant invisible fist had been launched directly at my navel. Could I even breathe anymore? Had all the air suddenly been sucked out of the room? Why had everything become a blur? And why was everything happening so quickly? I needed to get off the fucking phone. I couldn't hear any more from him.

"I want to remain friends."

Had he lost his mind? Had I lost my mind? Why was I even still listening?

It was bad enough that I'd invested three years into loving him, hanging on his every word. I listened to him all the time sounding like a scratched record on repeat. He was sure that there was nowhere for our relationship to go but marriage. Of course, he didn't ever want to marry, or so he'd always said.

When I finally got the courage to end it, he decided it was best to keep his toe in the pond, staying near the front and center of my world, stoking the embers of love in my heart, never letting the fire go out completely. He would never fully release me. And now this? Surely I had *fool* written across my forehead. *Pretend you love me. Play with me. Screw me. Never marry me.* The prick.

"Congratulations, I wish you all the best."

How I managed to belt those words out as strong as I did, I'll never know. I was already hurting, but he hadn't hurt me enough. No, he had to turn the knife, had to twist it in my back some more. He wanted to kill what little life was left in me completely. He insisted on sharing the details about her, about the two of them.

"I want you and me to stay friends. I'll call you in a couple of weeks," he said, ending the call.

Seriously? Mr. Heartcracker, who is currently extracting every bit of life from me, thinks we're going to "remain friends?" Oh hell no. My head was dizzy. The walls of my bedroom were starting to close in on me, getting closer and closer, as each paralyzing second ticked by.

I needed to get out of here. I was struggling to breathe, and I couldn't stand being in my own skin, let alone being home alone. It was time for me to use my lifeline, my *phone a friend.* I needed my girlfriends now more than ever. My promise of tomorrow, my man-future, my everything had just come crashing down all around me, shattering me into a thousand little pieces. I burst out in tears, sobbing aloud.

It was time for me to call my roadies. Time for us to find the nearest hot spot so I could drown in an endless row of tequila shots, where I could silence those ugly words. Until then, "I got married" would replay endlessly in my ears.

I grabbed my black leather messenger bag, twisting it over my shoulder against my favorite navy blue, leather-trimmed, quilted Burberry jacket. I stuffed some extra tissues in my dark five-pocket denim jeans to wipe my runny nose with. I slid on my black suede Louboutin shoe boots with the four-inch heels. I pulled my red cashmere scarf off the bed, wrapped it around my neck, and stuffed the matching red boy cap into the side of my bag.

Maya and Logan would surely remind me that the best revenge was looking good. If I was going to die of a broken heart, I needed to at least look like every penny's worth of the million-dollar princess he'd let slip right through his fingers.

www.ingramcontent.com/pod-product-compliance
Lightning Source LLC
Chambersburg PA
CBHW060540180626
46817CB00002B/652